The Smuggler Chief
A Novel

by

Gustave Aimard

The Smuggler Chief
A Novel
by Gustave Aimard

ISBN: 978-93-62201-08-9

Published by

DOUBLE 9 BOOKS

2/13-B, Ansari Road
Daryaganj, New Delhi – 110002
info@double9books.com
www.double9books.com
Tel. 011-40042856

ABOUT THE AUTHOR

Gustave Aimard wrote multiple volumes about Latin America and the American frontier. Oliver Aimard was born in Paris. As he previously stated, he was the offspring of two married individuals, "but not to each other". His father, François Sébastiani de la Porta (1775-1851), was a commander in Napoleon's army and a representative of the Louis Philippe government. Sebastiani was married to the Duchess of Coigny. In 1806, the couple had a daughter, Alatrice-Rosalba Fanny. The mother died shortly after she was born. Fanny was reared by her grandmother, Duchess of Coigny. Aimard was placed as a baby with a family that were paid to raise him. By the age of nine or twelve, he was sent off on a herring boat. Later, about 1838, he served briefly with the French Navy. After one more trip to America (when he claims he was adopted into a Comanche tribe), Aimard returned to Paris in 1847, the same year his half-sister, Duchess de Choiseul-Pralin, was cruelly killed by her noble husband. Reconciliation or acknowledgement by his biological family did not occur. After serving briefly in the Garde Mobil, Aimard returned to the Americas.

CONTENTS

PREFACE

The present is the most powerful story which Gustave Aimard has yet written. While there is enough of startling incident and hairbreadth escapes to satisfy the greatest craver after sensation, the plot is carefully elaborated, and great attention is paid to developing the character of the heroines. If there has been any fault in the author's previous works, it is that the ladies introduced are too subordinate; but in the present tale, the primary interest hinges upon them, and they are the most prominent characters. For this reason I am inclined to believe that the "Smuggler Chief" will become a greater favourite with readers than any of its predecessors.

Lascelles Wraxall, Bart.

CHAPTER I
THE PROCESSION

America, a land not yet thoroughly explored, and whose immense savannahs and gloomy virgin forests conceal so many mysterious secrets and unknown dramas, sees at this moment all eyes fixed upon her, for everyone is eager to know the strange customs of the semi-civilized Indians and the semi-savage Europeans who people the vast solitudes of that continent; for in the age of transformation in which we live, they alone have remained stationary, contending inch by inch against the civilization which invades and drives them back on all sides, and guarding with a religious obstinacy the faith, manners, and customs of their fathers—curious manners, full of interest, which require to be studied carefully and closely to be understood.

It is to America, then, that we invite the reader to accompany us. But he need not feel alarmed at the length of the voyage, for he can make it while comfortably seated in his easy chair by the fireside.

The story we propose to tell has its scene laid at Valparaíso—a Chilian city as regards the soil on which it is built, but English and French, European or American, through the strange composite of its population, which, is formed of people from all countries, who have introduced every possible language and brought with them every variety of trade.

Valparaíso! the name echoes in the ear like the soft sweet notes of a love strain!

Valparaíso! the city of Paradise—the vast depôt of the whole world. A coquettish, smiling, and frolicsome city, slothfully reclining, like a thoughtless Indian maid, at the base of three mountains and at the end of a glorious bay, dipping the tips of her roseate feet in the azure waters of the Pacific, and hiding her broad brilliant forehead in the tempest-swollen clouds which float along from the crests of the Cordilleras to make her a splendid diadem.

This city, the advanced sentinel of Transatlantic civilization, is the first land which the traveller discovers after doubling Cape Horn, of melancholy and ill-omened memory.

When at sunrise of a fine spring morning a vessel sails round the lighthouse point situated at the extremity of the Playa-Aucha, this charming oasis is perceived, half veiled by a transparent mist, only allowing the white houses and lofty edifices to be distinguished in a vague and fantastic way that conduces to reverie.

The atmosphere, impregnated with the sharp scents from the beach and the sweet emanations of the trees and flowers, deliciously expands the chest, and in a second causes the mariner, who comes back to life and hope, to forget the three months of suffering and incessant danger whose long hours have passed for him minute by minute, ere he reached this long-desired haven.

On August 25th, 1833, two men were seated in a posada situated in the Calle San Agostino, and kept by a Frenchman of the name of Crevel, long established in the country, at a table on which stood two glasses and a nearly empty bottle of aguardiente of Pisco, and were eagerly conversing in a low voice about a matter which seemed to interest them in the highest degree.

One of these men, about twenty-five years of age, wore a characteristic costume of the guasos, a name by which the inhabitants of the interior are designated; a wide poncho of llama wool, striped with different brilliant colours, covered his shoulders and surrounded his bare neck with an elegant and strangely-designed Indian embroidery. Long boots of dyed wool were fastened above his knees by silk cords, and armed at the heels with enormous silver spurs, whose wheels, large as saucers, compelled him to walk on tiptoe whenever he felt an inclination to leave his saddle for a moment—which, however, very rarely happened, for the life of a guaso consists in perpetual horse exercise.

He wore under his poncho a belt containing a pair of pistols, whose heavy butts could be distinguished under the folds each time that a hurried movement on the part of the young man evidenced the fire which he introduced into the conversation.

Between his legs rested a rifle richly damascened with silver, and the carved boss of a knife handle peeping out of the top of his right boot.

Lastly, to complete this accoutrement, a splendid Guayaquil straw hat, adorned with an eagle's plume, was lying on a table near the one which he occupied.

In spite of the young man's swarthy face, his long black hair falling in disorder on his shoulders, and the haughtiness of his features, it was easy to recognise by an examination of his features the type of the European under the exterior of the American; his eyes full of vivacity which announced boldness and intelligence, his frank and limpid glance, and his sarcastic lips, surmounted by a fine and coquettishly turned up black moustache, revealed a French origin.

In truth, this individual, who was no other than Leon Delbès, the most daring smuggler on the Chilian coast, was born at Bayonne, which city he left after the loss of an enormous fortune which he inherited from his father, and settled in South America, where in a short time he acquired an immense reputation for skill and courage, which extended from Talcahueno to Copiapó.

His comrade, who appeared to be a man of five-and-thirty years of age, formed the most perfect contrast with him.

He wore the same costume as Delbès, but there the resemblance ended.

He was tall and well built, and his thin, muscular limbs displayed a far from ordinary strength. He had a wide, receding forehead, and his black eyes, close to his long, bent nose, gave him a vague resemblance to a bird of prey. His projecting cheek bones, his large mouth, lined with white, sharp teeth, and his thin pinched-up lips, imparted to his face an indescribable expression of cruelty; a forest of greasy hair was imprisoned in a red and yellow silk handkerchief which covered his head, and whose points fell upon his back. He had an olive complexion, peculiar to individuals of the Indian race to which he belonged.

This man was well known to the inhabitants of Valparaíso, who experienced for him a hatred thoroughly justified by the acts of ferocity of which he had been guilty under various circumstances; and as no one knew his real name, it had grown into a custom to designate him by the name of the Vaquero, owing to his great skill in lassoing wild bulls on the Pampas.

"The fiend twist the necks of those accursed English captains!" the Frenchman exclaimed, as he passionately smote the table: "it is easy to see that they are heretics."

"Yes," the other replied; "they are thieves—a whole cargo of raw silver, which we had such difficulty in passing, and which cost us the lives of two men."

"It is my fault," Leon continued, with an oath. "I am an ass. We have made a long voyage for nothing, and I ought to have expected it, for with the English it is impossible to gain one's livelihood. I am sure that we should have done our business famously at Copiapó, and we were only eight leagues from there."

"That's true," said the half-breed; "and I cannot think how the mad idea occurred to us of coming, with thirty loaded mules, from Chanoccillo to Valparaíso."

"Well, what is done is done, my friend; but we lose one thousand piastres."

"*Vaya pués*. Captain, I promise you that I will make the first Englishman I catch on the sierra pay dearly for our misadventure. I would not give an ochavo for the life of the man who comes within range of my rifle."

"Another glass," said Leon, as he seized the bottle, and poured the last of the spirit into the glasses.

"Here's your health," said the half-breed, and raising his glass, he emptied it at a draught, and then put it back on the table, heaving a deep sigh.

"Now, Diego of my soul, let us be off, as nothing keeps us here any longer."

"*Caray*, captain, I am ready. I am anxious to reach the mountains, for my health fails me in these poisoned holes which are called towns."

"Where are our lads?"

"Near the Rio Claro, and so well hidden that the fiend himself could not discover them."

"Very good," Leon answered. "Hilloh, Crevel!" he shouted, raising his voice, "come hither."

At this summons the posadero, who was standing at the end of the room, and had not lost a syllable of the conversation between the two smugglers while pretending to be busy with his household duties, advanced with a servile bow.

He was a fellow of about forty years of age, sturdy built, and with a red face. His carbuncled nose did not speak at all in favour of his temperance, and his crafty and hypocritical manners and his foxy eyes rendered him a complete specimen of one of those men branded in the French colonies by the name of BANIANS, utter scoundrels, who swarm in America, and who, in the shadow of an almost honest trade, carry on a dozen others which expose them to the scaffold. True fishers in troubled waters, who take with both hands, and are ready for anything if they are well paid.

This worthy landlord was an old acquaintance of the smugglers, who had for a long time been able to appreciate him at his full value, and had employed him successfully in many ugly affairs; hence he came up to them with that low and meaning smile which is always found stereotyped on the ignoble face of these low class traffickers.

"What do you desire, señores?" he asked, as he respectfully doffed the cotton nightcap of equivocal whiteness which covered his greasy poll.

"To pay you, master rogue," his countryman replied, as he tapped him amicably on the shoulder; "how much do I owe you?"

"Fourteen reals, captain."

"The deuce! you sell your adulterated Pisco rather high."

"Well," said the other, assuming a pious look and raising his eyes to heaven, "the excise dues are so heavy."

"That is true," said Leon; "but you do not pay them."

"Do you think so?" the landlord continued.

"Why, hang it! it was I who sold you the Pisco we have just been drinking, and I remember that you would only pay me—"

"Unnecessary, unnecessary, captain," Crevel exclaimed, quickly; "I will not bargain with a customer like you; give me ten reals and say no more about it."

"Stay; here are six, and that's more than it is worth," the young man said as he felt in a long purse which he drew from his belt, and took out several lumps of silver marked with a punch which gave them a monetary value.

"The deuce take the fancy they have in this country of making such money," he continued, after paying the posadero; "a man feels as if he had pebbles in his belt. Come, gossip, our horses."

"What, are you off, señores?"

"Do you suppose we are going to sleep here?"

"It would not be the first time."

"That is possible, but today you will have to do without us. I have already asked whether our horses are ready."

"They are at the door, saddled and bridled."

"You have given them something to eat, at least?"

"Two trusses of Alfalfa."

"In that case, good-bye."

And, after taking their rifles on their arms, the smugglers left the room. At the door of the inn, two richly-harnessed and valuable horses were waiting for them; they lightly leaped into the saddle, and after giving the landlord a parting wave of the hand, went off at a trot in the direction of the Almendral.[1]

While riding side by side, Leon and Diego continued to converse about the ill success of their last operation, so unluckily interrupted by the sudden appearance of custom-house officers, who opposed the passage of a string of mules conveying a heavy load of raw silver, which it was intended to smuggle, on account of certain merchants of Santiago, on board English vessels.

A fight began between the officers and the smugglers, and two of the latter fell, to the great annoyance of Leon Delbès, who lost in them the two bravest men of his band. It was a vexatious check; still, as it was certain that regretting would not find a remedy, Leon soon resolved to endure it manfully.

"On my word," he said, all at once, as he threw away the end of his cigarette, which was beginning to burn his fingers, "I am not sorry, after all, that I came to Valparaíso, for it is a pretty town, which deserves a visit every now and then."

"Bah!" the half-breed growled, thrusting out his lips disdainfully. "I prefer the mountains, where at any rate you have elbow room."

"The mountain has certainly its charm, but—"

"Look out, animal!" Diego interrupted, addressing a fat Genovevan monk who was bird gazing in the middle of the street.

Before the monk had time to obey this sharp injunction, Diego's horse had hit him so violent a blow in the chest that he fell on his nose five or six paces farther on, amid the laughter of a group of sailors, who, however, we must do them the justice of saying, hastened to pick him up and place him again on his waddling legs.

"What is the matter here?" Leon asked, as he looked around him. "The streets seem to me to be crowded; I never saw such animation before. Can it be a festival, do you think?"

"It is possible!" Diego answered. "These people of towns are so indolent, that, in order to have an excuse to dispense them from working, they have invented a saint for every day in the year."

"It is true that the Spaniards are religious," Leon muttered, with a smile.

"A beastly race," the half-breed added, between his teeth.

We must observe to the reader that not only did Diego, like all the Indians, cordially detest the Spaniards, the descendants of the old conquerors, but he, moreover, seemed to have vowed, in addition to this old hereditary rancour, a private hatred through motives he alone knew; and this hatred he did not attempt to conceal, and its effect was displayed whenever he found the opportunity.

The remark made by Leon was well founded—a compact crowd occupied the entire length of the street in which they were, and they only advanced with great difficulty; but when they entered the Governor's square it was impossible for them to take another step, for a countless multitude of people on horseback and foot pressed upon all sides, and a line of troops stationed at regular distances made superhuman efforts to keep back the people, and leave a space of a few yards free in the centre of the square.

At all the windows, richly adorned with carpets and garlands of flowers, were grouped blooming female heads, anxiously gazing in the direction of the cathedral.

Leon and Diego, annoyed at being unable to advance, attempted to turn back, but it was too late; and they were forced to remain, whether they liked it or no, spectators of what was going to take place.

They had not long to wait however; and few minutes had scarce passed after their arrival ere two cannon shots were heard. At the same time the bells of all the churches sent their silvery peals into the air, the gates of the cathedral were noisily opened, and a religious chant began, joined in by the whole crowd, who immediately fell on their knees, excepting the horsemen, who contented themselves with taking off their hats.

Ere long a procession marched along majestically in the sight of all.

There was something at once affecting and imposing in the magnificent appearance which the Governor's square offered at this moment. Beneath a dazzling sky illumined by a burning sun, whose beams glistened and sparkled like a shower of diamonds, and through the crowd kneeling and praying devoutly, the army of Christ moved onwards, marching with a firm and measured step, and singing the exquisite psalms of the Roman litany, accompanied by the thousand voices of the faithful.

Then came the dais, the crosses and banners embroidered with gold, silver, and precious stones, and statues of male and female saints larger than life, some carved in marble and wood, others sculptured in massive gold or silver, and shining so brightly that it was impossible to keep the eyes fixed on them.

Then came long files of Franciscan, Benedictine, Recollet, Genovevan, and other monks, with their arms folded on their chest, and the cowl pulled over their eyes, singing in a falsetto voice.

Then marched at regular intervals detachments of troops, with their bands at their head, playing military marches.

And after the monasteries came the convents, after the monks the nuns, with their white veils and contemplative demeanour.

The procession had been marching past thus for nearly an hour, and the end could not be seen, when Leon's horse, startled by the movement of several persons who fell back and touched its head, reared, and in spite of the efforts made by its rider to restrain it, broke into formidable leaps; and then, maddened by the shouts of the persons that surrounded it, rushed impetuously forward, driving back the human wall opposed to it, and dashing down everything in its passage.

A frightful tumult broke out in the crowd. Everybody, overcome by terror, tried to fly; and the cries of the females, closely pressed in by all these people, who had only one thought—that of avoiding the mad course of the horse—could be heard all around. Suddenly the horse reached the middle of the procession, at the moment when the nuns of the Purísima Concepción were defiling past; and the ladies, forgetting all decorum, fled in every direction, while busily crossing themselves.

One alone, doubtless, more timid than her companions, or perhaps more terrified, had remained motionless, looking around her, and not knowing what resolution to form.

The horse advanced upon her with furious leaps.

The nun felt herself lost; her legs gave way, and she fell on her knees, bending her head as if to receive the mortal stroke.

Leon, despairing of being able to change his horse's direction, or stop it soon enough not to trample the maiden under foot, had a sudden inspiration: driving in both spurs, he lifted the animal with such dexterity that it bounded from the ground, and passed like lightning over the nun without even grazing her.

A universal shout escaped from every throat on seeing the horse, after this exploit, touch the ground, stop suddenly, and tremble in all its limbs.

The crisis was spent, and there was nothing more to fear. Leon left the horse in the hands of Diego, who had joined him with great difficulty, and leaping out of his saddle, ran to raise the fainting maiden.

Before anyone had time to approach her, he took her in his arms, and lifted the veil which concealed her face.

The poor girl had been unable to resist the terrible emotion she had undergone; her eyes were closed, and a deadly pallor covered her features.

She was a delicious creature, scarce fifteen years of age, and her face was ravishing in its elegance and delicacy, through its exquisite purity of outline.

Her complexion, of a dazzling whiteness, had that gilded reflection which the sun of America produces; long black and silky lashes fringed her downcast eyelids, and admirably designed eyebrows relieved by their dark hue the ivory features of her virgin forehead.

Her lips, which were parted, displayed a double row of small white teeth. Deprived of consciousness as she was, it seemed as if life had entirely withdrawn from this body.

Leon stood motionless with admiration. On feeling the maiden's waist yield upon his arm, an unknown emotion made his heart tremble, and heavy drops of perspiration beaded on his temples.

"What can be the matter with me?" he asked himself, with amazement.

The nun opened her eyes again; a sudden flush suffused her cheek, and quickly liberating herself from the young man's arms with a gesture full of modesty, she gave him a glance of indefinable meaning.

"Thanks, Signor Caballero," she said, in a soft and tremulous voice; "I should have been dead without you."

Leon felt troubled by the melodious accents of this voice, and could not find any answer.

The maiden smiled sadly, and raising her hand to her bosom, she quickly pulled out a small bag, which she wore on a ribbon, and offering it to the young man, said—

"Farewell! farewell for ever!"

"Oh no!" Leon answered, looking around him, as if defying the other nuns, who, now that the danger was past, hurried up to resume their place in the procession; "not farewell, for we shall meet again."

And, kissing the maiden's hand, he took the scapulary.

The procession had already set out again, and the hymns were resounding once more in the air, as Leon perceived that the nun had returned to her place among her companions, and was going away singing the praises of the Lord.

A hand was heavily laid on the smuggler's shoulder, and he raised his head.

"Well," the half-breed asked him, "what are you doing here?"

"Oh!" Leon answered; "I love that woman, brother. I love her!"

"Come," Diego said; "the procession has passed, and we can move now. To horse, and let us be off!"

A few minutes later the two men were galloping along the road to Rio Claro.

[1] A part of Valparaíso situated at the end of the bay, and so called from the great number of almond trees that grew there.

CHAPTER II
THE COUNTRY HOUSE

Between Valparaíso and Rio Claro, halfway to Santiago, stood a delicious country house, belonging to Don Juan de Dios-Souza y Soto-Mayor, a descendant of one of the noblest and richest families in Chili: several of its members have played an important part in the Spanish monarchy.

The Soto-Mayors are counted among the number of the bravest and proudest comrades of Fernando Cortez, Pizarro, and all those heroic adventurers who, confiding in their sword, conquered for Spain those vast and rich countries, the possession of which allowed Philip II. to say at a later date, with truth, that the sun never set on his states.

The Soto-Mayors have spread over the whole of South America; in Peru, Chili, and Mexico, branches of this powerful family are found, who, after the conquest, settled in these countries, which they have not quitted since. This has not prevented them, however, from keeping up relations which have ever enabled them to assist each other, and retain under all circumstances their power and their wealth.

A Soto-Mayor was for ten years a Viceroy of Peru, and in our time we have seen a member of this family prime minister and chief of the cabinet at the Court of Spain.

When the American Colonies raised the standard of revolt against the Peninsula, Don Juan de Dios, although already aged and father of a family, was one of the first who responded to the appeal of their new country, and ranged themselves under its banner at the head of all the forces and all the servants they could collect.

He had fought the War of Independence as a brave soldier, and had endured courageously, and, before all, philosophically, the numerous privations which he had been compelled to accept.

Appointed a general when Spain, at length constrained to recognise the nationality of her old colonies, gave up the struggle, he retired to one of his estates, a few leagues from Valparaíso, and there he lived in the midst of his family, who loved and respected him, like a country gentlemen, resting from his fatigues and awaiting his last hours with the calmness of mind of a man convinced that he has done his duty, and for whom death is a reward rather than a punishment.

Laying aside all political anxieties, devoid of ambition, and possessing an immense fortune, he had devoted himself to the education of his three children, Inez, Maria, and Juanito. Inez and Maria were two maidens whose beauty promised to equal that of their mother, Doña Isabel de Costafuentes. Maria, the younger, according to the custom prevalent in Chilian families, was forced into a convent in order to augment the dowry of her sister Inez, who was nearly sixteen, and only awaited Maria's taking the veil to solemnize her own marriage.

Juanito, the eldest of the three, was five-and-twenty; he was a handsome and worthy young man, who, following his father's example, entered the army, and was serving with the rank of Major.

It was eight in the evening, and the whole family, assembled in the garden, were quietly conversing, while enjoying the fresh air after a stifling day.

The weather seemed inclined to be stormy, heavy black clouds coursed athwart the sky, and the hollow moaning of the wind could be heard amid the distant mountains; the moon, half veiled, only spread a vague and uncertain light, and at times a splendid flash tore the horizon, illumining the space with a fantastic reflection.

"Holy Virgin!" Inez said, addressing the general, "only see, father, how quickly the flashes succeed each other."

"My dear child," the old gentleman answered affectionately, "if I may believe certain wounds, which are a barometer for me, we shall have a terrible storm tonight, for they cause me intense suffering."

And the general passed his hand along his leg, while the conversation was continued by the rest.

Don Juan de Soto-Mayor was at this period sixty-two years of age; he was a man of tall stature, rather thin, whose irreproachable demeanour evidenced dignity and nobility; his grey hair, abundantly on the temples, formed a crown round the top of his head, which was bald.

"Oh! I do not like storms," the young lady continued.

"You must say an orison for travellers, Inez."

"Am I to be counted among the number of travellers, señorita?" interrupted a dashing cavalier, dressed in a splendid military uniform, and who, carelessly leaning against an orange tree, was gazing at Inez with eyes full of love.

"You, Don Pedro; why so?" the latter said eagerly, as she gave a pout of adorable meaning. "You are not travelling."

"That is true, señorita; at least, not at this moment, but—"

"What Colonel!" Don Juan said, "are you returning to Santiago?"

"Shortly, sir. Ah! you served at a good time, general; you fought, at any rate, while we parade soldiers are fit for nothing now."

"Do not complain, my friend; you have your good moments too, and the war which you wage is at times more cruel than ours."

"Oh!" Inez exclaimed, with a tremor in her voice, "do not feel annoyed, Don Pedro, at your inaction; I fear lest those wicked Indians may begin again at any moment."

"Reassure yourself, Niña, the Araucanos are quiet, and we shall not hear anything of them for a long time; the last lesson they received will render them prudent, I hope."

"May heaven grant it!" the young lady remarked, as she crossed herself and raised her eyes to heaven; "But I doubt it."

"Come, come," the general exclaimed, gaily, "hold your tongue, little girl, and instead of talking about such serious things, try to be more amiable to the poor colonel, whom you take a pleasure in tormenting."

Inez pretended not to hear the words which her father had just said to her, and turning to her mother, who, seated by her side, was talking to her son in a low voice.

"Mamita," she said, coaxingly, "do you know that I am jealous of you?"

"Why so, Inez?" the good lady asked.

"Because, ever since dinner you have confiscated Juanito, and kept him so closely to you that it has been impossible for me to tease him once the whole evening."

"Have patience, my pet," the young man said, as he rose and leaned over the back of her chair; "you will make up for lost time; besides, we were talking about you."

"About me! Oh, brother, make haste and tell me what you were saying."

And the girl clapped her little childish hands together, while her eyes were lighted up by curiosity.

"Yes," said Don Juanito, maliciously; "we were talking about your approaching marriage with my friend, Colonel Don Pedro Sallazar."

"Fie! you naughty fellow," Inez said, with a mocking smile; "you always try to cause me pain."

While saying these words, the coquette shot a killing glance in the direction of the colonel.

"What! cause you pain!" her brother answered: "is not the marriage arranged?"

"I do not say no."

"Must it not be concluded when our sister Maria has pronounced her vows?"

"Poor Maria!" Inez said, with a sigh, but quickly resumed her usual good spirits.

"That is true; but they are not yet pronounced, as my dear Maria will be with us shortly."

"They will be so within three months at the most."

"Ah!" she exclaimed lightly, "before then the donkey and its driver will die, as the proverb says."

"My daughter," the general remarked, gravely, "the colonel holds your word, and what you have just said is wrong."

The girl blushed: two transparent tears sparkled on her long lashes; she rose quickly, and ran to embrace her father.

"Forgive me, father; I am a madcap."

Then she turned to the colonel, and offered him her hand.

"And do you also forgive me, Don Pedro? For I did not think of what I was saying."

"That is right," the general exclaimed; "peace is made, and I trust that nothing will disturb it in future."

"Thanks for the kind wish," said the colonel, as he covered with kisses the hand which Inez abandoned to him.

"Oh, oh!" Don Juan remarked, "here is the storm; let us be off."

In fact, the lightning flashed uninterruptedly, and heavy drops of rain began beating on the foliage which the gusts continued to agitate.

All began running toward the house, and were soon collected in the drawing room.

In Europe it is difficult to form an idea of the magnificence and wealth which American houses contain; for gold and silver, so precious and so rare with us, are profusely employed in Chili, Peru, and the entire southern region.

The description of the room in which the Soto-Mayor family sought refuge will give a sketch of what is called comfort in these countries, with which it is impossible for us to contend, as concerns everything that relates to splendour and veritable luxury.

It was a large octagonal room, containing rosewood furniture inlaid with ebony; the floor was covered with mats of Guayaquil straw of a fabulous price; the locks of the doors and window fastenings were of massive silver; mirrors of the height of the room reflected the light of pink wax candles, arranged in gold candelabra enriched with precious stones; and on the white and gold damask, covering the space below the looking glass, hung masterpieces of art signed by the leaders of the Spanish and Italian schools.

On the credence tables and whatnots, so deliciously carved that they seemed made of lacework, were arranged China ornaments of exquisite workmanship—trifles created to excite for a moment the pleasure of the eye, and whose manufacture had been a prodigy of patience, perfection, and invention. These thousand nothings,—on which glistened oriental gems, mother-o'-pearl, ivory, enamel, jasper, and all the products of the mineral kingdom, combined and mingled with fragrant woods; feathers, &c.,—would of themselves have absorbed a European fortune, owing to their inestimable value.

The lustre of the crystal girandoles, casting multicoloured fires, and the rarest flowers which grew down over enormous Japanese vases, gave a fairy like aspect to the apartment; and yet, of all those who had come there to seek shelter from the bad weather, there was not one who did not consider it quite usual.

The conversation interrupted in the garden had just been recommenced indoors, when a ring of the visitor's bell was heard.

"Who can arrive so late?" the general asked; "I am not expecting anybody."

The door opened, and a servant appeared.

"Mi amo," he said, after bowing respectfully; "two travellers, surprised by the storm, ask leave to take shelter in the house."

At the same time a vivid flash rendered the candles pale, and a tremendous peal of thunder burst forth. The ladies uttered a cry of alarm, and crossed themselves.

"Santa Virgin!" Señora Soto-Mayor exclaimed, "do not receive them, for these strangers might bring us some misfortune."

"Silence, madam," the old gentleman answered; "the house of a Spanish noble must ever be open to the unfortunate."

And he left the room, followed by the domestic. The Señora hung her head at her husband's reproach, but being enthralled by superstition, she kept her eyes anxiously fixed on the door through which the strangers would enter. In a few minutes the general re-appeared, conducting Delbès and Diego el Vaquero.

"This house is yours, gentlemen; enter, in Heaven's name;" he said to them, affably.

Leon bowed gracefully to the ladies, then to the two officers, and thanked the general for his cordial reception.

"So long as you deign to honour my poor house with your presence, gentlemen," the latter replied, courteously, "we are entirely at your service; and if it please you to drink maté with us, we shall feel flattered."

"I accept your proposal, sir, with thanks."

Diego contented himself with nodding his head in the affirmative; the general rang, and ordered the maté. A minute later, a butler came in, carrying a massive gold salver, on which were arranged exquisitely carved maté cups, each supplied with an amber tube. In the midst of the cups were a silver coffeepot full of water, and a sandalwood box containing the leaves. On golden saucers were piled regalias, and husk and paper cigarettes.

The butler placed the salver on a table to which the company sat down, and he then retired. After this, Señora Soto-Mayor prepared the decoction, poured the burning liquid into the cups, and placed them before the guests. Each took the one within reach, and was soon drawing up the maté, while observing deep silence and sitting in a contemplative attitude. The Chilians are very fond of this beverage, which they have borrowed from the Indians, and they display some degree of solemnity when they proceed to drink it.

When the first mouthfuls had been swallowed, the conversation began again. Leon took a husk cigarette from one of the saucers, unrolled it, rubbed the tobacco for a moment in the palm of his hand, then remade it with the consummate skill of the inhabitants of the country, lit it at the flame of a small gold lamp prepared for the purpose, and, after taking two or three whiffs, politely offered the cigarette to Doña Inez, who accepted it with a gracious smile, and placed it between her rosy lips.

Colonel Don Pedro had not seen the Frenchman's action without a certain twinge of jealousy; but at the moment when he was about to light the cigarette which he held in his hand, Inez offered him the one Leon had given her, and which she had half smoked, saying—

"Shall we change, Don Pedro?"

The colonel gladly accepted the exchange proffered to him, gave his cigarette to the young lady, and took hers, which he smoked with rapture.

Diego, even since his arrival at the house, had not once opened his lips; his face had grown clouded, and he sat with his eyes fixed on the general, whom he observed askance with an indefinable expression of hatred and passion.

Leon knew not to what he should attribute this silence, and felt alarmed at his comrade's strange behaviour, which might be noticed by the company, and produce an unpleasant effect in their minds.

Inez laughed and prattled merrily, and several times in listening to her voice Leon was struck by a vague resemblance to another voice he had heard, though he was unable to call to mind under what circumstances he had done so. Then on scrutinizing Señora Soto-Mayor's features, he thought he could detect a resemblance with someone he knew, but he could not remember who it was.

Believing himself the dupe of an illusion, he had to get rid of the notion of explaining to himself a resemblance which probably only existed in his imagination; then, all at once, on hearing a remark that fell from Inez's lips, he turned to recognise an intonation familiar to his ears, which plunged his mind once more into the same perplexity.

"Madre," said Inez to her mother, "Don Pedro informs me that his sister Rosita will take the veil at the convent of the Purísima Concepción on the same day as my beloved Maria."

"They are, indeed, of the same age," the Señora replied.

Leon started, and could not repress an exclamation.

"What is the matter, Caballero?" the general asked.

"Nothing, general; merely a spark from my cigarette that fell in my poncho," Leon replied, with visible embarrassment.

"The storm is lulling," Diego said, at length emerging from his silence; "and I believe that we can set out again."

"Can you think of such a thing, my guests? Certainly not; the roads are too bad for me to let you depart. Besides, your room is prepared, and your horses are resting in the corral."

Diego was about to refuse, but Leon did not allow him the time.

"Since you wish it, general, we will pass the night beneath your roof."

Diego was obliged to accept. Moreover, in spite of what he stated, the storm, instead of lulling, redoubled its intensity; but it could be seen that the Vaquero obeyed against his will the necessity in which he found himself of remaining, and that he experienced an invincible repugnance in submitting to it.

The evening passed without any further incident, and about ten o'clock, after prayers had been read, at which all the servants were present, they separated.

The general had the two smugglers conducted to their bedroom by a peon, after kindly wishing them good night, and making them promise not to leave his house the next morning without wishing him good-bye, Leon and Diego thanked him for the last time, and so soon as they reached their apartment, dismissed the servant, for they were eager to cross-question each other.

CHAPTER III
THE CONVENT OF THE
PURÍSIMA CONCEPCIÓN

Whatever may be asserted to the contrary, a religion frequently undergoes, unconsciously, the atmospheric influences of the country in which it is professed; and while remaining the same fundamentally, the forms vary infinitely, and make it change its aspect according as it penetrates into countries where climates are different.

This may at the first glance appear a paradox; and yet, if our readers will take the trouble to reflect, we doubt not but they will recognise the justice and truth of our assertion.

In some countries, like Germany and England, where thick fogs brood over the earth at certain periods of the year, the character of the inhabitants is tinged by the state of the gloomy nature that surrounds them. Their ideas assume a morose and mystical hue perfectly in harmony with what they see and feel. They are serious, sad, and severe, positive and material, because fog and cold remind them at every moment that they must think of themselves, take care, and wrestle, so to speak, with the abrupt and implacable nature which allows them no respite. Hence come the egotism and personality, which destroy all the poetry of religion which is so marvellously developed in southern nations.

If we look further back, we shall find the difference even more marked. For this purpose it is only necessary to compare Greek mythology — Paganism, with its smiling images which deified vices and passions, with the gloomy and terrible worship of Odin in Scandinavia, or with that even more sanguinary paid to the god Teutates in the Gaul of olden times, and in the sombre forests of Germany.

Can we deny the influence of the northern ice over the disciples of Odin? Is not the savage majesty of the immense forests which sheltered the priests of Teutates the principal cause of the mysteries which they celebrated? And, lastly, is not the benignity of the Greek mythology explained by the beauty of the sky in which it sprang up, the mildness of the climate, the freshness of the shadows, and the ever renewing charm of its magnificent landscapes?

The Catholic religion, which substitutes itself for all the rest, has been, and still is, subjected to the action of the temperature of those countries into which it has penetrated, and which it has fecundated.

In Chili it is, so to speak, entirely external. Its worship is composed of numerous festivals pompously celebrated in churches glittering with light, gold, silver, and precious stones, of interminable processions performed under a reign of flowers, and clouds of incense which burn uninterruptedly.

In this country, beloved of the sun, religion is full of love; the ardent hearts that populate it do not trouble themselves at all about theological discussions. They love God, the Virgin, and the saints with the adoration, self-denial and impulse which they display in all their actions.

Catholicism is changed with them, though they do not at all suspect it, into a sort of Paganism, which does not account for its existence, although that existence cannot be contested.

Thus they tacitly accord the same power to any saint as to deity; and when the majority of them address their prayer to the Virgin, they do not pray to Mary the Mother of our Saviour, but to Nuestra Señora de los Dolores, Nuestra Señora del Carmen, Nuestra Señora de Guadalupe, Nuestra Señora de la Soledad, Nuestra Señora del Pilar, Nuestra Señora de Guatananga, and ten thousand other Our ladies.

A Chilian woman will not hesitate to say, with perfect conviction, that she is devoted to Nuestra Señora de la Sierra, because she is far more powerful than Nuestra Señora del Carmen, and so on with the rest.

We remember hearing one day in the church of Nuestra Señora de la Merced, at Pilar, a worthy hacendero praying to God the Father to intercede for him with Nuestra Señora del Pilar, so as to obtain for him a good harvest!

Novenas are kept and masses ordered for the slightest pretext. If a Chilian lady be deserted by her lover, quick a mass to bring him back to her side; if a man wish to avenge himself on one of his fellow men, quick a mass that his revenge may be carried out!

There is also another way of insuring the protection of any saint, and that is by making a vow. A young man who wishes his beloved lady to give him a meeting, never fails to pledge himself by a vow addressed to San Francisco or San Antonio to perform some pious deed, if the saint will consent to advise the lady in his favour. And these practices must not be taken for juggling; the people who accomplish them do so in perfect good faith.

Such is the way in which the Catholic religion is understood in South America.

In all the ex-Spanish colonies members of the clergy swarm, and we are not afraid of being taxed with exaggeration when we assert that in Chili they form at least one-fourth of the population. Now, the clergy are composed of an infinite number of monks and nuns of every possible form, species, and colour, Franciscans, Benedictines, Genovevans, Barefooted Carmelites, Brothers of Mercy, Augustines, and many others whose names have escaped us. As will be easily understood, these religious communities, owing to their considerable number, are not paid by the government, whose resources would not nearly suffice for their support. Hence they are compelled to create a thousand trades, each more ingenious than the other, in order to be able to exist.

In these countries—and there will be no difficulty in understanding this—the clergy are excessively tolerant, for the very simple reason that they have need of everybody, and if they committed the mistake of alienating the inhabitants they would die of hunger in a fortnight. It is worth while seeing in Chili the extension given to the trade in indulgences. *Agnus Deis*, scapularies, blessed crosses, and miraculous images; everything has its price, everything is sold. So much for a prayer—so much for a confession—so much for a mass.

A Chilian sets out on a journey, and in order that no accident may happen to him on the road, he has a mass said. If, in spite of this precaution, he is plundered on the high road by the Salteadores, he does not fail on his return to go to the monk of whom he ordered the mass, and bitterly complain of his want of efficacy. The monk is accustomed to such recriminations, and knows what to answer.

"That does not surprise me, my son," the Franciscan, or the Benedictine, or whoever he may be, as the answer is always the same, replies; "what the deuce did you expect to have for a peso? Ah, if you had been willing to pay a half ounce, we should have had the beadle, the cross, the banner, two choristers, and eight candles, and then most assuredly nothing would have happened to you; but how could you expect the Virgin to put herself out of the way for a peso?"

The Chilian withdraws, convinced that he is in the wrong, and promising not to be niggardly on the next opportunity.

With the exception of the minor trades to which we have alluded, the monks are jolly fellows, smoking, drinking, swearing, and making love as well as a man of the world. It is not uncommon to see in a wine shop a fat monk with a red face and a cigarette in his mouth, merrily playing the vihuela as dance accompaniment to a loving couple whom he will confess next morning. Most of the monks carry their knife in their sleeve, and in a quarrel, which is a frequent thing in Chili, use it as well, and with as little remorse as the first comer.

With them religion is a trade by which they make the largest profit possible, and does not at all compel them to live without the pale of the common existence.

Let us add, too, in concluding this rather lengthy sketch, but which it was necessary to give the reader, in order that by knowing Chilian manners, he might be able to account for the strangest of the incidents which we are about to record, that, in spite of the reproaches which the light conduct of the monks at times deserves—regard being had to the sanctity of the gown they wear—they are not the less an object of respect to all, who, taking compassion on human weakness, excuse the man in the priest, and repay tolerance for tolerance.

The convent of the Purísima Concepción stands at the extremity of the Almendral. It is a vast edifice, entirely built of carved stone, nearly two hundred years old, and was founded by the Spaniards a short time after their arrival in Chili. The whole building is imposing and majestic, like all the Spanish convents; it is almost a small town, for it contains everything which may be useful and agreeable for life—a church, a hospital, a washhouse, a large kitchen garden, a shady and well-laid out park, reserved for the promenades of the nuns, and large cloisters lined with frescoes, representing scenes from the life of the Virgin, to whom the convent is consecrated. These cloisters, bordered by circular galleries, out of which, open the nuns' cells, enclose a sandy courtyard, containing a piece of water and a fountain, whose jet refreshes the air in the midday heat.

The cells are charming retreats, in which nothing that promotes comfort is wanting—a bed, two chairs covered with Cordovan leather, a prie-Dieu, a small toilet table, in the drawer of which you may be certain of finding a looking glass, and a few sacred pictures, occupy the principal space destined for necessary articles. In one corner of the room is visible, between a guitar and a scourge, a statue of the Virgin, with a wreath of roses on her head and a constantly-burning lamp before her. Such is the furniture which will be found, with but few exceptions, in the cells of the nuns.

The convent of the Concepción contains about one hundred and fifty nuns of the order of Mount Carmel, and some sixty novices. In this country of toleration, strict nunneries are rare; the sisters are allowed to go into town and pay or receive visits; the rule is extremely gentle, and with the exception of the offices which they are expected to attend with great punctuality, the nuns, when they have once entered their cells, are almost free to do what they think proper, no one apparently paying any attention to them.

After the incident which we recorded in our first chapter, the procession, momentarily interrupted by the furious attack of Leon's horses, was reorganized as well as it could be; all the persons comprising it returned to their places so soon as the first alarm was over, and two hours after the gates of the Purísima Concepción closed again upon the long file of nuns engulfed in its walls.

So soon as the crosses, banners, and statues of saints had been deposited with all proper ceremony in their usual places, after a short prayer repeated in community, the ranks were broken, and the nuns began chattering about the strange event which had suddenly interrupted them as they left the cathedral. Several of them were not tired of praising the bold rider who had so cleverly guided his runaway horse, and saved a great misfortune by the skill which he had displayed under the circumstances.

From the midst of a group of about a dozen sisters conversing together, there came forth two maidens, dressed in the white garb of novices, who, taking each other's arm, walked gently toward the most deserted part of the garden. They must have eagerly desired not to be disturbed in their private conversation, for, selecting the most shaded walk, they took great care to hide themselves from their companions' observation behind the shrubs that formed the borders.

They soon reached a marble seat hidden behind a clump of trees, in front of a basin filled with transparent water, whose completely motionless surface was as smooth as that of a mirror. No better place could have been selected for a confidential conversation; so they sat down, and raised the veil that covered their face.

They were two charming girls, who did not count thirty years between them, and whose delicate profile was gracefully designed under their pure and exquisitely white wimple. The first was Doña Maria de Souza y Soto-Mayor; the other was Doña Rosita Sallazar, sister of the dashing Don Pedro, of whom we have already got a glimpse as affianced husband of Inez.

Doña Maria's face displayed visible traces of emotion. Was it the result of the terror she had felt on seeing herself almost trampled on by the smuggler's horse, or did a cause, of which we are ignorant, produce the effect which we have just indicated?

The conversation of the young ladies will tell us.

"Well, sister," Rosita asked, "have you recovered from the terror which this morning's event caused you?"

Doña Maria, who seemed absorbed in secret thoughts, started, and hurriedly answered—

"Oh! I am well now; quite well, thank you."

"In what a way you say that, Maria! What is the matter? You are quite pale."

A short silence followed this appeal. The young ladies took each other's hand, and waited to see which would be the first to speak.

Maria and Rosita, who were nearly of the same age, loved each other like sisters. Both novices, and destined to take the veil at the same date, the identity of their position had produced between them an affectionate sympathy which never failed them. They placed in a common stock, with the simple confidence of youth, their hopes and sorrows, their plans and dreams—brilliant winged dreams, which the convent walls would pitilessly break. They had no secret from each other, and hence Rosita was grieved by the accent with which Maria had answered her when she asked her how she was. The latter evidently concealed something from her for the first time since she had entered the convent.

"Maria," she said to her, gently, "forgive me if I acted indiscreetly in asking after your dear health; but I feared, on noticing the pallor of your face—"

"Dear Rosita, how kind you are!" Maria interrupted, embracing her companion tenderly; "and how wrong I am! Yes, I am suffering, really; but I know not from what, and it only began just now."

"Oh! accursed be the wicked man, cause of so much terror!" Rosita continued, alluding to Leon the smuggler.

"Oh, silence, Rosita! Speak not so of that cavalier, for he has on his face such a noble expression of courage and goodness that—"

"So you looked at him, sister?" Rosita exclaimed.

"Yes, when I regained my senses and opened my eyes, his were fixed on me."

"What! he dared to raise your veil? But it is a great sin to let a man see your face, and you must confess it to dear Mother Superior; the convent rule demands it."

"I know it, and will conform."

"After all," Rosita continued, with volubility, "as you had fainted, you could not prevent him raising your veil; hence it is not your fault, but that young man's."

"He saved my life!" Maria murmured.

"That is true, and you are bound to feel grateful to him instead of hating him."

"Do you think I can remember him without sinning?"

"Certainly: is it not natural to remember those who have done us a great service?"

"Yes, yes; you are right," Maria exclaimed, joyfully. "Thanks, sister—thanks, sister: your words do me good, for I was afraid it would be wrong to think of him who saved me."

"On the contrary, sister," Rosita said, with a little doctorial tone which rendered her ravishing, "you know that Mother Abbess daily repeats to us that ingratitude is one of the most odious vices."

"Oh, in that case, I did right in giving him my scapulary as a pledge of remembrance."

"What! did you give him that holy object?"

"Oh, poor young man! he seemed so affected, his glance was so full of sorrow and grief—"

While Maria was speaking, Rosita was examining her, and after the last words, entertained no doubt as to the feelings which animated her friend.

"Maria," she said to her, bending down to her ear and speaking so low that no other but the one for whom it was meant could hear it—"Maria, you love him, do you not?"

"Alas!" Maria exclaimed, all trembling—"do I know? Oh, silence, for mercy's sake!" she continued, impetuously. "I love him! But who would have taught me to love? A poor creature, hurled within the walls of this convent at the tenderest age, I have up to this day known nought but the slavery in which my entire life must be spent. Excepting you, my kind Rosita, is there a creature in the world that takes an interest in my fate, is happy at my smile or grieved at my tears? Have I ever known since the day when reason began to enlighten my heart, the ineffable sweetness of maternal caresses—those caresses which are said to warm the heart, make the sky look blue, the water more limpid, and the sun more brilliant? No; I have ever been alone. My mother, whom I could have loved so dearly—my sister, whom I sought without knowing her, and whose kisses my childish lips yearned for—both shun me and abandon me. I am in their way; they are anxious to get rid of me; and as all the world repulses me, I am given to God!"

A torrent of tears prevented the young lady from continuing. Rosita was terrified by this so true grief, and tried to restore her friend's calmness, while unable to check the tears that stood in her own eyes.

"Maria! why speak thus? it is an offence to God to complain so bitterly of the destiny which He has imposed on us."

"It is because I am suffering extraordinary torture! I know not what I feel, but I fancy that during the last hour the bandage which covered my eyes has suddenly fallen, and allowed them to catch a glimpse of an unknown light. Up to this day I have lived as the birds of the air live, without care for the morrow and remembrance of yesterday; and in my ignorance of the things which are accomplished outside these walls I could not regret them. I was told: You will be a nun; and I accepted, thinking that it would be easy for me to find happiness wherever my life passed gently and calmly; but now it is no longer possible."

And the maiden's eyes flashed with such a brilliancy that Rosita dared not interrupt her, and listened, checking with difficulty the beating of her own heart.

"Listen, sister!" Maria continued, "I hear an undefinable music in my ears; it is the intoxicating promises which the joys of the world wake in me, which I am forbidden to know, and which my soul has divined. Look! for I saw strange visions pass before my dazzled eyes. They are laughing pictures of an existence of pleasures and joys which flash and revolve around me in an infernal whirlwind. Take care; for I feel within me sensations which horrify me; shudders that traverse my whole being and cause me impossible suffering and pleasure. Oh, when that young man's hand touched mine this morning, I trembled as if I had seized a red-hot iron; when I regained my senses, and felt his breath on my face, I fancied that life was going to abandon me; and when I was obliged to leave him, it seemed to me as if there were an utter darkness around me; I saw nothing more, and was annihilated. His fiery glance cast eternal trouble and desolation into my soul. Yes, I love him: if loving be suffering, I love him! For, on hearing the convent gates close after the procession, a terrible agony contracted my heart, an icy coldness seized upon me, and I felt as if the cold tombstone were falling again on my head."

Overcome by the extreme emotion which held possession of her, the maiden had risen; her face was flushed with a feverish tinge; her eyes flashed fire; her voice had assumed a strange accent of terror and passion; her bosom heaved wildly, and she appeared to be transfigured! Suddenly she burst into sobs, and hiding her face in her hands, yielded to her despair.

"Poor Maria!" said Rosita, affected by this so simply poignant desolation, and seeking in vain by her caresses to restore calmness, "how she suffers!"

For a long time the two maidens remained seated at the same spot, mingling their tears and sighs. Still a complete prostration eventually succeeded the frenzy which had seized on Maria; and she was preparing, on her companion's entreaties, to return to her cell, when several voices, repeating her name, were heard at a short distance from the thicket where she had sought refuge.

"They are seeking us, I think," said Rosita.

"They are calling me," Maria continued; "what can they want with me?"

"Well, beloved sister, we will go and learn."

The two maidens rose, and soon found themselves in the presence of two or three sisters, who were looking for them.

"Ah, there you are!" the latter exclaimed; "Holy Mother Superior is asking after you, Maria; and we have been seeking you for the last ten minutes."

"Thanks, sisters," Maria answered; "I will obey the summons of our good mother."

"Be calm," Rosita whispered to her, with some amount of anxiety.

"Fear nothing; I will manage to hide my feelings." And all returned in the direction of the convent.

CHAPTER IV
THE SMUGGLERS

Three years prior to the events which we have just recorded, that is to say, about the month of May, 1830, Diego the Vaquero, who at that period was one of the bravest gauchos on the pampas of Buenos Aires, was returning to his rancho one evening after a day's hunting, when suddenly, before he could notice it, a magnificent panther, probably pursuing him in the tall grass, leaped, with an enormous bound, on his horse's neck. The animal, startled by this attack, which it was far from expecting, neighed with pain, and reared so violently that it fell back on its master, who had not had time to leap on the ground, but was held down by the weight of his steed.

It was, doubtless, all over with man and horse when Diego, who, in his desperation, was commending his soul to all the saints in paradise, and reciting, in a choking voice, all the scraps of prayers which he could call to mind, saw a long knife pass between his face and the head of the foetid brute, whose breath he could feel on his forehead.

The panther burst into a frightful howl, writhed, vomited a stream of black blood, and after a terrible convulsion, which set all the muscles of his body in action, fell dead by his side.

At the same moment the horse was restored to its trembling feet, and a man helped the Vaquero to rise, while saying, good-humouredly—

"Come, tell me, comrade, do you think of sleeping here, eh?"

Diego rose, and, with an anxious glance around him, felt all his limbs to make sure they were intact; then, when he was quite certain that he was perfectly sound and free from any wound, he gave a sigh of satisfaction, devoutly crossed himself, and said to his defender, who, with folded arms and a smile on his lips, had followed all his movements with the utmost interest—

"Thanks, man. Tell me your name, that I may retain it in my heart along with my father's."

"Leon," the other answered.

"Leon," the gaucho repeated, "it is well; my name is Diego; you have saved my life; at present we are brothers, and do with me as you will."

"Thanks," said Leon, affectionately pressing the hard, rugged hand which the half-breed offered him.

"Brother, where is your rancho?"

"I have none," Leon answered, with a cloud of sorrow over his face.

"You have none? What were you doing all alone, then, in the middle of the Pampas at this hour of the night?"

The young man hesitated for a moment, and then, regaining his good spirits, replied—

"Well, if I must confess to you, comrade, I was dying of hunger in the most philosophical way in the world: I have eaten nothing for two days."

"Caray," Diego exclaimed; "die of hunger! Come with me, brother; we will not part again; I have some charqui in my rancho. I repeat to you, you have saved my life, and henceforth all must be in common between us. You look like a daring fellow, so remain with me."

From this day Leon and Diego never parted again; and the friendship of these two men grew with time so great that they could not live without one another; but however great was the intimacy existing between them, never had a word been exchanged concerning their past life; and this mutual secret, mutually respected, was the only one that existed between them.

Diego certainly knew that Leon was a Frenchman, and had also noticed his great aptitude in bodily exercises, his skill as an excellent horseman, and, above all, the depth of his ideas and far from ordinary conceptions.

Recognising of what great use the young man's intellect had been to him in critical moments to get out of a difficulty, Diego regarded him with a species of veneration, and endured his moral superiority without even perceiving it.

With the sublime self-denial of virgin natures whom the narrow civilization of towns has not degraded, he had grown to regard Leon as a being placed on his path by Providence, in order that he might have someone to love; and finding in Leon a perfect reciprocity of friendship, he felt ready to sacrifice to Leon the life which he owed him.

On his side, Leon, captivated by the frank advances which the Vaquero had made him, had gradually come to feel for him a sincere affection, which was evidenced by a deep and unbounded devotion.

A short time after their meeting, Diego communicated to Leon the plan he had of going to Chili, and proposed to him to accompany him. The idle life on the pampas could not suit Leon, who had dreamed of an active and brilliant existence when he set foot on American soil. Gifted with an adventurous and enterprising character, he had left his native land to tempt fortune, and hitherto chance had not favoured his hopes. As nothing, therefore, prevented him from trying whether Chili might not be more lucky, he accepted.

One morning, therefore, the pair, mounted on Indian horses, crossed the pampas, and then, after resting for some days at San Luis de Mendoza, they entered the passes of the Cordilleras, which they got through with great difficulties and dangers of every description, and at length reached their journey's end.

On arriving at Chili, Leon, powerfully supported by Diego, organized the contraband trade on a vast scale, and a few months later fifty men obeyed his orders and those of Diego, whom he made his lieutenant. From this moment Captain Leon Delbès found the mode of life which suited his tastes.

Now that we have explained the nature of the ties which bound the two principal characters of our story, we will resume our narrative at the moment when we left our smugglers in the room which Don Juan y Soto-Mayor ordered to be got ready for them.

Scarce had the peon left the room ere Leon, after assuring himself that no one could hear his words, walked up to Diego, who was sitting gloomy and silent on a folding chair, and said—

"What is the matter with you tonight? Why did you remain so silent? Is it that General Soto-Mayor—"

"There is nothing the matter with me," the half-breed sharply interrupted; "but by the way," he added, looking Leon in the face, "you appear yourself to be suffering from extraordinary agitation."

"You are right; but if you wish to learn the cause, confidence for confidence, and tell me what you have on your mind."

"Leon, do not question me on this subject. You are not mistaken; I allow I have been thoughtful and silent ever since I have crossed the threshold of this house; but do not try to penetrate the motive. It is not the time yet to tell you the things which you must know some day. Thanks for the interest you take in my annoyances and my sorrows; but once again I implore you, in the name of our friendship, do not press me."

"Since such is the case, brother, I will refrain from any questions," Leon answered.

"And now, if you please, tell me why I saw you turn pale and tremble when a word that fell from the lips of the Señora Inez, and which I did not catch, struck your ear."

"Brother, do you remember that this morning, after saving from a certain death the novice of the convent of the Purísima Concepción, I told you that my heart knew love for the first time in my life?"

"But what is there in common between that girl and Señora Inez?"

"Do you remember also," Leon continued, without answering the Vaquero's observation, "that I swore to see the maiden again, even if I were obliged to lay down my life in satisfying my desire?"

"But again I say—"

"Well, know then, brother, that I have learned her name, and it is Doña Maria y Soto-Mayor."

"What are you saying?"

"And that she is the daughter of our host, Don Juan de Dios-Souza y Soto-Mayor."

"And you love her?" Diego exclaimed.

"Must I repeat it again?" Leon remarked impetuously.

"Malediction!" said the half-breed.

"Yes, malediction, is it not? for Maria is eternally lost to me; she will take the veil shortly, and the hopes I entertained of being able to drag her out of the walls of that convent are blighted."

"To marry her?" Diego remarked, mockingly.

"Nonsense, Leon, my friend: you are mad. What, you, the smuggler, marry a Señora, the daughter of a gentleman! No, you cannot suppose such a thing."

"Silence, Diego, silence! for the more that I feel the impossibility of possessing the girl, the more I feel that I love her."

And the young man, crushed by sorrow, fell into a seat by Diego's side.

"And do you believe," the latter continued, after a moment's silence, "that there is no hope of delaying her in taking the veil?"

"How do I know? Besides, of what good is it, as you said just now—can I think of the daughter of General Soto-Mayor? No, all is lost!"

"Remember the Spanish proverb—'Nothing is certain but death and the tax gatherer.'"

For a moment past, the half-breed's face had become animated with a singular expression, which would not have escaped Leon, had not the latter been entirely absorbed in the thought of losing her whom he loved.

"What do you mean?" he asked Diego.

"Listen patiently, for the question I am going to ask you is intended to fix an important determination in my mind."

"I am listening," the young man said.

"Do you really love Doña Maria?"

At this question, which might seem, at the least, inopportune after what Leon had just stated, the latter frowned angrily; but on noticing the half-breed's serious face, he understood that it was not for the purpose of making a jest of his despair that Diego had revived the fire which was burning in his bosom.

"If I do not see her again, I shall die," the young man replied, simply.

"You shall not die, brother, for within a fortnight she will be at your knees."

Leon knew the half-breed, and that he was a man who never promised in vain: hence he did not dare doubt, and merely raised his eyes and questioned him with a look.

"Within a fortnight she will be at your knees," the half-breed slowly repeated; "but till then, not a word, not a sign of recollection, reproach, impatience, or amazement, but passive obedience."

"Thanks, brother," Leon contented himself with answering, as he held out his hand to Diego, who pressed it in his.

"And now let us sleep, so that tomorrow our foreheads may be less burning, and we may be able to set to work."

Then, putting out the candles, the two men threw themselves on their beds, without exchanging another word, for each was anxious to reflect upon the course he should pursue.

Neither slept: Leon thought of Maria and the means Diego might employ to fulfil the pledge he had made; while Diego had in his head a ready-traced plan, whose success appeared to him certain, as it was connected with a far more dangerous affair.

At daybreak they rose, and kneeling down in the middle of the room, took each other by the hand, and devoutly said their prayers. Anyone would have been astonished who had overheard what these two men asked of God—the God of mercy and goodness! Their prayer ended, they went down into the garden; the night storm had entirely passed away, the sun was rising in a flood of transparent vapour, and everything announced a magnificent day.

Shortly after their arrival, they perceived the general, who came to meet them with a regular step and a joyous face.

"Well, gentlemen," he shouted to them, so soon as he saw them, "how did you pass the night?"

"Excellently, general," Leon replied; "and my friend and myself both thank you sincerely for your kind hospitality."

"At your age a man can sleep anywhere," the general continued, with a pleasant smile. "Oh, youth!" he added, with a sigh of regret, "happy time, which flies, alas! too quickly." Then becoming serious; "As for the slight service which I have had the pleasure of rendering you, you will disoblige me by thanking me for so simple a thing."

After a few more words from him, dictated by politeness, the three men walked round the garden several times, and, to Leon's great surprise, Diego did not allude to their departure; but as the young man did not know the Vaquero's line of conduct as to the prospects which he nursed, he waited.

Don Juan was the first to break the silence.

"Gentlemen," he said, stopping at the corner of a shady walk, "be good enough, I pray, not to take in ill part what I am about to say—you are smugglers, I believe?"

"Yes, sir," replied Diego, amazed at the old gentleman's perspicuity.

"This discovery does not injure you at all in my opinion," continued the general, who had noticed the look of surprise exchanged by the two friends. "I have frequently had dealings with gentlemen of your profession, and have had always cause to be pleased with them; and I trust that the relations which may be established between us will prove advantageous to both parties."

"Speak, sir."

The Vaquero was all ears, and examined the general with a distrust which the latter did not notice, or feigned not to notice.

"This is the matter, gentlemen. I am obliged, owing to certain family reasons, to undertake a journey to Valdivia, where my brother Don Louis resides; now, your arrival at my house has made me think of making the journey under your escort, and I wish to propose to you, as I shall take Señora y Soto-Mayor and my whole family with me, that you and your men should escort us, leaving it to you to fix the price as you think right."

"General," Leon answered, "you have guessed correctly in regarding us as smugglers; I have the honour of being the captain of a band of fifty men, who know how to put down the customs' dues when they are too high; but you are mistaken in supposing that we can accompany you."

"Why so?" the Vaquero eagerly interrupted, on whose features a strange gleam of satisfaction had appeared. "It is true that it is not our habit to undertake business of that nature; but the general has shown himself too hospitable to us to refuse him our assistance. Captain, remember, too, that we have something to do within a few days in the neighbourhood of Valdivia, and hence we shall merely make our journey the sooner, which is a trifle."

"That is true," muttered the captain, whom a glance of Diego's had told that he must accept. "I fancied that I must return to Valparaíso; but what my friend has just said is perfectly correct, so you can dispose of us as you please."

"In that case, gentlemen," said the general, who had only seen in this opposition on the part of the captain a mode of demanding a large sum, "be good enough to step into my study, and while drinking a glass of Alicante, we will settle money matters."

"We are at your orders."

And all three proceeded to the general's apartments. It was arranged that, instead of bargaining with an arriero, the captain was to supply a dozen mules to carry the baggage, and that they should start the following morning. When this arrangement was made, Leon and Diego asked the general's permission to go and join their men, and give orders for the departure; but he would not consent until they had breakfasted.

They therefore waited, and soon found themselves again in the company of the members of the Soto-Mayor family, as well as of Don Pedro Sallazar, who had decided on spending the night at the country house before setting out for Santiago. Leon was dying to turn the conversation to the Convent of the Purísima Concepción, and could have most easily done so by telling the event of the previous day; but he remembered the promise made to Diego, and fearing lest he might commit some folly injurious to his interests, he held his tongue; still he learned, on hearing the talk, that the general's major-domo had started that morning for Valparaíso entrusted with a message for the Señora Doña Maria.

When breakfast was over, the two friends took leave of their hosts, and, after finally arranging the hour for starting, they left the house, and found in the courtyard their horses ready saddled and held by a peon. At the moment of starting, Don Pedro de Sallazar waved his hand to them, and disappeared in the direction of Santiago, accompanied by the general's son.

The two smugglers arrived before midday at the spot where their men, somewhat alarmed at their prolonged absence, were encamped. It was a narrow gorge between two lofty mountains, and at a sufficient distance from the beaten road for the band to be safe from any surprise, of which there was not much apprehension, by the way, as in this country smugglers enjoy almost complete immunity, and have only to fear the excessively rare cases of being caught in the act.

The horses were browsing at liberty, and the men, seated on a hearth made of two lumps of stone, were finishing their breakfast of charqui and tortillas. They were mostly men in the prime of life, whose resolute air sufficiently evidenced the carelessness they felt for every species of danger.

Belonging to all nations, they formed a whole which was not without originality, but each of them, whether he were German or Portuguese, Sicilian or Dutchman, as he found in the existence which he led the charm of an adventurous life studded with perils, pleasures, and emotions, had completely forgotten the name of his country, only to remember the memorable days on which, indulging in his dangerous profession, he had put the custom house officers to flight, and passed under their very noses bales of merchandize.

Enemies of a yoke and servitude, under whatever form they might appear, they obeyed with rigorous exactness the discipline which Leon Delbès had imposed on them—a discipline which, by the way, allowed them to do whatever they pleased when not actually engaged with their smuggling duties. Some were drunkards, others gamblers, and others libertines; but all ransomed their faults, which they regarded almost as qualities, by a well-tried courage, and a perfect devotion to Leon and Diego.

Their dress varied but slightly from that of their chief; all wore a poncho, which covered their weapons, and the boots of wood rangers, which, while protecting their legs from the stings of reptiles, left them perfect liberty of motion. Their hats alone might be regarded as the distinctive mark either of their nationality or the difference of their tastes. There were broad-brimmed, pointed, and round hats; every shape came into strange contact there, from the worn silk hat of Europe to that of the American Bolivar.

They uttered a shout of joy on perceiving their chiefs, and, eagerly rising, ran to meet them.

"Good day, gentlemen," Leon said, as he leaped from his horse. "I am rather behind my time, but you must blame the night storm, which compelled us to halt on the road. Is there any news?"

"None, captain," they answered.

"In that case listen to me. Ten of you will stay here, and at four o'clock tomorrow morning proceed with twelve mules to the house of Don Juan y Soto-Mayor, and place yourselves at the orders of that gentleman, whom you will accompany to Valdivia." Diego set about selecting the men whom he thought the best fitted for the expedition; and after he had done so, Leon addressed the others.

"You will start for Valparaíso and await my orders there; you will lodge at Crevel's, in the Calle San Agostino, and at Dominique the Italian's, at the Almendral. Above all," he added, "be prudent, and do not attract attention; amuse yourselves like good fellows, but do not quarrel with the señores, or have any fights with the sailors. You understand me, I suppose?"

"Yes, captain," they all answered.

"Very well. Now I will give each of you five ounces to cover your expenses, and do not forget that I may want you at any moment, and you must be ever ready to obey my summons."

He gave them the money, and after repeating his recommendations, he retired, leaving it to Diego to give the men who were proceeding to Valparaíso the final instructions which they might need. The smugglers removed all traces of their meal, and each of them hurried to saddle his horse. A few minutes later, forty men of the band set out under the guidance of the oldest among them.

Diego watched them start, and then returned to Leon, who was resting from his fatigue on a small turf mound, overshadowed by a magnificent clump of trees. The Vaquero held in his hand the alforjas which he had taken off his horse; he examined the place where Leon was seated, and finding it as he wished, he sat down by his side; then taking out of the bag a clumsy carved earthern pipe, into which he fitted a long stem, he began to strike a light over a small horn box filled with burnt rags, which soon caught fire. When his pipe was lighted, he began smoking silently.

Leon, on seeing these preparations, understood that something important was about to take place between him and Diego, and waited. At the expiration of five minutes, the latter passed him his pipe; Leon drew several puffs and then returned it to him. These preliminaries completed, Diego began to speak.

"Leon, three years have passed since Heaven brought us together on the pampas of Buenos Aires; since that moment—and I shall never forget it, brother—everything has been in common between us—pleasure and pain, joy and sorrow."

Leon bowed his head in the affirmative, and the half-breed continued:

"Still, there is one point upon which our mouths have ever remained silent, and it is the one which refers to the life of each of us before that which we now lead together."

Leon looked at him in amazement.

"It is not a want of confidence," Diego hastily added, "but the slight interest we felt in cross-questioning each other, which alone is the cause. Of what use is it to know the past life of a man, if from the day when you first saw him he has not ceased to be honest and loyal? Besides, the hours are too short in the pampas for men to dream of asking such questions."

"What are you coming to?" Leon at length asked.

"Listen, brother. I will not question you about what I care little to know, but I wish to tell you something you must know. The moment has arrived to speak; and though the story I have to tell you is gloomy and terrible, I am accomplishing a duty."

"Speak, then," said Leon.

The half-breed passed his hand over his forehead, and for a moment collected his recollections. Leon waited in silence.

CHAPTER V
THE INCA OF THE NINETEENTH CENTURY

"Long ago, very long ago," Diego, the Vaquero, began, "all the lands bordering the bay of Valparaíso belonged to the Indians, whose vast hunting grounds extended on one side from the lofty peaks of the Cordilleras down to the sea, and on the other covered the Pampas of Buenos Aires, of Paraguay—in a word, all the splendid countries from which they have eternally disappeared, and it is impossible to find a trace of the moccasins which trod them during centuries."

"The Indians were at that day free, happy, powerful, and more numerous than the grains of sand in the bed of the sea. But one day strange news spread among them: it was said that white men, who had come no one knew whence, and mounted on immense winged horses, had suddenly appeared in Peru."

"I need not remind you of all that occurred in consequence of this news, which was only too true, or describe to you the hideous massacres committed by the Spaniards, in order to reduce the unhappy Indians to slavery, for it is a story which everybody knows. But what you are possibly ignorant of is, that during one of the dark and stormy nights which followed this invasion, a dozen men of majestic demeanour, with haughty though care-laden brows, were seen to land from a canoe half broken by the waves and jagged rocks."

"They were Indians who had miraculously escaped from the sack of Quito, and had come to present themselves as suppliants to the elders of the Araucano nation. Among them was a man whom they respectfully obeyed. He was the son of the sister of the valiant Atahualpa, King of Quito, and his name was Tahi-Mari. When in the presence of the elders, Tahi-Mari gave them a narration of the misfortunes which had struck him."

"He had a daughter, Mikaa, the purest and loveliest of the daughters of the Sun. When conquered by the Spaniards, who, after killing two of his sons, set fire to his palace, Tahi-Mari, followed by his three sons left home, rushed toward the palace of the Sun, in order to save his daughter, if there were still time."

"It was night: the volcano was roaring hoarsely, and hurling into the air long jets of fire, whose lurid and sinister gleams combined with the flames of the fire kindled by the conquerors of this unhappy city. The squares and streets were encumbered with a terrified multitude, who fled in all directions with terrible cries from the pursuit of the Spanish soldiers, who, intoxicated with blood and carnage, massacred mercilessly old men, women, and children, in order to tear from their quivering bodies the gold collars and ornaments which they wore. Neither tears, prayers, nor entreaties succeeded in moving their ferocious executioners, who with yells and shrill whistles excited their dogs to help them in this horrible manhunt."

"When Tahi-Mari reached the Temple of the Sun, that magnificent edifice, which contained such riches, had become a prey to the flames; a girdle of fire surrounded it on all sides, and from the interior could be heard the groans of the hapless virgins who were expiring in the tortures of a horrible death. Without calculating the imminency of the peril, the poor father mad with grief and despair, rushed into the burning furnace which opened its yawning mouth before him."

"'My daughter! my daughter!' he cried. In vain did the flames singe his clothing; in vain did frightful burns devour his hands and face: he felt nothing, saw nothing; from his panting chest constantly issued the piercing cry—"

"'My daughter! my daughter!'"

"Suddenly a half-naked virgin, with dishevelled hair, and her features frightfully contracted, escaped from the flames; it was Mikaa. Tahi-Mari, forgetting all that he had suffered, weepingly opened his arms to the maiden, when a Spaniard, dressed in a brilliant garb, and holding a sword in his hand, rushed upon Mikaa, and ere her father had time to make a gesture thrust his weapon into her chest!"

"Oh, it is frightful!" Leon, who had hitherto listened to his comrade's story in silence, could not refrain from exclaiming.

Diego made no reply, but a sinister smile played round his livid lips.

"The maiden fell bathed in her blood, and Tahi-Mari was about to avenge her, when the Spaniard dealt him such a fierce blow that he lost his consciousness. When he regained his senses the officer had disappeared."

"It is infamous," Leon said again.

"And that officer's name was Don Ruíz de Soto-Mayor," Diego said, in a hollow voice.

"Oh!" Leon muttered.

"Wait a moment, brother; let us continue, for I have not finished yet."

"Though tracked like a wild beast, and incessantly hunted by the Spaniards, Tahi-Mari, accompanied by his three sons and some faithful friends, succeeded in getting away from Quito and reaching the country of the Araucanos."

"After the Inca had recounted his misfortunes to the great Indian Chief, the latter welcomed the fugitives with hearty marks of affection; one of them, the venerable Kouni-hous-koui (he who is respected), a descendant of one of the oldest families of the Sagamores of the nation, exchanging his calumet with Tahi-Mari, declared to him, in the name of the Araucanos, that the Council of Elders adopted him as one of their caciques."

"From this day Tahi-Mari, owing to his courage and wisdom, acquired the esteem of those who had given him a new country to love and defend."

"Several years passed thus, and no sign led the Araucanos to suspect that the Spaniards would ever dare to attack them; they lived in a perfect state of security, when suddenly and without any justification for the aggression, a Spanish fleet consisting of more than thirty brigantines sailed into the bay of Valparaíso. They had no sooner disembarked than they built a city, which soon saw the flag of conquest floating from its walls."

"Still the Araucanos, although driven back by their terrible enemies, were aroused by the voice of Tahi-Mari, and resolved to keep the Spaniards constantly on their defence, by carrying on against them a war of snares and ambushes, in which the enemy, owing to their ignorance of the places where they fought, did not always get the best of it."

"In the course of time, this perpetual war made them lose a great number of soldiers, and feeling desperate at seeing several of their men fall daily under the blows of invisible enemies, who seemed to inhabit hollow trees, the tops of mountains, or the entrails of the earth, they turned all their rage against Tahi-Mari, whose influence over all the men who surrounded him they were aware of, and resolved to get hold of him."

"But it was no easy matter, for the Inca was on his guard against every attack, and was too well versed in the tactics of his enemy to let himself be caught by cunning or treachery. And yet this was destined to happen. There was among the Indian prisoners—alas! it is disgraceful to say it, but it was so—a man who, given to habits of intoxication and brought to Peru by the Spaniards, did not recoil before the offer made him to betray his brothers, on condition that they should give him as much aguardiente as he could drink."

"The Spanish captain, fertile in expedients, who had proposed this cowardly bargain to the Indian, induced the latter to go to Tahi-Mari, give himself out as an escaped prisoner, and, after inquiring into his plans, urge him to surprise the Spaniards, of whose numbers, position, and plan of campaign he was to give a false account. Once that Tahi-Mari was in the power of the Spaniards, firewater would amply compensate the traitor."

"All was carried out in the way the officer suggested; for could Tahi-Mari suspect that an Araucano would betray him? He received him on his arrival among his brothers with transports of joy, and then questioned him as to the enemy's strength and means of defence. This was what the Indian was waiting for: he answered the questions asked him by adroitly dissimulating the truth, and ended by asserting that nothing was easier than to take the Spanish troops prisoners, and he offered to guide the expedition in person."

"The hope of a certain victory animated the Araucanos, who joyfully greeted this proposition, and all was soon arranged for the start. During the night following the traitor's arrival, five hundred men picked from the bravest, and led by Tahi-Mari, descended the mountain under the guidance of the treacherous Indian, and marched silently upon a Spanish redoubt, in which they expected to find the principal chiefs of the enemy and surprise them."

"But as they advanced they perceived a dark line which was almost blended with the darkness, but which could not escape the piercing glances of the Indians. This line formed an immense circle, which surrounded them and became more contracted every moment. It was the Spanish horse coming to meet them and preparing to attack them."

"All at once Tahi-Mari uttered a yell of fury, and the head of the traitor who had drawn them into the snare rolled at his feet; but ere the Araucanos had time to retire, a number of horsemen, holding in leash twenty of those ferocious dogs trained for man hunting, rushed upon them. They were compelled to fight, and a terrible massacre began, which lasted all night. Tahi-Mari performed prodigies of valour. In the height of the action his eyes were injected with blood and a lurid pallor covered his face; he had recognised among those who were fighting the Spanish officer who killed his daughter Mikaa on the threshold of the Temple of the Sun in so dastardly a way. On his side the Spaniard rushed with incredible fury upon the Inca."

"It was a sublime moment! The two men attacked each other with equal fury, and the blood that flowed from their wounds stained their weapons. The axe which the Inca held was already whirling above the head of the Spaniard to deal him the final blow, when Tahi-Mari fell back, uttering a yell of pain: an enormous hound coming to the officer's assistance, had ripped open the Inca's stomach. Taking advantage of Tahi-Mari's defenceless state, Don Ruíz de Soto-Mayor despatched him by passing his sword right through his body."

"The next day the Inca's body, frightfully mutilated, was burnt on the public square of Valdivia, in the presence of a few Indians, who had only escaped the sword of their murderers to die at a later date in the punishment of a horrible captivity."

"Oh!" Leon exclaimed, who had felt his heart quiver; "it is frightful!"

"What shall I say, then?" Diego asked in his turn; "I who am the last of the descendants of Tahi-Mari!"

At this unexpected revelation Leon started; he looked at Diego, and understood that there was in this man's heart a hatred so deeply rooted, and, above all, so long repressed, that on the day when it broke out no power in the world would be strong enough to check the terrible effects of its explosion. He hung his head, for he knew not what to reply to this man who had to avenge such blood-stained recollections. Diego took his friend's hand, and remarking the emotion he had produced, added—

"I have told you, brother, what the ancestors of Don Juan de Souza y Soto-Mayor made mine suffer, and your heart has bounded with indignation, because you are loyal and brave; but what you do not yet know is that the descendants of that family have faithfully followed the conduct of the murderers of Tahi-Mari. Oh! there are strange fatalities in a man's life! One day—and that day is close at hand—you shall know the details of the existence which I have led, and the sufferings which I have endured without a murmur; but at the present day I will only speak of those of my race; afterwards I will speak of myself."

While uttering the last words, a flash of joy like that which a tiger feels when it holds a quivering prey under its claws passed into the half-breed's eyes. He continued—

"My father died a victim to the cruelty of the Spaniards, who put him to death because he dreamed of the independence of his country; his brother followed him to the tomb, weeping for his loss."

"Diego! God has cruelly tried thee."

"I had a mother," Diego went on, with a slight tremor in his voice; "she was the object of my father's dearest affections, and was young and lovely. One day when she left the mountain to visit my father, who was expiating within the walls of Valparaíso prison his participation in a movement which had broken out among the Araucanos, she met on the road a brilliant Spanish cavalier who wore a lieutenant's epaulettes."

"The Spaniard fixed upon her an impassioned glance; she was alarmed, and tried to fly, but the horseman prevented her, and in spite of her prayers and supplications, she could not liberate herself from the villain's arms. On the morrow Lieutenant Don Juan de Soto-Mayor was able to boast among his friends, the noble chiefs of the Spanish army, that he had possessed the chaste wife of Tahi-Mari the Indian."

"Yes, it was again a Soto-Mayor. This accursed name has ever hovered over the head of each member of my family, to crush it under punishment, sorrow, shame, or humiliation. Each time that one of us has reddened American soil with his blood, it was a Soto-Mayor that shed it. Each time that a member of this family met a member of mine, one was the executioner, the other the victim."

"And now, brother, you will ask me why, knowing that General Don Juan de Souza y Soto-Mayor is the man who dishonoured my mother, I did not choose among the weapons which hung from my girdle the one which should pierce his heart?—why I have not some night, when all were sleeping at the hacienda, carried within its walls the all-devouring fire, and taken, according to Indian custom, eye for eye and tooth for tooth?"

"Yes, I confess it; I should have quivered with pleasure had I seen all the Soto-Mayors, who live calm and happy a few leagues from us, writhing in the agonies of death. But I am the son of Tahi-Mari, and I have another cause to defend beside my own—that of my nation. And on the day when my arm falls on those whom I execrate, it will not be the Soto-Mayors alone who perish, but all the Spaniards who inhabit these countries."

"Ah! is it not strange to dream of enfranchisement after three hundred years of slavery? Well, brother, the supreme moment is close at hand; the blood of the Spaniard will again inundate the soil of Peru, and the nineteenth century will avenge the sixteenth."

"That is the reason why you saw me so silent at the general's house; that is why I agreed to escort him and his family to Valdivia, for my plans are marvellously served by this journey. As for the girl you love, as I told you, you shall see her again, and it will be the beginning of the punishment which is destined to fall on this family."

Diego had risen, but a moment later he resumed his ordinary stoicism.

"I have told you what you ought to know, in order to understand and excuse what you may see me undertake against the Spaniards; but before going further it is right that I should know if I can count on your help, and if I shall find in you the faithful and devoted friend who never failed me up to this day."

A violent contest was going on in Leon's heart. He asked himself whether he, who had no cause of complaint against the Spaniards, had any right to join those who were meditating their ruin. On the other hand, the sincere friendship which he felt for the Vaquero, whose life he had shared during the last four years, rendered it a duty to assist him, and did not permit him to abandon him in the moment of danger. Still he hesitated, for a secret anxiety kept him undecided, and prevented him forming a resolution.

"Diego," he asked the Vaquero in his turn, "before answering you, let me ask you one question?"

"Speak, brother!" Diego answered.

"What do you mean to do with Doña Maria?"

"I have promised you to bring her to your knees. If she love you, she will be my sister; if she refuse your love, I shall have the right to dispose of her."

"And she will have nothing to fear till I have seen her again?" Leon asked further.

"Nothing! I swear to you."

"In that case," said Leon, "I will take part in your enterprise. Your success shall be mine, and whatever be the road you follow, or the means you employ to gain the object of your designs, I will do all that you do."

"Thanks, brother; I was well aware that you would support me in the struggle, for it is in the cause of justice. Now I will set out."

"Do you go alone?"

"Yes, I must."

"When shall I see you again?"

"Tomorrow morning, at Don Juan's, unless I am compelled to remain at the place where I am going longer than I think; in that case I will join you on the Talca road. Besides, you do not require me to escort the general: our men will be at their post tomorrow, and you can say something about my going on ahead."

"That is true; but Doña Maria?"

"You will see her again soon. But start alone tomorrow for the country house, and I will meet you this day week, whatever may happen, in the Del Solar wood, at the San Francisco Solano quarry, where you will order a halt."

"Agreed, and I leave you to act as you think proper. Next Wednesday at the Del Solar wood, and if you wish to join us before then, we shall follow the ordinary road."

"Very good; now I am off."

Ten minutes after this long interview, Diego was galloping away from his comrade, who watched him depart, while striving to conjecture in what direction he was going. Profoundly affected by the varied events of the preceding day, and the story which Diego had told him, Leon reflected deeply as he walked toward the smugglers remaining with him, and who were engaged in getting their weapons in order.

Although nothing in his exterior announced the preoccupation from which the was suffering, it could be guessed that he was in a state of lively anxiety. The image of Doña Maria floated before his eyes; he saw her pale and trembling after he had saved her from his horse's rush, and then, carrying himself mentally within the walls of the convent of the Purísima Concepción, he thought of the barrier which separated them. Then suddenly the half-breed's words returned to his ear—"If she refuse your love," he had said, "I shall have the right to dispose of her!"

An involuntary terror seized on the young man at this recollection. In fact, was it presumable that Doña Maria loved him? and would not the Vaquero be compelled to employ violence in carrying out his promise of bringing him into the presence of the novice? In that case, how could he hope to make himself loved?

These reflections painfully agitated Leon Delbès, who, obeying that spontaneity of action peculiar to his quick and impetuous character, resolved to fix his uncertainty by assuring himself of the impression which he had produced on the heart of the maiden, whom he loved with all the strength and energy of a real passion.

Such a sudden birth of love would appear strange in northern countries, where this exquisite feeling is only developed in conformity with the claims of the laws of civilization; but in Chili, as in the whole of South America, love, ardent as the fires of the sun which illumines it, bursts forth suddenly and displays itself in its full power. The look of a Chilian girl is the flush which enkindles hearts of fire which beat in breasts of iron.

Leon was a Frenchman, but several years' residence in these parts, and his complete adoption of American manners, customs, and usages had so metamorphosed him, that gradually his tastes, habits, and wants had become identified with those of the inhabitants of Chili, whom he regarded as his brothers and countrymen. Without further delay, then, Leon prepared to return to Valparaíso, and make inquiries about Doña Maria.

"It is two o'clock," he said to himself, after consulting his watch; "I have time to ride to Ciudad, set Crevel to work, and be at the general's by the appointed hour."

And leaping on his horse, he galloped off in the direction of the Port, after bidding the ten men of the escort to start with or without him the next morning for the country house.

CHAPTER VI
THE BANIAN'S HOUSE

Valparaíso, like nearly all the commercial centres of South America, is a collection of shapeless huts and magnificent palaces, standing side by side and hanging in long clusters from the sided of the three mountains which command the town. The streets are narrow, dirty, and almost deprived of air, for the houses, as in all American towns, have a tendency to approach each other, and at a certain height form a projection of four, or even six feet over the street. Paving is perfectly unknown; and the consequence is, that in winter, when the deluging rains, which fall for three months almost without leaving off, have saturated the ground, these streets become veritable sewers, in which pedestrians sink up to the knee. This renders the use of a horse indispensable.

Putrid and pestilential miasmas exhale from these gutters, which are filled with rubbish of every description, resulting from the daily sweepings of the houses. On the other hand, the squares are large, square, perfectly airy, and lined with wide verandahs, which at midday offer a healthy protection from the sun. These verandahs contain handsome shops, in which the dealers have collected, at great cost, all that can tempt purchasers. It is a medley of the most discordant shops and booths, grouped side by side. A magnificent jeweller displays behind his window diamond necklaces, silver spurs, weighing from fifteen to twenty marcs, rings, bracelets, &c.; between a modest grocer quarrelling with his customers about the weight, and the seller of massamorra broth, who, with sleeves tucked up to the elbow, is selling his stuff by spoonfuls to every scamp who has an ochavo to regale himself with.

The smuggler captain passed gloomily and thoughtfully through the joyous population, whose bursts of laughter echoed far and wide, and whose merry songs escaped in gay zambacuecas from all the spirit shops which are so frequent at Valparaíso. In this way he reached Señor Crevel's inn, who uttered a cry of joy on perceiving the captain, and ran out to hold his horse.

"Are my men here?" Leon asked civilly, as he dismounted.

"They arrived nearly two hours back," Crevel answered, respectfully.

"It is well. Is the green chamber empty?"

Every landlord, in whatever country he may hang out his sign, possesses a separate room adorned with the names of blue, red, or green, and which he lets at a fabulous price, under the excuse that it is far superior to all the others in the house. Señor Crevel knew his trade too well not to have adopted this habit common to all his brethren; but he had given the name of the green room to a charming little quiet nook, which only his regular customers entered. Now, as we have said, the smugglers were very old friends of Crevel.

The door of the green room, perfectly concealed in the wall, did not allow its existence to be suspected; and it was in this room that the bold plans of the landlord's mysterious trade, whose profits were far greater than those which he drew from his avowed trade, were elaborated.

On hearing Leon's question, the Banian's face assumed an expression even more joyous than that with which he had greeted the young man's arrival, for he scented, in the simple question asked him, a meeting of smugglers and the settlement of some affairs in which he would have his share as usual. Hence he replied by an intelligent nod, and added aloud, "Yes, señor; it is ready for your reception."

After handing the traveller's horse to a greasy waiter, whom he ordered to take the greatest care of it, he led Leon into the interior of the inn. We are bound to confess that if the architect who undertook to build this house had been more than saving in the distribution of ornamentation, it was admirably adapted for its owner's trade. It was a cottage built of pebbles and beams, which it had in common with the greater portion of the houses in Valparaíso. Its front looked, as we know, upon the Calle San Agostino, while the opposite side faced the sea, over which it jutted out on piles for some distance. An enormous advantage for the worthy landlord, who frequently profited by dark or stormy nights to avoid payment of customs dues, by receiving through the windows the goods which the smugglers sold him; and it also favoured the expeditions of the latter, by serving as a depôt for the bales which they undertook to bring in on account of people who dealt with them.

This vicinity of the sea also enabled the Frenchman, whose customers were a strange medley of all sorts of men, not to trouble himself about the result of the frequent quarrels which took place at his house, and which might have caused an unpleasantness with the police, who at Valparaíso, as in other places where this estimable institution is in vogue, sometimes found it necessary to make an example. Hence, so soon as the squadron of lanceros was signalled in the distance, Señor Crevel at once warned his guests; so that when the soldiers arrived, and fancied they were about to make a good haul, they found that the birds had flown. We need scarce say that they had simply escaped through the back window into a boat always kept fastened in case of need to a ring in the wooden platform, which served as a landing stage to the house. The lanceros did not understand this sudden disappearance, and went off with a hangdog air.

Differing from European houses, which fall back in proportion to their elevation from the ground, Señor Crevel's establishment bulged outwards, so that the top was spacious and well lighted, while the ground floor rooms were narrow and dark. The landlord had always taken advantage of this architectural arrangement by having a room made on the second floor, which was reached by a turning staircase, and a perfect ear of Dionysius, as all external sounds reached the inmates, while the noise they made either in fighting or talking was deadened. The result of this was that a man might be most easily killed in the green room without a soul suspecting it.

It was into this room, then, witness of so many secret councils, that the landlord introduced, with the greatest ceremony, the captain of the smugglers, who walked behind him. On regarding the interior of the room, nothing indicated the origin of its name; for it was entirely hung with red damask. Had this succeeded a green hanging? This seems to be a more probable explanation.

It received light from above, by means of a large skylight. The walls were hung with pictures in equivocal taste, representing subjects passably erotic and even slightly obscene. A large four-post bed, adorned with its tester, occupied all one side of the room, and a mahogany chest of drawers stood facing it: in a corner was a small table covered with the indispensable toilette articles—combs, brushes, &c. A small looking glass over the table, chairs surrounding a large round table, and, lastly, an alabaster clock, which for the last ten years had invariably marked the same hour between its two flower vases, completed the furniture of this famous green room. We must also mention a bell, whose string hung behind the landlord's bar, and was useful to give an alarm under the circumstances to which we have referred. Leon paid no attention to these objects, which had long been familiar to him.

"Now, then," he said, as he took off his hat and poncho, and threw himself into an easy chair, "bring me some dinner at once."

"What would you like, captain?"

"The first thing ready: some puchero, some pepperpot—in short, whatever you please, provided it be at once, as I am in a hurry."

"What will you drink?"

"Wine, confound it! and try to find some that is good."

"All right."

"Decamp then, and make haste to bring me all I require."

"Directly, captain."

And Señor Crevel withdrew to attend to the preparation of the young man's dinner. During this time Leon walked up and down the room, and seemed to be arranging in his head the details of some plan he was meditating.

Crevel soon returned to lay the table, which he performed without opening his lips for fear of attracting some disagreeable remark from the captain, who, for his part, did not appear at all disposed for conversation. In an instant all was arranged with that coquettish symmetry which belongs to the French alone.

"Dinner is ready, captain," said Crevel, when he re-entered the room.

"Very well. Leave me; when I want you I will call you."

The landlord went out. Leon sat down to the table, and drawing the knife which he wore in his boot, vigorously attacked the appetizing dishes placed before him.

It is a fact worthy of remark, that with great and energetic natures, moral sufferings have scarce any influence over physical wants. It might be said that they understand the necessity of renewing or redoubling their strength, in order to resist more easily and more victoriously the griefs which oppress them, and they require all their vigour to contend worthily against them.

Chilian meals in no way resemble ours. Among us people drink while eating, in order to facilitate the absorption and digestion of the food; but in America it is quite different—there people eat without drinking. It is only when the pastry and sweets have been eaten that they drink a large glass of water for digestion; then comes the wines and liqueurs, always in small quantities, for the inhabitants of hot countries are generally very sober, and not addicted to the interminable sittings round a table covered with bottles, in an atmosphere impregnated with the steam of dishes.

When the meal was ended, Leon took his tobacco pouch from his pocket and rolled a cigarette, after wiping his fingers on the cloth. As this action may appear improper to the reader, it is as well that he should know that all Americans do so without scruple, as the use of the napkin is entirely unknown. Another custom worth mentioning is that of employing the fingers in lieu of a fork. This is the process among the Americans. They cut a piece of bread crumb, which they hold in their hand, and pick up with it the articles on their plate with great rapidity and cleanliness.

Nor must it be thought that they act in this way through ignorance of the fork; they are perfectly well acquainted with that utensil, and can manage it as well as we do when required; but though it is present on every table, both rich and poor regard it as an object of luxury, and say that it is far more convenient to do without it, and remark that the food has considerably more flavour when eaten in this fashion.

Leon lit his cigarette, and fell again into his reflections. All at once he rose and rang the bell, and Crevel at once appeared.

"Take all this away," said Leon, pointing to the table.

The landlord removed all traces of the meal.

"And now bring me the articles to make a glass of punch."

Crevel gazed for a moment in amazement at the man who had given this order. The sobriety of the smuggler was proverbial at Valparaíso; he had never been seen to drink more than one or two glasses of Pisco, and then it was only on great occasions, or to please his friend Diego, whom he knew to be very fond of strong liquors, like all the Indians. When a bottle of aguardiente was served to the two men, the Indian finished it alone, for Leon scarce wet his lips. Hence the landlord was almost knocked off his feet on receiving his guest's unusual order.

"Well, did you not hear me?" Leon resumed, impatiently.

"Yes, yes, sir," Crevel replied; "but—"

"But it surprises you, I suppose?"

"I confess it."

"It is true," Leon said, with a mocking smile, "that it is not my habit to drink."

"That it is not," said Crevel.

"Well, I am going to take to it, that's all. And what do you find surprising in that?"

"Nothing, of course."

"Then bring me what I asked for."

"Directly, directly, captain."

"On my soul, something extraordinary is taking place," Crevel said to himself as he descended to his bar. "The captain never had a very agreeable way with him, but, on the word of Crevel, I never saw him as he is tonight; it would be dangerous to touch him with a pair of tongs. What can have happened to him? Ah, stuff, it concerns him, after all: and then, who knows; perhaps he is on the point of becoming a drunkard."

After this aside, the worthy landlord manufactured a splendid bowl of punch, which he carried up to Leon so soon as it was ready.

"There," he said, as he placed the bowl on the table; "I think that will please you, captain."

"Thanks! but what is this?" Leon said, as he looked at what Crevel had brought—"there is only one glass."

"Why, you are alone."

"That is true; but I trust you will do me the pleasure of drinking with me."

"I should be most unwilling, captain, to deprive myself of the honour of drinking with you, but—"

Crevel, through his stupefaction, was unable to complete his sentence, for the invitation which the captain gave him surprised him beyond all expression. Let us add that it was the first time such an honour had been done him.

"In that case bring a glass for yourself."

Crevel, without further hesitation, fetched the glass, and seated himself facing the captain.

"Now, my dear Crevel," Leon said, as he dipped into the bowl and filled the glasses to the brim, "here's to your health, and let us talk."

The landlord was all ears.

"Do you know the convent of the Purísima Concepción?"

At this question Crevel opened his eyes to their fullest extent.

"What the deuce can the captain have to do with the nuns of the Purísima Concepción?" he asked himself, and then replied, "Certainly, captain."

"Very good; and could you contrive to get in there under some pretext?"

The landlord appeared to reflect for a moment.

"I have it," he said; "I will get in whenever you like."

"In that case get ready, for I want to send you there this very moment."

"What to do?"

"A trifle. I want you to see the Señora Maria," Leon said to him, after describing the accident of which he had been the involuntary cause, "and deliver her a message from me."

"The deuce! that is more difficult," Crevel muttered.

"Did you not tell me that you could get into the convent?"

"Yes; but seeing a novice is very different."

"Still you must do so, unless you refuse to undertake the task. I thought of you, because I believed you to be a clever and resolute fellow; if I am mistaken, I will apply to someone else, and I feel certain that I shall find more than one ingenious man who will not be sorry to earn four ounces."

"Four ounces, did you say?" and the Parisian's eyes sparkled with a flash of covetousness.

"Tell me if that suits you?"

"I accept."

"In that case, make haste. Have my horse saddled for I shall accompany you."

"We will start within a quarter of an hour; but in order that I may take my precautions, tell me what I have to do when I see the Señora?"

"You will hand her this scapulary, and say to her that the cavalier who wore it is lying at your house in danger of death. Pay careful attention to the expression which her face assumes, and manage to describe it to me. That is all I want."

"I understand."

And the landlord went down to make his preparations.

"In that way, I shall know whether she loves me," Leon exclaimed, so soon as he was alone.

Then, taking up his poncho and montera, he rolled a cigarette in his fingers, and went to join Crevel in the ground floor room.

"Do not be impatient, captain; I shall be with you in a moment," the banian said on perceiving him; "I only ask of you the time to run to my cellar."

"Make haste, for time is slipping away."

"Do not be alarmed; I shall be at the convent within half an hour."

On returning from the cellar the landlord brought with him three bottles covered with a thick coating of mould, bearing witness to the long stay they had made in the shadow of the sun, and adorned with a skullcap of pitch, whose colour time had changed.

"What is that?" Leon asked.

"The keys of the convent of the Purísima Concepción," Crevel replied, with a crafty smile. "We can start now."

In a moment Leon, on horseback, was going down the Calle San Agostino a few paces a head of Crevel, who was on foot.

CHAPTER VII
THE NOVICE

We left Doña Maria in the garden of the convent, preparing to obey the summons of the venerable abbess, Doña Madeline Aguirre Frías, in religion, Sister Santa Marta de los Dolores, the Mother Superior of the community, not doubting but that she was summoned to give a detailed account of the morning's events. Doña Maria expected to receive some reproof for the involuntary fault she had committed by letting her face be seen by the cavalier who raised her when in a fainting state.

But, in her present state of mind, far from upbraiding herself for not having quickly lowered her veil so soon as she regained possession of her senses, she was quite prepared to confess the impression which the sight of the young man had produced on her, and the present she had made him of her scapulary, for she had only one thought, one desire, one wish, and that was, to see again the man whom she loved.

Still, in consequence of the remonstrances which her companion, Rosita, made to her, and in order not to give anybody the opportunity of reading in her eyes what was passing in her soul, she removed all traces of her tears, overcame the feeling of sorrow which had invaded her whole being, and proceeded with a firm step toward the cell of the Mother Superior, while Rosita regained her own.

We have described the interior of the cells of the nuns or novices dwelling in the convent of the Purísima Concepción, which, with but rare exceptions, are all alike, but that of the Mother Superior deserves a special description, owing to the difference that exists between it and those of the other nuns. Nothing could be more religious, more worldly, and more luxurious than its whole appearance. It was an immense square room, with two large pointed windows, with small panes set in lead, on which were painted holy subjects with an admirable delicacy and surety of touch. The walls were covered with long gilt and embossed Cordovan leather tapestry; and valuable pictures, representing the chief events in the life of the patron saint of the convent, were grouped with that symmetry and taste which are only found among ecclesiastics.

Between the two windows was a magnificent Virgin by Raphael, before which was an altar; a silver lamp, full of odoriferous oil, hung from the ceiling and burnt night and day in front of the altar, which could be concealed by thick damask curtains when required. The furniture consisted of a large Chinese screen, behind which was concealed the abbess's bed, a simple couch of carved oak, surrounded by a mosquito net of white gauze. A square table, also in oak, supporting a few books and a desk, was in the centre of the room; and in one corner a large library filled with books relating to religious matters, allowed the rich gilding of scarce tomes to be seen through the glass doors. A few chairs with twisted legs were arranged against the wall. Lastly, a brasero of brilliant brass, filled with olive kernels, faced a superb press, whose fine carving was a work of art.

The sunshine, subdued by the coloured glass of the windows, spread a soft and mystical light, which made the visitor undergo a feeling of respect and contemplation, by giving this large room a stern and almost lugubrious aspect.

At the moment when the maiden was introduced to the abbess, the latter was seated in a large, straight-backed chair, surmounted by the abbatial crown, and whose seat, covered with gilt leather, was adorned with a double fringe of gold and silk. She held an open book in her hand and seemed plunged in profound meditation. Doña Maria waited till the abbess raised her eyes to her.

"Ah, you are here, my child," the abbess at length said, on perceiving the presence of the novice. "Come hither."

Maria advanced towards her.

"You were nearly the victim of an accident which cast trouble and confusion upon the progress of the procession, and it is slightly your own fault; you ought to have got out of the way of the horse as your dear sister did; but, after all, though the fear exposed your life to danger, I see with satisfaction that you have, thanks to the omnipotent protection of Nuestra Señora de la Purísima Concepción, escaped from the peril, and hence I order you to thank her by reciting an orison morning and night for eight days."

"I will do so, buena Madre," Maria replied.

"And now, chica, in order to efface every trace of the emotion which the event must have caused you, I recommend you to drink a few spoonfuls of my miraculous water; it is, as you are aware, a sovereign remedy against every sort of attack. Worthy Don Francisco Solano, the reverend Pater-Guardian of los Carmelitos Descalzos, gave me the receipt for it, and on many occasions we have recognised the truly surprising qualities of this water."

"I will not fail to do so," the young lady replied, with the firm intention of doing nothing of the sort, as she knew the perfect inefficiency of the good lady's panacea.

"Good! You must take care of your health, Maria, for you know that my great object is to watch over the welfare of all our sisters, and to render their abode in this peaceful retreat in which we live in the peace of the Lord, full of attractions and sweetness."

Maria looked at the abbess; she had expected some sort of reprimand, and the honeyed words of the worthy Mother Superior had a tinge of benignity which was not habitual to them. Emboldened by the abbess's kind manner, Maria felt a great desire to tell her of the deep aversion she felt for a monastic life, but fearing lest she might be mistaken as to the purport of the words which fell from the unctuous lips of the holy person, she awaited the end of her discourse, and contented herself with saying, with all the appearance of a submission full of humility—

"I know, buena Madre, how great your anxiety is for all of us; but I do not yet merit such kindness, and—"

"It is true that you are but a novice, and the solemn vows have not eternally consecrated you to the pious destination which Heaven has reserved for you, but the blessed day is approaching, and soon—"

"Madre!" Maria impetuously interrupted, about to speak and display the wound in her heart which was painfully bleeding at the thought of taking the veil.

"What is the matter, my child? you are impatient. I understand the lively desire which animates you, and am delighted at it, for it would be painful for me to employ with you, whom I love so dearly, any other means than those of persuasion to oblige you to take the gown which is destined for you."

On hearing the abbess speak thus, Maria understood that her fate was settled, and that no supplication would produce any change in what was resolved. Moreover, the air of hypocritical satisfaction spread over the face of the Mother Superior sufficiently proved that the conversation which she had begun had no other object than to adroitly sound the young lady as to her feelings about taking the veil, and that, if necessary, she would employ her right and power to force her into submission.—

Maria, consequently, bowed her head and made no reply. Either the abbess took this silence for a sign of obedience, or regarded it as a manifestation of utter indifference, for a faint smile played round her lips, and she continued the conversation.

"While congratulating you on the good sentiments which have taken root in your mind, it is my duty to inform you of the orders which I received this morning from your father, General Soto-Mayor."

Maria raised her head, trying to read in the abbess's looks what these orders might signify.

"You are not ignorant, chica, that the rule of our convent grants novices who are preparing to take the veil, permission to spend a month with their family before beginning the retreat which must precede the ceremony of their vows."

Here Maria, who was anxiously listening, felt her heart beat as if it would burst her bosom. The abbess continued —

"In obedience to this custom, your father, before affiancing you to God, informed me this morning that he wished to have you near him, and employ the month which you will spend out of the convent in taking you to Valdivia to see his brother, that worthy servant of the Lord, Don Luis."

A cry of joy, restrained by the fear of letting what was taking place in her mind be seen, was on the point of bursting from her bosom.

"Dear father!" she said, clasping her hands.

"You will set out tomorrow," the abbess continued; "a servant of your family will come to fetch you in the morning."

"Oh, thanks, madam," Maria could not refrain from exclaiming, as she was intoxicated with joy at the thought of leaving the convent.

Assuredly, under any other circumstances, the announcement of this holiday would have been received by the maiden, if not with coldness, at the least with indifference; but her meeting with Leon had so changed her ideas, that she fancied she saw in this departure a means which Providence gave her to escape from a cloistered life. The poor child fancied that her parents were thinking of restoring her to the world; then, reflecting on the slight probability which this hypothesis seemed to possess, she said to herself that, at any rate, she might see again within the month *him* whose memory excited so great an influence over her mind. There was still hope for her, and hope is nearly happiness. The abbess had not failed to notice the look of pleasure which had suddenly illumined the maiden's features.

"You are very happy, then, at the thought of leaving us, Maria," she said, with an attempt at a smile.

"Oh, do not think that, Mamita," Maria said, as she threw herself on her neck. "You are so kind and so indulgent that I should be ungrateful did I not love you."

At this moment the maiden's heart, inundated with delight, overflowed with love. The aversion which she had felt an hour previously for all that surrounded her had faded away and made room for a warm expression of joy. A sunbeam on high had sufficed to dissipate the dark cloud which had formed on the blue sky.

In spite of the lively desire which Maria had to bear the good news to Rosita, she was obliged to listen to the perusal of General Soto-Mayor's letter, which the abbess gave her, as well as a long exhortation which the latter thought it her duty to address to her about the conduct she should assume when she found herself in the bosom of her family. Nothing was forgotten, neither the recommendation to perform her religious vows exactly, nor that of preparing to return to the convent worthily at the close of the month, animated with the pious desire of devoting herself to it joyfully, as the trial of the world would serve to show her the slight happiness which those forced to live in it found there. Maria promised all that the superior wished; she only saw through the pompous phrases of the holy woman the temporary liberty offered to her, and this sufficed her to listen patiently to the rest of the peroration. At length the harangue was finished, and Maria rushed towards Rosita's cell; on seeing her companion with a radiant brow and a smile on her lip, the latter remained stupefied. Amid the transports of joy, Maria informed her of the happy event which had occurred so opportunely to calm her anguish, and embraced her affectionately.

"How happy you seem!" Rosita could not refrain from saying to her.

"Oh! I really am so. Do you understand, Rosita, a whole month out of the convent, and who knows whether I may not see during the month the man who so boldly saved me from peril."

"Can you think of it?"

"Yes; I confess to you that it is my dearest wish to see him again and tell him that I love him."

"Maria!"

"Forgive me, dear Rosita, for, selfish that I am, I only think of myself, and forget that you, too, might perhaps like to leave these convent walls in order to embrace your brother."

"You are mistaken, sister; I am happy here; and though my brother loves me as much as I love him, he will not call me to his side, for he would be alone to protect me, and what should I do in the world when he was compelled to remain with his soldiers? Ah! I have no father or mother!"

"Poor Rosita!"

"Hence," the latter said, gaily, "speak no more of me, but let me rejoice at finding you smiling after having left you so sad."

The maidens soon after separated, and Maria went to make the necessary preparations for her departure. On entering her cell, her first care was to throw herself on her knees before the image of the Virgin and thank her. Then the rest of the day passed as usual. But anyone who had seen the novice before her interview with the Mother Superior, and met her after the latter had made the general's letter known to her, would have noticed a singular change in her. A lovely flush had driven the pallor from her lips, her eyes had regained their expression of vivacity, and her lips, red as the pomegranate flower, parted to let her heaving breath pass through.

The morrow Maria was up at daybreak, still under the impression of the sweet dreams which had lulled her slumbers. The whole night Leon's image had been before her, flashing in her ravished eye the dazzling prism of a new existence. It was striking ten by the convent clock when General Soto-Mayor's major-domo presented himself at the door of the house of God.

CHAPTER VIII
A VISIT TO THE CONVENT

It was about five in the evening when Leon Delbès left the posada in the company of Crevel. The great heat of midday had been succeeded by a refreshing sea breeze, which was beginning to rise and blow softly, producing an exquisite temperature, of which all took advantage to rush from their houses, and join the numerous promenaders crowding the streets, squares, and the shore of the ocean, whose calm and smooth surface was tinged by the ardent beams of the sun, which had spent two-thirds of its course. It was a saint's day, and the people, dressed in their best clothes, whose varied colours offer the eye such a piquant effect, hurried along with shouts, song, and laughter, of which no idea can be formed in Europe. In South America a holiday is the occasion for all the pleasures which it is given to man to enjoy, and the Americans do not neglect it. Marvellously endowed by nature, which has given them strength, vigour, and unalterable health, their powerful organization allows them to do anything. Born for love and pleasure, the South Americans make of their life one long enjoyment: it is the ideal of refined sensualism.

The two Frenchmen, with their hats pulled over their eyes, and carefully wrapped in their ponchos, so as not to be recognised and delayed, mingled with the crowd, and elbowing and elbowed, pushing and pushed, they advanced as quickly as they could, moving with great difficulty through the mob that surrounded them.

The reader will be doubtless astonished to see, in a country so hot as Chili, Leon Delbès and Crevel enveloped, as we have just said, in heavy cloaks. In Chili, Peru, and generally in all the ex-Spanish colonies, the cloak is constantly in use, and almost indispensable! It is worn everywhere and always in all weathers and all places, at every hour of the night and of the day. There is a Spanish proverb which says that the cloak protects from heat and cold, from rain and sun. This is true to a certain extent, but is not the sole reason why it has become obligatory.

The South Americans, as well as the descendants of the Spaniards, have retained the two chief vices which distinguished their ancestors, that is to say, a mad pride and invincible indolence. The American never works save when driven into his last entrenchments, when hunger forces him to lay aside his careless and contemplative habits in order to earn means to support himself. Hence it follows very naturally, that it is impossible for him to obtain the fine clothes which he covets, and whose price is so heavy, that he despairs of ever possessing them.

In order to remedy this misfortune, and save, at the same time, his pride, which prohibits him from appearing badly dressed, he works just long enough to save the money to buy himself a Panama hat, a pair of trousers, and a cloak. When he has succeeded in obtaining these objects of permanent necessity, he is all right and his honour is saved, for thanks to the exceptional talent which he possesses of draping himself elegantly and majestically in a piece of cloth, he can boldly present himself anywhere, and no one will ever suspect what hideous rags and frightful misery are covered by the splendid cloak which he bears on his shoulders.

In addition to the motive which we have just explained, it is fair to state that, owing to the excessive heat of the climate, the advantage of the cloak is felt in the fact that it is ample and wide, leaves the limbs liberty of movement, and does not scorch the body, as well-fitting clothes do when heated by the sunbeams. Hence rich and poor have all adopted it.

After a ride interrupted at every moment by the people who encumbered the streets, the two Frenchmen reached their destination, and stopped before the church adjoining the convent. There they separated: Crevel proceeded toward the gate of the community, and Leon, after dismounting and fastening his horse to an iron ring fixed in the wall, entered the church, and leant against a pillar to wait.

The church of Nuestra Señora del Carmo, belonging to the Convent of the Purísima Concepción, is one of the finest and richest of those existing in Valparaíso. It was built a short time after the conquest of Chili, in the Renaissance style. It is lofty, large, and well lighted by a number of arched windows, whose coloured glass is among the finest specimens of the art. A double row of columns delicately carved, supports a circular gallery, with a balcony in open work, made with that patience which the Spaniards appear to have inherited from the Arabs, and which produced the marvellous details of the great mosque of Cordova.

The choir is separated from the nave by a massive silver grating, modelled by some rival of Benvenuto Cellini. The high altar is of lapis lazuli, and sixteen silver columns support a dome painted blue, and studded! with gold stars, above the splendid table covered with a rich pall of English point, on which stand the magnificent golden reliquary containing the Holy Sacrament.

In the aisles, eight chapels, placed under the protection of different saints, and adorned with, extraordinary wealth, each contains a confessional which closes hermetically, and in which it is impossible to catch a glimpse of the male or female penitent asking remission of sins. Nothing can be imagined more aërial or coquettish than the ebony pulpit, inlaid with mother-of-pearl, used by the preacher. This pulpit is a masterpiece, and it is said that a Spanish workman, finding himself in great danger, made a vow to Nuestra Señora del Carmen that he would give her a pulpit if he escaped. Having escaped the danger, he devoted hourly years of his life to the accomplishment of the work he had promised, and which he only completed a few months prior to his death. If we may judge of the danger this man incurred by the finish of the execution and the merit of the work, it must have been immense.

Lastly, there are at regular distances large holy water vessels of carved marble, covered with plates of silver. When Leon entered the church it was full of faithful people. Upwards of two thousand candles spread a dazzling light, and a cloud of incense brooded over the congregation, who were plunged into a profound contemplation.

In American churches that impudent traffic in chairs, which goes on so shamelessly elsewhere during the holiest or more sorrowful ceremonies, is unknown. There are no seats, but the men stand, and the women bring with them small square carpets on which they kneel. This custom may perhaps injure the symmetry, but it certainly imparts to the assembly of the faithful a more religious appearance. We do not see, as in France, individuals stretching themselves, taking their ease, throwing themselves back, or sleeping in their chairs, and we are not at each movement disturbed by the rattling of wood upon the slabs.

On hearing the chants of the nuns, which rose in gentle and melodious notes, accompanied by the grave sound of the organ, Leon Delbès felt himself involuntarily assailed by a melancholy feeling. Gradually forgetting the motive of his presence at this sacred spot, he let his head fall upon his chest, and yielded entirely to the ecstasy into which the mighty harmony that filled his ears plunged him.

In the meanwhile Crevel, after leaving the captain of the smugglers, took a half turn and proceeded, as we said, toward the gate of the convent, on which he knocked thrice, after looking around him rather through habit than distrust, in order to make certain that he was not followed. The door was not opened, but a trap in the niche of the upper panel was pulled back, and an old woman's face appeared in the aperture. Crevel assumed his most sanctimonious look, and giving a mighty bow, he said, as he doffed his broad-brimmed straw hat—

"Ave Maria Purísima, sister."

"Sin pecado concebida, brother," the old woman replied, who was no other than the sister porter, "what can I do for you?"

"I am ill, sister, very ill," Crevel repeated in a moaning voice.

"Good gracious, brother, what is the matter with you? But I am not mistaken," she added, after looking at the newcomer more attentively, "you are the worthy Frenchman established in the Calle San Agostino, who brings from time to time a few bottles of old French wine to the abbess for her cramp."

"Alas! yes, sister, it is myself; and I have brought two under my cloak, which I beg her to accept." Crevel, like a good many of his fellow traders, had the praiseworthy habit of giving alms to the rich, in order to rob the poor with greater facility.

"They are welcome," said the sister porter, whose small eyes glistened with covetousness; "wait a minute, brother, and I will open the gate for you."

"Do so, sister, and I will wait as long as you please."

Crevel soon heard the formidable sound of bolts being drawn and locks turned, and at the end of a quarter of an hour the door was opened just wide enough to leave passage for a man. The landlord glided like a snake through the opening offered him, and the door closed again at once.

"Sit down, brother," said the sister porter; "it is a long way from your house to the convent."

"Thanks, sister," said Crevel, taking advantage of the invitation; "I am really extremely tired."

He then took from under his poncho the two bottles, which he placed on the table.

"Be good enough, sister," he said, "to give these bottles to your Mother Superior, begging her not to forget me in her prayers."

"I will not fail, brother, I assure you."

"I am certain of it, sister; and stay," he added, drawing out a third bottle, "take this, which I brought for you, and which will do you good, for it is justly said in France that wine is the milk of aged people."

"That is true, brother, and I thank you; but tell me the nature of the illness you are suffering from."

"For some time past, sister, I have been subject to a sudden dizziness, and as your convent possesses a miraculous water which cures all diseases, I have come to buy a phial."

"With the greatest pleasure, brother," the sister porter replied. "I am sorry that I cannot make you a present of it; but this water is deposited in my hands, and is the property of the poor, to whom we must render an account of it."

We will remark parenthetically that the convents of Valparaíso willingly accept anything offered them, but never give anything away. Crevel was perfectly aware of this fact; hence, without offering the slightest observation, he drew four piastres from his pocket, which he placed in the sister's hand. The latter put them out of sight with a vivacity which astonished the banian himself: then running to a chest of drawers, the sole article of furniture which adorned the room, she opened it and took a small white glass bottle, carefully corked and sealed, which lay there along with some sixty others, and brought it to Crevel.

The landlord received it with marks of profound gratitude.

"I hope that this water will do me good," he said, striving to prolong the interview.

"Do not doubt it, brother."

And the sister porter looked at Crevel in a way which made him comprehend that nothing need detain him now that he had what he came to seek. The banian understood it and prepared to rise.

"Now, sister, I will ask your permission to retire, in spite of the charm which your conversation has for me; but business before everything."

"That is true," the sister porter replied; "hence I will not keep you; you know that you will always be welcome to the convent."

"Thanks, sister, thanks. And now I am off."

"Farewell, my brother."

He walked a few steps toward the door, but then hurriedly turned back.

"By the bye," he said, as if remembering something which he had forgotten, "I trust that the accident which happened to one of your sisters during the procession had no serious consequences."

"No, thanks to Heaven, brother."

"Ah, all the better; then she has quite recovered."

"So perfectly," said the sister porter, "that she is travelling at this moment."

"What! the Señora Maria de Soto-Mayor travelling?"

"You know her name?"

"Of course; for I was formerly butler to the general her father."

"Well, then, it was through an order of the general that Sister Maria left this morning for the country house which he possesses a few leagues from here."

"Well, then, sister, good-bye, and I hope we shall meet again soon," Crevel exclaimed, hurrying this time to reach the gate.

"¡Anda Ve con Dios!" said the sister, surprised at this hurried movement.

"Thanks, thanks."

Crevel was already in the street.

Now, while he was conscientiously performing the commission which Leon had entrusted to him, the latter was still waiting for Crevel to rejoin him. After remaining a quarter of an hour in the church, he left it, and was beginning to grow impatient, when the landlord's shadow was thrown on the convent wall.

In a second he was by his side.

"Well?" he asked, on approaching him.

"Come, come," said Crevel, with satisfaction, "I fancy I bring good news."

"Speak at once."

"In the first place, Doña Maria is perfectly well, and feels no effects from the terror which your horse caused her."

"Next?"

"That is something, surely."

"Go on, go on! scoundrel," the smuggler cried, as he shook Crevel's arm.

"Good heavens! a little calmness, Señor Caballero; you will never correct yourself of your vivacity."

Leon's brows were contracted, and he stamped his foot passionately, so Crevel hastened to obey.

"Learn, then, that this morning the young lady left the convent to rejoin her family."

"What do you say?" Leon asked, utterly astounded.

"The truth; for the sister porter assures me of the fact."

"In that case, I am off, too."

"Why?"

"What would you have me do here?"

And, not troubling himself further about his companion, the captain unfastened his horse and leaped on its back. Then, throwing his purse to the landlord, he said that he should see him again soon, and started at a gallop.

"Hum!" Crevel said, quite confounded; "the devil's certainly in that fellow, or he has a slate loose. What a pace he rides at!"

And, after giving a last glance at the rider, who was disappearing round the corner of the square, the worthy landlord quietly bent his steps in the direction of his posada.

"For all that, he is a good customer."

CHAPTER IX
ON THE SIERRA

The traveller who, proceeding south, leaves one fine morning the city of Santiago, that magnificent capital of Chili which is destined ere long (if it be not destroyed by an earthquake, as has already happened twice), to become the finest city of South America, experiences—according as he belongs to one of the two classes of travellers called by Sterne positive or enthusiastic travellers—a sudden disillusion or a complete charm at the sight of the landscape spread out before him.

In fact, for a radius of fifty or sixty leagues round the capital, the country offers, with but few differences, the same appearance as we meet with when we traverse the smiling plains of Beauce, or the delicious province of Touraine, so poetically named the garden of France.

On either side of wide and well-kept roads, lined with lofty trees, whose tufted crests meet and form a natural arch, which affords a shelter against the heat of the day, extend for an enormous distance vast fields covered with crops of wheat, barley, rice, and alfalfa, and orchards filled with apple, pear, and peach trees, and all the other fruit trees which grow prolifically in these superb countries. On the horizon, upon hills exposed to the rising sun, countless patches of that vine which Chili alone has succeeded in cultivating, and which produces a wine highly esteemed by connoisseurs, rejoice the eye which contemplates to satiety these enormous masses of gilded grapes destined to supply the whole of South America with wine.

In the distance are seen on the prairies horses, mules, vicunas, viscachas, and llamas, which raise their head on the passage of the caravans, and regard the travellers with their large eyes full of gentleness and intelligence. An infinite number of small streams wind with capricious turns through this country, which they fertilize, and their limpid and silvery track is covered with formidable bands of majestic, black-headed swans.

But, after a journey of four days, when you leave the province of Santiago to enter that of Colchagua, the country assumes a more abrupt appearance. You can already begin to feel the rising of the ground which gradually reaches, with undulation upon undulation, the Cordilleras of the Andes. The soil, ruder to the eye and more rebellious to cultivation, although it has not yet completely acquired those sublime, savage beauties which, a few leagues further on, will cause the blessings of civilization to be forgotten, holds a mid place between that nature of which man has made a conquest, which he changes and modifies according to his caprices, and that invincible nature against which all his efforts are impotent, and which victoriously retains the independence of its diversified, wild, and imposing scenery.

It was the sixth day after that fixed for the journey projected by General Don Juan, and on the road that runs from Currio to Talca, that at about midday, a large party of travellers composed of fifteen men, both masters and peons, and three ladies whose features it was impossible to distinguish, as they were careful to conceal them so thoroughly under their rebozos, was advancing with difficulty, trying in vain to shelter themselves against the burning sunbeams which fell vertically.

No shadow allowed the men or beasts to breathe for a moment; there was not a single tree whose foliage might offer a little refreshment. Ahead of the horsemen a dozen mules, trotting one after the other, and each loaded with two heavy bales, followed with a firm step the bell of the yegua madrina, which alone had the privilege of marching at liberty, and with no burthen, at the head of the caravan.

All our travellers, armed to the teeth, rode in groups behind the mules, and were mounted on those capital Chilian horses which have no equals for speed, and of which we might almost say that they are indefatigable.

The heat was stifling, and with the exception of the *area mula!* uttered from time to time by the muleteers, in order to stimulate the vigour of the poor brutes, no one said a word. Nothing was audible save the sharp footfall of the animals echoing on the stones, and the clang of the heavy spurs which each rider had on his heels.

The road wound round a vast quebrada along the brink of which it ran, growing narrower every moment, which soon compelled the travellers to ride one by one, having on their right a precipice of more than twelve hundred yards in depth, down which the slightest slip on the part of their steeds might hurl them, and on their left a wall of granite rising perpendicularly to an incalculable height. Still this precarious situation, far from causing a feeling of terror among the persons of whom we are speaking, seemed, on the contrary, to give them a sensation of undefinable comfort.

This resulted from the fact that on this gorge the sun did not reach them, and they were able to refresh their lungs by inhaling a little fresh air, which it had been impossible for them to do during the last three hours. Hence, without troubling themselves about the spot which they had reached, any more than if they had been in a forest glade, they threw off the folds in which they had wrapped themselves, in order to avoid the heat, and prepared to enjoy for a few minutes the truce which the sun had granted them. Gaiety had returned, the muleteers were beginning to strike up those interminable complaints with which, if we may be allowed to use the expression, they seem to keep the mules in step, and the masters lit their paper cigarettes. They rode on thus for about half an hour, and then, after having followed the thousand windings of the mountains, the caravan came out upon an immense plain covered with a tall close grass, of a dark green hue, in which the horses disappeared up to the chest, and on which clumps of trees grew at intervals. The mountains opened on the right and left like a fan, and displayed on the horizon their denuded and desolate crests.

"Baya Pius, gentlemen," one of the horsemen said, as he spurred his horse and wiped his forehead; "we shall halt within two hours."

"I hope so, captain; for I frankly confess to you that I am exhausted with fatigue."

"Stay, Don Juan," the first of the two men continued, as he stretched out his hand in the direction they were following; "do you perceive a little to the left that larch tree wood stretching out at the foot of the mound, down which a torrent rushes?"

"Yes, yes, I see it, Señor Leon," the general, whom our readers have doubtless recognized, answered the captain of the smugglers.

"Well, general, that is where we shall camp tonight."

"Heaven be praised!" a sweet maiden voice exclaimed, mingling in the conversation; "but are you not mistaken, Señor Captain, in saying that we shall not reach that spot before two hours?"

Leon eagerly turned his head, and replied, while accompanying his words with a look in which the love he felt was seen—

"I have been about the mountains too long, Doña Maria, to be mistaken as to a thing so simple for us sons of the Sierra as a calculation of distance; but if you feel too fatigued, señorita, speak, and we will camp here."

"Oh, no," the maiden quickly replied, "on the contrary, let us go on; for the great heat has now passed, and the rising breeze is so agreeable, that I feel as if I could canter thus all night."

Leon bent to his saddle-bow, and after courteously saluting Doña Maria and the ladies with her, he hurried on and joined Diego, who was marching ahead, with his eye on the watch and a frown on his brow, in the attitude of a man who seems afraid he shall not find the traces which he is in search of. He had rejoined the caravan two days before, and as yet not a syllable had been exchanged between him and Leon: still the latter had noticed in the half-breed's countenance, since his arrival, an air of satisfaction, which proved that he had succeeded in his plans.

And yet, though Doña Maria was riding a few yards from him, had Diego brought the two young people together according to his promises? Evidently not; since at the hour when the Vaquero left Leon, the young lady arrived under the safeguard of one of her father's servants. Hence the half-breed's satisfaction must be attributed to some other motive.

While Leon was striving to divine it—while curiously examining his friend's slightest gesture, let us relate, in a few words, what had taken place between the captain and the Soto-Mayor family during the six days which had elapsed since his visit to the Convent of the Purísima Concepción. Returning at full speed, Leon reached the Rio Claro during the night, and after two or three hours' repose among the smugglers, he started at the head of his men for the general's country house, where the persons whom he had engaged to escort as far as Valdivia were awaiting him.

At the moment when Leon entered the drawing room to announce that the mules and the horses were ready to start, a loud exclamation burst from a young lady whom the captain's eyes had been greedily seeking ever since his entrance into the house. It was Maria, who recognised her saviour.

Not one of the persons present, who were engaged with the final preparations for the start, noticed the cry of surprise uttered by the maiden. Leon at once felt it echo to his heart, and a flash of joy escaping from his glance illuminated Maria's soul. In the space of a second they both understood that they were loved.

The journey they were about to undertake appeared to them a more splendid festival than their imagination could conceive. They had scarce hoped to see each other again, and they were about to live side by side for a week. Was not this such perfect happiness that it seemed a miracle?

An hour later, the young couple were riding along together. Although the captain was obliged to remain pretty constantly at the head of the small party which he commanded, he seized the slightest excuse to get near Maria, who, forgetting everything else in this world, kept her eyes incessantly fixed on this man, the mere sight of whom caused her heart to beat. And there was no lack of excuses: at one moment he must encourage by a shout or a signal the young lady's horse which was checking its speed; at another he must recommend her to guard herself against a whirlwind of dust, or remove a stone from her horse's hoof. And Maria ever thanked him with a smile of indescribable meaning.

As he was obliged, in order not to excite suspicion, to pay similar attention to the Señora Soto-Mayor and her other daughter, the smuggler's manner delighted the general, who applauded himself with all his heart for having laid his hand on such a polite and attentive man.

During the first night's bivouac, Leon managed for a few moments to leave the rest of the party and approach Maria, who was admiring the magnificent spectacle which the moonlight offered, by casting its opaline rays over the lofty trees which surrounded the spot where they had halted.

"Señorita," he said to her, in a voice trembling with emotion, "do you not fear lest the fresh night breeze may injure your health?"

"Thanks, Señor Leon," the maiden replied; "I am about to return to camp, but the night is so long that I cannot weary of admiring this superb landscape. I am so happy in contemplating all that I see around me."

"Then you do not regret your abode in the convent, señorita?"

"Regret it! when I feel as if God had wished to inundate my heart with all the joy which it can feel! Oh, Caballero, you do not think so. But why do you say it to me?"

"Forgive me," Leon continued, noticing the expression of sorrow which had suddenly overclouded the maiden's features; "the fact is, that my thoughts ever revert to the moment when I saw you, pale and dumb with terror, leave the ranks of the nuns of the Purísima Concepción."

"Oh, speak not so; and since Heaven has permitted that I should leave those convent walls to see you again, do not remind me that I must soon return to them, to remain there till death liberates me from them."

"What!" Leon exclaimed, "see you again and then lose you! Oh; forgive me, señorita; forgive my speaking to you thus; but I am mad, and sorrow renders me distracted."

"What do you say?"

"Nothing! nothing! señorita: forget what I may have said to you, but believe that if I were called on to sacrifice my life to save you any pain, however slight in its nature, I would do so at a moment," said Leon.

Maria replied, raising her eyes to heaven, "God is my witness that the words which you have just uttered will never pass from my mind: but as I told you, I am happy now, and when the convent gate has again closed on me, I shall have neither pain nor sorrow to endure, for I shall die."

A dull cry burst from Leon's breast; he looked at the maiden, who was smiling calmly and tranquilly.

"And now," she said to Leon, "I will join my sister again, for I fancy I am beginning to be chilled."

And hurriedly proceeding to the tent, under which the principal members of her family were assembled, she left Leon to his thoughts. From this moment, Leon abandoned himself with delight to the irresistible charm of the love which he felt for Maria. This man, with the nerves of steel, who had witnessed the most terrible scenes without turning pale, who with a smile on his lips had braved the greatest dangers, found himself without the strength to combat the strange feeling which had unconsciously settled in his heart. Hitherto squandering his youth's energy in wild saturnalia, Leon felt for the first time in his life that he loved, and he did not question the future, reserved for a passion whose issue could not be favourable.

Still, and although illusion was almost impossible, the young man, with that want of logic of love which seems to grow in proportion to the insurmountable obstacles opposed to it, yielded to the torrent which bore him away, confiding to chance, which may at any moment effect a miracle.

In addition to the numberless obstacles which Leon might expect to find on the road, Diego's plans of vengeance alarmed him more than all the rest. He knew that the half-breed's will did not recoil before any excess; that if he had resolved to avenge himself on the Soto-Mayor family, no power would be strong enough to prevent him. Hence a shudder passed through Leon's veins when he was rejoined by Diego, and the latter, on perceiving Leon, had said to him—

"The girl you love is near you without any interference on my part; all the better, brother, it is your duty to watch over her henceforth, and I will take charge of the others."

Leon was about to open his mouth to reply, but a look from the half-breed caused the words to expire on his lips. The reader now knows why the captain, after saluting the ladies, started to place himself at the head of the band and watch Diego.

The sun was on the point of disappearing upon the horizon when the party reached the wood which Leon had indicated to Don Juan as the spot where they would pass the night. All halted, and the preparations for camping were made.

In Chili, and generally throughout South America, you do not find on the roads that infinite number of inns and hostelries which encumber ours, and where travellers are so pitilessly plundered. In these countries, which are almost deserted, owing to the tyrannical rule of the Spaniards and the philanthropy of the English, this is how people behave in order to obtain rest after a long day's journey.

The travellers choose the spot which appears to them most suitable, generally on the banks of a river, the mules are unloaded, and they are left for the night to their own instincts, which never deceive them, and enable them to find pasture. The bales are placed upon one another in a circle of sixty or eighty feet; in the middle of this enclosure a large fire is lit and carefully kept up in order to keep wild beasts at bay, and each man placing his weapons by his side arranges himself to pass the night as comfortably as he can.

Our travellers installed themselves in the way we have described, with this distinction, that as General Soto-Mayor had a tent among his baggage, the peons put it up in the centre of the camp, and as it was divided into two parts, it formed sleeping rooms for Don Juan, his wife, and his daughters. After a supper of jerked beef and ham, the muleteers, wearied with their day's journey, took a glance around to see that all was in order, and then lay down, with the exception of one who remained up as sentry.

Diego, Leon, and the Soto-Mayor family were sitting round the fire and talking of the distance they still had to go before reaching their destination. In these countries there is no twilight, and the supper was hardly over before it became pitch dark.

"Miguel!" the general said to a peon standing close behind him, "give me the bota."

The peon fetched a large goatskin, which might contain some fifteen quarts, and was full of rum.

"Gentlemen!" the general continued, addressing the smugglers, "be kind enough to taste this rum; it is a present made me by General Saint Martin, in memory of the battle of Maypa, in which I was wounded while charging a Spanish square."

The bota passed from hand to hand, while the ladies, seated on carpets, were sipping water and smoking their cigarettes.

"It is excellent," said Leon, after swallowing a mouthful; "it is real Jamaica."

"I am delighted that it pleases you," Don Juan continued, kindly; "for in that case, you will not refuse to accept this bota, which will remind you of our journey when we have separated."

"Oh!" Leon exclaimed, casting a fiery look at Maria, whose cheeks turned purple, "I shall remember it, believe me, and I thank you sincerely for this present."

"Say no more about it, pray, my dear captain; and tell me whether you think we are still far from Talca."

"By starting early tomorrow we shall be by ten in the forenoon at the mountain of Amehisto, and two hours later at Talca."

"So soon?" Maria murmured.

Leon looked at the maiden, and there was a silence; the general calculated the distance that separated Talca from Valdivia, the ladies smoked, and Diego was deep in thought. Suddenly the sound of galloping horses could be heard, the sound soon grew louder, and the sentry shouted, "Who goes there?"

In a second everybody was up, the men leaped to their weapons, and the ladies, by Leon's orders, went into the tent to lie down on the ground and remain perfectly motionless. No one had answered the sentry's challenge.

"Who goes there?" he repeated, as he cocked his piece.

"Amigos!" a powerful voice answered, which re-echoed in the silence of the night.

Every heart beat anxiously; a dozen horsemen could be noticed moving in the darkness about thirty yards off; but the gloom was so dense that it was impossible to recognise them, or know with whom they had to deal.

"Say what you want or I fire," the sentry shouted for the third time, as he levelled his piece.

"Down with your arms, friends," the same voice, still perfectly calm, repeated; "I am Don Pedro Sallazar."

"Yes! yes!" the general exclaimed, joyfully, as he threw down his gun, "I recognise him: let Don Pedro enter, my friends."

Four men hastily removed some bales to make a passage for the officer who entered the camp, while his escort remained outside. The general stepped forward to meet the newcomer.

"How is it you are here?" he asked him. "I fancied you were at Santiago."

"You will soon learn," Pedro replied, "for I have important communications to make to you. But first permit me to give some instructions to the men who accompany me."

Then turning to his soldiers, he said, "Cabo Lopez, take care that no one leaves the camp, and post yourself here, and try to be on good terms with the worthy persons here present."

"Yes, general," the corporal answered, with a bow.

"What? general!" Don Juan asked, with surprise. "Are you really a general, my dear Don Pedro?"

"I will explain all that to you," Don Pedro replied, with a smile; "in the meanwhile, however, lead me to your tent, for what I have to communicate to you does not require any witnesses."

"Certainly; and make haste, that I may present you to these ladies, who will be agreeably surprised at seeing you."

Don Pedro bowed, and followed the general, who led him into the tent where the ladies had taken refuge in apprehension of an attack. During this time the smugglers did the honours of the camp to the soldiers with all the courtesy they were capable of displaying under such circumstances. At the end of a quarter of an hour they fraternized in the most cordial way, thanks to the aguardiente of Pisco, with which the lanceros were abundantly provided.

CHAPTER X
INSIDE THE TENT

When the alarm was given by the sentry, Diego, usually so prompt to go and meet danger, rose cautiously, and without making a single gesture which could reveal any anxiety, stood leaning on his rifle with a smile on his lips. So soon as the Spaniards had disappeared in the tent, Leon turned to him with an inquiring glance, which the latter only replied to by a very careless nod.

"Did you know, then, that we should meet Don Pedro?"

"I presumed so," Diego replied, laconically.

"In truth, for some days past, brother," said Leon, "things have occurred of which you keep the secret to yourself."

"What are they?"

"In the first place, this journey which you consented to make with the Soto-Mayor family as far as Valdivia."

"What, you complain of it, and your beauty is with you?"

"Certainly not; but after all, we have nothing to do at Valdivia."

"You are right, if you are referring to our commercial trips; but as regards my personal interests," the half-breed added, his large eyes flashing in the darkness, "the case is very different."

"What do you mean?"

"That we must go there because we are expected there. However, if you wish to know more, come, and you will see that the two days I spent in Valparaíso were put to good purpose."

And leading his friend, and warning him to be silent, he cautiously passed to the other side of the tent. On reaching that point, Diego lay down on the ground, invited Leon to imitate him, and gently raising a corner of the tent, he listened to what was being said inside.

"We are doing wrong," said Leon.

"Silence," the other replied, "and listen."

The captain obeyed, and looked at the persons who were conversing, while not losing one of the words which they interchanged.

"I cannot imagine," said Don Juan, "how it is that you, whom I fancied at Santiago, are now only a few leagues from Talca."

"It is because a good many strange things have happened since my arrival in that city."

"What are they?" asked Inez, whose curiosity was aroused.

"Speak, Don Pedro, I implore you," said Don Juan in his turn.

"I will do so, general. The Chilian government, which, as you are aware, is unable to cope with the incessant invasions of the Araucano Indians, reluctantly agreed to treat with them, and supply them annually with necessaries, such as corn, tools, and weapons which they might have need of. At various times, however, it attempted to shake off this disgraceful yoke; and the Indians, beaten and dispersed in various encounters, appeared to comprehend how ridiculous these claims were, and have refrained, during the last two years, from claiming the tribute, and making incursions into the territory of the republic. Hence, what was our astonishment when, four days ago, we saw arrive at Santiago a dozen Indian bravos in their war paint, who marched haughtily in Indian file, and proceeded with the silence that characterizes them toward the Government Palace."

"'What do you want?' the officer of the guard asked them at the moment when they passed through the gates."

"'Art thou a chief?' one of the Indians replied, who appeared to exercise a certain authority over the rest."

"'Yes,' the officer replied, without hesitation."

"'Maitai,' said the Indian, 'tell our great white father that his Indian sons of the Pere Mapou have held a great deliberation round the council fire, at the end of which they resolved to send him a deputation of twelve warriors, chosen from the twelve great Molucho nations, in order that the dissensions which have, up to this day, reigned between our great white father and his Indian sons may be eternally extinguished, and the war hatchet buried so deeply in the earth that it can never be found again.'"

"The officer then informed the President of the Republic of the strange visitors who had arrived; and, as the senate was assembled, orders were at once given to introduce the Indians with all the respect due to their ambassadorial quality, and the lofty mission with which they were entrusted."

"When the twelve envoys entered the Senate Hall, which was splendidly decorated and filled with officers dressed in magnificent uniforms, they did not appear at all dazzled by the sight of this unexpected pomp; they slowly advanced towards the foot of the dais on which the President of the Republic was standing to receive them, and after bowing they folded their arms on their chests and waited."

"'My Indian sons are welcome,' the President said, in a soft and insinuating voice."

"'My father is a great chief,' the Indian who had hitherto spoken replied. 'Guatechu will protect him because he is good.'"

"The President bowed his thanks."

"'What do my Indian sons desire?'" he asked.

"'The Ulmens,' the orator resumed, 'assembled in the seventh moon of this year round the council fire and asked themselves the following questions:—'"

"'Why are not our white fathers satisfied with the possession of the lands which we left to them on the seashore?'"

"'Why do they refuse to pay us the tribute they consented to, as they have done up to this day?'"

"'Why, instead of kindly treating the Indians whom they capture, do they use them cruelly?'"

"'Why, lastly, do they wish to compel the sons of Bheman to renounce the faith of their fathers?'"

"You can understand," Don Pedro continued, "the amazement produced in the minds of the senate by the Indian's speech, which demanded the establishment of the Chilian frontiers, the payment of the impost, and the liberation of the plundering and vagabond Indians. Only one reply was possible, a pure and simple refusal. This was given; but then the Indian, whose stoicism had not failed him for a single instant, drew, without a word, a packet from under his poncho, and laid it on the dais at the President's feet. It was a bundle of arrows, whose points were dipped in blood, and which were fastened together by a cascabel's skin."

"Then, taking advantage of the general stupor, the ambassadors withdrew, and when, a quarter of an hour later, the President ordered them to be pursued, it was too late; they appeared to have become suddenly invisible."

"Why, it is war," the old general suddenly interrupted, who had been listening with sustained attention to Don Pedro's narrative; "war with the Indians."

"Yes; a war such as they carry on, without truce or mercy, and which, incredible to relate, has already begun."

"What?" said Don Juan.

"Alas! yes; two hours after the strange disappearance of the Indians, a courier reached Santiago at full gallop, announcing that the Araucanos, more than fifty thousand in number, had crossed the Bio Bio, and were firing and destroying all the villages up to the gates of Valdivia, while another band had arrived under the very walls of Ports Araucos and Incapel."

"On hearing this news, the President of the Republic offered me the command of the province of Valdivia, while ordering me at the same time to explore the neighbourhood of Talca. I eagerly accepted, and set out with the rank of general, following at only a few hours' interval your son Don Juan, who has received orders to defend Incapel."

"What, Don Juan!" the señorita Soto-Mayor interrupted.

"Yes, your son, madam, or, if you prefer it, Lieutenant-Colonel Don Juan, for lie, too, has received the reward due to his merit; but, now that I think of it, he must have passed in the vicinity, and I am surprised that you have not seen him, for as he was aware of your departure for Valdivia, he hoped like myself, to meet you on the road."

"It is probable," the old gentleman remarked, "that he passed at a distance during one of your night halts; and yet we have not left the usual road."

"Oh," said Inez, "I am very sorry that my brother was unable to embrace us before proceeding to his post."

"I regret it, too, my child; but he did well in avoiding a meeting with us, if the time he might have given us could be employed in making speed. The duty of a soldier is superior to family joys. As for you, Don Pedro, though the news you have brought us is afflicting to the heart of a Chilian, I thank you for having come to inform me, and I implore you to continue your journey, while we make sincere vows for the success of your arms."

"I thank you, general, but I can remain with you without any inconvenience. As I told you, I am marching at easy stages, in order to assure myself of the state of the roads as far as Valdivia, and if you intend to continue your journey as far as that town, I will ask your permission to join your party with my men."

"Most willingly. My plan is most assuredly to go to Valdivia, and as we are close to Talca, it would be folly to turn back."

"Pardon me, general, if I insist, but it is because I have not yet told you all you ought to know."

And Don Pedro seemed to hesitate before proceeding.

"Speak, speak," the general and his wife said in chorus; "what is it?"

"If the reports which have reached Santiago are correct, the Indians have plundered and burnt your fine haciendas between the Bio Bio and the Valdivia."

"It is the fortune of war," Don Juan answered in a hollow voice; "and if I have only that misfortune to deplore, I shall console myself."

"It is also stated," Don Pedro continued, anxious to finish the sad story he was telling, "that your brother Don Luis has been utterly ruined by a band of Indian bravos, who suddenly attacked his estates with fire and sword, and devastated them."

General Soto-Mayor had remained motionless on hearing of the misfortune which personally affected him, but on learning that which had assailed his brother, he could not restrain the indignation which he felt against those of whom he was the victim.

"Oh, these villains! these villains!" he exclaimed, stamping his foot passionately; "will they never be weary of persecuting my unhappy family? Oh, you know not, my children, what this accursed race is, these Indians! Oh, why cannot I crush to the last of these impious cowards who have done me so much injury? Don Pedro, fight them, make them perish in the most cruel tortures, and bid my son remember that the Soto-Mayors have ever been the implacable foes of these obstinate demons; let him avenge his family, since the sword of his father is now in his hands."

The old man was suffering from an agitation impossible to describe, his face was covered with a sallow pallor, and a nervous tremor agitated his limbs. The remembrance of all the hatreds of former days was rekindled in his heart. The ladies, terrified at the state in which he was, strove to calm him.

"Oh, you are right," Don Juan said, a moment later; "I did wrong to break out thus in empty words, for throughout the wide republic of Chili there will be no want of arms to crush my enemies under their blows, and since a Soto-Mayor is fighting, I ought rather to bless heaven for not allowing me to die ere I had seen the triumph of my race. My brother has recovered, you say, Don Pedro; hence it is more than ever my duty to go to him and console him, and offer him one half of what is left to me. I am still rich enough to relieve one of my family."

"Come," Diego said at this moment to Leon, making him a sign to rise; "you have heard enough."

"Oh!" the young man exclaimed, sorrowfully, "all this is frightful."

"Why so?" the half-breed said. "As the old man remarked, it is the fortune of war."

"Oh, ill-fated family!"

"To which do you allude?—to mine or that man's? Yes;" he added, with a terrible accent, "unhappy is the family which, born to command millions of men, finds itself reduced to wander about without shelter or friend among his enemies. Is that what you are pitying, brother?"

"Forgive me, Diego. I swore to help your vengeance because it is just, so dispose of me."

"Good!"

"But why stoop so low as to wish to torture women?" Leon continued; "would the noble lion murder timid hares? Avenge yourselves on men, face to face, chest to chest, but not on women."

"Leon, the woman who loves my brother is my sister, and she shall be happy and respected, because in exchange my brother has left me at liberty to dispose of the others. Remember that a Tahi-Mari was the brother of Mikaa, and that the mistress of Don Ruíz de Soto-Mayor, was the wife of a Tahi-Mari."

"Enough, brother; I remember it."

The two men had returned to the middle of the camp, and were now walking side by side; a deep silence had followed the last words of the smuggler captain. It was hardly nine in the evening; the night was calm; thousands of stars glittered in the azure of the celestial vault, spreading over the peaks of the mountains which bordered the horizon a vaporous light; the moon shone brilliantly, and a light breeze made the leaves of the large palm trees that surrounded the camp rustle.

Suddenly a shrill whistle traversed the air: Diego startled, stretched out his head, and with his eyes fixed on the distance, listened attentively.

"It is a coral snake!" Leon exclaimed, as he looked round him with instinctive terror.

A few seconds passed and another whistle was heard in the same direction, but nearer.

"It is a coral snake, I tell you," Leon repeated.

"Silence!" said Diego, seizing his arm.

And taking from his lips the cigarette which he was smoking, the half-breed shook off the ash, and threw it in the air, where it described a luminous parabola; then he turned to his friend.

"Come with me," he said to him.

"Where to?"

"There," Diego replied, pointing to the wood, in front of which the camp was pitched.

"What to do?"

"You will learn."

"But they?" Leon said, hesitatingly, as he pointed to the tent in which the Soto-Mayor family was assembled.

"Be at rest."

"But really—"

"The moment has arrived, brother," Diego said, fixing his flashing eyes on the young man; "I have need of you."

"In that case I am ready."

"Thanks, brother."

And the two smugglers, forcing a passage through the trunks and bales which formed the outer wall of the camp, disappeared unseen by the sentry, and buried themselves in the tall grass.

CHAPTER XI
THE SONS OF THE TORTOISE

After walking for about ten minutes the two smugglers stopped; then Diego, looking around him inquiringly, imitated the whistle which had served as a signal to him, with such perfection that Leon at the first moment could not refrain from starting, although he knew it was his friend who had uttered it. Almost at the same instant, an Indian in full war paint rose before them: with his motionless body carelessly leaning on his rifle, he contemplated them silently, doubtless waiting to be addressed.

He was a man of about thirty years of age, of a height exceeding six feet, perfectly proportioned in all his limbs, and who offered the true type of Indian beauty—strength united to elegance of figure: his solidly attached and muscular limbs seemed to possess incredible elasticity and suppleness; his forehead was lofty and open; his eyes covered by thick brows and fringed with long lashes, were black, piercing, and restless; his bent nose, and his handsomely chiselled mouth, lined with teeth of dazzling whiteness, produced an *ensemble* really stamped with grandeur, but slightly obscured by the expression of pride, disdain, and cunning, which animated his countenance.

NO tattooing disfigured his face, which was of a dark copper colour. His dress was extremely simple; his long black hair, drawn up and fastened on the top of his head by a thong made of a snakeskin, fell in large curls on his shoulders, while an eagle's feather placed on the side indicated his rank as chief. He was wrapped up in a poncho, and through the girdle which served to hold up the wide drawers, which fell to his knees, were passed an axe, a machete, an ox horn, which served as a powder flask, and a bullet bag of llama skin. His legs were covered with boots of oxhide, unassailable by the bites of the reptiles so dangerous in these countries, round which he wore human scalp locks as garters. A second poncho, much wider and larger than the other, fell carelessly from his right shoulder to the ground, and was employed as a mantle. On seeing the Indian, Diego waved his hand, and said to him—"My brother is welcome."

The Indian bowed without replying.

"What does my brother desire?" Diego continued.

"Iskarre is growing on the holy Inapere and the hour has arrived; all the Molucho warriors are assembled; is the descendant of the great Tahi-Mari ready to answer his brothers?"

"My brother will guide me," Diego replied, without any further remark.

"Matai! my brother can come, then, and he will see the great Molucho chiefs."

While uttering these words the Indian looked at Leon with marked suspicion, but whether that he did not dare question Diego about him, or expected an explanation from the latter, he resolved to show the road to the two men. The further he advanced the thicker the wood became, but the Indian marched lightly, without any hesitation, and like a man perfectly acquainted with the locality. Turning his head repeatedly to the right and left, he examined the thickets and clumps of trees, and after half an hour of this rapid and silent march he halted. They had reached the entrance of a vast clearing, in the centre of which some forty men were assembled; the Indian made the smugglers a sign not to advance, and went off with the straightness of an arrow in the direction of the Indians. A strange spectacle was then offered to Leon.

The Indians were smoking round a large fire, whose reddish glare illumined them, and a dozen huts of boughs hastily constructed, proved that this temporary encampment was not a mere night halt. A few Indians walked up and down before these huts, while others, rifle in hand, seemed to be guarding two European prisoners, whose features the distance and scene prevented the smugglers from distinguishing, and who were lying at the foot of a tree with their limbs bound.

The Indian who had guided Diego and Leon went up to those of his brothers who seemed to be the oldest, and spoke to them with great animation. They soon rose and entered a hut, and then came out again almost immediately, addressing a few words to the men who were guarding the prisoners. The latter raised the Europeans from the ground and carried them into the hut.

"All this is inexplicable," Leon said to his companion; "what mean these comings and goings?—who are the two men being dragged away?"

And he made a movement as if to rush forward.

"Do not stir," Diego exclaimed, as he held him back: "no imprudence, for the slightest movement would ruin us; do you not know that we are surrounded by invisible watchers? Know that behind every one of the trees that surround us is hidden a man, whose eye is fixed upon us."

Leon made no reply, but continued to observe, till their Indian guide reappeared.

"My brothers will follow me," he said, so soon as he was a few steps from the smugglers.

They bowed and obeyed; and Longscalp led them right down the clearing, and introduced them into the most spacious hut. It to some extent resembled a beehive, except that its base was square, and might be thirty feet in depth, by the same in width. The narrow, low door only allowed passage for one man at a time, and he was obliged to stoop. In the roof a hole was made for the smoke which escaped from a fire of dried branches that occupied the centre of the hut.

Twelve or fourteen Indians, gravely squatting on their heels, smoked while listening in the most religious silence to a Sayotkatta, who could be easily recognised by his pacific costume, which consisted of a long white dress of llama hair, fastened round his hips by a blue and red girdle. His hair, parted on his forehead, fell on his neck, and he wore on his head a species of diadem composed of a gold fillet surmounted by an image representing a tortoise supporting the sun. His features, though grave and stern, had something gentle and majestic about them which inspired respect.

It was he who pointed out to Diego and Leon a place at the lire, and without appearing to pay any further attention to the newcomers, he began speaking, all raising their eyes to him.

"At the beginning of ages," he said, in a guttural and marked voice, "when Guatechu only reigned over the chaos of the worlds, there existed but six men, who, tossed about by the winds, wandered on the backs of clouds, which allowed them to soar over the immensity of space. These men were sad, because they understood that their race was accursed and could not be perpetuated."

"One day, when they met, they all passed onto the same cloud, and held a council, in order to arrange a plan for avoiding such a misfortune. For a long time they had been talking together and proposing measures one more impracticable than the other, when suddenly Mayoba appeared in the midst of them. He gazed at them for a moment in silence, then an ironical smile curled his upper lip, and he said to them, in a voice that resembled the hoarse howling of a distant storm—"

"What you are seeking exists; choose the bravest and handsomest from among you, for he alone can attempt the adventure: let him go to Paradise, where he will find Ataentsic, the woman; it is she who will prevent your race from perishing, and that is the reason why Guatechu keeps her far from you, in order that you may perish, for he repents having made you."

"After uttering these words Mayoba disappeared with a burst of savage and shrill laughter, which caused the men to shudder with terror. Our first fathers held another council, and pointed out one among them, the handsomest and whitest among them, of the name of Hoquaho, to go and conquer Ataentsic."

"Hoquaho accepted the mission entrusted to him, and aided by his five companions, he piled up the clouds on each other in order to scale Paradise: but, in spite of all their efforts, the distance seemed ever to remain the same, and they began to despair of succeeding in this bold enterprise on seeing the inutility of their efforts, when the birds of heaven that had followed their movements anxiously had pity on them, and forming into a compact flock, made a convenient seat for Hoquaho, whom they bore away on their wings."

"On reaching Paradise, Hoquaho concealed himself behind a tree opposite the wigwam in which Ataentsic was, and he waited till she came out, as she was accustomed to do every morning, to go and draw water at the spring. As soon as she appeared, he went up to her and offered her some grizzly bear's grease to eat, of which he had laid in a stock."

"The woman, surprised and charmed by the appearance of Hoquaho, easily let herself be seduced, and they soon came to a perfect understanding; but Guatechu soon perceived what had happened, and furious at seeing his plans overthrown by the fault of a woman, he expelled the two unhappy beings from Paradise, and hurled them into space."

"They fell thus for nine days and nine nights, imploring, but in vain, the mercy of Guatechu, for he had stopped up his ears with wax, and did not hear. At length a tortoise took pity on the wretched couple, and placed itself under their feet to stop the fearful fall. Then the otters, cayonans, and sea fish went to the bottom of the waters to fetch clay, which they brought up and fixed all round the shell of the tortoise, and thus they formed a small island, which gradually increased through their incessant labour, and ended by forming the earth such as you see it at present."

"Thus, sons of Hoquaho, the first man, you come," said the Sayotkatta, in conclusion, "to respect and adore Chemiin, who is the soul of the world, and the centre of the universe, which his shell alone supports and enables to float in immensity."

"Matai!" cried the Indians, inflamed by their priest's narrative, "Chemiin Aulon (the Tortoise-sun) is the master of the world."

The Sayotkatta hung his head on his breast, and throwing over his eyes the corner of the ample poncho which floated from his shoulders, he remained plunged in deep meditation. After this a gloomy silence fell upon this strange assembly. Then an Indian, whose great age was indicated by his noble but worn features, and his long grey hair, took up a calumet full of tobacco, lit it at the fire, took a few whiffs, and passed it to his right hand neighbour, who did the same. The calumet thus went round the circle till it returned to the old Indian, who seemed to preside over the meeting.

He finished the tobacco, and when the last grain was consumed, shook the ash out on his hand, and threw it in the fire, saying —

"This is the supreme council at which the great Molucho chiefs are present. May Agrikoué come to our assistance, for the war hatchet is dug up, and the Sons of the Tortoise are about to recapture their territory, unjustly invaded by the palefaces."

"May Agrikoué aid us!" the Indians repeated.

"Which are the nations," the old man continued, "ready to take part in the struggle?"

Then one of the Indians spoke in reply,

"The Tecuitles of the Curuhi, whose hunting ground extends from the town of Valparaíso to the Gulf of Guapatika, has raised the war cry, and six thousand fighting men have answered his appeal. I have spoken."

Another spoke as follows —

"The Tecuitles of the Huiliches has assembled seven thousand warriors."

Then another said in his turn —

"Four thousand Oumas are awaiting the signal."

"Ten thousand Puelches are ready to utter the war cry," said a fourth.

"Eight thousand Tehuels are under arms," continued another.

After the chief who had last spoken rose a man whose features had a singular blending of the European and Indian tribe. In fact, his tribe was descended from the crews of three Spanish ships, who, having mutinied, abandoned their officers, and landed on the American coast, where they settled. By degrees they became allied with the Indians, whose religion and customs they adopted, and multiplied to such an extent as to form a tribe.

"The Aigueles," he said, "have five thousand warriors round the war stake."

"My brothers the Ulmens have done well," the president replied, "and the great confederation will be complete; nearly all the nations have risen, and Guatechu will give us the victory. The Moluchos count thirty thousand warriors, who, with twenty-five thousand of the sacred tribe of the great Toltoru, have passed the Bio Bio, and are encamped on the banks of the Valdivia: one nation, however, has not sent a deputy to the great council, and the valiant Jaos alone are not represented here."

"My father is mistaken," replied a young Indian of martial aspect, whose face, bathed in perspiration and clothes covered with dust, indicated the speed he had displayed in covering the ground which separated his territory from the place of council. "It is a long distance from the country of the Jaos to that of the Moluchos, but twelve thousand men are following me."

A quiver of enthusiasm ran round, the assembly.

"My son is welcome," replied the aged man. "The Jaos honour us by sending us a chief so celebrated as Tcharanguii, the invincible Ulmen."

A flush of satisfaction passed over the features of the young chief of the Jaos.

"You see," the old Indian continued, "that one hundred thousand warriors will march along the war trail, resolved at length to take back the territory which the Spaniards have so long unjustly held. Everything is at length ready. The great confederation which has enveloped them for the last twenty years in its thousand folds is about to draw closer and crush them. War to the death upon the cruel invaders, and let us drive them into the sea which vomited them up. No truce, no pity, and to the courage of the Lion let us add the prudence of the Serpent."

Then, turning to Diego, who, during the whole period that this scene had lasted, remained motionless by the side of Leon, whose anxiety was increasing, he said—

"The hour has arrived for my son Tahi-Mari to rise and give us a report of the manner in which he has carried out the mission entrusted to him twenty years ago by the assembled chiefs of the great Molucho nations. Our ears are open, and all my sons will listen, for it is a great chief who is about to speak!"

For the first time since Leon had known Diego, the face of the latter grew animated, and a smile of triumph had taken the place of the cold expression of indifference which seemed stereotyped on his lips. He bowed to the chief, whose eyes were fixed on him, and leaning on his long rifle, he raised his head and answered in a firm voice—

"I am ready to reply to my father, Unacha Cuayac, and to the great chiefs of the twelve nations. I am the son of the tortoise, and my race supports the world. Let them question and I will answer."

"My brother will speak, for, as he has said, he is the son of the Chemiin which supports the world," the Indian remarked, "and the words that fall from his lips rejoice our heart."

Diego began—

"Twenty years ago the great chiefs, fatigued with the continued vexations of the Spaniards, formed a vast confederation, and assembled, as on the present day, in a supreme council to consider the means to be employed in order to end the struggle which they had supported so long, and finally free themselves from those sanguinary and perfidious strangers, who had in one day stolen from us our gods, our hunting grounds, and our wealth. As at the present day, more than one hundred thousand warriors dug up the war hatchet, assembled to invoke Guatechu at the foot of the war post, and took an oath to live free or die. The signal was about to be given, and Okikiouasa was already waving his fatal torch ready to bear fire and death among our ferocious enemies, when a chief rose in the council and asked permission to speak. This chief was my father, Tahi-Mari, a warrior renowned for his valour in combat, and an old man revered for his wisdom at the council fire; he alone, when all loudly demanded war, dared to speak in favour of peace; but Tahi-Mari was so respected by the other chiefs, that far from bursting into fury against the man who tried to overthrow their projects, they listened to him in silence. What he said you all know, and hence I need not repeat it; the chiefs accepted his advice, and it was resolved that a young Molucho warrior, chosen among the most worthy, should leave his tribe and go among the Spaniards, whose manners and religion he should pretend to adopt; that he should pass five years among them, trying to surprise all the secrets which rendered them invincible, and after that period should come and give an account of his mission to the great council of the nations."

"This mission was delicate and difficult to carry out; continual dissimulation was imposed on the man who undertook it; an hourly torture, by forcing him to live with his most cruel enemies, and feign for them friendship and attachment. The choice fell upon me, not because I was the most worthy, but because I was the son of Tahi-Mari, the great beloved Inca chief of the Moluchos. I joyfully accepted the painful though honourable distinction offered me; I at that time counted eighteen summers; life appeared to me happy and smiling: I had a bride to whom I was to be married at the next melting of the snow, but I was compelled to abandon this sweet dream, renounce the happiness which I had promised myself, and devote myself to the service of my country. I left everything without regret, for the chiefs had spoken, and I ought to feel jealous of the honour they had done me. The five years passed, then five others, but the hour for deliverance did not strike; for twenty years, in fine, I wandered about all the countries subjected to the Spaniards, listening at each step that I took to the maledictions which fell upon those of my race. My father died, and I was unable to close his eyes and sing the tabouré at his interment; my betrothed has left the earth, summoning me, but I was unable to reply to her voice; my whole family is extinct, and has gone to join Garonhea in the paradise of the blest. I have remained alone and abandoned, but my courage has not weakened; hesitation has not entered my heart, and I have continued to walk in the path which I traced for myself, because Tahi-Mari had made a sacrifice of his life and his happiness to his brothers. Today my mission is accomplished; I know in what the strength of the Spaniards resides and how they may be laid low; all their towns and fortresses are known to me; I can give the numbers of their soldiers, indicate their hopes and projects, and I have infallible means to break every one of the springs which set their government in motion. In a word, nothing has been omitted or forgotten by me, and I can answer beforehand for the success of our cause. I have spoken."

Diego ceased speaking and waited, and a solemn silence followed on the narration which he had just made. The Indians were profoundly affected by the sublime self-denial and perfect devotion of the man, whose heroic will had not failed him for a single moment during the long trial which he had undergone.

Leon shared the general enthusiasm. The great character of his friend was perfectly revealed to him, and, measuring the importance of the sacrifice the Indian had made of the twenty fairest years of his life with that of his own love for Maria, which he had been unable to make up his mind to relinquish, he confessed to himself that there was in Diego's heart a paternal devotion far superior to any that he was capable of feeling.

At length the Sayotkatta rose and walked towards the Inca with a slow and majestic step: on coming in front of him, he stopped and gazed at him with pride, and then said—

"The piaies are right, you are really a descendant of the race of the Tortoise. Son of Tahi-Mari," he added, as he took off his gold diadem and placed it on Diego's brow, "be our chief."

"Yes, yes," the Indians exclaimed, eagerly rising; "Tahi-Mari! Tahi-Mari! he alone ought to command us; he alone is worthy to be the Toqui of the Twelve Nations."

CHAPTER XII
A HUMAN SACRIFICE

When the first moment of effervescence was over, and tranquillity was beginning to be restored, Diego made a sign that he wished to speak, and all were silent.

"I thank," he said, "the chiefs of the Twelve Nations for the honour which they do me, and I accept, because I believe myself worthy of it: but the war we are about to undertake is decisive, and must only terminate with the utter extermination of our enemies. We shall have terrible contests to endure and extraordinary difficulties to overcome. Now, one man, whatever his genius may be, and however great his knowledge, cannot satisfy such claims."

"My son speaks like a sage; let him tell us what to do, and we will approve it," Huachacuyac answered.

"We must continue," Diego went on, "in the track which has been followed up to this day; a man must remain among the Spaniards, as in the past, in order to know the secret of their operations. Let me remain this man, and I will transmit to the chiefs whom you select to take my place the orders they will have to carry out, and the information which I may think useful for them, up to the time when I resume the command of the great army."

Universal assent was testified by the great assembly, and Diego continued—

"Perhaps I shall return among you soon, if circumstances decree it, but I propose for the present to attach to myself three chiefs renowned for their wisdom."

"Speak," the Indians replied, "for you are our sole master."

"In that case appoint as my assistants our venerable Sayotkatta, Vitzetpulzli, and Huachacuyac, if the choice suit my brothers."

"Matai," said the Indians, "Tahi-Mari is a great chief."

Then Diego turned to Leon and invited him to rise, and the latter obeyed, without knowing what his friend wanted of him. Diego, or rather Tahi-

Mari, laid his hand on the young man's head and addressed the Indians, who gazed at him curiously.

"Chiefs," he said, "I have still one request to make to you; this is my brother; he has saved my life and his heart belongs to me. He is a Frenchman, and his nation has frequently fought against our enemies. I ask that he may be regarded as a son of the Twelve Molucho Nations, and beloved by you as I love him."

The chiefs bowed to Leon, whose heart beat violently: then Huachacuyac taking him by the hand, said to him in a voice full of gentleness and gravity, after kissing him on both cheeks:

"My brother, thou art no longer a stranger among us. I adopt thee as my son."

Then, addressing the Indians:

"Molucho warriors! let this man be for ever sacred to you, for he is the son of the Twelve Nations."

And taking off the gold necklace he wore, he threw it over the young man's shoulders, adding:

"Here is my turbo, do you consent to receive the adoption of the Moluchos and march with them?"

"I do, brother," Leon answered, with some emotion.

"Be it so, then, and may Guatechu protect thee!" Then each of the Indians came to kiss the young man on the face, make him the present of adoption, and change with him a portion of their weapons. Diego followed with interest the details of this scene, which profoundly affected Leon, who was sensible of the new mark of friendship which the half-breed gave him: and when his turn came to give him the embrace, a tear of joy sparkled in his black eye. This ceremony terminated, the Sayotkatta advanced into the centre of the assembly.

"Ikarri is in the middle of his course," he exclaimed, "the piaies are waiting; let us make the war sacrifice in order to keep the evil spirits at bay and appease them, so that Guatechu may grant us the victory."

All the Indians present seemed to be anxiously awaiting these words: hence, so soon as they were pronounced they hastened from the hut, and proceeded to a much larger spot, in the centre of which was a pedestal, a colossal statue of the sun, called in Indian Areskoui, and which was supported by a tortoise.

In front of this statue was a sort of stone table sustained by four blocks of rock. The table, slightly hollowed in the centre, was provided with a trough intended for the blood to flow into; and a few paces from it was a figure, formed of resinous wood. Six piaies surrounded the table: they were dressed in long white robes, and all wore a golden fillet resembling the one which surrounded the Sayotkatta's head, but of smaller dimensions. The hut was also guarded by forty armed Indians, who preserved a religious silence. During the short walk from the council hut to the one we have just described, Diego took aside Leon, and said as he pressed his hand fiercely:

"Brother, in the name of all that you hold dearest in the world, shut up in your heart any trace of emotion: I should have liked to spare you the horrible spectacle you are about to witness, but it was impossible: not a word, not a gesture of disapprobation, or you will destroy us both."

"What is going to happen?" Leon asked, in terror.

"Something frightful, brother; but take courage, remain by my side, and whatever may happen, be calm."

"I will try," said Leon.

"You must," Diego repeated; "swear to me to check your emotion."

"I swear it," the smuggler repeated, more and more surprised.

"It is well: now we can enter;" and both went into the hut and mingled with the crowd of spectators. One of those awful dramas which seem impossible in the nineteenth century, and which unfortunately are still in vogue in remote regions, was about to begin. The Sayotkatta, with his head bowed on his chest, was standing at the base of the Statue of the sun, with six piaies on the right, and six on the left. Two young Indians held a torch, whose red and flickering glare cast light and shadow with sinister reflections. The Sayotkatta at length spoke:

"The hatchet is dug up, the toqui has just been proclaimed, and the hour has arrived to stain the hatchet. Ikarri demands blood."

"Let us give blood to Ikarri," the Indians shouted, "so that he may give us victory."

The Sayotkatta made a sign, and two piaies left the hut; then all present fell on their knees, and began a chorus to a slow and monotonous rhythm. A moment after the piaies returned, bringing a man between them. The Indians rose, and there was a deep silence, during which every man waited with feverish impatience.

The individual whom the piaies brought into the hut wore the uniform of the Chilian lanceros. He was a young man of twenty-four or twenty-six years of age, with an open face and elegant and bold features. All about him revealed the mocking carelessness peculiar to soldiers of every country.

"Asses!" he said, laughing at his guardians, who pushed him on before them, "could you not wait till tomorrow to perform all your mummeries? Caray! I was so sound asleep! the devil take you!"

The piaies contented themselves with shaking him rather roughly.

"Miserable bandits," he added, "if I had my sabre, I would show you certain cuts which would make you sink six feet into the ground. But all right; what I cannot do, my comrades will do, and you will lose nothing by waiting."

"The papagay is a chattering bird, that speaks without knowing what it says," a piaie interrupted in a hollow voice: "the eagle of the Andes is dumb in the hour of danger."

"In truth," the lancero continued, with a laugh, "this old rogue is right; let us show these Indian brutes how a Spanish hidalgo dies. Hum!" he added, taking a curious look around him, "these fellows are very ugly, and I should almost thank them for killing me, for they will do me a real service by freeing me from their villainous society."

After this last sally, the soldier haughtily raised his head and remained silent and calm in the presence of the danger which he had before his eyes. Leon had not lost one of the words uttered by the young man; and he felt moved with compassion, and thinking of the sorrowful fate which was reserved for the hapless prisoner. Leaning against one of the walls of the hut, he admired with a sort of irresistible fascination the bright glance of the soldier, so haughty and careless, and asked himself with tears to what punishment he was going to be condemned.

He had not long to wait; the Sayotkatta gave a signal, and two piaies began stripping off the lancero's uniform; after which they removed his shirt, and only left him his trousers. The young man did not attempt to make any resistance, and the muscles of his face remained motionless; but when one of his assassins tried to remove the scapulary, which, like all Spaniards, he wore round his neck suspended from a black ribbon, he frowned, his eyes sparkled, and he cried in so terrible a voice that the Indian recoiled in terror—

"Brigand! leave me my scapulary!"

The Indian hesitated for a moment, and then returned to his victim.

"Nonsense, no weakness!" the prisoner added, and held his tongue.

The Indian seized the string, and without taking the trouble to remove it from his neck, pulled so violently that a red mark was produced on the soldier's skin. Suddenly a sudden pallor discoloured the prisoner's cheeks; the Sayotkatta advanced upon him, holding up in his hand a long-bladed, thin, and sharp knife. Then came a moment of indescribable agony for Leon, who felt his hair bathed in a cold perspiration, while his temples were contracted by pain. He saw the man with the knife attentively seeking on the victim's chest the position of the heart, and a smile of satisfaction passed over his lips when he had found it; then pressing very lightly the sharp point of the knife on the flesh, he drove it inch by inch, and as slowly as was possible, into the soldier's chest.

The latter kept his enormously dilated eyes fixed on those of the Sayotkatta, all whose movements he watched; ere long the pallor that covered his features became now livid, his lips blanched, and he threw himself back, stammering—

"Santa Maria, ora pro nobis!"

The Sayotkatta was pressing the hilt of the knife against the body, and the Indians struck up a mournful hymn. The knife was drawn out—a jet of blood came from the wound—a convulsion agitated the body, which the piaies supported in their arms, and all was over. The lancero was dead!

Leon bit his poncho to prevent his crying out. A hundred times had the captain of the smugglers' band braved death in his encounters with the custom's officers and lanceros, and his arm had never failed him when he was obliged to cleave a man's head with a sabre cut, or level him by the help of his rifle, but at the sight of the cowardly and cruel assassination being performed he stood as if petrified by disgust and horror. He gave a start when the lancero drew his last breath; but Diego, who was watching him, went up to him.

"Silence! or you are a dead man," he said.

Leon restrained himself, but he had not reached the end of his amazement yet. The piaies raised the corpse, laid it on the stone table, after removing the rest of the clothes, and the Sayotkatta pronounced a few mysterious words, to which the Indians replied by chanting.

Then the latter, taking his knife up again, cut the victim's chest down the whole length, and examined with scrupulous attention the liver, heart, and lungs, which he pulled out to lay on the prepared pyre. All at once he turned round and addressed the spectators with an inspired accent—

"Sons of Chemiin, Guatechu protects you. Everything is favourable, and our cruel enemies will at length fall under our blows."

Then one of the piaies collected in a vessel the blood which dripped from the table, and carefully placed it outside. It was not enough to have mutilated the corpse. This horrible butchery was succeeded by an operation which completely froze Leon's blood, and he could hardly restrain the feeling of repulsion which the hideous spectacle aroused in him.

One of the Indians brandished a cutlass with a gesture of furious joy over the cold head of the assassinated lancero; and while with the left hand he seized the pendant hair, with the other adroitly scalped him. The sight of this despoiled head produced a lively movement of satisfaction among all the spectators, who resumed their chanting.

At length the other four piaies seized the bleeding body, and carried it, quivering as it was, to the centre of the camp, followed by all the other Indians, who sang, accompanying themselves with furious gestures and yells. As we stated, it was in the middle of the nineteenth century that this scene—which our readers might be inclined to fancy borrowed from the history of barbarous times, but of which we were an eye-witness—occurred.

On the command of the Sayotkatta, the piaies stopped near a young tree, which he stripped of its branches by the help of an axe. All the Indians halted, and formed a sort of thick hedge several rows in depth. Chanting sacred prayers, the piaies deposited the corpse at the foot of the tree, from which they stripped the bark. Then the Indians who held the vessel of human blood poured it over the stem, after which the one who had scalped the lancero attached the scalp to it.

The strange songs recommenced with fresh energy, and ere long the piaies, bringing piece by piece the wood employed to construct the pyre in the hut of sacrifice, built it up again at the foot of the tree, and laid the corpse upon it, carefully placing near it the heart, liver, and lungs. When all these preparations were ended, the Indians formed a circle round the tree, and the Sayotkatta ascended the pyre.

The scene then assumed a character at once savage, majestic, and imposing. In fact, it was something striking to see on this magnificent night, by the light of the torches which illumined with fantastic flashes the dark foliage of the trees, all these Indians, with their harsh and stern faces, arrayed round a pyre on which stood an old man dressed in a long white robe, who with inspired eye and superb gestures contemptuously trampled underfoot a blood-stained corpse.

The Sayotkatta took a scrutinizing glance around him, and then said in a loud and solemn voice—

"The victim is immolated, and Ikarri is satisfied. Guatechu protects us. The victory will be faithful to the right, and our enemies will fall never to rise again. Sons of the Tortoise, this is the war stake!" he continued, as he pointed to the tree; "It is for me to strike the first blow in the name of Guatechu and Ikarri."

And, raising the axe, which he held in his right hand, the old man dealt the tree a blow, and descended. This was the signal for a frenzied assault; each Indian, drunk with fury, advanced with horrible yells to the tree, which he struck, and each blow that re-echoed seemed to arouse such ardour among those who were waiting their turn, that they soon all rushed with deafening noise upon the tree, which could not endure such an attack for any length of time. Long after it had fallen, furious men were assailing a few inches of the trunk which stood out of the ground.

The kindling of the pyre by the Sayotkatta by means of a torch could alone interrupt these attacks on the tree, which they treated as if they were dealing with a real enemy. A few minutes later, the flames whirled up, the snapping of wood and the cracking of bones which were being calcined in the midst of the fire became audible. A dense smoke escaped from the furnace, and driven by the wind, suffocated the birds sleeping in the aspens and larch trees that surrounded the clearing.

It was the finale of the festival, and, like most Indian festivals, was accompanied by a dance, if such a name can be given to the mad round which the Indians performed. Taking each other by the hand, without distinction of rank or dignity, they began whirling round the pyre, forcing Leon, who did not dare decline, to share in this horror.

Ere long, overexcited by the sound of the Molucho war song, which they struck up in chorus, they went round so hurriedly and quickly, that at the end of ten minutes it would have been impossible for any human being to distinguish a single ring of the chain, which seemed to be moved by a spring. Imagine an immense wheel turning on its axle with the speed of a railway carriage wheel, and you will have an idea of the exercise which the bravest and most brilliant warriors of the twelve Molucho tribes indulged in with gaiety of heart.

They did not stop till the pyre had become a pile of ashes. Carefully collecting these ashes the piaies went with great pomp to throw them into a torrent which leaped no great distance from the camp. A portion of the Indians, that is to say, those among them still able to use their limbs, accompanied them with a new dance and fresh songs. As for Leon, utterly exhausted, he had fallen almost in a fainting state near a hut.

"Come, brother," Diego said to him, as he helped him to rise, and pointed to the dawn which was beginning to whiten the horizon, "let us depart; it is late, and we must be back in camp before daylight."

"Let us go—let us go," said Leon, "for my head is turning. The smell of blood chokes me, and the atmosphere here is poisoned."

Diego looked at him without replying; then, after exchanging a few words with the great chief Huachacuyac and the Sayotkatta, he took the arm of the smuggler captain, and went with him toward the camp where the Soto-Mayor family were resting.

CHAPTER XIII
THE BALAS RUBY

The sun was rising radiantly when Señor Don Juan de Soto-Mayor, with pale face and features worn by the unhappy news which Don Pedro de Sallazar brought him on the previous evening, raised the canvass of the tent in which he had spent the night, and stepped forth. General Don Pedro accompanied him.

The morning was superb, and the arrieros were engaged in loading the mules and saddling of horses; Leon, seated apart on a fallen tree, seemed plunged in deep and bitter thoughts. The old gentleman approached, and he did not seem to notice his presence.

"Good morning, Señor Captain," he said to him, lightly touching his shoulder.

The young man started at the sound of this voice; then rising, he slightly raised his hat off his head, and bowed to the old general, while replying, mechanically—

"May heaven grant it be good to you, caballero."

"What is the matter, my friend?" the speaker asked him, kindly; "has anything unpleasant occurred during your sleep?"

"Nothing, sir," Leon said, hastily; "I trust that the ladies have slept well."

"Yes, yes; at least, I suppose so, for I have not seen them yet."

"Here are the señoras," Don Pedro, who had remained a little behind, said to the general: "and what is more, all ready to mount."

The two gentlemen advanced to meet them. "Ah! ah!" said Diego, good humouredly, "everybody is up; all the better, for the sooner we start, the sooner we shall reach our journey's end."

"Gentlemen, one word with you, if you please," General Don Juan said to the two smuggler chiefs, after inquiring the health of his wife and daughters.

"We are at your orders, general," Leon and Diego said. And they followed Don Juan, who led them apart from the muleteers.

"Gentlemen," he said to them, when he fancied himself out of earshot, "I received strange news last night; it seems that the Indians have risen, and are disturbing the province of Valdivia; hence we must try to reach the city as speedily as possible."

Diego affected surprise.

"Really," he said, "that is extraordinary."

Then, after appearing to reflect for a moment, he added—

"Must you absolutely pass through Talca?"

"No; but why that question?"

"Because," Diego answered, "I know a road across the mountain which shortens the journey twenty leagues."

"That is true," said Leon; "by crossing the mountain we shall save a day's march."

"In that case, gentlemen, let us do so, for when a man is in a hurry to arrive, he must choose the shortest road. Ah! bye-the-bye," he added, "before forming a determination, I must consult with General Don Pedro, in order to know if he consents to accompany us without stopping at Talca."

Don Pedro did not consider it advisable to oppose the plan; on the contrary, his plan of inspecting the vicinity of Talca was served by the measure, which would allow him to reconnoitre whether the Indians had as yet entered the wood skirting the forest.

For a moment the fear of some surprise seemed to occupy his mind; but reflecting that his escort, joined to that of Don Juan, would be sufficient to protect the caravan, he saw no inconvenience in adopting the change of route proposed by Diego.

The latter had not seen, without some displeasure, the caravan swelled by Don Pedro and his soldiers; but, too clever to let it be seen, he pretended to be extremely pleased by this increase of men, who, in the event of an attack, would serve as a reinforcement. However this may be, Don Pedro ordered four of his lanceros to march about a hundred paces ahead of the column, and then they started. Each horseman, fully armed, advanced with his eye on the watch, and in profound silence, while two other lanceros, forming the rearguard, rode fifty yards behind. The small troop was composed altogether of five-and-thirty persons.

Leon scarce dared to raise his eyes to Maria, who rode by her mother's side. Each time that the maiden's glance met his, a sort of confusion or remorse was depicted on his features, in spite of the efforts which he made to recover his usual coolness. Doña Maria knew not to what to attribute this change in the young man's manner, and seemed to be striving to discover the cause.

"Can it be the arrival of Don Pedro that thus brings a cloud to his brow?" she asked herself; "perhaps he is jealous of that cavalier. Oh! if that be the case, it is because he loves me."

And turning her face once again toward the smuggler, she smiled on him in a way that must remove his error; but he, far from deriving from the marks of love which the maiden gave him, the joy which the heart feels on knowing itself beloved, he found in it a motive for secret grief.

The scene he had witnessed during the previous night in the Indian camp had produced so deep an impression upon him, that he could not refrain from thinking of the mournful consequences it must have for the Soto-Mayor family, which was, doubtless, devoted to death.

Although Doña Maria's life had been guaranteed by Diego, he trembled at the grief which must assail her, when struck in her dearest and tenderest affections; and, while recognising the apparent justice in the name of which Diego had condemned the general, his wife, and his other children, he was horrified by the terrible position in which the half-breed had placed him by making him swear to aid his revenge.

"What!" he said, "I love Doña Maria, and not only must I allow the death of her family to be carried out without opposition, but if the contest breaks out between them and the Indians, my duty orders me to join the latter. Oh, no! for I feel that I shall never commit such an unworthy action, and I would sooner let myself be killed than array myself against those whom I am pledged to serve, or those whom I have sworn to defend."

And the young man's cheeks were flushed by the action of the internal fever which devoured him; his burning forehead, and his sharp, quick gestures announced the agitation which the combat going on in his mind produced.

The caravan had entered the wood where the Indians had assembled on the past night, and they soon reached the middle of the clearing where they had camped. The sons of the Tortoise had disappeared, but the huts built by them, though half destroyed, still stood, as well as the trace of the ashes of the pyre on which the body of the ill-fated lancero had been burnt. Leon could not see the spot again without feeling a shudder of awe and terror. Diego looked around him carelessly, and whistled a sambacueca between his teeth.

"Oh, oh!" said Don Pedro, looking all around; "what have we here?"

And with the experience which he had acquired in wars in which he had taken part against the Indians, he began to rummage all the huts, after giving Leon a sign to follow him, and the rest orders to go on ahead. Leon acceded to his wishes, and both remained behind; and at the moment when they entered one of the huts, Leon saw something glistening on the ground, which he fancied was a precious stone.

He suddenly stooped, and eagerly picking up the article, examined it; it was a gold ring, set with a balas ruby of inestimable value. The young man thrust it into his belt with a vague feeling of alarm. He asked himself to whom this ring could belong, for it was not probable that an Indian had lost it: moreover, he fancied that he had already seen one like it, though he could not remember on whose finger.

"On the lancero's, perhaps?" he said to himself, thinking of the soldier who had been assassinated in his presence; but this latter supposition was speedily abandoned, for it was impossible that a simple private could be the possessor of such a jewel. Then he thought of the other prisoner, and a terrible presentiment was rising in his mind, when Don Pedro called him. The latter had completed his inspection, and was preparing to rejoin the travellers, apparently knowing all that he desired to know. Leon was soon at his side.

"I have two words to say to you, sir," Don Pedro remarked to him.

"Speak, sir," the smuggler answered, affected by the tone in which the general had uttered these words.

"I do not know you, sir," the general continued, "nor do I know your usual mode of conduct with the travellers whom you may escort."

"Do you wish to insult me, general?" Leon interrupted, as he drew himself up and fixed his firm and haughty glance on the speaker.

"Not the least in the world; still, as I do not share the friendship which the Soto-Mayor family—whether rightly or wrongly—displays for you, I wish to inform you of the reflections I have made on your score, and give you a piece of advice."

"Speak, sir," said Leon, disdainfully; "but in the first place, you know that I do not care for your reflections, and shall not accept your advice."

"Perhaps so, señor captain. At any rate, you shall have them," Don Pedro continued, not deigning to notice the arrogance which the smuggler placed on his remarks. "The place where we are at this moment is an Indian camp; if I doubted the fact, this," he added, as he knocked over a broken pipe, "would afford me a certainty. This camp was but a few hours ago still occupied by Indians, and here is the proof," he said, stooping down; "the ashes are quite warm."

"Sir," said Leon in his turn, who felt a cold perspiration beading on his temples, "what you are saying appears to me highly probable, but I do not see how that can personally interest me, or form any motive for what you said to me just now. Be good enough to explain yourself more clearly."

"I will do so, sir, and frankly," the general replied; "for I am a soldier, and do not like any prefacing."

"Nor I, sir; so to facts."

"They are these. Last night, after a lengthened conversation with General Don Juan, I had a fancy to go and smoke my cigar in the open air; the night was magnificent and invited a walk. Now, at the moment when I raised the tent curtain to go out, I saw two men glide between the bales and leave camp without warning the sentry."

"What next, sir?"

"Next? Good gracious! that is very simple. I asked myself what these two men could have to do outside the camp at that hour, when duty imposed on them the obligation of remaining at their post; but as I could learn nothing at that moment, I resolved to satisfy my curiosity by awaiting their return. I waited a long time, captain; but that did not cause me much annoyance, for I am naturally very patient, as you will say, when I tell you that I saw these two men go out and also saw them return, although they did not do so till a few minutes before daybreak. Now, I conclude by begging you to tell me where they went, for one of the two men was yourself."

"It is true, sir, I left the camp, and only returned at daybreak."

"But what important reason urged you to do so?"

"That I cannot tell you, sir," Leon said with firmness. "Suffice it for you to know that I allow nobody, not even you, general, the right to inquire into my conduct, and that, moreover, the step which I took in no way compromised the safety of the persons confided to my charge."

"Very good! that answer does not surprise me; but bear this in mind—at the first mysterious sortie you make in future—at the first action which appears to me suspicious—I will simply have you seized by my lanceros and give them orders to shoot you within an hour. You have understood me, I suppose?"

"Perfectly, general; and whenever you please, you will find me at your orders," the smuggler replied, with a tinge of irony; "but, in the meanwhile, I think it would be more useful to rejoin the caravan."

"You are warned, sir," the general continued, "and will only have yourself to blame if anything unpleasant happen to you. Now let us start."

"Very good, general."

And the two men, leaping into the saddle, galloped in the direction of the small party, which they soon, rejoined. Don Pedro placed himself at the head, and rode by the side of Diego, still silently, while Leon, who had remained a few paces in the rear, drew from the belt the ring which he had found, and regarded it afresh with sustained attention.

"I have certainly seen this ring before," he said, after turning it over and over in all directions; "but on whose finger, in Heaven's name?"

Then, thrusting it on to his finger and pulling it off again, he continued in vain to rack his brains in recalling his recollections, but could not succeed in fixing his doubts. Then pressing his horse's flank, he rode up to the travellers, and soon found himself by Doña Maria's side.

"Señor captain," the latter said to him, "shall we go through this wood for any length of time?"

"For about two hours, Señora."

"Oh, all the better, for there is an exquisite freshness in it. I am delighted that we have left the road which we were following yesterday; here it is so picturesque, that I am never weary of admiring the scenery."

"And then it will shorten our journey by a day," Leon said, sadly.

"That is true," the maiden answered, each of whose words was overheard by her mother and sister.

But at the same moment she gave the smuggler a glance which signified how much she regretted to see him so badly interpret the words to which she was far from giving the meaning which he attributed to them. The journey ended, what hope would remain to the maiden of seeing again the man whom she loved.

Leon understood the reproach, and bending down his head, he concealed his trouble by spurring his mustang, which soon carried him up to General Don Juan, who was engaged in a conversation with Don Pedro.

"For all that, general," the latter was saying to Don Juan, "I am astonished that your son did not meet you when you were following the Talca road, for I do not know any other which he could have taken in order to arrive sooner."

"Did he command any detachment of troops?" the general asked.

"No; he started for Tulcapel, merely accompanied by two lanceros."

Leon did not hear the close of the conversation, for a sudden revelation had been made to him. Suddenly his blood was frozen and his teeth were clenched. He remembered that young Don Juan de Soto-Mayor wore on his right hand, on the night which he spent at the general's country house, a ring resembling the one which he had in his belt. He perfectly remembered having noticed the sparkling of the ruby, whose exceptional size had attracted his attention.

But in proportion as his thoughts, becoming more lucid, rendered the truth more distinct, he saw with horror the dark drama of which he scarce dared to seek the meaning, so afraid was he of finding the reality in it. He had picked up the ring in the tent into which he had seen the prisoners carried on the previous evening; one was a lancero, and he was dead; but the other. Was not the other Don Juan, the son of the old general in front of him? And if, as he feared he was certain, this prisoner was Don Juan, what had become of him? Perhaps, at that very hour, he might be expiring under the frightful sufferings which the Indians were making him undergo.

Leon wished at once to question Diego on the point, for he must know the truth, but the fear of not being able to master his emotion in the presence of the two generals prevented him from doing so, and he resolved to await the first halt to satisfy his anxious curiosity. But, agitated by a thousand conflicting emotions, he did not dare look at Maria, for he was already afraid lest the maiden should ask him, with tears in her voice, what he had done with her brother's blood, as he was the accomplice of those who had assassinated him.

The caravan still advanced, and soon left the wood to debouch upon a plain intersected by numerous rivulets, which wound through a hard and rocky soil. At the moment when the last man left the edge of the forest, the dense shrubs that bordered the road noiselessly parted and made room for the head of an Indian, who looked out cautiously, after having, so to speak, smelt the air around him. His eyes settled on the little troop, which they followed until it had bent to the left and entirely disappeared; then carefully removing the twigs, the Indian thrust forward the rest of his body and crawled out. He soon found himself in the middle of the road, and began looking around him again in all directions, after which his face assumed a marked expression of satisfaction.

"Matai," he said, smiling so as to show his long white teeth.

And then he began running with the lightness of a llama in the traces of the caravan. On reaching the spot where the road formed a bend, he thrust out his head, and then hurriedly withdrawing it, climbed up the side of a wood-clad height and disappeared.

This man was Tcharanguii, the feared and formidable chief of the Jaos, one of the most powerful tribes of the twelve Molucho nations. For some minutes the rustling of parted branches might be heard, then all became silent again, the sole interruption being the imposing sounds of the desert.

CHAPTER XIV
THE RUPTURE

They travelled the whole day without any incidents: the heat which had so incommoded them all during the first few days, had been succeeded by a temperature which hourly became colder. The foliage of the trees assumed a deeper tinge of green; the singing birds of the llanos, whose sweet notes ravished the ear, had been succeeded by the eagles, vultures, and other birds of prey, which formed immense circles in space while uttering the hoarse and strange cries peculiar to them.

The sky, which had hitherto been of such a pure blue, was beginning here and there to assume greyish tones and coppery reflections, which formed a contrast with the dull whiteness of the water of the torrents which fell in cascades from the snowy peaks of the mountains, down whose flanks they dragged with a dull roar masses of rock and enormous firs which they uprooted in their passage.

A wild llama or vicuna might be seen balanced on a point of granite, and at times in the openings of the thick wood which bordered the road, the flashing eyes of a puma, or the black muzzle of a bee hunting bear, could be seen stretched out over a branch. All, in a word, announced the vicinity of the Cordillera of the Andes.

When night set in, the caravan had reached a narrow plateau, situated in what is called the temperate region, the last station of travellers before entering the vast and gloomy solitudes of the Andes, which are as yet very little known or explored, owing to the difficulty of means of transport, and the absence of a sedentary population.

The camp was made by the side of the road, under an immense natural arch, formed by means of rock, which overhung the road for more than two hundred yards, and formed a shelter for travellers by being hollowed out at its base. The fires were lighted, one in the centre of the camp, and the other at each corner, in order to keep off the wild beasts whose attacks were beginning to be apprehended with reason.

When supper was ended, sentries were posted, and each prepared his couch in order to spend his night in the enjoyment of that sleep which restores the strength. If the expression we have just used, that each prepared his couch, were to be taken literally, it would be a great mistake, if this performance were at all supposed to be like what is done in Europe in similar cases.

In fact, with a European a bed generally consists of at least one mattress, or something analogous to take its place, a bolster, a pillow, sheets, blankets, &c.; but in Chili things are very different. Although luxury and comfort are things well known in towns, beds at all like ours are only found in the houses of rich people, and then, great heavens! what beds. As for the one which the Chilians employ when travelling, it is most convenient and ingenious, since it serves them as a saddle by day, as we shall proceed to show.

The horse's equipment consists, in the first place, of three ponchos, folded square, and laid one upon the other on the back of the horse; in these ponchos are laid four sheepskins with the wool on, and on these again is placed a wooden seat, representing a saddle, which supports a pair of heavy wooden stirrups, hollowed out in a triangular form. A surcingle, fastened under the horse's belly, keep these various articles in their places, and four more ponchos and four more skins are laid on them. Lastly, another poncho is thrown over the whole, and serves as chabraque, a second strap holding this edifice in its place.

We can see from the description of what enters into the formation of Chilian horse accoutrement that it can advantageously take the place of our scanty English saddle, and that the rider is able to find the materials for a very soft bed. When the latter arrives at his sleeping place, he unsaddles his horse, which he leaves at liberty to find its food where it thinks proper, and then makes the aforesaid bed in the following way.

He first lays the saddle on the ground to act as pillow, then spreads his first sheepskins, over a space six feet in length, and two or three in width; he covers these with three ponchos, on which he lies down, and then pulls over him the four other skins and the remaining ponchos, and eventually disappears under this pile of stuff so entirely that it is impossible to perceive him, for even his head is hidden.

It happens at times that when a man is passing the night on the Cordilleras, under the protection of this formidable rampart of skins and blankets, a few feet of snow literally bury the sleeper, who, on awaking, is compelled to throw his legs and arms about for some minutes, in order to liberate himself and see daylight again.

Diego was preparing his bed in the manner which we have just described, and displaying all the attention of a man who feels the need of a sound sleep, when he saw Leon Delbès coming towards him, who since the morning had not spoken to him, and seemed to avoid him. We must suppose that the smuggler's face betrayed a lively emotion, for Diego on looking up to him, felt ill at ease, and saw that something extraordinary had taken place in his friend's mind. From the way in which the young man looked at him, it was certain that he was preparing to ask of him an explanation about some fact, and understanding that it could only refer to the Soto-Mayor family, he could not suppress a start of impatience which did not escape Leon.

The latter, on his side, was asking himself how he should manage the conversation as to lead Diego to tell him what he wanted to learn, and not knowing how to begin, he waited till the latter should address him. Both were afraid of reverting to the past, and yet each felt that the moment had arrived to behave frankly and expose the nature of his grievances.

When we speak of grievances, we know perfectly that neither had to reproach the other for any deed of a reprehensible nature in what concerned their mutual pledge to help each other; but if Leon involuntarily revolted against the implacable revenge which the half-breed had begun to exercise against the Soto-Mayors, while confessing to himself that, in spite of the friendship which united him to Diego, he could never lend a hand to excesses like the one which he had seen committed on the previous night by the Indians, Diego had not failed to comprehend that the love which Leon entertained for Maria would be an invincible obstacle to the support which the latter had sworn to give him. Without accusing him of treachery, he still taxed him with softness of heart and irresolution, or rather pitied him for having surrendered himself, bound hand and foot, to a wild passion which paralyzed all the goodwill which he might under other circumstances have expected from him.

As we see, the respective position of the two men toward each other had been too false for them not to feel in their hearts a lively desire to put an end to it; the difficulty was to manage it without injuring their self-esteem and interests.

Leon had hoped that Diego would at length inquire the motive which had brought him to his friend, but on seeing that the latter affected not to address a syllable to him, he resolved to break the silence.

"You are going to sleep, brother," he said to him.

"Yes," Diego replied: "I am tired."

"You tired!" Leon remarked, with a smile of incredulity, "tired by a ten leagues' ride, when I have seen you hunt on the Pampas for eight or ten days in succession without dreaming of resting for a moment; nonsense!"

"Tired or no, I wish to sleep: besides, what is there extraordinary in that? Has not everybody in camp lain down?"

"That is true."

"Then I invite you to do the same, unless love keeps you awake," he added, laconically. "In that case, the best thing you can do is to spend the night in walking round the hut in which your fair one is reposing, that her sleep may not be disturbed; and much good may it do you."

"Diego," Leon answered, sorrowfully, "what you are saying to me is not right. What have I done to you that you should address me so roughly?"

"Nothing," the half-breed said, with a regretful tone. "But come," he said, kicking the bed over which he had taken so much pains in preparing, "you really seem so anxious to speak to me that I might fancy that you had important business."

"What makes you suppose that I want to speak to you?"

"Oh, good Heaven! Leon, we have lived together long enough for us to be able to read on one another's faces what our thoughts are. Confess that you are suffering, that you are anxious, and that you have come to ask some explanation of me. Come, if it be so, tell me frankly what you want of me, and I will answer. For on my side I also have to speak with you about the grief and sorrow which seem to have assailed you since yesterday. Speak; is it the engagement you made to support me in the struggle I am preparing, for that seems to you too heavy to carry out? Only say one word: there is still time, and I will give you back your word; but speak, for I am anxious to come to a decision."

"Brother," said Leon, without replying directly to Diego's injunction, "I notice bitterness in your words and mocking on your lips: still, in order to remove from the discussion anything that might resemble passion or annoyance, I have let the whole day pass over the event about which I wish to speak to you, for it is the friend I am addressing, and not Tahi-Mari."

"Well, what do you want?"

"I will tell you."

Leon drew from his belt the ring which he had found, and handed it to Diego.

"Do you know this?" he asked him.

"What is it?" said the half-breed, taking it and turning it over in his fingers, while giving the young man an inquiring glance.

"A ring."

"Hang it, I can see that, and a very handsome ring too; but I ask you what meaning it has in your hands?"

"Do you not know?"

"How would you have me know?"

"Is it true that you do not know to whom it belongs?"

"Certain."

"Then you did not notice it on anybody's hand?"

"No; and I assure you that if I had seen it twenty times I should not recognise it now, for I pay no attention to such futilities."

"Well, since you do not know to whom it belongs, I will tell you."

"If you insist on my knowing, very good. But," he added, with a smile, "if I could have thought that you wished to speak to me so anxiously in order to talk about a pearl, I should have begged you to let me sleep."

"A little patience, for this ring is more important than you seem to fancy."

"In that case tell me for what reason, and how it comes in your hands."

Leon looked at Diego's face, which indicated his entire good faith, and continued:

"You remember that when we reached the Indians' camp together, two Spanish prisoners were in their power."

"Yes, certainly."

"Now, this morning, when passing again through that camp with the caravan, Don Pedro Sallazar, after examining the sign, divined an Indian sojourn, and invited me to enter the huts with him. I found this ring in the one to which I saw the prisoners transported."

"In that case," said Diego, "it must have belonged to one of them, that is incontestable. But how do those prisoners concern us?"

"Our second, as victim of the barbarous sacrifice which I saw accomplished before my eyes, and he was a lancero. I allow that I saw that hapless man for the first time in my life. But the other."

"The other!" Diego interrupted, who was curiously listening to Leon's narrative.

"The other we both know, for he was Don Juan de Soto-Mayor, the general's son, and this ring is the same which he wore on the day when his father sheltered us under his roof."

"Don Juan!" Diego said, with a start, while a flash of savage joy illuminated his eyes. "What! it was he?"

"Did you not know it?"

"No, on my soul! It is probable that he was following the same road as ourselves; and the Indians, who were ahead of us, seized him."

"And what has become of him? What have they done to him?"

"How do I know? A Soto-Mayor!" Diego repeated, on whom the announcement of this news produced unequivocal satisfaction. "Thanks, Leon, for having been the first to inform me of the fact."

"What do you mean? I came to you to ask you whether this man has not found among the Indians the horrible death that smote the lancero who accompanied him!"

"No; and I thank Heaven for it, for I gave orders that all prisoners should be kept in a place of safety, with the exception of the one selected for sacrifice, and I shall soon be able to find Don Juan, who belongs to me, and whose blood shall be shed by me in expiation of the great Tahi-Mari, my father. At length," the half-breed exclaimed, growing animated, "you are about to be avenged, my glorious ancestors! and may every head which my hand causes to fall, rejoice your irritated manes!"

At this moment, Diego's attitude had something so imposing about it that Leon felt himself gradually overcome by its terrible expression; because he resolved to oppose to the force of hatred which burned in the half-breed's heart that of love which consumed his own, by striking a grand blow.

"Brother," he said, "you are strangely in error if you fancy that I told you the name of the wearer of this ring in order to satisfy your vengeance."

"What do you mean?" Diego replied.

"That in the name of the friendship which unites us, in the name of the love which I have for Doña Maria, I have come to ask you to restore to liberty the brother of her whom I love."

And Leon ceased speaking.

The man who, walking along a road bordered by flowers and turf, suddenly saw the ground open under his feet, and a bottomless precipice present itself, would not feel a greater commotion of surprise than that which assailed the descendant of Tahi-Mari: his lips were clenched, his cheeks turned livid, and he fell crushed on the ponchos which remained on the ground.

"Have I rightly understood? Leon, it is at the moment when after waiting twenty years for the solemn hour of victory I at length hear it strike, that you ask me to surrender my enemy to you! What I should have broken all the obstacles which opposed the success of the holy cause which I am defending; I should have sacrificed without pity for myself all that attached me to life, after tearing from my heart all the illusions of my youth, in order only to leave my hatred, and all that in order to renounce the hope of attaining the object which I was pursuing! Oh, no, that is not possible; and it is not you, Leon, my friend, my brother, who would ask such a sacrifice of me. No!"

"Brother, forgive me!" Leon exclaimed; "but I love this woman."

"Yes, you love her; and if I give you the life of the brother, you will ask me tomorrow for that of the father; and each day, implored by you, I must, I suppose, abandoning one by one the victims I have marked, efface from my memory every recollection of the past, and allow the assassins of Tahi-Mari to live amid the joys which power and wealth produce. No, no! I pity you, brother, for you must have left all your reason at the bottom of that love to which you refer when you dare to make me such a proposal."

"Enough, Diego; enough! I implored you in the name of our friendship, and I was wrong, since you believe that you are committing an act of justice in killing those for whom I implore your mercy. Pardon me; and now farewell, brother, I will leave you."

"Where are you going, madman?" Diego asked, as he held him back.

"I do not know, but I wish to fly far from here."

"What! leave me! thus break a friendship like ours! You cannot think of such a thing."

"Do you not know that I love Maria with all the strength of my soul: as I told you it is an impossibility to give up that love, and yet I do not wish to betray your cause; so let me go and seek far from her, if not oblivion, at least death."

"Grief leads you astray, Leon. Come, listen to me."

"What!—your justification! I do not accuse you; but once again I say we must separate, for if Maria were to ask me for her brother and I should not give him to her, she would curse me, do you hear? Because she would refuse to believe that I love her, as I did not know how to die to save him whom your hatred has condemned! You see plainly that I must depart."

"Well, then," said Diego, with some amount of emotion, "an insurmountable barrier is raised between us."

"Yes, brother; but though we are parted the memory of our friendship will survive our separation."

A silence of some minutes' duration followed these words, and nothing could be heard but the hurried breathing of the two men. Diego was the first to speak.

"Leon," he suddenly exclaimed, making a violent effort over himself; "you have spoken the truth; one of us must depart, as we are both following a different road; but it shall be I, for my place is at the head of the Indians, my brothers. As for you, remain with those whom you are protecting, and ere I go to resume the life of the proscript, and continue in broad daylight the struggle which I have been carrying on for so many years in the darkness, give me your hand, that I may press it in mine for the last time; and then, to the mercy of God!"

"Oh!" Leon replied, eagerly, "most gladly so, or rather let us embrace, for we are still worthy of each other."

And the two smugglers fell into each other's arms.

"Be happy, Diego," said Leon.

"God grant that you may find happiness in the love of Doña Maria," said Diego.

Then the latter, taking his lasso, whistled to his colt, which came up at the appeal, and, after saddling it, he leaped lightly on its back. He remained motionless for a moment, taking a sorrowful glance at the men sleeping a short distance from him; and then, after breathing a deep sigh, he addressed Leon once again.

"Farewell!" he said to him: "remember that you are an adopted son of the Araucanos, and that if you please one day to come among your brothers to seek a supporter or a defender, you will find one and the other."

"Farewell!" murmured Leon, whose eyes were moist.

Ere long the half-breed's mustang, sharply spurred, leaped at one bound over the bales which formed the enclosure of the camp, and darted across the plain with the rapidity of an arrow.

CHAPTER XV
A FIRST LOSS

After Diego's departure, Leon remained for a long time leaning on the baggage which he had before him; the last words of his departing friend rang in his ear like the sound of a knell; a deep sorrow, a deadly discouragement had seized upon him, and a state of undefinable morbidness preyed on his whole being.

A friendship like that which united him to the Vaquero is not broken so suddenly without the heart suffering from it, and in spite of the exceptional circumstances which had caused the separation of the two men, Leon could not refrain from a species of remorse.

Turning over in his mind the different phases of his past existence and those of the four last years of his life, spent in the midst of llanos and Pampas, he asked himself whether he had not consciously exchanged the quietude of an unclouded present for the painful agitation of a future big with tempests.

With his eye fixed on the dark and bold outline of Diego, which was vaguely designed on the horizon, and was gradually disappearing in space, twenty times he was on the point of dashing forward and begging him to return, while swearing to give up the ardent passion which mastered him; but an invincible force nailed him to the ground, his choking voice died away on his lips, and his courage failed him. Ere long an impenetrable mist spread between the eyes of the young man and his friend, who entirely disappeared.

Then Leon began cursing the fatal love which had come to torture his heart, and the hours of the night passed away unnoticed by him, so greatly were his thoughts concentrated in his soul.

The sky was gloomy; heavy black clouds strangely edged, and driven from the south-west by a cold wind, coursed through the air with extreme velocity. When, at rare intervals, the moon appeared during the short period which separated a cloud on the horizon from the advent of another which dashed after it, its pale and sickly rays hardly lit up the objects on which they cast their vague light.

The scenery, plunged in darkness at each new obscuration of the moon, was mournful and silent, and nothing could be heard but the regular footfall of the sentry echoing on the hardened soil. All were asleep in the camp, save the sentry and Leon, and the latter, not afraid of being seen, gave a free course to his grief, and heavy tears fell from his eyes.

What secret and acrid sorrows are contained in each of these drops of burning water which trickle down a man's face. Tears! the supreme expression of impotence and despair. Tears! the height of weakness and despondency which brutally restore man to his place, by showing him the vanity of his pride, and the nullity of his pretended strength.

The captain of the smugglers was still weeping when a hand was laid on, or rather slightly touched, his shoulder. He quickly raised his head, and with difficulty restrained a cry of surprise. Doña Maria was standing before him, with her finger laid on her lip, in order to recommend silence.

Half hidden by the white lace which surrounded her face, and fell in long streamers on her shoulders, the maiden presented herself to Leon's astonished gaze, like a celestial apparition which had come from on high to restore him hope and courage.

"You!" he murmured, with a tenderness of expression impossible to render.

"Speak lower," the maiden replied, and she pointed to the sentry, who had stopped, and seemed to be spying her movements. Leon looked for a moment at the man to whom the guard of the camp was temporarily confided.

"Reassure yourself," he said to her; "he is the bravest and most devoted man in my band. Stop here for a moment."

Then walking a few paces, Leon made a signal to the sentry to come to him.

"Wilhelm," he said to him, "stop as sentry till I give you orders myself to call one of your comrades, and look out."

"Yes, captain," the man replied, with a marked German accent; "I understand."

"Very good," Leon replied; "begone."

The sentry retired, and Leon returned to the maiden, whose bosom was hurriedly heaving. The captain knew Wilhelm, and that at the slightest movement which took place in the Soto-Mayor's tent, he should be warned. Hence he was enabled to talk freely with her whom he loved, without fear of being surprised.

"You here so close to me!" Leon went on, seizing one of the maiden's hands. "Oh, Doña Maria, how kind you are!"

"You are suffering," she said, as she bent on the young man a glance in which the signs of a sympathising interest were visible; "you are suffering, and seem to avoid and shun me, and that is why I have resolved on asking you the cause of your sorrow."

"Oh, no! I am no longer suffering since I see you; since I hear fall from your lips sweet words which dilate my heart with hope and joy."

"Oh, be silent!" Maria replied; "for I only wish to know the cause of the sorrow which I have remarked, since this morning, on your countenance."

"What! has your attention been so directed to me as to make you feel anxious on seeing me sad and despondent?"

"Do you not know that I love you?" Maria said, with an accent of such sublime simplicity, that Leon fancied himself the sport of a dream.

There was a moment of supreme silence, which the maiden was the first to break.

"I know," she said, "how strange and unusual is the step which I am now taking, and how dangerous it would be with a man whose heart was not so noble or so great as yours; but, alas! we are at this moment in a situation so different from all the ordinary laws of life, that I thought I must frankly come and find you."

"You were right, señorita," muttered Leon, with his eyes ardently fixed upon her.

"Let me," she continued, "express to you all the gratitude I feel to you for your conduct, so full of self-denial and so loyal."

"Oh!" he said.

"I know all; I was an invisible hearer of your conversation; and nothing said by you or your friend escaped my ear. I thank you from the bottom of my heart for your devotion to our family. Alas!" she said, as if speaking to herself, "perhaps it would have been better for you and for us had you abandoned us."

"I will carry out, whatever may happen, the oath which I took to you, señorita, to lead you in safety to your destination."

"But," she said, with a movement of fear, "that man, your friend, that gloomy and stern individual, I tremble lest he may try to make us fall into some horrible trap. I have a dark foreboding that a danger menaces us."

"Whatever may be the danger, señorita," the young man exclaimed passionately, "be convinced that my friend will have no share in it; his word is sacred, and I place the most perfect confidence in him."

"Heaven grant that you are not mistaken!" she said, with a stifled sigh.

"Moreover," he continued, "whatever may happen, I shall be there, and no one will reach you without passing over my body. I have sworn to escort you and your family safe and sound to the end of this long journey, and that oath I will keep, whatever may happen."

"Thanks," she murmured, with emotion, as she offered him her white and delicate hand; "thanks, Leon—I love you!" and she disappeared light as a shadow, leaving the young man plunged into indescribable ecstasy.

The rest of the night passed without further incident, and at daybreak Leon, who had not slept for an instant, gave the signal for starting. In spite of himself, the young man felt a vague terror for which he could not account. The maiden's parting words echoed in his ear and the presentiment which she stated that she felt, caused him a preoccupation which he sought in vain to dissipate, by proving to himself that no possible danger could threaten the persons whom he was escorting.

Still, before reaching the districts where any fear would become chimerical owing to the distance from the country frequented by the Indians, the caravan would be obliged to pass through a passage called the Parumo de San Juan Bautista, a very difficult pass to cross, and which, as it served as the extreme limit of the Indian border, was the more favourable for the preparation of an ambush.

The captain wished to arrive before nightfall at this pass, in order to reconnoitre the approaches carefully, and guard against any surprise. But to do this speed was required. Gene Soto-Mayor asked the young man why he raised the camp at so early an hour, but the latter without telling him all his thoughts, managed to give him reasons which, without being good, closed his mouth, and the caravan started. The three ladies, carefully wrapped up in their ponchos and rebozos in order to protect themselves from the cold, rode side by side, preceded by General Soto-Mayor and Don Pedro Sallazar.

Leon was a few paces ahead plunged into serious reflections.

"Eh, Caballero!" Don Pedro shouted to him, "I should like, with your permission, to ask you a question."

The captain stopped.

"A question, señor," he said; "what is it, if you please?"

"Well, I fancy it very simple; still if, unconsciously, I am guilty of any indiscretion, I beg you beforehand to excuse me, and I authorize your not answering me."

The young man bowed.

"Let me hear the question," he said.

"Since we have started," Don Pedro continued, "I have sought your friend in vain, but could not find him; can he have left us, or has he gone ahead to reconnoitre?"

"My friend, señor," the young man answered, somewhat drily, "has left us not to return. He went away last night while you were asleep, but I have remained, and shall not abandon you. Does this explanation suit you, señor? Or have you any other questions to ask me?"

"Hum!" Don Pedro replied, internally offended by the way in which the young man had answered him, and checking his horse, so as to let the others pass.

The caravan continued its journey, and not one of those who composed it—numbed by the cold which gradually grew more intense, and which they had great difficulty in guarding themselves against—attempted to stripe up even the most frivolous conversation.

The nearer the travellers came to the Parumo de San Juan Bautista, the more nervous did the captain grow, though he could not guess the reason; at length this anxiety became so great, that, after temporarily entrusting the command of the troop to Wilhelm, he made a signal to four of his adventurers to follow him; and, putting himself at their head, he dashed his horse at the flanks of the mountain which the travellers were ascending at the moment. As he passed Doña Maria, the latter slightly pulled aside the rebozo that covered her face, and bent down to him.

"Are you leaving us in that way, Leon?" she murmured, in a voice faint as a sigh.

The young man started at the sound of the beloved voice.

"No!" he answered; "on the contrary, I am going to watch over your safety." And dashing off, he at once disappeared among the trees.

"Heaven grant," the maiden said as she crossed herself, "that my fears are chimerical, and that the danger which I apprehend may only exist in my imagination."

And wrapping herself once more in her rebozo, the maiden rode pensively on by the side of her mother and sister, who seemed not to have paid any attention to the few words she had exchanged with the captain.

CHAPTER XVI
THE PARUMO DE SAN JUAN BAUTISTA

The Cordilleras of the Andes are strange mountains, with which no others in the world could be compared, and they form, so to speak, the backbone of the New World, the entire length of which they traverse. It is in Chili, whose natural frontier they form, that they assume the sternest and most gloomy proportions; raising to the clouds their snow-covered heads, it seems as if it were under the pressure of an omnipotent will, as Ervilla, the poet of Araucania, says, that they allow at certain periods daring travellers to enter their dark gorges and cross their denuded peaks.

The Cordilleras cannot at any season be everywhere crossed, and it is only during four months at the most that at certain spots caravans are enabled to make their way through the snow, escalade the crests of these inhospitable mountains, and descend the opposite sides.

These spots, called passages, are very few in number: they are only three in Chili, and they are quebradas, or gaps, the dried beds of torrents, or streams, through which men, horses, and mules pass with great difficulty, at the expense of extraordinary cost and privations.

The most frequented of these passages is the Parumo of San Juan Bautista, a narrow gorge between two lofty mountains, which can only be reached by a track a yard in width, bordered on the right by a forest, which rises in an amphitheatrical shape, and on the left by a precipice of immense depth, at the bottom of which an invisible stream may be heard murmuring.

This was the road which the caravan was following.

About four in the evening, at the moment when night was beginning to brood over these elevated regions, the travellers came out on a plateau of about forty yards in circumference; before them, nearly at their feet, and half bathed in the early mist of night, were vaguely designed the plains to which they would descend on the morrow, while around them were dark, inextricable forests, which seemed to enfold them.

Wilhelm, in obedience to the orders which he had received from his captain, commanded a halt, and all preparations to be made for the night encampment, as going any further would have been committing great imprudence, especially during the darkness. No one raised any objection, but all dismounted, and began actively unloading the mules and pitching the tent set apart for the Soto-Mayor family.

While some were piling up the bales, and others unsaddling the horses and draught animals, several adventurers, selected by the leader, entered the forest, in order to seek for dry wood necessary to keep up the watch fires.

The duties were thus allotted, in order that they might be completed as speedily as possible, when suddenly a terrible yell was heard, and a band of Indians burst forth from the forest, and rushed at the travellers with brandished weapons.

There was a moment of disorder which it is impossible to describe. The travellers, so suddenly surprised, and for the most part unarmed, offered but a feeble resistance to their assailants; but, speedily obeying the voice of Wilhelm, and excited by the shouts of General Soto-Mayor, and of Don Pedro Sallazar, they collected round the tent in which the three ladies had sought shelter, and arming themselves with any weapon they came across, they bravely resisted the Indians; not hoping, it is true, to emerge as victors from the contest they were sustaining, but resolved to sell their lives dearly, and only yield to death.

The combat then assumed gigantic proportions; the white men knew that they had no quarter to expect from their ferocious enemies, while the latter, whose great number heightened their boldness, and who counted on an easy victory, exasperated by the resistance offered them, redoubled their efforts to finish with the white men, whom they execrated.

The fight became with each instant more terrible; Chilians and Indians were engaged in a hand-to-hand fight, rending each other like wild beasts, and howling like tigers when a combatant fell on either side.

The issue of this frightful butchery was impossible to foresee, when suddenly several shots were fired, and a band of horsemen rushed desperately into the thickest of the fight. They were Leon, and his adventurers, who, after a futile search, when returning to join their friends, heard the sound of the battle, and hurried up to take their part in the danger, and claim the right of dying with their comrades.

It was time that this succour arrived, for the Chilians who, crushed by numbers, did not feel their courage give way, but the moment approaching when they would fall not to rise again in front of the tent which they had undertaken to defend with the last drop of their blood. Hence the unforeseen and almost providential arrival of the captain changed the aspect of the fight.

The Indians, astonished at this unforeseen attack, and not knowing what enemy they had to combat, hesitated for an instant, which Leon took advantage of to redouble his blows. A ray of hope animated the Spaniards, who regained their courage, and their resistance threatened to become fatal to the Indians; but this triumph, alas! was of short duration.

All at once a Redskin of colossal height rushed to meet the smuggler captain, with the evident intention of fighting him. When the two adversaries faced, they looked at each other with attention, each in his heart doing justice to the elegant form and muscular appearance of his opponent.

As frequently happens under such circumstances, Indians and Spaniards suspended the blows they were dealing one another, in order to be spectators of the combat in which Leon was about to engage with the Indian, who appeared to be one of the chiefs of the band. On the issue of this struggle the fate of the combatants on either side might depend. By a common agreement, the Redskin threw his axe on the ground and Leon his gun. Then after drawing their machetes, the two men looked at each other attentively, and suddenly making a bound forward, seized each other round the body, but neither could make use of his knife, as each had seized his enemy's right arm with his left hand. Activity and skill could alone triumph.

For some minutes they could be seen intertwined like serpents, with frowning brows, haggard eyes, and set teeth; they writhed in a hundred ways, and tried, to throw each other, but in vain. The panting breath of both combatants could be heard escaping from their heaving chests like a whistle. The perspiration poured down their faces, and a whitish foam gathered at the corners of their mouths.

At length the Indian chief uttered a savage yell, and, collecting all his strength in a supreme effort, threw Leon, who dragged him down with him. Both rolled on the hardened snow. A long cry of joy burst from the Indians, and a cry of despair from the Spaniards; and, as if they had only expected this denouement to renew the combat, they rushed upon each other with fresh strength.

In the midst of this dark forest, which was plunged into a sort of demi-obscurity, these scenes had something awful and sinister. The groans of the ladies, and the cries of agony from the men, who fell before the bullets and the blade, echoed mournfully far and wide; add to these lugubrious sounds the plaintive howling raised by the animals at the sight of the fire which was devouring the rest of the baggage, and the reader will have an idea of the sad picture which we are drawing.

In the meanwhile the Indian who had thrown Leon had set his knee on his chest with ferocious delight, and was brandishing his knife; but all was not yet over for Leon; by a movement rapid as thought he hurled away his foe, who fell, letting his knife slip from his grasp. It was now the Indian's turn to tremble. Leon seized him by the throat, and throttled him by the pressure of his left hand, while in his right he raised his machete to kill him.

"Die, scoundrel!" he shouted.

He had not finished the sentence when a blow from the butt end of a gun fell on his head, and the smuggler captain fell senseless, while his enemy was dragged away by the man who had thus saved him from a certain death.

When Leon recovered his senses, the Indians had disappeared; of his twenty-five companions, ten still lived, while the others, scalped and horribly mutilated, were stretched out on the ground. Don Pedro Sallazar was stanching, as well as he could, a wound which he had received in the chest; while General Soto-Mayor was on his knees, and holding in his arms the body of his wife, who had been killed by a bullet through the temples.

The old man looked at the wound with a lacklustre eye, and seemed to be no longer conscious of what was going on around him; still the heavy tears that coursed down his pallid cheeks fell one by one on the face of the dead woman.

"And the young ladies?" Leon anxiously asked, as he rose with great difficulty; "I do not see them."

"They have been carried off by the Indians," Don Pedro replied, in a hollow, sullen voice.

"Oh!" said Leon, mad with despair, "I am accursed!"

And, overcome by grief, he fell as if stunned to the ground. At this moment a horseman entered the clearing; it was Major Don Juan, the son of General Soto-Mayor.

CHAPTER XVII
THE ABDUCTION

After the infernal dance performed by the Indians round the tree of war, Tcharanguii, one of them, exhausted by fatigue, fell at the foot of the tree, in order to rest, and whether voluntarily or through excessive weariness, fell asleep. When he awoke, he found himself alone; his comrades had abandoned the camp.

Without loss of time, he set off to join a party of his friends, whom he knew had gone in the direction of the Cordilleras. He came up with the caravan, as we described in a previous chapter, at the moment when it was continuing its journey towards Valdivia, and the sudden impression produced on him by the sight of the two young ladies aroused in him an eager desire to seize them.

In all probability, the Indian had instantly followed the trail of the travellers, and so soon as they had established their bivouac in the wood, Tcharanguii had hastened off to warn his companions, exhorting them not to lose the magnificent opportunity that presented itself of massacring some thirty Spaniards—that is to say, deadly enemies.

As for the maidens, he had been very careful not to allude to them, through fear of arousing in the others the feelings which he experienced. Besides, it was far more simple that the rape should become the result of the fight, than the fight the result of the rape.

The Indians greeted Tcharanguii's project with great demonstrations of joy, and swore by common agreement the destruction of the caravan. We have seen what the consequences of the attack on the travellers' camp were for the Indians, who did not give up the struggle till they had made numerous victims, and their chief Tcharanguii had seized Doña Inez and Doña Maria de Soto-Mayor; that is to say, the Redskin had succeeded in obtaining what he desired.

A thrill of extraordinary pleasure coursed through the Indian's veins so soon as he had rendered it impossible for the two maidens to escape, by himself escorting the horses on which he had compelled them to mount. His eyes, sparkling with pleasure, turned from Maria to Inez, and could not dwell with greater complacency on one than on the other. He considered them both so lovely, that he was never weary of contemplating them with the frenzied admiration that Indians feel at the sight of Spanish women, whom they infinitely prefer to those of their tribe.

Now, in drawing our readers' attention to this peculiarity, we must add that, for their part, the Spaniards eagerly seek the good graces of the Indian squaws, in whom they find irresistible attractions. Is this one of the effects of a wise combination of Providence, desiring to accomplish the fusion of the two races in a complete fashion? No one knows; but what cannot be denied is, that there are few Spaniards in South America who have not Indian blood in their veins.

On this subject we may perhaps be allowed to leave for a moment the framework of this romance, in order to establish the enormous difference which exists at the present time between the situation of the aborigines of South America to the Spaniards, their conquerors, and that of the North American Indians toward the Yankees, their masters. It is a difference that is destined to weigh heavily in the balance of the destinies of the New World.

The Spaniards who rushed upon South America sword and fire in hand, who conquered those ill-fated countries amid the glare of arson and the despairing shrieks of the unhappy inhabitants, whom they killed with horrible sufferings, ended, however, though without suspecting it, in gradually becoming blended with them, by contracting marriages with Indian girls, while the natives chose squaws among the Spanish women.

Then, still following the incline down which they were gliding, they eventually recognised the intelligence and political influence of the various tribes they have conquered, but which they respect by dealing and trafficking with them.

Let us now see what has been the conduct of the English in North America. Disembarking on this portion of the New World, under the guidance of William Penn, they purchased the territories which they possess, and continually treated the Indians on equal terms, while having always words of peace on their lips. They succeeded in this way, and under the deceitful appearances of an entire good faith and perfect loyalty, in gradually becoming aggrandized, though they were not willing to regard the men whom they plundered as their equals, or lower the pride of their race so far as to mingle their blood with that of the Indians.

Even more. The English, impelled by that philanthropic spirit that distinguishes them, and to which we have already had occasion to refer, were too humane to shoot down the men whose wealth they coveted, and found it far more simple to inoculate them with all the vices of old Europe; above all, that of drunkenness, which brutalizes and decimates them.

What are the results of the opposite systems adopted by the two nations? North America is losing its aborigines with frightful rapidity, while South America, on the contrary, is covered with innumerable Indian tribes.

After the organic law of the world, which wishes that the old and exhausted blood of the ancient races should be renewed and regenerated by a young and vigorous blood, it is easy to foresee that, in spite of the present state of the great Republic of the United States, which strives to invade everything, and behaves with that shorthanded system peculiar to the English character, it is only a colossus with feet of clay, which has not and cannot find in itself the necessary vital strength to accomplish the task laid down for itself by this youthful Republic, formed of heterogeneous elements which come into collision and thwart each other at every step. Its blood, vitiated by a long servitude in Europe, would require to be completely rejuvenated.

This bastard nation, without father or country, whose ancestors do not exist, and which has a pretension to be regenerating, will suddenly and eternally collapse, when, in its fury for possession, it has devoured all the so-called Spanish republics on the seaboard, and dashes against the wide chests of those men of bronze who are called the Moluchos.

In order to regenerate peoples, a nation must itself possess the regenerating virtues; but it has been said for a long time, with great truth, that the republicans of North America possessed all the vices of the old world without one of its virtues. Besides, the puerile debates, insensate utopias, and absurd follies of these honourable citizens gave us, many years ago, the measure of their strength. The future will decide the question and say whether we are deceived in the severe but impartial judgment which we pass on them. But to return to Tcharanguii, from whom this long digression has carried us away.

The young Indian chief, on getting possession of his two captives, had at the outset the idea of conveying them among his tribe, and afterwards decide which of the two he would select as his squaw; but on reflecting upon the distance which separated the Cordillera from the territory of the Jaos, and not wishing to confide such a precious booty to the warriors who had fought with him, he resolved to get ahead of his comrades, who were proceeding to the north, and conduct General Soto-Mayor's two daughters to Schymi-Tou, the Sayotkatta of Garakouaïti, who in his quality of High Priest of the Sun, would be enabled to conceal them from all eyes up to the day when Tcharanguii came to ask for an account of the deposit he had made with him.

It was, therefore, towards Garakouaïti that the ravisher was proceeding. The two unhappy girls, violently separated from their parents and friends, whom they never hoped to see again, had fallen into a state of prostration which almost deprived them of a consciousness of the frightful position in which the fatal issue of the fight had placed them. Surrendered without defence to the will of a savage, who might at any moment display the utmost violence toward them, they had no human succour to await. They were, therefore, compelled to leave their fate to God, and resign themselves in a Christian spirit to the harsh trials which He inflicted on them.

Employing our privilege of narrator, we will precede the Indian chief, and sketch the character of the country he had to pass through before reaching the city which was his destination. We will at the same time give a description which will enable the reader to form an idea of the manners and customs of the inhabitants, while Tcharanguii is hurrying to arrive, and displaying a certain respect to his prisoners, and lavishing on them attentions which might seem surprising on the part of a man like the formidable chief of the Jaos. What were the reasons that induced Tcharanguii to act in this way?—we may probably know hereafter.

The Cordillera of the Andes, that immense backbone of the American continent, which it traverses through its whole length from north to south, has several peaks forming immense llanos on which tribes reside at an elevation where in Europe all vegetation ceases.

After passing through the Parumo of San Juan Bautista and entering the templada region, which extends for about sixty leagues, the traveller finds himself in face of a virgin forest which is no less than eighty leagues in depth, and some twenty odd in width.

The most practised pen is powerless to describe the unnumbered marvels to be found in that inextricable vegetation called a virgin forest, which is at once strange and fascinating, majestic, and imposing. The most fanciful imagination recoils before this prodigious fecundity of an elementary nature, which is necessarily born again from its own destruction with every new strength and vigour.

Lianas running from tree to tree and from branch to branch, plunge here and there into the soil to rise again further on skywards, and form by crossing and interlacing an almost impassable barrier, as if jealous Nature wished to conceal from profane eyes the secret mysteries of these forests, in whose shadows the footsteps of men have only echoed at rare intervals and never with impunity. Trees of all ages and species grow without order or symmetry, as if they had been sown haphazard like grains of wheat in a furrow. Some, slight and tall, count but a few years, and the ends of their branches are covered by the wide and grand foliage of others whose haughty crowns have seen centuries pass.

Beneath the foliage sweetly murmur pure and limpid streams, which escape from fissures in the rocks, and after a thousand windings are lost in some lake or unknown river, whose free waters have as yet only reflected on their calm mirror the arcana of the solitude. Here are found, pell-mell and in a picturesque disorder, all the magnificent products of tropical regions— the mahogany, the ebony, the satinwood, the oak, the maple, the mimosa, with its silvery frondage, and the tamarind, thrusting out in all directions its branches covered with flowers, fruit, and leaves, which form a dome impenetrable by the sunbeams.

From the vast and unexplored depths of these forests issue at times inexplicable sounds—ferocious howls, mocking cries, mingled with shrill whistles, joyous strains full of harmony, or expressions of fury, rage and terror from the formidable guests that people them.

After resolutely entering this chaos, and struggling hand to hand with this untended and savage nature, the traveller succeeds, axe in hand, in cutting step by step a path impossible of description. At one moment he crawls like a reptile on the detritus of leaves, dead wood, and birds' deposits, piled up for centuries; at another, he leaps from branch to branch at the top of the trees, and travels, so to speak, in the air.

But woe to the man who neglects to have his eye constantly open to all that surrounds him, and his ear strained, for he has to fear, in addition to the obstacles of the vegetation, the venomous bites of snakes disturbed in their retreat, and the no less dangerous teeth of ferocious animals. He must also carefully watch the course of the rivers and streams which he comes across, and settle the position of the sun by day, and guide himself at night by the Southern Cross; for once lost in a virgin forest it is impossible to get out of it; it is a labyrinth of which Ariadne's thread would be powerless to find the issue.

At last when the traveller has succeeded in surmounting the dangers we have described and a thousand others no less terrible which we have passed over in silence, he finds himself in front of an Indian city. That is to say, he is before one of those mysterious cities into which no European has ever penetrated, whose exact position is ever unknown, and which since the conquest have served as the refuge of the Araucanian civilization.

The fabulous tales told by some travellers about the incalculable riches contained in these cities have inflamed the greed and avarice of a great number of adventurers, who, at various periods, have attempted to find the lost road to these queens of the llanos and Pampas of the Cordillera. Others merely impelled by the irresistible attractions which extraordinary enterprises offer to, vagabond imaginations, have also started, during the last fifty years, in search of the Indian cities, but, up to the present day, success has not crowned a single one of these expeditions.

Some of the travellers have returned disenchanted and half killed by this journey toward the unknown; a certain number left their bodies at the base of precipices or in the quebradas to serve as food for birds of prey; and, lastly, others, more unhappy still, have disappeared without leaving a trace, and no one has ever known what became of them.

We, in consequence of circumstances too lengthy to repeat here, but which we may possibly narrate some day, have involuntarily inhabited one of these impenetrable cities, and, more fortunate than our predecessors, we succeeded in escaping through a thousand perils, all miraculously avoided. The description we are about to give is therefore scrupulously exact, and will not admit of doubt, since we speak from personal knowledge.

Garakouaïti, the city which appears before us, when we have at last crossed the virgin forest, extends from north to south in the form of a rectangle. A wide stream, over which are thrown several stone bridges of incredible lightness and elegance, passes through its entire length. At each corner of the square an enormous block of rock, cut perpendicularly on the side facing the country, serves as an almost impregnable fortification. These four citadels are also connected together by a wall, twenty feet thick at the top, and forty high, which inside the town forms an incline whose base is sixty feet in width. This wall is built of the bricks of the country, which are about a yard long, and called adobes, and surrounds the town. A wide deep ditch doubles the height of the walls.

Two gates alone offer entrance to the city: they are flanked by turrets, exactly like a mediæval castle; and what supports our comparison is, that an extremely narrow and light bridge of planks, which can be removed upon the slightest alarm, is the sole communication between the gate and the exterior.

The houses are low, and have terraced roofs connected with each other: they are light, and built of reeds and canaverales covered with cement, owing to the earthquakes so frequent in these countries; but they are large, airy, and have numerous windows. They are all one storey high, and their front is covered with a varnish of dazzling whiteness.

The narrow streets, which intersect each other at right angles, converge upon an immense square, situated in the centre of the city, and bearing the name of Ikarepantou (the square of the sun). It is probable that it was in honour of the sun that the Indians designed this square, whence all the streets of the city radiate, for it is impossible to imagine a more correct representation of the planet which they venerate, than this symmetrical arrangement.

Four magnificent palaces stand in the direction of the four cardinal points, and on the western side is the great temple of Chemiin-Sona, surrounded by an infinite number of carved gold and silver columns. The appearance, of this building is most beautiful: it is reached by a flight of twenty steps, each made of a single marble slab ten yards long; the walls are excessively lofty, and the roof, like that of the other buildings, is terraced, for the Indians, who are well versed in the art of constructing subterranean vaults, are ignorant of the formation of domes.

The interior of the temple is relatively most simple. Long pieces of tapestry, worked with feathers of a thousand hues, and representing the entire history of the Indian religion, cover the walls. In the centre stands an isolated altar surmounted by a sun glistening with gold and precious stones, and supported by the sacred tortoise. By an ingenious artifice, the first beams of the rising sun fall on this splendid idol, and make it flash with the most brilliant colours, so that it appears to become animated, and really illumines all surrounding objects. In front of this altar stands the sacrificing table, which resembles the one we described when relating the ceremony which Leon Delbès witnessed in the Indian camp. We will state at once that human sacrifices are daily becoming rarer, and now only take place under entirely exceptional circumstances. The victims are selected from persons condemned to death, or prisoners of war.

At the end of the temple is a space closed by heavy curtains, to which the public are refused admission. These curtains conceal the entrance of a flight of steps leading to vast vaults that run underneath the temple, and to which the priests alone have the right to descend. The ground is covered with leaves and flowers, which are daily renewed.

On the south side of the square stands the Ulmen Faré, or Palace of the Chief. It is merely a succession of reception rooms, in which everybody has a right to appear, and of immense courtyards which serve for the martial exercises of the nation. A separate building, to which visitors are not admitted, is occupied by the chief's family, and the building serves as an arsenal and contains all the weapons of the nations, from Indian bows and arrows, sagaies, lances and shields, up to European sabres, swords, and muskets, which the Indians, after fearing them so greatly, have now learned to employ as well as ourselves, if not better.

On the same square is the famous Jouimion Faré, or Palace of the Vestals, where the Virgins of the Sun live and die. No man, the high priest excepted, is allowed to enter the interior of this building, which is reserved for the maidens devoted to the sun: a terrible death would immediately punish the daring man who attempted to transgress this law.

The life of the Indian virgins has many points of resemblance with that of the nuns who people European convents. They are immured, take an oath of perpetual chastity, and pledge themselves never to speak to a man, unless he be their father or brother, and in that case, are only allowed to converse with him through a paling in the presence of a third person, and must carefully hide their faces.

When they appear in public and are present at the religious festivals in the temple, they are veiled from head to foot. A vestal convicted of having allowed a man to see her face is condemned to death. In the interior of their abode, they occupy themselves with feminine tasks, and fervently perform the rites of their religion. The vows are voluntary: a maiden cannot be admitted among the Virgins of the Sun until the high priest has acquired the certainty that no one has forced her to take this determination, and that she is really following her vocation.

Lastly, the fourth palace, situate on the east side of the square, is the most splendid and at the same time most gloomy of all. It is the Houdaskon Faré, or Palace of the Genii, and serves as the residence of the Sayotkatta and piaies. It is impossible to express the mysterious, sad, and cold air of this residence, whose windows are covered with a trelliswork of osiers, so closely interwoven that it almost entirely obstructs the light of day.

A gloomy silence perpetually prevails in this enclosure, but at times, in the middle of the night, sleeping Indians are aroused in terror by strange clamours, which seem to issue from the interior of the Houdaskon Faré. What is the life of the men who inhabit it?—in what do they pass their time? No one knows. Woe to the imprudent man who, desirous of information on this point, might try to detect secrets of which he ought to be ignorant.

If the vow of chastity is imposed on the vestals it does not exist for the piaies; still few of these marry, and all abstain from any ostensible connexion with the other sex. The novitiate of the priests lasts ten years, and it is only at the expiration of that period, and after undergoing numberless trials, that the novices assume the title of piaies. Till then they can recall their determination, and embrace another profession; but such cases are extremely rare. It is true that, if they took advantage of the permission, they would be infallibly assassinated by the priests, through a fear of a part of their secrets being revealed to laymen. However, they are greatly respected by the Indians, by whom they continue to make themselves loved; and we may say that next to the Ulmen, the Sayotkatta is the most powerful man in the tribe.

Among peoples where religion is so formidable a lever, it is remarkable that the spiritual and temporal powers never clash; each knows how far his attributes extend, and follows the line traced for him without trying to encroach on the rights of the other. Thanks to this intelligent diplomacy, priests and chiefs work amicably together, and double each other's strength.

Now that we have made our readers acquainted with Garakouaïti, let us end this chapter by saying that Tcharanguii, according to his desires, found in the Sayotkatta Schymi-Tou a complacent ally, who promised him on his head to watch with scrupulous attention over the prisoners whom he undertook to hold in trust.

It is as well to add that Tcharanguii told the Sayotkatta that they were the daughters of one of the most powerful gentlemen in Chili, and that, in order to force him to make common cause with the chief of the Jaos, he had decided on taking one of them for his wife. And lastly, he added, that a magnificent present would amply reward him for the watch which he begged him to keep.

CHAPTER XVIII
AFTER THE COMBAT

We left the unhappy relics of the caravan suffering from the impression which the fatal result of their struggle with the Indians produced on them. At the moment when young Don Juan made his appearance in the camp a triple exclamation of joy, interest, and surprise greeted him.

"My son! my Juan!" the general exclaimed, sobs choking his voice.

"My dear colonel," said Don Pedro, "Heaven be praised that you are safe!"

"Ah!" muttered Leon, whom the arrival of the young man aroused from the despondency into which the disappearance of the maidens had plunged him.

The colonel rushed weeping into his father's arms, who showed him the body of his murdered wife.

"You arrive too late, my son! This is the work of the Indians."

"My mother!" the young man said, as he fell on his knees before the corpse.

"Yes, your mother! who died beneath their blows, while your sisters have been torn from me for ever."

"What do you say, father?"

"The truth," Don Pedro remarked. "Your sisters have been carried off, in spite of all the efforts we made to oppose it."

"Oh, father! father!" was all that Don Juan could answer, as he gave the old gentleman a look of painful regret.

The old general's features were frightfully contracted by the crushing grief that oppressed his heart as a husband and father, and yet, overcoming it by the strength of his will, he seized his son's hand:

"Don Juan, thirty years of happiness have passed since the day when the wife whom I lament for the first time laid her hand in mine, and now Heaven has taken her from me again! Two children, whom I love as I love you, Juan, were, with you, the fruits of that union, and Heaven has allowed them to be torn from my side! Still, I bow before His omnipotent will, because I am a Christian, and in the midst of my profound affliction, you are left to me, my son, to punish the cowards who attack women when they have men to face them. Don Juan, will you avenge your mother and sisters?"

The spectacle offered by this scene was very painful. Old Don Juan, bareheaded, was striving to appear calm, but the heavy tears that fell on his grey moustache were a flagrant contradiction of the resignation which he affected. Behind the old man's studied countenance could be discerned an immense grief, which was betrayed by the very violence of the stoicism which he displayed. Choked by sobs, the colonel remained dumb to his father's exhortations.

"Have you understood what I demand of you?" Don Juan again said to his son.

"Yes, father," the latter at length replied. "Oh!" he added, "why was I not here to defend them? but the scoundrels kept me back."

"Who did?" Don Pedro asked; "have you not come from Santiago?"

"No, general; and it was within an ace that I never saw the light of day again."

"What has happened, then?"

"In the environs of Talca, while I was travelling post haste in the hope of joining you on the road, I was made prisoner by an Indian party, whose presence I was far from suspecting. My lancero was put to death after one of their barbarous ceremonies, and I was preparing to undergo the same fate, when this night I was suddenly set at liberty by the order of an Indian chief of the name of Tahi-Mari, whom I did not see."

"Tahi-Mari!" the old general immediately interrupted him. "What! there is still a man bearing that name, and you owe your liberty to him? Oh! he must, in that case, be meditating some treachery, for a Tahi-Mari would have killed you, in order to enjoy the sight of your agony."

"My father, calm yourself," Don Juan remarked.

"General," Leon said at length, who had paid great attention to the young man's words, "whatever may be the motive which caused the man who liberated the colonel to act so, we must take advantage of the help which he is able to give us, in order to escape from the wood."

"My daughters! my daughters!" the old gentleman exclaimed, "must I then give up all hope of seeing them again?"

"Oh!" said Don Pedro, "we must follow up the track of these accursed Indians, or—no, we will hasten to Valdivia, and once arrived there, I will organize an expedition."

"That is not the way to find them again," Leon remarked, anxiously.

"What do you mean?" Don Pedro asked.

"Nothing—except that you will lose your time in sending an army against the Indians: the two Señoras are at this moment secure among some tribe that will sedulously keep them at a distance from the spot where your troops are fighting."

"In that case they are lost!" General Soto-Mayor exclaimed, wildly.

"Perhaps not," Leon answered, struck by a sudden inspiration.

"Oh, sir!" the old gentleman continued, "if you suspect the spot where they are, speak—fix yourself the sum I am to pay you for such a service, and I will pay it. Stay, sir; yesterday I was rich, powerful, and honoured; today I am only a poor old man, whose heart is broken; but I swear to you on my honour as a gentleman, that if you restore me my daughters, I will love you as a son, and will bless you with tears of joy and gratitude."

On seeing the old general so crushed by despair, Leon felt himself moved by a pity and compassion which he did not attempt to check.

"I only ask your esteem, general, if I succeed."

"Speak, then, sir," Don Juan de Soto-Mayor and Don Pedro said together; "do you really think that you can place us on the track of the ravishers?"

A ray of hope had illumined the old man's heart on hearing Leon speak in such a way as to suggest a possibility of finding the maidens again, and he awaited with feverish anxiety the captain's answer, who kept silence, and seemed plunged in deep reflection. Still, as Leon seemed to be reflecting on the weight of the words which he was going to utter, and whose meaning might cause those who listened to him either an immense consolation or a bitter deception, neither of the two gentlemen dared to interrupt him.

The fact was that Leon was asking himself whether he could undertake the liberation of the maidens. He had but one resource, that of going to find Tahi-Mari, and threatening to kill himself in his presence, unless he restored to the father the daughters whom he was bewailing.

Assuredly, after the conversation which had caused the separation between the captain and Diego, it was at least a bold step to think of imploring the Inca's clemency again; but since the latter had voluntarily broken the bonds which held young Don Juan captive, it was but reasonable to assume that Diego was animated by a different purpose. Perhaps he had renounced, if not his vengeance, still that which he had selected in vowing the death of all the Soto-Mayors. And then, again, if he thirsted for victims, had not the general's beloved wife been killed by Indians under his orders?

Leon, while revolving all these arguments, did not doubt but that the maidens were in the power of Tahi-Mari, and either that he considered them sufficient to feel certain of entire success, or more probably that the desire he had of saving Maria made him mentally smooth down all difficulties, and he resolved to attempt the adventure with a firm determination to die if he failed.

"I cannot put you on the track of the Indians who have carried off the Señoras," he at length answered the generals; "but I pledge myself to restore them to you."

"How?" Don Pedro Sallazar asked.

Don Juan contented himself with raising his hand to Heaven, and calling down blessings on the young man.

"By starting alone in search of them," Leon said, "while the few men left me continue to escort you to Valdivia."

"Alone! But why cannot we accompany you?" Don Pedro resumed, in whom the feeling of distrust which he had already displayed to the captain was again aroused.

"That is true," Don Juan said, in his turn. "Guide us to these villains, since you know where to find them, and although I am old, I will follow you with all the ardour of youth, for I feel within me the strength to overcome all dangers for the sake of tearing my poor children from the hands of these cowardly ravishers."

"Do you think, sir," said the young colonel, who had just kissed his mother's icy forehead, "that we would leave to others the duty of avenging us?"

"In that case, sir, it is impossible; your duty calls you, Don Pedro, to Valdivia, and you would not have time to carry out the expedition which I hope to bring to a successful result. You," the young man continued, addressing General Soto-Mayor, "although your heart may bleed at it, must give up all thought of accompanying me, for ere we had reached the spot where I believe the Señoras to be, fatigue would exhaust your strength, and you would find it impossible to follow me."

"But, sir—" the colonel remarked.

"Pray do not insist, sir," said Leon; "for once again I repeat that, if you wish me to succeed, you must let me act as I think proper."

"What do you propose doing, Leon, that you are afraid of letting us be witnesses of it?" Don Pedro observed haughtily.

"The same as I did when the Indians attacked us," the captain answered, who felt anger flush his face on remarking the insolent expression which the speaker's countenance had assumed — "risk my life in the service of those to whom I have promised assistance and succour."

"Sir!"

"Yes," Leon continued; "for the rude task I am about to undertake demands utter self-denial; manhunting on the llanos and Pampas requires more than courage, for cunning and craft are needed, and if I refuse your help in this expedition, it is because your presence would impede my progress. Alone, I am certain of joining Tahi-Mari, but with you we should all be lost."

A feverish excitement had seized on the young man, who seemed most anxious to efface the suspicions of which he was the object.

"I have lived among the Indians who attacked us, and know their strange manners and customs. At this very moment, the forests are full of invisible eyes that watch and spy us; if we advance in a body toward the spot where they are, we may be certain of being all massacred. Believe me, in order to enter their encampment, I must glide like a snake through the lianas that grow in the forest. Such is the reason, gentlemen, why I refuse to let you accompany me, for you are ignorant of their infernal skill. And now I am at your disposal: if you absolutely insist on following me, I am at your orders; but, in that case, I answer for nothing, for we shall have every unfavourable chance against us."

These few words, uttered with an accent of conviction and frankness which could not be suspected, produced on the mind of the three men a favourable impression; no further objection was raised, and Leon was left at liberty to act as he pleased. Once the four gentlemen were agreed on this point, they had to turn their attention to the burial of the dead, and collecting the mules and horses, which the cries of the Indians and the gleam of the flames had terrified and driven from the camp.

All set to work: while Don Pedro gave orders to his lanceros to restore a little order among the bales and other articles, Leon gave a signal to two of his men, who began digging a grave at the foot of a pine tree with their machetes. It was intended to receive the mortal remains of the Señora Soto-Mayor. Another, somewhat larger, was dug a few paces off in which to bury pell-mell the bodies of the Spaniards and Indians killed during the fight. After this melancholy task was completed, Leon went up to the Señora's corpse, and prepared to wrap it in a poncho before laying it in the earth.

"No one must touch that body," old Don Juan exclaimed as he dashed upon it with incredible speed, "for it is mine."

And, thrusting Leon away, he called his son, and both, their faces inundated with tears, commenced the melancholy duty. The old man's chest heaved under the pressure of the sobs which he tried in vain to stifle. Long after the body had disappeared under the woollen poncho that covered it, the general was unable to depart from the spot where lay the remains of her who had been dearest to him in the world.

At length Leon made an effort, and breaking off the affecting scene, he with the help of Don Pedro, raised the corpse, which he placed in the grave in spite of the final convulsions of grief on the part of Don Juan, who clung to the body from which he was unable to separate. Then came the turn of the dead friends and foes who encumbered the ground.

A deep silence had presided over this mournful ceremony; two branches of trees formed into a cross were placed over either tomb, and all was ended. During this time Wilhelm the smuggler, whom we have already introduced to the reader, and who had started with one of his comrades in search of the mustangs and mules, returned to the camp, bringing back the intelligent animals, which had come up of their own accord on his signal.

All was soon ready for a start, but one thing still troubled Leon—the difficulty of transporting the wounded. One of the smugglers had his arm broken by a bullet, and was suffering atrocious pain; a lancero had a contusion on the head, and two peons were wounded in the legs. The fatigue of the journey might prove most injurious to them.

Don Pedro himself, in spite of the firmness he displayed, was suffering severely from the gunshot wound in his chest; and although, thanks to the medical knowledge of Leon, who, accustomed to see blood flow in the frequent fights which he and his men carried on against the custom-house officers, was enabled to dress a wound, each of the men injured by the Indians had received the first necessary attention, they could not venture to travel for any length of time without danger.

Still it was absolutely necessary to get out of the difficulty, and after selecting the horses whose pace was the easiest, a sort of litter made of thongs, skins, and ponchos was laid on their backs, and the wounded were hoisted on them, with exhortations to remain patient till they reached Valdivia, where they would find repose and attention.

Once these arrangements were made, Leon counted the hearty men left of his comrades, and ordered three to escort the two generals and Colonel Don Juan, along with Don Pedro's lanceros; then turning to the other five, he said to them—

"My friends, I shall require you to second me in what I am going to undertake; we are going to rescue from the Indians General Soto-Mayor's two daughters."

"What are we to do?" the smugglers asked; "we are ready."

"Wilhelm," said Leon, addressing one of them, "and you, Harrison, will come with me."

"Very good, captain."

"You others," he continued, pointing to the other men who were awaiting his instructions, "will return at once to Valparaíso; the road is a long one, but you must cover it with the greatest promptitude, and I reckon on your punctuality."

"You can."

"In eight days we shall be at Valparaíso."

"Very good. So soon as you arrive, you will collect the band, and if Crevel has at his disposal twenty resolute fellows, you will enrol them, and I will give you the money for the purpose; but be very careful only to take bold companions like yourselves, and wood rangers accustomed to a life on the Pampas. You understand me?"

"Yes, captain," said Hernandez, a tall fellow, with a hangdog face and of herculean stature, "you can feel perfectly assured."

"And where is the band to go?" his comrade Joaquin asked, as he twisted his black moustache.

"You will return here at full speed."

"Very good, captain," Hernandez again said; "but are you going to encamp here till we come?"

"No. Harrison alone will be here, and lead you to the spot which I shall inform him of."

"All right."

Hernandez, Joaquin, and Enrique took leave of the party, and soon found themselves on the road that led to Valparaíso, while the three men told off to serve as an escort to the generals only awaited an order from the latter to place themselves at their disposal.

All at once General Soto-Mayor addressed Leon, who was watching all that went on.

"We are going," the old gentleman said, as he took a parting glance at his wife's tomb; "and I bear with me the assurance which you have given me that you will start at once in search of my daughters."

"You can reckon on it, general; all that it is humanly possible to do I will do, and I hope to have succeeded within two months."

"May Heaven hear you! For my part, so soon as I arrive at Valdivia, I will obtain, with the help of General Don Pedro, all the information that may serve to discover the spot where they are; for I suspect that the Indians are concentrated in the vicinity of that town, the capture of which would be of such great utility to them."

"I told you, general, that I not only have the means to learn where they are, but also to bring them back."

"But, in that case, and if Heaven permit you to find them, how shall I be informed of it, and whither will you take them?"

"War is declared," Leon answered, "and possibly within a week the communications with Valdivia will be interrupted. It would, therefore, be the height of imprudence to try and join you in that town."

"That is true, great Heavens! But in that case what is to be done?"

"A very simple thing; so soon as I have succeeded in rescuing them from the Indians, I will take them both to the convent of the Purísima Concepción at Valparaíso."

"Yes, you are right; that is the best place for them."

"In two months, then, they will be there, or I shall be dead."

"Thanks," said the old gentleman, as he held out his hand to the young man, who pressed it in his.

A quarter of an hour later, the little party was proceeding toward Valdivia, and the only persons left in camp were Leon, Harrison, Wilhelm, and Giacomo.

CHAPTER XIX
THE MANHUNT

So soon as the party had quite disappeared in the forest, Leon turned to his men, who were carelessly seated round the fire and smoking their cigarettes.

"Comrades," he said, "our expedition is about to change its course. We have no longer to escort travellers, but must go manhunting."

"All the better," remarked Wilhelm, "I prefer that; it is a lazy trade to act as guide to Spaniards."

"It is a trade which is sometimes dangerous, and our brave comrades who sleep there," Leon said, pointing to one of the tombs, "are a proof of it."

"That is true," Giacomo remarked; "but no matter; it is better to die while smuggling a few bottles of aguardiente under the very noses of the officers."

"However that may be," the captain resumed, "they are dead, and they were brave fellows. As for you, listen carefully to this;—While I, Wilhelm, and Giacomo go into the mountains to seek Indian sign, Harrison will remain here, and await the arrival of the band under Joaquin's orders."

"The deuce!" Harrison exclaimed; "I would sooner go about the country with you."

"Yes, but I require that a courageous and resolute man should remain at the meeting place I have fixed, and I could not apply to a better one than yourself."

Leon was acquainted with the character of his comrades, and could always manage, by the clever employment of a bit of flattery, to make himself obeyed not only punctually but enthusiastically. Harrison, on hearing the homage rendered by the captain to his martial virtues, drew up his head proudly, and manifested by a certain movement of the muscles, how flattered he felt at the good opinion Leon had of him.

"And you have done well, captain," he replied, proudly.

"You must not stir from here. As we know not what road we shall have to follow, we will leave you our horses, which you will take care of. Build a hut; hunt; do all that you think proper, but remember that you must not leave the Parumo of San Juan Bautista without my orders."

"That is settled, captain; and you can start when you please. You may remain absent six months, and be certain of finding me here on your return."

Leon rose.

"Very good," he said; "I reckon on you."

Then he whistled to his mustang, which ran up at his call, and laid its intelligent head on its master's shoulder to be petted. It was a noble animal, of considerable height, with a small head, but its eyes sparkled with animation, while its broad chest and fine nervous legs denoted a blood horse.

Leon seized the lasso which hung from the horse's saddle, and knotted it round his body; then, lightly tapping the croup of the animal, he watched it retire. Wilhelm and Giacomo were provided with their weapons and provisions, such as charqui, queso, and dried beans.

"Come let us be off," said Leon, as he laid his long rifle on his shoulder.

"We are ready," the two men said.

"Good luck!" Harrison shouted to them, though unable to prevent a sigh accompanying these words, which proved how vexed he was at not being allowed to join them.

"Thanks!" his comrades replied.

On leaving the clearing they began marching in Indian file, that is to say, one after the other, the second placing his feet exactly in the footsteps of the first, and the third in those of the second. The last one took the additional precaution of effacing as well as he could the traces left by his predecessors. Harrison, after looking after them for some time, sat down again by the fireside.

"No matter," he said, talking to himself. "I shall not have much fun here, but what must be must."

And after this philosophic reflection he lit a cigarette, and began quietly smoking, while eagerly following the wreaths which the smoke produced, and inhaling its fragrance with the methodical phlegm of a true Indian Sagamore.

In America, when a man is travelling through the Indian regions in war time, and does not wish to be tracked by the Araucanos, he must go North if he has business in the South, and vice versa, and behave like a vessel which, when surprised by a contrary wind, is obliged to make constant tacks, which gradually bring it to the desired point.

Leon Delbès was too well acquainted with the intelligence and skill of the Indians not to act in the same way. Assuredly, his adoption by the Araucanos, which the captain had received in the council of the chief of the twelve Molucho tribes, rendered him sacred to the latter; but not knowing what Indian party he might fall in with, he judged it more prudent to avoid any encounter. Moreover, he had fought the men who had attacked the caravan, and it would have been ill grace to claim the benefit of his adoption after the active part which he had taken in the struggle. Hence he had a twofold reason to act on the defensive, and only advance with the most extreme prudence.

Fenimore Cooper, the immortal historian of the Indians of North America, has initiated us in his excellent works into the tricks employed by the Mohicans and Hurons, when they wish to foil the search of their enemies; but without offence to those persons who have so greatly admired the sagacity of young Uncas, that magnificent type of the Delaware nation, of which he was the last hero, the Indians of the North are mere children when compared with the Moluchos, who may be regarded as their masters in every respect.

The reason for this is very simple and easy to understand. The Northern tribes never really existed as a political power; each of them exercise a separate government; the Indians composing them rarely intermarry with their neighbours, and constantly lead a nomadic life. Hence they have never possessed more than the instincts, highly developed we allow, of men who incessantly inhabit the woods,—that is to say, a marvellous agility, a great fineness of hearing, and a miraculous length of sight, qualities, however, which are found to the same extent among the Arabs, and generally with all wandering nations, no matter what corner of the earth they dwell in. As for artfulness and craft, they learned these from the wild beasts, and merely imitated them.

The South American Indians join to these advantages the remains of an advanced civilization—a civilization which, since the conquest, has sought a refuge in inaccessible lurking places, but for all that does not the less exist. The tribes or families regard themselves as parts of the same whole—the nation.

Now the aborigines, continually on terms of hostility with the Spaniards, have felt the necessity of doubling their strength in order to triumph, and their descendants have gradually modified whatever might be injurious in their manners, to appropriate those of their oppressors, and fight them with their own weapons. They have carried these tactics—which, by the way, have saved them from the yoke up to the present day—so far that they are thorough masters in roguery and trickery; their ideas have been enlarged, their intellect is developed, and they have succeeded in surpassing their enemies in astuteness and diplomacy, if we may be allowed to employ that expression.

This is so true, that not only have the Spaniards been unable to subjugate them during the past three hundred years, but have been actually obliged to pay them, with more or less goodwill, an annual tribute. Can we really regard as savages these men who, formerly driven back by their terror of firearms and dogs—animals of whose existence they were ignorant—to the heart of the Cordilleras, have defended their territory inch by inch, and in some regions have reconquered a portion of their native soil?

We know better than anybody that savages exist in America—savages in the full meaning of the term; but these are daily disappearing from the surface of the globe, as they have neither the necessary intellect to understand nor the energy to defend themselves. These are the Indians who, before being subjected to the Spaniards, were so to the Mexicans or Moluchos, owing to their intellectual organization, which scarce raises them above the brute.

These tribes which are but exceptions in the species, must not be confounded, then, with the great Molucho nations of which we are speaking, and whose manners we are describing—manners which are necessarily being modified; for, in spite of the efforts they make to escape from it, the European civilization, which they despise more through hereditary hatred of their conquerors than for any other motive, crushes and invades them on all sides.

Within a hundred years of this time the emancipated Indians, who smile with pity at the paltry struggles carried on by the phantom republics that surround them, will take their place in the world again and carry their heads high. And this will be just, for they are heroic men with richly endowed characters, and capable of undertaking and successfully carrying out great things. We will quote in support of this statement one fact which will speak better than words:—The best history of South America which has been published in Spanish up to this day was written by an Inca. Is not this conclusive?

Let us return to Leon and his two comrades Wilhelm and Giacomo. They were three determined men. Our readers know Leon, so we will say no more of him; but we will sketch in a few outlines the appearance of

Wilhelm and his comrade Giacomo. These worthy gentlemen, who were bound together by a hearty friendship, formed the most singular contrast imaginable.

Giacomo, a native of Naples, whence he escaped one morning under the excuse that the house he lived in was too near Vesuvius, but in reality on account of the visits paid him repeatedly by the sbirri, whom he was not particularly anxious to see, was the real type of a lazzarone, careless, slothful, thievish, and yet capable of extraordinary bravery, and bursts of energy and devotion. Well built, with an intelligent and crafty face, and endowed with far from common muscular strength, he seemed to be born for the smuggler's trade.

Wilhelm, on the contrary, was one of those cold and systematic Germans who do nothing save by weights and measures. Only speaking when he was compelled, he seemed ever to be dreaming though he thought of nothing, and concealed, under an apparent simplicity and proverbial phlegm, an excellent disposition, and a certain amount of intelligence. He was tall, smoke-dried, thin, and angular, and his flat face, disfigured by the smallpox, was rendered still uglier by gimlet eyes deep set in their orbits.

His hair, of a flaxen hue, fell in flat curls on his enormous ears, and gave him one of those countenances which provoke hilarity. His magnificent teeth, however, and a mouth which had a remarkably clever expression, formed a happy diversion with the grotesqueness of his features. He had been a member of the Cuadrilla for two years, and had entered it, as he said, in consequence of a violent love disappointment.

On leaving the clearing, the three smugglers took the road to Talca, which they followed the whole day; at nightfall they encamped in the neighbourhood, and then next morning, after a hasty breakfast on a piece of queso saturated with pimento, they went down to the bottom of the quebrada, by clinging with hands and feet to the asperities of the ground. Here they found themselves in a species of canyon, and were obliged to march on the bed of a half-dried torrent, where their footsteps left no imprint.

After two days' journeying which offered no incident worthy of mention, our adventurers reached the beginning of the llanos of the templada region, situated on the other watershed of the Cordilleras, which they had just crossed.

The verdure came back, and the heat began to be felt again. Our men were perfectly revived by this gentle and balmy atmosphere, the azure sky and dazzling sun, which took the place of the grey sullen sky of the Cordilleras, and the narrow horizon covered by mist and fog. On the third day Leon perceived in the distance the green crest of a forest, toward which he had directed his march, and gave vent to a cry of satisfaction.

"Courage, my friends," he said to his comrades, "we shall soon have the shadow and freshness which we want for here."

"In truth, captain, I confess that I should infinitely prefer the slightest tree, provided that its branches afforded us means to rest for a moment in their shadow, to a forced march with this great rogue of a sun who burns our bones."

It was Giacomo who spoke; the poor lad seemed to be troubled by the heat, and could scarce succeed in mopping up the perspiration which poured down his face. It was midday, the time for the siesta, and the ex-lazzarone, who every day of his life never failed to sacrifice an hour to this pleasant habit, said to himself with reason, that it was more than ever advisable to enjoy it now, because, in addition to the hour which invited them, they were also strongly impelled by the ardent heat which they could not guard against, and their fatigue.

"And where the deuce do you mean to take your siesta?" Leon asked. "Don't you see, on the contrary, that we must push on in order to gain some shelter?"

"Alas!" said Giacomo. And patiently enduring his woes, the smuggler continued his march without uttering a word.

"Hallo!" Wilhelm suddenly exclaimed, as he stooped down, "what is this?"

And rising, he showed Leon a small gold cross hanging from a narrow velvet ribbon.

"Maria's cross!" Leon exclaimed; "yes, I recognise it! We are on the traces of the ravishers!"

"In that case," said Wilhelm, "we must move ahead."

Leon kissed the precious relic, and carefully hid it in his bosom.

"My lads, we must now learn where the Moluchos have sought refuge; we are on the right track, and the forest which we perceive ahead of us serves as a retreat for some tribe, I imagine."

Then examining with scrupulous attention the ground they trod on, they continued to advance, seeking, but in vain, signs corroborating that of the cross which they had found. At the end of two hours they at length reached a spot suitable for a halt. Four magnificent royal palms, whose branches were intertwined and formed a dome of foliage, appeared a smiling oasis on this denuded prairie, which was burnt up by the beams of a fiery sun.

Wilhelm and Giacomo fell asleep, but Leon remained awake, and while inhaling the smoke of his papelito, sought to determine the direction in which the Indians had proceeded. Suddenly a fresh idea germinated in his brain. He remembered that, on several occasions, when conversing with Diego, the latter had spoken of an Indian town which the Araucanos regarded as sacred, and which no European could enter. This town was called Garakouaïti, and was about sixty leagues from the Parumo of San Juan Bautista, hidden in a virgin forest.

It was there, Diego had also told him, that the Moluchos hid all their most precious articles, as they felt sure that no one would come to find them. A secret presentiment made Leon suppose that the Indians, after carrying off the two young ladies, must have conveyed them to Garakouaïti as an inaccessible spot.

It was to that city, then, that he must proceed. But he remembered that, as the entrance to the city was interdicted to Europeans, he could not hope to obtain admission, and he sought for an excuse for introducing himself by imagining some stratagem. As the advice of his companions might be useful to him, he woke them, and consulted as to the way he should contrive to enter Garakouaïti, supposing that he discovered that city.

The means were not so easy to find, and as the most pressing thing at present was to march toward the city, the three smugglers set out again, while reflecting on the plan of conduct which they should follow. All the rest of the day was passed in this way, and night surprised them on the banks of a rather wide stream, whose proximity the branches had hidden from them, though they had heard the murmurs of its waters for some time past.

As it was quite dark, Leon resolved to wait till the morrow, to look for a ford by which to cross it. They therefore halted, but through prudence lit no fire, and the three men were soon lying on the ground, wrapped in their ponchos. The moon was descending on the horizon, the stars were glistening in the heavens, and Leon, whose eyes were closed by fatigue, was on the point of falling asleep, when a strange and unexpected sound made him start. He listened. A slight tremor agitated the leaves bordering the stream, whose calm waters looked like a long silver ribbon. There was not a breath of wind in the air. Leon nudged his comrades, who opened their eyes.

"The Indians!" the captain whispered to them. "Silence."

Then, crawling on his hands and knees, he went down the bank and entered the water. He looked round him and saw nothing; all was calm, and he waited with fixed eye and expanded ear. Half an hour passed thus, and the sound which had attracted his attention was not repeated. It was in vain that he tried to pierce the obscurity; the night was so dark, that at ten yards off he could distinguish nothing; and though he listened attentively, no sound troubled the silence of the night.

Plunged as he was up to the waist in the water, an icy coldness gradually spread over his whole body. At length, feeling worn out and fancying himself mistaken, he was preparing to remount the bank, when, just at the moment when he was about to beat a retreat, a hard log slightly grazed his chest.

He looked down and instinctively thrust out his hand. It was the gunwale of a canoe, which was gliding noiselessly through the reeds, which it parted in its passage. This canoe, like nearly all Indian vessels, was simply the stem of a tree hollowed out by the help of fire. Leon regarded this mysterious canoe, which seemed to be advancing without the help of any human being, and rather drifting with the current, than being guided in a straight line. Still, what astonished him was, that it went straight on without any oscillation. Evidently some invisible being, an Indian probably, was directing it; but where was he stationed, and was he alone? These facts it was impossible to know.

The captain's anxiety was extreme; he dared not make the slightest movement through fear of being surprised, and yet the canoe was still there. Desirous, however, of knowing how matters really stood, Leon softly drew his knife from his boot, and, holding his breath, crouched down in the river, only leaving his face above water.

All at once he gave a start; he had seen flashing in the dark, like two live coals, the eyes of a savage, who, swimming behind the canoe, was pushing it forward with his arm. The Indian held his head above water, and was looking about him inquiringly.

Suddenly Leon, on whom the eyes had first been fixed, leaped forward with the activity of a panther, seized the Indian by the throat, and before he was able to defend himself or utter a cry of alarm, plunged his knife into his heart.

The Indian's face became black; his eyes were enormously dilated; he beat the water with his legs and arms, then his limbs stiffened and he sank, carried away by the current, and leaving behind him a slight reddish track. He was dead.

Leon, without the loss of a moment, got into the canoe, and holding by the reeds, looked in the direction where he had left his comrades. Both had followed him, bringing with them the rifle which Leon had laid on the ground, and which they were careful to keep above water, as well as their own.

Then the three men, making as little noise as possible, disengaged the canoe from the reeds which had barred its progress, and lay down in the bottom, after placing it in mid-stream, and making it feel the current. They went on thus for some time, believing themselves already safe from the invisible enemies who surrounded them, when all at once a terrible clamour broke out, and awoke the echoes.

CHAPTER XX
THE REDSKINS

The body of the Indian killed by Leon had followed for some minutes the course of the river, then had become entangled in the reeds, and eventually stopped exactly in the centre of the Indian camp, in whose proximity Leon and his comrades halted that night without suspecting it.

At the sight of their brother's corpse, the redskins had uttered the formidable yell which the smugglers heard, and rushed tumultuously to the bank, pointing to the canoe. Leon seized the paddles, which were in the boat, and, aided by Wilhelm, was soon out of reach.

The disconcerted Indians, who did not know with whom they had to deal, gesticulated and bespattered the fugitives with all the insults which the Indian language could supply them with, calling them dogs, asses, ducks, and other epithets borrowed from the nomenclature of the animals which they hate and despise. Leon troubled himself but little about their insults, and continued to paddle, which re-established the circulation of the blood, which the cold had interrupted.

A few bullets, meant for the fugitives, were sent after them, but they merely dashed up the water.

The night passed thus: the smugglers paddled eagerly, for they had noticed that the stream, owing to repeated windings, was sensibly approaching the forest which was their destination. Still, having nothing more to fear from their enemies, they drew in the paddles for a few minutes' rest, and each feeling in his alforjas, drew out some provisions, which he hurriedly devoured. As day had arrived, there was no harm in their letting the canoe drift for awhile, though they kept a sharp lookout.

Leon and Giacomo had lit their cigarettes, and Wilhelm his magnificent porcelain pipe, from which he never separated, when the latter, who was beginning to inhale with gentle satisfaction the enormous jets of smoke which he drew from the stem, let his pipe fall in the bottom of the canoe, while exclaiming with an expression of terror and surprise—

"Der Teufel!"

"What is it?" Leon at once said, who understood that Wilhelm had seen something extraordinary.

"Look!" the German replied, as he stretched out his arm in the direction whence they had come.

"Sacrebleu!" Leon shouted; "two canoes in pursuit of us! We must look out."

"Sangre de Cristo!" Giacomo said, with a start which nearly upset the canoe.

"What now?" Leon asked.

"Look!"

"A thousand fiends!" Leon exclaimed, "we are surrounded!"

Two canoes were really coming up rapidly behind the smugglers, while two others, which had started from the opposite banks, were arriving with the manifest intention of barring their passage and cutting off their retreat.

"These gentlemen," said Giacomo, "wish to make us dance a funny sambacueca; what do you say to it, captain?"

"We will pay for their music, my fine fellows. In the meanwhile, paddle firmly, and look out for the attack."

And seizing the paddles again, Wilhelm and Giacomo gave such an impulse to the canoe that it seemed to fly through the water. Leon, who was standing up, was calculating the chances of the encounter. He was not afraid of the boats that were following them, for they were still at too great a distance to hope to catch him, but all his anxiety was directed to those coming toward them, and between which they must infallibly pass. Each paddle stroke brought them nearer to the hostile canoes, which seemed overloaded with men, and to move with considerable difficulty.

Leon formed a bold resolution, the only one that could save him and his. Instead of trying to pass between the canoes, in which he ran a risk of being sunk, he kept to the left, and advanced in a straight line on the canoe nearest to him.

On seeing this manoeuvre, the Indians broke out in shouts of joy and triumph. The smugglers made no reply, but continued to advance. A smile played round Leon's lips. As he steered the canoe toward the Indians, he noticed that the left bank of the stream formed an inlet, behind an island, which, though very near the land, left a passage sufficiently wide for his boat, which thus would avoid a detour, and at the same time gain ground on their pursuers. The great thing was, to reach the point of the island before the Indians in the first canoe.

The latter, who suspected their enemy's intentions, had changed their tactics, and, instead of coming up to meet the Europeans, tacked and paddled actively for the island. Leon understood that he must delay their progress at all risks.

Not a shot had as yet been fired on either side; the redskins felt themselves so sure of seizing the smugglers that they had thought it unnecessary, to proceed to such extremities, while the smugglers, who felt the need of saving their powder in a hostile country, where it would be impossible for them to renew their stock, had imitated their prudence, however desirous they might feel to attack.

The Indian canoe was only fifty yards from the island, when Leon stooped down to his comrades and whispered a few words. The latter shipped their paddies, and seizing their rifles, knelt down, and rested the barrels on the gunwale of the canoe, after driving home a second bullet. Leon had done the same.

"Are you ready?" he asked a moment after.

"Yes," the two men replied.

"Fire, then, and aim low."

The three discharges were blended in one. We have said that the two canoes were excessively close.

"Now to your paddles—quick!" the captain said.

Four arms seized them, and the light canoe recommenced its rapid course. Leon alone reloaded his rifle and knelt down in readiness to fire. The effect of the firing was soon visible; the three bullets, striking at the same spot, had formed an enormous breach in the side of the canoe, just at the line of floatation.

Cries of terror were raised by the Indians, who leaped into the water one after the other, and swam in different directions. As for the canoe, left to itself, it drifted for a little while, gradually filled, and sank. Fancying themselves freed from their enemies, the smugglers relaxed their efforts; but all at once Wilhelm raised his paddle, while Leon seized his rifle by the barrel.

Two Indians, with athletic limbs and savage looks, were trying to catch hold of the canoe and upset it, but they soon fell back with cloven skulls and drifted down the stream. A few moments later the smugglers reached the passage. The Indians who had left the water pursued them by running along the bank, and threw stones at them, as they were unable to use their muskets, which had been wetted by the plunge into the water.

Leon again recommended his men to redouble their vigour, in order to escape as soon as possible from the enormous projectiles which fell around the canoe from every tuft of grass; for the Indians, according to their habit, were careful not to show themselves in the open through fear of bullets.

The captain saw, a few paces from him, a thicket of aquatic plants shaking, so he aimed at it and fired on the chance. A terrible yell burst from the tangled mass of canaverales and lianas, and an Indian rushed forth to seek shelter behind the tree that grew on the bank. Leon, who had reloaded his piece in all haste, pointed it in the direction of the fugitive, but raised it again directly. The man had just fallen, and was writhing in the last convulsions of death.

Several redskins rushed upon him, carried him away and disappeared. A suddenly calm and extraordinary tranquillity succeeded the extreme agitation and cries which had aroused the echoes a few minutes before.

"There!" said Leon as he laid the gun in the bottom of the boat, and seizing a pair of paddles to help Giacomo—"they have enough; now that they know the range of my rifle, they will leave us at peace."

In fact, the Indians gave no further sign of life; but this must not surprise the reader. The redskins are accustomed never to expose themselves unnecessarily. With them success alone can justify their actions, and when they do not consider themselves the stronger, they give up with the greatest facility any plans which they have formed, for the most inveterate pursuit.

At this moment the smugglers doubled the point of the island. The second canoe was already far behind them; as for those which they had first perceived, they were mere specks on the horizon. When the Indians in the second canoe perceived that the smugglers were escaping from them, and had got ahead of them, they gave a general discharge which wounded nobody, and turned back to join their companions on land.

Leon and his men were saved. After paddling for about an hour in order to put a great distance between themselves and their enemies, they took a moment's rest to recover from this warm alarm, and wash the contusions which they had received, for some of the stones had struck them. In the heat of the action they had not noticed this, but now that the danger was passed, they began to feel them.

The forest, which in the morning had been so distant from them, was now excessively close, and they had hopes of reaching it before night. They therefore took up the paddles again with fresh ardour and continued their route. At sunset the canoe disappeared beneath the immense dome of foliage of the virgin forest which the stream intersected obliquely.

At nightfall the yells of wild beasts were heard hoarsely in the depths of the forest. Leon did not consider it prudent to venture at this hour into unknown regions, which contained dangers of every description. Consequently after tacking about for some time, the captain gave orders to pull for a rocky point which jutted out into the water, and which they could approach without any difficulty. After they had landed, Leon walked round the rock in order to reconnoitre the neighbourhood, and find out in what part of the forest they were.

Chance served him better than he could have hoped for. After parting with great difficulty and extraordinary precautions the creepers and shrubs which obstructed his progress, he suddenly found himself at the entrance of a natural grotto formed by one of the volcanic convulsions so frequent in these regions.

On seeing this he stopped, and lopping with his machete a branch of the resinous tree, which the Indians call the candle tree, and which grows profusely in that part of America, he struck a light, lit the torch, and then boldly entered the grotto, followed by Wilhelm and Giacomo. The smuggler's sudden appearance startled a swarm of night birds and bats, which began flying heavily in all directions and attempting to escape.

Leon continued his march without troubling himself about these gloomy denizens, whose sports he so unexpectedly interrupted. All at once a hoarse and prolonged growl was audible in a remote corner of the grotto. The three men remained nailed to the ground. They found themselves face to face with a magnificent bear, of which the cavern was doubtless the usual abode, and which, standing on its hind legs with widely-opened mouth, showed the troublesome visitors, who had disturbed it in its retreat, a tongue red as blood, and glistening claws of a remarkable length. Its round and staring eyes were fixed on the smugglers in a way that caused them to reflect. Luckily the latter were not the men to let themselves be intimidated for long.

"There's a fellow who seems inclined to sup with us," said Giacomo, looking at the animal.

"Silence! My piece will make us, on the contrary, sup with him. Here, Giacomo, take my torch, lad."

"Take care, captain," the latter observed. "A shot fired at this spot will make a frightful din, and bring a band of red devils on our back."

"You are right, by Heaven!" the captain replied; "We must run no risk."

Then, laying his rifle along the side of the grotto, he undid the lasso which he rolled round his body.

"Get behind me," he said to his comrades, "and be in readiness to help me."

Then, after carefully preparing the lasso, he whirled it round his head, while whistling in a peculiar manner. At this unexpected apparition the bear shambled two or three paces toward him, and that was its ruin. The running knot fell on its shoulders, and the three smugglers, laying hold of the end of the lasso, began running backwards, while pulling with all their strength.

The poor animal thus strangled and putting out a tongue of a foot long, tottered about, while trying in vain to free itself with its heavy paws from the necklace which squeezed its throat. The smugglers did not relax their efforts till the bear had heaved its last sigh.

"Now," said Leon, when he was certain that the bear was really dead, "for the canoe."

The three men returned to the boat, drew it out of the water, and taking it on their shoulders, carried it to the end of the grotto. Then, with a patience of which Indians and wood rangers are alone capable, they effaced every trace which might have led to a discovery of their landing, and the retreat which they had chosen. The smallest bent blade of grass was straightened; the lianas and shrubs which they had parted were brought together again, and after this operation was completed, no one could have suspected that human beings had passed that way. After this, making an ample provision of dead wood and torches, they re-entered the grotto with the manifest intention of at length taking the rest which they so greatly needed.

All this had required time; hence, so soon as they were free from anxiety, Giacomo, who was a mighty hunter, began flaying the bear, while Wilhelm lit a colossal fire. The queso and charque remained in the alforjas, thanks to the succulent steaks which Giacomo adroitly cut off the animal, and which, being roasted on the embers, procured them a delicious supper.

When quite satisfied, the three men crowned this feast with a few drops of rum which Leon had about him, and after smoking for some ten minutes, they wrapped themselves in their ponchos, with their feet to the fire and their hands on their weapons. Nothing disturbed their rest, which lasted till long after the first sunbeams had purpled the horizon, and it was Leon who awoke his comrades.

"Up!" he shouted to them, "the sun has risen and we must think of business."

"Ah!" said Wilhelm, as he rubbed his eyes, "what a pity! I was dreaming that we were carrying a cargo of pisco past the custom-house officers, who presented arms to us."

"I was not dreaming," said Giacomo, "but I was having a glorious snooze."

In a minute he was on his legs, while Leon was reflecting on his best course.

"Giacomo," he said to the Italian, who was making arrangements for a start, "we have arrived at the spot where our search will really begin. It is impossible for all three of us to dream of entering the city, which must be in the heart of this forest. On the other hand, I may have occasion to require men here in whom I can trust; you will therefore go back to the Parumo of San Juan Bautista. So soon as the band arrives you will take the command and lead it to the spot where we now are."

"What! I am to leave you!"

"It must be. Take careful note of the road we have followed, so as to make no mistake."

"All right, captain."

"However, when you return with our comrades, you will try to find a shorter and more direct route."

"Yes, captain."

"This grotto is large enough to shelter you all; you will remain in it with your horses, and not quit it, save on an order from me—you hear?"

"And understand—all right."

"One last recommendation. I have told you that it was important for the success of the enterprise I am undertaking that I should find all my men here in case of need. Remember, then, that I expressly forbid you letting yourselves be trapped by the Redskins, and you must show them that they are but asses when compared with a clever smuggler."

"We will prove it to them, captain, and I will take it on myself."

"In that case, you will set out directly, while we proceed through this forest, which seems the most entangled that I ever saw."

"One moment—hang it!" Wilhelm exclaimed; "do you not see, captain, that breakfast is ready?"

In fact, Wilhelm, as a man who did not care to run after adventures on an empty stomach, had blown up the fire smouldering in the ashes, and roasted some superb slices of bear meat.

"Wilhelm, you are growing greedy," said Leon, affecting a tone of reproach.

"Captain, when a man has his stomach full he can march a long distance without feeling fatigued," the German answered sententiously; "besides, the morning air sharpens the appetite."

"Very good, then, but we must make haste," Leon resumed, amazed at this long sentence.

"There, captain, it is first-rate."

Wilhelm had spoken the truth in asserting that the morning air sharpened the appetite, for, in spite of the toughness of the meat which composed the staple of their meal, it was disposed of in a twinkling, which leads to the supposition that the idea which the German had was not inopportune.

"Giacomo," Leon said again, "Wilhelm and I have provisions enough for a few days, and the forest will not let us want for game, if we require it; so you had better take the rest of the bear with you."

"Thanks, captain. At my first halt I will cut up all the best meat left."

"Take it while we put the canoe in the water."

The three men then left the grotto, though not till they had looked all around to see whether any danger existed for them. Giacomo had thrown the bear's hide over his shoulders, and walked in front, Leon and Wilhelm following, and bearing on their shoulders the canoe, in the bottom of which they had deposited the remaining bear meat. The skiff was soon balancing lightly on the water; Giacomo leaped in, seized the paddles and went off.

"Good-bye, captain—good-bye, Wilhelm, till we meet again," he said for the last time.

"Good-bye and good luck," the latter replied, and the smuggler proceeded in the direction of the Parumo of San Juan Bautista. Leon looked after him for a moment, and then addressed Wilhelm, who was awaiting his orders.

"My friend," he said to him, "I fear that we may have many difficulties to face if we cross the forest together. Suppose I left you in the grotto to await Giacomo's return? Once I have arrived at Garakouaïti, I could easily find means to warn you."

"What are you thinking of, captain? Suppose you were to be taken prisoner, or wounded, in that case there would be no chance of helping you if you were alone. At any rate, if anything happen on the road while we are travelling together, I will return at full speed to warn my comrades."

"Still, you will be forced to leave me after we have crossed the forest; for, as I told you, admission to the city is interdicted to all those who are not Indians, and the means which I imagine I have discovered to enter can only be used by myself."

"Well, then, captain, let me accompany you to the vicinity of the city, and then I will turn back."

"Very good; that is settled."

The two men re-entered the grotto, fetched their travelling utensils, and came out again, rifle on shoulders, and axe in hand. They then buried themselves in the virgin forest which lay expanded before them.

CHAPTER XXI
THE INDIAN CITY

Tcharanguii, the chief of the Jaos, had rejoined his warriors, after entrusting Inez and Maria de Soto-Mayor to the care of the Sayotkatta of Garakouaïti. Immediately after he had departed, the young ladies were imprisoned in the Jouimion Faré, inhabited by the Virgins of the Sun.

Although prisoners, they were treated with the greatest respect, according to the orders which Tcharanguii had given, and might perhaps have endured the weariness of their captivity with patience, had not a profound anxiety as to the fate reserved for them and an invincible sadness resulting from their brutal separation from those whom they loved, and the terrible circumstances under which they had left them, seized upon them.

It was then that the difference of character in the two sisters was displayed. Inez, accustomed to the eager attentions of the brilliant gentlemen who frequented her father's house, and to the enjoyment of the slothful and luxurious life which is that of all rich Spanish families, suffered on finding herself deprived of the delights and caresses by which her childhood had been surrounded, and, being incapable to resist the grief that devoured her, she fell into a state of discouragement and torpor, which she made no attempt to combat.

Maria, on the contrary, who found in her present condition but little change from her novitiate, while deploring the blow that struck her, endured it with courage and resignation. Her powerful mind accepted the misfortune as a chastisement for the fervent affection which she had devoted to Leon; but, confiding in the purity of that love, she had drawn from it the hope that she would one day emerge from the trial by the help of the man whom she loved, and who had rendered her aid and protection.

When the two sisters conversed together about the probabilities of deliverance, Inez trusted to the power of her father's name and fortune, while Maria contented herself with confiding in the bravery and intrepidity of the young smuggler chief who had escorted them up to the moment when they were carried off by the Indians. Inez did not understand what relations could exist between this captain and the future, and cross-questioned Maria; but the latter either did not answer the question or evaded it.

"In truth, sister," Inez said to her, "you incessantly speak about Captain Leon. Do you think then, that our father, Don Juan, and Don Pedro, who loves me and is going to marry me, cannot succeed without Leon in delivering us from the hands of the wicked Redskins who keep us prisoners here?"

"Sister Inez," Maria answered her, "I hope for the help of the smuggler, because he engaged to escort us to Valdivia, where we should arrive safely; and he is too honourable and brave a man not to set everything in motion to remedy the fatal event which has prevented him from keeping his word."

This last sentence was uttered by the maiden with so much conviction that Inez was surprised at it, and raised her eyes to her sister, who blushed beneath this searching glance. Inez said no more, but asked herself what could be the nature of the feeling which thus compelled her sister to defend a man whom she did not know, and whose relations with the family were of so low a nature. From that day no further allusion was made to Leon.

It is a strange fact, but one that is incontestably true, that priests, no matter to what country or religion they belong, are continually devoured by the desire of making proselytes. The Sayotkatta of Garakouaïti had not let the opportunity slip which appeared to offer itself in the persons of Inez and her sister. Endowed with a great mind, thoroughly convinced of the excellence of the religious principles which he professed; and, in addition, an obstinate enemy of the Spaniards, he conceived the plan of making the young ladies priestesses of the sun, so soon as they were entrusted to him by Tcharanguii.

In America there is no lack of such conversions; and though they may appear monstrous to us, they are perfectly natural in that country. He therefore prepared his batteries very artfully. The young ladies did not speak Indian; and he, on his side, did not know a word of Spanish; but this difficulty, apparently enormous, was speedily got over by Schymi-Tou.

He was related to a renowned warrior of the name of Meli-Antou (the four suns), whose wife, reared not far from Valdivia, spoke Spanish well enough to make herself comprehended. In spite of the law which interdicted the introduction of strangers into the Jouimion Faré, the high priest took it on himself to let Mahiaa (My Eyes), Meli-Antou's wife, visit the young ladies.

We can imagine the satisfaction which the latter must have felt on receiving the visit of someone who could talk with them, and help them to overcome the ennui in which they passed their whole time. The Indian squaw was welcomed as a friend, and her presence as a most agreeable distraction. But in the second interview they saw for what an interested object these visits were permitted, and a real tyranny succeeded the short conversations of the first days.

This was a permanent punishment for the maidens. As Spanish girls, and attached to the religion of their fathers, they could not at any price respond to the Sayotkatta's hopes, and still the squaw had not concealed from them, that in spite of the honeyed words and insinuating manners of Schymi-Tou, they must expect to suffer the most frightful torture if they refused to devote themselves to the worship of the Sun.

The prospect was far from being reassuring; hence, while pledging themselves in their hearts to remain faithful to the Catholic faith, the young girls experienced a deadly anxiety. Time slipped away, and the Sayotkatta was beginning to grow impatient at the slowness of the conversion; and the slight hopes which the maidens had retained of being able to escape the sacrifice demanded of them gradually abandoned them.

This painful situation, which was further aggravated by the absence of any news from outside, eventually produced an illness, whose progress was so rapid, that the Sayotkatta considered it prudent to suspend the execution of his ardent wish. Let us leave the unhappy prisoners almost congratulating themselves on the alteration which had taken place in their health, and which freed them from the annoyance to which they were subjected, and take up the thread of the events which happened to other persons who figure in this history.

A month after the arrival of Maria and Inez within the walls of Garakouaïti—that is to say, on a fine October evening—two men, whose features or dress it would have been impossible to distinguish owing to the obscurity, debouched from the forest which we previously described, and stopped for a moment with marked indecision upon the extreme verge of the wood.

Before them rose a mound, whose summit, though of no great elevation, cut the horizon in a straight line. After exchanging a few whispered words, the two travellers laid down on their stomach, and crawling on their hands and feet, advanced through the giant grass, which they caused to undulate, and which entirely concealed their bodies. On reaching the top of the mount, they looked down, and were struck with amazement.

The eminence on which they found themselves was quite perpendicular, as was the whole of the ridge that extended on their right and left. A magnificent plain stretched out a hundred feet beneath them, and in the centre of this plain—that is to say, at a distance of about a thousand yards—stood an Indian city, haughty and imposing, defended by a hundred massive towers and its stout walls.

The sight of this vast city produced a lively feeling of pleasure on the mind of the two men, for one of them turned to his comrade and said to him with an accent of indescribable satisfaction—

"That must be the city which Diego told me of: it is Garakouaïti! At last we have arrived."

"And it was not without trouble, captain," the other remarked, who was no other than Wilhelm; "we may compliment ourselves on it."

"What matter, since we have arrived?"

"Before the city, yes: but inside it, no."

Leon smiled.

"Don't be alarmed, comrade; I shall be inside tomorrow."

"I hope so, captain; but in the meanwhile I do not think it advisable to spend the night here in contemplating what there is at the base of this species of precipice, and I think we should not do wrong in returning to the forest, or seeking the road that leads to the place that lies before us."

"It is too late to dream of getting any nearer the city today. As for the road, we shall find it by bearing a little to the right, for the ground seems to trend in that direction."

"In that case, captain, we must put off the affair till tomorrow."

"Yes; and now let us return to the llama."

And joining action to words, Leon turned back, and exactly following the track which his body had left in the grass, he soon found himself—as did Wilhelm, who followed all his movements—once again on the skirt of the forest.

The silence which reigns at midday beneath these gloomy arches of foliage and branches had been succeeded by the hoarse sounds of a savage concert composed of the shrill cries of the nocturnal birds, which awoke, and prepared to dash at the loritos and hummingbirds belated far from their nests; of the yells of the pumas, and the hypocritical and plaintive miaulings of the tigers and panthers, whose echoes were hurled back in mournful notes by the roofs of the inaccessible caverns and the yawning pits which served as the lurking places of these dangerous guests.

Going back along the road which they had traced with the axe, the smugglers soon afterwards found themselves close to a fire of dead leaves and branches burning in the centre of a clearing. Some fifteen yards from them a magnificent llama, carelessly lying at the foot of a tree, watched them approach, and fixed on them its large eyes as melancholy and intelligent as those of a stag, though it did not appear at all astonished or startled by their presence.

"Well, Jemmy, my boy, you were not tired of waiting for us?" Wilhelm said, as he went up to the animal and patted it on the neck.

Leon threw a few branches on the fire, which was beginning to decay.

"On my honour, captain, I am not curious," the German continued, "but I should like to know what you intend doing with this llama which we have dragged after us for the last fortnight? Now that we have reached our journey's end, do you not think it time to kill and roast it?"

"For Heaven's sake, no, my friend; for if I have spared this llama, it is simply that it may serve me as a passport to enter the city which we saw just now."

"How so?"

"I will explain that to you tomorrow, till then let us keep up a good fire, as the wild beasts seem out of temper tonight, and sleep."

"Done for sleep!" the German answered, phlegmatically.

And without farther ceremony he prepared to obey his captain's orders. The latter, who felt that the hopes which he had conceived were on the point of being realized, was, as frequently happens in such cases, overcome by the fear that he had deceived himself in the supposition he had formed of the young ladies' captivity in the city of Garakouaïti. In vain did he recall the details which Diego had furnished him with about the customs of the Indians, and the art among others which they had of conveying to, and concealing in, the holy city everything they took from their enemies; the fear of being mistaken constantly reverted to his mind.

"Oh, no!" he said to himself, "I cannot have deceived myself; it is love which guides my footsteps, and I feel here," he continued, as he laid his hand on his chest, "something which tells me that I am going to see her again. Oh! see her, and then save her! It would be too great happiness, and I would give ten years of my life to be sure of success."

Then, following the current of his thoughts, Leon saw himself leading Maria back to the general, and receiving her hand as a recompense for the service which he had rendered him. Then, a moment after, he asked himself whether he could endure life hence-forward were he to fail in his plans; and, looking at the rifle he held, he vowed that it should help him not to survive his sorrow.

"Come," he said to himself, suddenly, "this is not the moment for doubt. Besides, if Maria is not in Garakouaïti, Diego will be there, or someone who can tell me where to find him; and in that case he must restore me her whom I love, for he swore that she should be sacred to him."

After the young man had to some extent regained the courage which had momentarily failed him, he removed from his brow the anxiety which had overshadowed it, and asked of sleep the calmness necessary for his thoughts and forgetfulness of his anxious cares. He therefore lay down by the side of Wilhelm, whose irregular snores added an additional note to the melody which the wild denizens of the forest were performing with a full orchestra.

The first beams of dawn had just begun to tinge the sky with a whitish reflection, when the smuggler captain opened his eyes and shook his comrade's arm. The latter turned—turned again—and at last awoke, suppressing an enormous yawn, which almost cleft his face to the ears—

"Hilloh, skulk!" Leon shouted to him, "make haste and get on your legs; for we have no time to lose. The red devils are still asleep, but they will soon spread over the plain, and they must not find us here."

"Let us decamp," Wilhelm replied, who had been quite restored by his long sleep; "I shall not be sorry to have a peep at an Indian city. It must be funny."

"My poor Wilhelm, in spite of all the desire I might have to procure you this satisfaction, I am compelled to beg you to abstain from it, because I have already told, I must go on alone."

"Der Teufel! But in that case what am I to do while waiting for you? for I do not suppose that you intend remaining any length of time in that confounded capital?"

"I will tell you. In the first place, help me to dress."

"Dress?"

"Yes; hang it all! Do you fancy I shall present myself at the city gates in Spanish costume?"

"What! are you going to disguise yourself?"

"Exactly."

"But as what?"

"As an Indian, you donkey."

"Oh! famous—famous!" Wilhelm exclaimed, bursting into a hearty laugh. "I'm your man."

"In that case make haste."

"I am ready, captain; I am ready."

The travestissement did not take long to effect; in a few minutes Leon took from his alforjas a razor, with which he removed his whiskers and moustache; and during this Wilhelm went to pluck a plant that grew abundantly in the forest. After extracting the juice, Leon, who had stripped off all his clothes, dyed his face and body with it.

Then Wilhelm drew on his chest, as well as he could, a tortoise, accompanied by some fantastic ornaments which had no warlike character about them, and which he reproduced on the face. He gave his magnificent black hair a whitish tinge, intended to make him look older than he really was, knotted it upon his head in the Indian fashion, and thrust into the knob the feather of an aras, which Leon had picked up some days previously in the forest, being careful to place it on the left side, in order to show that it adorned the head of a peaceful man, since the warriors are accustomed to fix their plumes in the centre of their top-knot. When these preparations were completed, Leon asked Wilhelm whether he could present himself among the Indians without risk?

"You are so like a redskin, captain, that, if I had not helped to transform you, I should not be able to recognise you, for you are really frightful."

"In that case, I have nothing to fear."

Leon, feeling once again in his alforjas, brought out his travelling case, and a small box of medicaments, which he always carried with him, a precious article to which he and his men had had recourse on many occasions; joining to these articles his pistols, he made the whole into a small packet, which he wrapped up in his poncho and fastened on the back of the llama, whose taming had so greatly excited Wilhelm's curiosity.

"Now," he said, addressing the German, "pay careful attention to what I am about to say to you."

"I am listening, captain."

"You will collect my clothes, and as soon as I have left the forest, start at once for the grotto, where I left Giacomo; our comrades must have reached it some days back. You have only twenty leagues to go, and the road is ready traced, since it cost us three weeks' labour; by travelling day and night, you can arrive soon."

"I will not lose an hour, captain."

"Good: you will tell Harrison where I am, and return here with all the men who have been enlisted at Valparaíso to reinforce our troops. Do you thoroughly understand?"

"Yes, captain."

"You will bring the horses with you, for they can pass. When you have all assembled at this spot, Harrison will place sentries in the environs day and night, while careful to hide them so that they cannot be noticed, and so soon as you hear the cry of the eagle of the Cordilleras, which I shall imitate, you will answer me, so that I may know your exact position; and if I repeat it twice, you will hold yourselves in readiness to help, for in that case I shall be attacked. You will remember all these instructions?"

"Perfectly, captain; and I will repeat them to you word for word."

"Good!" Leon resumed, after Wilhelm had repeated his orders word by word. "One thing more. It is possible that when I return I may bring two or three persons with me; do not be troubled by that, nor stir till you hear the agreed on signal."

"Yes, captain."

"Keep watch before all at night, for I shall probably leave the city after sunset."

"All right—a good guard shall be kept."

"And if I have not given the signal within a week, it will be because I am dead; and, in that case, you can be off and choose another chief, as you cannot hope to see Leon again."

"Oh! captain, do not say that."

"We must foresee everything, my worthy fellow; but I have hopes that, with the help of Heaven, nothing disagreeable will happen to me. Here is the day, and it is time to set out; so let us separate. Good-bye, my excellent Wilhelm, my trust is in you."

"Good-bye, captain, and distrust those scamps of Indians, for they are as treacherous as they are cowardly."

The two men shook hands, and Leon made his llama get up from the ground, while Wilhelm, after making a bundle of the clothes which his captain had bidden him remove, threw it on his shoulder with a desperate air, opened his enormous compasses of legs, and went off into the forest with long strides, and a melancholy shake of the head. Leon looked after him for a moment.

"It is, perhaps, the last friendly face that I shall ever see," he said to himself, with a sigh.

A moment after he resolutely raised his head.

"The die is cast, and I will go on."

Then, assuming the quiet, careless slouch of an Indian, he went slowly toward the plain, followed by his llama, though continually looking searchingly around him.

CHAPTER XXII
THE JAGOUAS OF THE HUILICHES

In the sparkling beams of the sun which had risen radiant, the great landscape which Leon was passing through assumed a really enchanting appearance. Nature was, so to speak, animated, and a varied spectacle had taken the place of the gloomy and solitary aspect which it had offered on the previous evening to the captain and his comrade.

From the gates of the city, which were now open, poured forth groups of Indians, mounted and on foot, who scattered in all directions with shouts of joy and bursts of noisy laughter. Numerous canoes dashed about the river, and the fields were peopled with flocks of llamas and vicunas, guided by Indians armed with long wands, who were proceeding to the city from their neighbouring farms.

Strangely-attired women, sturdily bearing on their heads long wicker baskets filled with meat, fruit, or vegetables, walked along conversing together and accompanying each sentence with that continued sharp metallic laugh of which the Indian tribes have the secret, and whose sound bears a near resemblance to that which the fall of a number of pebbles on a copper dish would produce.

Leon, who, by the aid of his new exterior, could examine at his leisure all that was taking place around him, looked curiously at the animated picture which he had before his eyes; but what most fixed his attention was a troop of horsemen in their war paint, armed with the enormous Molucho lances, which they wield with such great dexterity, and whose wounds are so dangerous. All, also, carried a slung rifle, a lasso at their girdle, and advanced at a trot in the direction of the city; they seemed to have come from the opposite direction to the one by which Leon was arriving.

The numerous persons scattered over the plain stopped to gaze at them; and Leon, taking advantage of this circumstance, hurried on so as to be mixed up with the curious crowd. The horsemen still advanced at the same pace, not noticing the attention which they excited, and arrived within fifty yards of the principal gate, where they halted. At the same moment three men quitted the city at a gallop, crossed in two bounds the bridge thrown across the moat, and came to join them.

Three warriors came out of the ranks of the troop to which we have alluded, and approached them. After a short conversation all six horsemen rejoined the squadron, which started once again, and entered the town with it. Leon, who followed them, reached the gate at the moment when the last men of the detachment disappeared within the city. Assuming the most careless air he could, although his heart beat as if to break his chest, he presented himself in his turn to enter. After crossing the wooden bridge with a firm step, he entered the gateway, where a lance was levelled at his breast and barred his passage.

An Indian of lofty stature, to whom his grey hair and the numerous wrinkles on his face imparted a certain character of gentleness, cleverness, and majesty, advanced with measured steps, and looked attentively at him.

"My brother is welcome at Garakouaïti," he said to Leon. "What does my brother desire?"

"Yourana," answered Leon, who, thanks to the life he had led in the Pampas, talked Indian with as much facility as his mother tongue—"is my father a chief?"

"I am a chief," the Indian answered.

"My father can question me," Leon said.

"My brother seems to have come a long distance?" the other went on, looking at the smuggler's worn boots.

"I left my tribe four moons back."

"Which is my brother's tribe?"

"I am a son of the Huiliches."

"Matai. My brother is not a warrior. I can see."

"My father is right; I am a Jagouas."

"Good! my brother is beloved by Chemiin."

Leon bowed, but said nothing.

"And where are the hunting grounds of my brother's tribe situated?"

"On the banks of the Great Salt Lake."

"And why has my brother left his tribe?"

"To come to Garakouaïti to exercise the skill with which Chemiin has endowed me, and to adore Agriskoui in the magnificent temple which the piety of the Indians has raised to him in the city of the sun."

"Very good! my brother is a wise man."

Leon bowed a second time to this compliment, although his anxiety was extreme, and he knew not how the examination he was undergoing would terminate.

"What is my brother's name?" the Indian asked.

"Cari-Lemon," Leon at once answered.

"My brother is truly a man of peace," the other remarked, with a smile. "I," he added, drawing himself up haughtily, "am called Meli-Antou."

"My father is a great chief."

It was Meli-Antou's turn to bow with superb modesty on receiving this flattering qualification.

"My skill supports the world: I am a son of the sacred tribe of the great Chemiin."

"My father is blessed in his race."

"My brother will follow me, and my house will be his during the period that he sojourns in Garakouaïti."

"I am not worthy to shake the dust of my moccasins off on the threshold of his door," Leon replied, modestly.

"Chemiin blesses those who practise hospitality. My brother Cari-Lemon is the guest of a chief; he will therefore follow me."

"I will follow my father, since such is his wish."

And he began walking behind the old Indian, delighted in his heart at having escaped so well from the first trial. Before starting, Meli-Antou entrusted to another Indian the post which he occupied at the city gate, and then turned to Leon.

"Arami!" he said to him.

Both, without further remark, proceeded toward the house inhabited by the chief, which was at the other extremity of Garakouaïti. The European, accustomed to the tumult, bustle, and confusion of the streets of the old world, which are constantly encumbered with vehicles of every description and busy passers-by, who run against each other and jostle at every step, would be strangely surprised at the sight of the interior of an Indian city.

There are no noisy thoroughfares bordered by magnificent shops, offering to the curiosity and covetousness of buyers or rogues, superb and dazzling specimens of European trade. There are no carriages—not even carts; the silence is only troubled by the footfall of a few passers-by who are anxious to reach their homes, and walk with the gravity of savants or of magistrates in all countries. The houses, which are all hermetically closed, do not allow any sound from within to be heard outside. Indian life is concentrated. The manners are patriarchal, and the public way is never, as among us, the scene of disputes, quarrels, or fights.

The dealers assemble in immense bazaars until midday, and sell their wares—that is to say, their fruit, vegetables, and quarters of meat, for any other trade is unknown among the Indians, as every family weaves and manufactures its own clothing and the objects which it requires. When the sun has attained one-half of its course, the bazaars are closed, and the Indian traders, who all live in the country, quit the city only to return on the morrow.

Everybody has by that time laid in the provisions for the day. Among the Indians the men never work: the women undertake the purchases, the household duties, and the preparation for everything that is indispensable for existence. The men hunt or make war. The payment for what is bought and sold is not effected as among us, by means of coins, which are only accepted by the Indians on the seaboard who traffic with Europeans, but by means of a free exchange, which is carried on by all the tribes residing in the interior of the country. This system is exceedingly simple: the buyer exchanges some object for the one which he wishes to acquire: and nothing more is said.

The two men, after walking right through Garakouaïti, at length reached the lodge of Meli-Antou, in which happened to be Mahiaa, his squaw, whom our readers know as the Indian woman whom the Sayotkatta had placed with General Soto-Mayor's daughters, in order to aid in their conversion to the worship of the Sun. Since the illness of the young ladies she had suspended her visits to the Jouimion Faré, but intended to renew them so soon as she received instructions to that effect.

She was a woman of about thirty years of age, though she looked at least fifty. In these regions, where growth is so rapid, a woman is generally married when she is twelve or thirteen. Continually forced to undertake rude tasks, which in other countries fall to the men, their freshness soon disappears, and on reaching the age of thirty, they are attacked by a precocious decrepitude which, twenty years later, makes hideous and repulsive beings of women who, in their youth, were generally endowed with great beauty and exquisite grace, of which many European ladies might be fairly jealous.

Mahiaa, seated cross-legged on a mat of Indian corn straw, was grinding wheat between two stones. By her side stood two female slaves, belonging to that bastard race to which we have already referred, and to whom the title of savage is applicable. At the moment when Leon entered the lodge, Mahiaa and her women looked up curiously at him.

"Mahiaa," said Meli-Antou to his squaw, as he laid his hand on the captain's shoulder, "this is my brother Cari-Lemon, the great Jagouas of the Huiliches; he will dwell with us."

"My brother Cari-Lemon is welcome to the lodge of Meli-Antou," the squaw replied, with a rather sweet smile. "Mahiaa is his slave."

"Will my mother permit me to kiss her feet?" said Leon.

"My brother will kiss my face!" the chiefs wife replied, as she offered her cheek to Leon, who respectfully touched it with his lips.

"Will my son take maté?" Mahiaa continued. "Maté relieves the traveller's parched throat."

The introduction was over. Meli-Antou sat down, while his wife ordered her slaves to unload the llama and lead it to the corral, after which the maté was served. Leon, while imbibing the favourite beverage of the Spaniards and Indians, looked at the house in which he now was. It was a rather spacious square room, whose whitewashed walls were adorned with human scalps, and a rack of weapons, kept remarkably clean. Folded up puma skins and ponchos were piled up in a corner, until they were arranged as beds. Wooden chairs, excessively low and carved with some degree of art, furnished this room, in the centre of which stood a table, only some fifteen inches above the ground.

This interior, which is very simple, as we see, is reproduced in all the Indian lodges; which are composed of six rooms. The first of these is the one which we have just described, and the one in which the family generally keep. The second is set aside for the children. The third is used as a bedroom. The fourth contains the looms, which are made of bamboo, and display an admirable simplicity of mechanism. The fifth contains provisions of every description; and lastly, the sixth is set apart for the slaves. As for the kitchen there is none, for the food is prepared in the corral, that is to say, in the open air. Chimneys are equally unknown, and each room is warmed by means of an earthenware brasero.

The household duties are entrusted to the slaves, who work under the inspection of the mistress of the house. These slaves are not all savages; many of them are unhappy Spaniards made prisoners of war, or who have fallen into the ambushes which the Indians incessantly set for them.

The lot of the latter is even more sad than that of their companions in slavery, for they have not the prospect of being free some day, and must expect to perish sooner or later as victims to the spite of their cruel masters, who avenge themselves on them for the numberless vexations which they suffer at the hands of the Spaniards. It is truly in this harsh captivity that a man can apply to himself the words which Dante inscribed over the gates of the Inferno, "Lasciate ogni speranza."

Meli-Antou, to whom accident had led Leon, was one of the most respected chiefs among the warriors of Garakouaïti: he had lived among Europeans, and the experience which he had acquired by passing through countries remote from his home, had rendered him more polite and sociable than the majority of his countrymen.

He informed Leon that he was the father of four sons, who had joined the great Moluchos army, and were fighting against the Spaniards: he told him of the journeys he had made, and seemed anxious to prove to the medicine man, Cari-Lemon, that his great courage as a warrior, and his military virtues, did not prevent him recognising all that there was noble and respectable in science.

The captain seemed deeply touched by the consideration which Meli-Antou paid to the character he was invested with, and resolved to profit by his host's good temper to sound him cleverly as to what he desired to know as to the presence of Diego, Tahi-Mari, and the young ladies in the city. Still, in the fear of arousing the Indian's suspicions, he waited till the latter furnished him with the opportunity to question him.

An hour about had elapsed, and Leon had not yet been able to approach the question without danger, when an Indian presented himself in the doorway.

"Agriskoui rejoices," said the newcomer.

"My brother is welcome," said Meli-Antou; "my ears are open."

"The great council of the Ulmens is assembled," the Indian said, "and awaits my brother Meli-Antou."

"What is there new then?"

"Tcharanguii has just arrived with his warriors, his heart is full of bitterness, and he wishes to speak to the council."

"Tcharanguii returned!" exclaimed Meli-Antou, in surprise; "that is strange."

"He has just arrived in the city."

"Was he in command of the warriors who arrived about an hour ago?"

"Himself. My brother did not look in his face when he passed before him? What answer shall I give the chief?"

"That I am coming to the council."

The Indian bowed and departed, and the old chief rose, and, after courteously taking leave of Leon, went to the council. The captain took advantage of the freedom granted him to take a turn round the city, and try to pick up the topographical information of which he stood in need.

Not knowing how his stay in the city would terminate, or how he should get out of it, he studied most carefully the formation of the streets and the situation of the buildings, in the event of an attack or an escape. When he returned to Meli-Antou's lodge, the latter had got back and was awaiting him with a certain amount of impatience. On remarking the animation depicted on the Indian's features, Leon thought that he had, perhaps, discovered something concerning him, and advanced with a considerable amount of suspicion.

"My brother is really a great Jagouas?" Meli-Antou asked, as he looked searchingly at him.

"Did I not tell my father so?" Leon answered, who began to believe himself seriously menaced.

"My brother will come with me, then, and bring the implements of his art."

It would not have been prudent to refuse; besides, nothing as yet proved that Meli-Antou had any evil intentions; hence Leon accepted.

"My father can go on, and I will follow him," he contented himself with answering.

"Does my brother speak the language of the Spanish barbarians?"

"I have lived for a long time on the banks of the Salt Lake, and I understand the idiom which they employ."

"All the better."

"Have I to cure a Spaniard?" Leon asked, who wished to make sure of what was expected of him.

"No," said Meli-Antou, "one of the great Moluchos chiefs brought here some time back two paleface women; it is they who are ill; the evil spirit has seized on them, and they are at this moment in danger of death."

Leon started at this unexpected revelation; his heart all but stopped beating, and an involuntary shudder agitated all his limbs. He was compelled to make a superhuman effort to drive back the profound emotion which he experienced, and to answer Meli-Antou in a calm voice:

"I am at my father's orders."

"Let us go, then," the Indian answered.

Leon took up his box of medicaments, followed the old man, and both, leaving the lodge, proceeded towards the Palace of the Vestals.

CHAPTER XXIII
A MIRACULOUS CURE

Tcharanguii had returned to Garakouaïti, with orders to fetch reinforcements for the Molucho army, which, under Tahi-Mari's orders, had seized by surprise Valdivia and Concepción, and was advancing on Talca. The young chief had been delighted at this mission, which gave him an opportunity for seeing again his two captives, with whom he was so struck. Hence, after explaining to the council the motive of his presence in the city, he hastened to seek the Sayotkatta to whom he had entrusted them. But the latter, on learning the return of the young Indian chief, proceeded to Mahiaa to warn her and recommend her silence about the active part which she had taken in the attempted conversion of the young ladies. Mahiaa promised to remain dumb, and informed the old man of the arrival of Cari-Lemon the Jagouas, whose knowledge might be useful in re-establishing the health of the prisoners.

The Sayotkatta thanked the Indian squaw for her devotion, and begged her to send the Jagouas of the Huiliches to him. Meli-Antou himself promised to bring him to the palace as soon as he came in again. After this the Sayotkatta, henceforth at rest, awaited the visit of Tcharanguii, for which he had nerved himself.

At the first words which the chief uttered as to the lively desire he felt to see his prisoners, the old man replied that, for the sake of guarding them more effectually, he had removed them to the Palace of the Vestals until they were restored to their legitimate owner.

"My father will promptly deliver them into my hands, then," Tcharanguii said, "for they belong to me alone."

"My son," the high priest continued, "my heart is filled with affliction, but I cannot satisfy my son's just demand, for the maidens whom he confided to my charge have been sorely tried by Chemiin, who has sent on them the scourge of illness."

"Is their life menaced?" the young chief exclaimed.

"Gualichu alone holds in his hand the existence of his creatures; but still I believe that the danger may be avoided. I am awaiting an illustrious Jagouas, belonging to the Huiliche tribe, who, by the help of his knowledge, may restore strength and health to the slaves whom my son won from the barbarous Spaniards."

Tcharanguii, on hearing this bad news, had not been able to repress a movement of annoyance, which seemed to show that he was not entirely the Sayotkatta's dupe, and suspected what had really happened. Still, either through respect or a fear of being mistaken in his suppositions, he constrained himself, and contented himself with begging the old man to neglect nothing to save his captives, adding that he would know how to display his gratitude to him for the attention which he might pay them.

At this very moment Leon entered, accompanied by Meli-Antou. The Sayotkatta looked at him with close scrutiny, and made him undergo a cross-examination precisely like Meli-Antou's. His answers satisfied the high priest, for a few minutes after he led him away to the Jouimion Faré, to examine into the illness of the señoras, while Meli-Antou and Tcharanguii followed them.

Leon's heart was beating with the most violent emotion, and heavy drops of perspiration stood on his forehead. The critical position in which he found himself was, indeed, of a nature to cause him lively anxiety. He was not at all afraid about retaining his own coolness and stoicism in the presence of the young ladies, for he had too great an interest in not betraying himself to lack the strength of remaining his own master; whatever might happen.

But what he feared above all was the effect which his presence might produce on the señoras if they recognised him at the first glance, or when he made himself known, for it was indispensable for the success of the stratagem which he wished to employ that the young ladies should know with whom they had to deal.

In the meanwhile they had arrived; the four men saw the palace gates open before them; but so soon as they had entered a large room, which, through the absence of all furniture, might be compared to a vestibule, Tcharanguii received orders to remain there with Meli-Antou, while the Sayotkatta and Leon proceeded to visit the captives. As we said, all the Indians, except the Sayotkatta, were interdicted from entering the residence of the Virgins of the Sun; still one person—the medicine man—was of course an exception to the rule.

Following the Sayotkatta, then, Leon crossed a long courtyard, entirely paved with brick, and going up a few steps, found himself in a small building entirely separate from the main building in which were the Virgins of the Sun.

In a hammock of cocoa fibre, suspended from two golden rings at about eighteen inches from the ground, a maiden was lying, whose excessively pale face bore the stamp of great sorrow. It was Doña Inez de Soto-Mayor. By her side stood her sister Maria, with her arms folded on her chest, and her eyes, full of her state of despondency, proved that she had for a long time abandoned all hopes of emerging from the prison in which she was confined, and that the illness had also assailed her. This room, which received no light from without, was merely illumined by a torch fixed in a bracket in the wall, and whose vacillating flame cast a sickly reflection over the persons present. At the sight of the two men, Maria gave a start of terror. Leon turned to his guide.

"Chemiin alone is powerful, for his skill supports the world," he said. "Ghialichu inspires me; but I must be alone in order to read on the face of the sufferers the nature of their malady."

The Sayotkatta hesitated for a moment, and then left the room. Leon rushed to the door, fastened it on the inside, and returned to Maria, who, more and more terrified, was crouching in a corner.

"Maria! it is I—I, Leon, who has come to save you—"

A cry escaped from the maiden's breast.

"Silence," said the smuggler; "perhaps he is listening."

Inez was awake, and looking at this scene, whose meaning escaped her.

"You, Leon?" Maria at length said, as she cast her arms round the young man's neck. "Oh, thank heaven! thanks!"

"For mercy's sake, listen to me! The moments are precious."

"Oh! take me away, if you love me! Take me away at once!"

"Soon."

"Oh, sir," Inez said, in her turn, "save me, and my father will reward you."

Leon smiled, and looked at Maria, who raised to him her lovely eyes, radiant with joy and love.

"My father—where is he?" she asked him. "My sister reminds me that we left him in the midst of the contest."

"He is in safety, so calm yourself."

Footsteps were heard approaching the room in which the young people were assembled.

"Someone is coming," said Leon; "take care."

"But what must we do?" Maria asked.

"Wait, and have confidence."

"What! you are going away?"

"I shall return. Once again, hope and patience."

"Leon, if you do not save us, we shall die."

"Oh yes, Señor Captain, have pity on us," Inez added.

Maria's curls grazed Leon's lips, who felt his soul pass away in the kiss which he gave them.

"Whatever happens, whatever you may hear, trust in me, for I am watching."

"Thanks."

The footsteps had stopped after drawing nearer still; Leon opened the door, and without uttering a syllable, passed before the Sayotkatta, displaying marks of the greatest agitation, and ran toward the vestibule, making incomprehensible gestures. The maidens asked themselves whether they were not the sport of a dream, while the Sayotkatta was dumb with surprise.

Closing the door again, he followed Leon, but as if he did not dare approach him. At the moment when he entered the room in which Meli-Antou and Tcharanguii were waiting, Leon had rejoined the latter, and still seemed possessed by thought which absorbed him.

"Well, brother?" the two Indians said. "Speak," the Sayotkatta added; "what is the matter with you?"

"The sons of Chemiin must arm themselves with courage," Leon slowly answered.

"What does my son mean?" the old man resumed.

"Mayoba has seized on these women, and from this night the evil spirit will smite all those who approach them; for the learning which Gualichu has given me has enabled me to assure myself of the malign influences which they can exert."

The three Indians, credulous like all of their race, fell back a step; and Leon still continued apparently to wrestle against the influence of Mayoba.

"What must be done to deliver them?" Tcharanguii asked.

"All strength and wisdom come from Gualichu," said Leon. "I ask my father, the Sayotkatta, to let me pass this night in prayer in the Chemiin sona."

The Indians exchanged a glance of admiration.

"Be it as my son desires," the Sayotkatta answered.

"Until tomorrow, let no one approach the Spanish women, and Gualichu will grant my prayer by indicating to me the remedy to be applied."

The men bowed their assent, and left the palace with Leon. On arriving in front of the Temple of the Sun, Tcharanguii and Meli-Antou parted, and the Sayotkatta led Leon into the interior.

"Tomorrow, after morning prayer, I will let my father know the will of Gualichu."

"I will wait, my son," the old man said; and, leaving Leon alone, he retired.

In order to make our readers properly understand the confidence with which the Indians accepted Leon's statements, it is necessary to add that, in these countries, soothsayers are regarded as the favourites of the Deity, and enjoying an unlimited supernatural power. And it must not be supposed that the lower classes are alone imbued with this opinion: the chief of the warriors, and the priests themselves, though they do not grant them such an absolute power, recognise a marked superiority over themselves.

Leon passed the whole night in arranging in his mind the details of the plan which he had formed to rescue the two maidens. The next morning he paid a visit in the company of the Sayotkatta to them, in which he acquired the certainty that Inez could without danger support the fatigue of being removed from the Palace of the Vestals. In fact, the Niña, who had suddenly recovered the hope which had abandoned her, found the illness which was undermining her health dissipated as if by enchantment. As for Maria, the captain's presence had given her more than hope, in the unlimited confidence resulting from reciprocated love.

As on the previous day, Leon was careful to remain alone with the young ladies, and begged them to hold themselves in readiness to quit the Jouimion Faré. As on the previous day, too, Tcharanguii and Meli-Antou anxiously awaited in the first room the result of the visit, where Leon found them, and the young chief questioned him as to the state of the patients. He pretended to reflect for a moment, and then replied—

"My brother Tcharanguii is a great chief, and the palefaces tremble at his appearance; his heart can rejoice, for his captives will soon be delivered from the wicked spirit."

"Is my son speaking the truth?" the Sayotkatta asked, as he tried to read in the countenance of the false medicine man the degree of confidence that he could place in his words.

"I am a simple man, whose strength resides in the protection which Gualichu grants me, and it is he who has revealed to me the means of restoring health to those who are suffering."

The Sayotkatta bowed submissively, and invited Leon to let him know what he ought to do.

"Matai!" Leon answered; "on the coming of the third day following the present one, so soon as Iskarre spreads abroad his beneficent light, my brother, the young chief of the Jaos, will take the skin of a llama, which my father, the venerated Sayotkatta of the Moluchos, will kill in the interval, and bless in the name of Chemiin. He will spread out this skin on a mound which I will show him, and which must exist in the vicinity of the city, so that Mayoba, on leaving the maidens, cannot enter any person belonging to Garakouaïti; after which he will lead the two captives to the spot where the skin is stretched out."

"But," the Sayotkatta interrupted, "one of them is unable to leave the hammock in which her body reposes."

"The wisdom of my father dwells in each of his words; but Gualichu has given the strength to her whom he wishes to save to leave her bed."

For a second time the Sayotkatta yielded to the subtlety of these unanswerable arguments.

"That done," Leon continued, "he will select four of his bravest warriors to help him to guard the captives through the night; and then, after I have given my brother, as well as the men who accompany him, a drink to protect them against all evil influences, I will expel Mayoba, who is torturing the paleface squaws."

Meli-Antou and Tcharanguii listened in silence, while the Sayotkatta seemed to reflect; Leon noticed this, and hastened to add—

"Although Gualichu assists me, and allows me to triumph over the wicked spirit, it is necessary that my brother and the four warriors whom he selects should pass the night preceding the cure in the Chemiin sona, and deliver to the wise Sayotkatta twenty brood mares which have not yet foaled, that they may be sacrificed to Gualichu. Will my brother do this?"

"If I do it, will my prisoners be restored to me?" Tcharanguii objected, with a certain hesitation.

"The Spanish girls will not only be restored to my brother, but they will also feel the most lively gratitude to him. If he refuse, they will die."

"I will do it," Tcharanguii said, quickly.

"My son is a wise man," remarked the Sayotkatta, whose forehead grew clearer when Leon mentioned the gift of the mares; "Gualichu protects him."

"My father is too kind," Leon contented himself with answering with a feigned humility, while rejoicing in his heart at seeing the plan he had conceived so facilely accepted by the Indian.

Nothing could be more simple than this plan, which consisted in carrying off the maidens when they were on the hillock whence, a few days previously, he and Wilhelm had seen for the first time the walls of Garakouaïti. It was the sole chance of success possible, for he could not dream of carrying them off from the Jouimion Faré, and even admitting that Tahi-Mari had been willing to use his authority over the chief of the Jaos, by forcing him to restore his prisoners to liberty, Leon could not have recourse to him, as he was fighting far away from the holy city.

The delay of three days fixed by Leon before attempting his plan was necessary to give Wilhelm time to find Giacomo and return with him and the band commanded by Harrison to the spot where the captain had metamorphosed himself into an Indian.

These three days were employed in visits to the young ladies and prayers in the Temple of the Sun.

Still the time seemed long to the captain and the daughters of General Soto-Mayor, who continually trembled lest some fortuitous circumstances might derange their plan. On the last day, Leon, as usual, was conversing with Maria, recommending her passive obedience, when he heard a peculiar rustling at the door of the room in which the young ladies were. Immediately reassuming his borrowed face, he opened the door, and found himself face to face with the Sayotkatta, who recoiled with the promptness of a man caught in the act of spying. Had he heard what they had been saying in Spanish? Leon did not think so, still he considered it prudent to keep on his guard.

The night at length arrived. The young ladies, each carried in a hammock borne on the shoulders of powerful Indians, were taken to the hillock, which

Leon had pointed out on the previous day to Tcharanguii, and deposited on the llama skin stretched out upon it. Leon made Tcharanguii a sign to post as sentries the four men who had carried the maidens. Then, after uttering a few mysterious sentences, and burning a handful of odoriferous herbs, he ordered the Indians and their chief to kneel down and implore Agriskoui.

During this time he looked down into the city, striving to see if anything extraordinary were happening in it. So soon as he was assured that all was calm, and that the deepest silence prevailed in the city, he rose to his feet.

"Let my brother listen to me," he said; "I am going to compel Mayoba to retire from the bodies of the palefaced squaws."

At this moment Maria and Inez gave a start of terror, but Leon did not appear to notice it.

"My brothers will come hither!" he commanded. The four sentries advanced with a hesitation which threatened to degenerate into terror at the slightest movement on the part of the smuggler.

"I am going to pray; but in order to prevent Mayoba from assailing you when he quits the maidens, drink this firewater which Gualichu has endowed with the virtue of causing those who drink it to resist the assaults of the evil spirit, and then return each of you to your place."

At the words "firewater," the Indians quivered, and their eyes sparkled with greed. Leon poured them out, as well as Tcharanguii, half a calabash of spirits, amply doctored with opium, which they swallowed at a draught.

"Now, on your knees, all of you!" said Leon.

The Indians obeyed. He alone remained on his feet, holding out his right hand in the direction of the East, and with the other making a gesture commanding Mayoba to obey his authority. A minute after he changed his posture, and began turning round, while making an evocation.

Half an hour had passed, and during this time one of the Indians had fallen with his face on the ground, as if prostrating himself through humility. Another followed his example, and Tcharanguii imitated him. In a word, the five men were soon all in the same position. Then Leon slightly touched with his foot the man nearest to him, and rolled him over on his side. The opium had thrown him into such a lethargy, that he could have been stripped without waking him. He did the same with the other four, who were equally stupefied by the opium. Then, suddenly turning to the young ladies, who were awaiting the close of this scene with ever-growing anxiety,

"Let us go," he said. "Collect all your strength and follow me, for it is a matter of life or death."

Taking a pistol in either hand, he went down the hillock, preceding Inez and Maria, and ran with them in the direction of the forest. On reaching its skirt they stopped, for the young ladies, exhausted with fatigue, felt that they could go no farther. Leon did not press them, but making them a signal to listen, he imitated with rare perfection the cry of an eagle of the Cordilleras, which he repeated twice. Within a minute, which seemed an hour to the smuggler, the same cry answered him. A quarter of an hour did not elapse ere sixty riders, having Wilhelm and Harrison at their head, debouched from the forest and surrounded the captain and the young ladies, whom they lifted on their saddles.

"Saved! great Heavens!" Leon exclaimed; "they are saved!"

At the same moment a flash crossed the horizon, a whistling was heard, and a bullet broke the branch of a tree a couple of feet from the captain.

"The Indians!" Leon exclaimed; "we must gallop, my lads."

CHAPTER XXIV
THE RUINS OF THE HACIENDA

It was indeed the Indians, who guided by Meli-Antou, were pursuing the smugglers with terrible imprecations. This is what had occurred.

We said that on the day of the escape Leon surprised the Sayotkatta in the act of listening at the door. He had not deceived himself; still, as Schymi-Tou was ignorant of Spanish, he had been unable to understand the young people's conversation, but he had noticed a certain animation which appeared to him suspicious. He did not dare, however, oppose the ceremony of exorcism which was about to take place, and contented himself with imparting his suspicions to Meli-Antou, who was astonished at the Sayotkatta's doubts, and treated them as chimeras.

But, as the old man seemed strongly inclined to suppose some machination, or, at least, some jugglery, on the part of the pretended conjuror, he resolved to watch what took place on the eminence, and hold himself in readiness to march with twenty men, to the help of Tcharanguii, if he were the dupe of the medicine man's trickery. A little while, then, after the young ladies started for the hillock, he followed on their track, accompanied by his warriors; and, on reaching the hill, he crawled up through the tall grass, and listened.

He first heard the prayers of the five men, and was on the point of regretting that he had followed the Sayotkatta's advice, when Leon suddenly ceased speaking. He thought, however, that whispered prayers had succeeded the former ones. Still, as this silence was prolonged, he went a little higher, and was staggered at only seeing Tcharanguii and his four warriors, lying on the ground. Thinking them dead, he rushed toward them, and shouted to his men, whom he had left at the foot of the mound. They were soon with him, and shook the five sleepers, who at last woke up with a very confused idea of what had happened to them.

Meli-Antou guessed a portion of the truth, and, not doubting but that the fugitives had gone into the forest, he gave orders to pursue them. At the moment when they were setting out, they heard the eagle cries which had served as a signal to the smugglers, and dashed toward the spot whence they came. Meli-Antou was the first to perceive the fugitives, and fired at them, and, though he missed his mark, he hoped very soon to recapture them.

Before the smugglers had time to select the route which they must follow, the Indians were upon them. The young ladies were in the middle of the little band and in safety. Leon, therefore, gave orders to accept the fight and charge the enemy. Seizing a mace which had just fallen from the grasp of a wounded Indian, Leon rushed into the centre of the medley with the bounds of a tiger. The combatants, who were too close together to employ their firearms, fought with their knives, and dealt furious blows with their clubbed rifles or maces.

This frightful carnage lasted for more than half an hour, animated by the yells of the Indians and the shouts of the smugglers, who killed them to the last man—thanks to their numerical superiority—by a determined charge, which decided the victory. The victory, however, cost the smugglers eight of their party.

The next great point was to get away from the vicinity of the Indians before the news of the fight spread in Garakouaïti; for if it did so they would not have to contend only against twenty men, but against an entire army of redskins, animated with the desire to avenge their brothers. Leon assembled all his men, and they started for the forest, along the path which he and Wilhelm had cut, and which the smugglers were well acquainted with, through having come along it.

At sunrise they had got through the forest, and found themselves on the banks of the river where the captain, Wilhelm, and Giacomo had been so hotly pursued. Leon gave orders to halt—and it was high time, for the horses were panting with fatigue. Besides, whatever diligence the Indians might display to catch up the smugglers, the latter had a whole night's start of them; hence they could rest in perfect security.

While the men, in various groups, were preparing the meal or dressing their wounds, and the young ladies were sleeping on a pile of ponchos and sheepskins, Leon went to bathe, in order to remove the Indian paint that disfigured him; and, after resuming his European dress, he stationed himself near the spot where the ladies were reposing.

The first words of the latter, on awaking, were a torrent of thanks, which amply rewarded the captain for all that he had done to save them. Maria could not find expressions sufficiently strong to testify to Leon the joy which she felt at being restored to liberty by his assistance; and Inez, herself, gradually felt her heart expanding to a feeling more lively than that of gratitude.

Betrothed to Don Pedro Sallazar by her father's wish, she had accepted this alliance with perfect indifference, only seeing in this marriage greater liberty of action, and the pleasure of being the wife of a rich and brilliant gentlemen, who would devote his entire attention to satisfying her slightest caprices. But her heart had never beaten more violently than usual in the presence of the husband destined for her.

Such was the state of her heart, when the attack of the Indians at the Parumo of San Juan Bautista had suddenly modified her ideas by causing her to reflect on the conduct of the captain, who had not hesitated to risk his life to save her, while her betrothed husband had not even followed her track. Thus she guessed the grandeur and nobility of the smuggler's character, and at the same time conceived a love for him, which was the more violent because the man who was the object of it did not seem to notice it.

It was only at this moment that she understood why her sister had so often praised the young man's courageous qualities, and that she recognised the passion which they entertained for each other. A cruel grief gnawed at her heart, and it was in vain that she struggled against the horrible torture of a frenzied jealousy. She felt that she had no chance of being loved by Leon, who only lived for Maria; and yet, in spite of herself, she could not dispel the charm with which he inspired her. As for Leon, intoxicated with happiness, he revelled in the felicity with which the presence of Maria, who was seated by his side, inundated him.

After a few hours halt, they set out again, and on the morning of the fourth day reached the Parumo of San Juan Bautista, without having been molested in any way. Here they halted, and so soon as the camp was pitched, Leon went up to the maidens, and taking them by the hand, led them to the grave in which the Señora Soto-Mayor was interred.

"Kneel down," he said to them in a grave voice, "and pray, for here rests the body of your mother, whose soul is in heaven."

Maria and Inez mingled their prayers and sobs over the tomb of her who had taken care of their childhood, and both remained absorbed in profound grief. Leon had discreetly withdrawn, leaving the maidens to weep without witnesses: but at the expiration of an hour he went up to them, and by gentle words recalled them to a sense of the things of this world by speaking to them of their father, to whom he had pledged himself to restore them.

On hearing their father's name, the sisters wiped their tears and went back to join the smugglers, who were conversing about the combat which they had waged five weeks previously at that very spot. The men whom Hernandez and Joaquin had enlisted at Valparaíso listened to the narration with the greatest interest, and resolved, on the first opportunity, to avenge those whose places they had taken in Leon's band. The way in which they had behaved before Garakouaïti was, however, a sufficient guarantee of their good disposition.

From the Parumo of San Juan Bautista, the party proceeded to Talca; and after two days' march, the lofty peaks of the Cordilleras had gradually sunk behind the smugglers, who found themselves in the hot regions of the llanos, uninhabited by the Chilians.

Leon, who for more than a month had been unable to receive any news about the political events which had occurred during the period, and who desired to obtain some information about General Soto-Mayor, and whether on his return from Valdivia he had passed through Talca, gave orders to march straight on the latter town, where he intended to let the young ladies rest for two or three days. The nearer they drew to it the darker the captain's brow became; he frowned anxiously, and the glances which he cast in all directions revealed a profound preoccupation.

A great change had, indeed, taken place in these parts during the last month; the country had no longer that rich appearance which it formerly offered to the eye. Fields trampled by horses, the remains of burnt haciendas, and the ashes heaped up at places where flour mills had stood a few weeks previously—all these signs indicated that war had passed that way.

Two or three leagues farther, however, the houses of Talca could be seen on the horizon glistening in the sun. All was perfectly calm in the vicinity; no human being showed himself: no flocks grazed on the devastated prairies; on all sides, a leaden silence and a lugubrious tranquillity brooded over the landscape, and imparted a heart-breaking effect to the cheerful sunbeams.

All at once Wilhelm, who was riding a few paces ahead of the troop, stopped his horse with a start of terror, and anxiously leaned over his saddle. Leon dashed his spurs into his horse's flanks, and joined the smuggler. A hideous spectacle was presented to the two men; in a ditch bordering the road lay, pell-mell, a pile of Spanish corpses horridly disfigured, and all deprived of their scalps.

Leon commanded a halt, while asking himself what he had better do. Should he turn back, or advance on the town, which was evidently in the hands of the Indians? Hesitation was permissible. Still the captain understood that a determination, no matter what its nature, must be formed at once, and looking around him, he noticed a ruined hacienda about a league distant. It was a shelter, and it was better to seek refuge there, than remain on the open plain.

Twenty minutes had not elapsed before Leon leaped from his horse and rushed into the farm. The house bore traces of fire and devastation. The cracked walls were blackened with smoke, the windows broken, and amid the ruins that encumbered the patios lay the bodies of several men and women, assassinated and partly burnt.

Leon conducted the trembling ladies to a room which was cleared of the rubbish that obstructed the entrance; then, after recommending them not to leave it, he rejoined his comrades, who were establishing themselves as well as they could among the ruins.

"Caballeros," he said to them, "we are going to entrench ourselves here while four of you go out to reconnoitre; for we should commit a grave imprudence by entering the town before knowing in whose hands it is. Who are the four men who will undertake the duty?"

"I!—I!" all the smugglers replied, in chorus.

"Very good," Leon remarked, with a smile; "I shall be obliged to choose."

They were all silent.

"Giacomo, Hernandez, Joaquin, and Harrison, leave the ranks!"

The four advanced.

"You will go out," Leon said to them, "in four different directions as scouts. Do not stay away more than two hours, and find out what is going on. Above all, do not let yourselves be caught. Begone!"

The smugglers rushed to their horses, and set out at a gallop.

"Now," said Leon, addressing Wilhelm, "how many are there of us?"

"Fifty-four," a voice answered.

Leon felt himself strong. With fifty-four men he thought a good, deal could be done. His first care was to fortify the house in the best way he could; it was surrounded by a breast-high wall, like all the Chilian haciendas; he had the gateway blocked up, and then, returning to the house, he had loopholes pierced, and placed sentries near the wall and on the terrace. Then summoning Wilhelm, he gave him the command of twenty-five resolute men, and ordered him to ambuscade with this band behind a hillock, which was about two hundred yards from the house.

All these precautions taken, he waited. The scouts soon after returned, and their report was not reassuring:—The grand Molucho army, commanded by Tahi-Mari, had seized on Talca by surprise; the town was given over to pillage; and the Chilians, defeated in several engagements, were flying in the direction of Santiago. Parties of Indians were beating up the country on all sides; and it appeared evident that the smugglers could not go a league beyond the hacienda without falling into an ambuscade.

Hernandez, who was the last to arrive, brought with him some thirty Chilian soldiers and guasos, who had been wandering about for two days at the risk of being caught at any moment by the Indians, who pitilessly massacred all the white men that fell into their hands. Leon gladly welcomed the newcomers, for a reinforcement of thirty men was not to be despised. They were well armed, and could render him a great service. After distributing his men at the spots most exposed to attack, the captain went up on the terrace, and after lying down, carefully examined the country in the direction of Talca.

Nothing had altered, and the country was still deserted. This calmness appeared to him to be of evil augury. The sun set in a reddish mist, the light suddenly decreased, and night arrived with its darkness and mysteries. Leon went down, and proceeded to the room serving as refuge to the two sisters, in order to reassure them, and give them hopes which he was far from feeling. The maidens were sitting on the ground silently.

"Niñas," Leon said to them, "regain your courage. We are numerous, and shall be able to start again tomorrow morning without any fear of being disquieted by the Indians."

"Captain," Maria answered him, "it is vain for you to try and tranquillize us; we have heard what the soldiers are saying to one another, and they are prepared for an attack which appears to them inevitable."

"Señor Captain," Inez said, in her turn, "we are the daughters and sisters of soldiers, so you can tell us frankly to what we are exposed."

"Good heavens! do I know it myself?" Leon remarked. "I have taken all the precautions necessary to defend the hacienda dearly, but still I hope that we shall not be discovered."

"You are deceiving us again," Maria said with a smile, which was sorrowful, though full of grace and charms.

"Besides," Leon continued, without replying to the young lady's interruption, "be assured that, in the event of an attack, both I and my men will be dead ere an Indian crosses the threshold of this door."

"The Indians!" the young ladies could not help exclaiming, for they had before them the recollection of their captivity at Garakouaïti, and trembled at the mere thought of falling into their hands again.

Still, this terror was but momentary. Maria's face soon reassumed the delicious expression which was habitual to it, and it was with the softest inflexion of her voice that she addressed him.

"Captain," she said to him, "my sister and I wish to ask a favour of you—will you promise to grant it to us?"

"What is it, Señora? Speak, for you know that I am only too happy to obey the slightest wish of yours."

"Then you swear to grant it me, whatever it may be?"

"Without doubt," Leon answered; "but what is it?"

"Give me the pistols hanging from your girdle."

"Pistols! Great Heaven! what would you do with them?"

"Kill ourselves," Maria said, simply, "sooner than return to the Indian city."

"Oh! am I not here to defend you?"

"We know it," Inez added, "and know, too, that you are the noblest and bravest of all your comrades: but I join my entreaty to that of my sister, and beg you not to refuse us."

"If you were killed, Leon," Maria at length said, "must not I die too?"

Inez looked at her sister, and was silent.

Leon started, and drew the pistols from his girdle.

"Here they are," he said, as he handed them to the ladies.

And, without adding a word, he left the room, with his face buried in his hands. Maria and Inez threw themselves into each other's arms, and passionately embraced.

At the moment when Leon re-entered the patio, Harrison walked up to him, and said, as he pointed to several rows of black dots, which seemed crawling at no great distance from the hacienda—

"Look there, captain."

"They are Indians," Leon answered; "every man to his post."

An hour passed in horrible anxiety. All at once, the hideous head of a redskin appeared above the enclosing wall, and took a ferocious glance into the patio. Leon raised his axe, and the Indian's body fell back outside, while the head rolled at the captain's feet. Several attempts of the same nature, made at different points of the wall, were repulsed with equal success.

Then the Indians, who had expected to surprise a few sleepy guasos, on seeing themselves so unpleasantly received, raised their war yell, and rising tumultuously from the ground on which they had hitherto been crawling, bounded upon the wall, which they tried to escalade on all sides at once. A belt of flame then flashed forth round the hacienda, and a shower of bullets greeted them. Several fell, but their impetuosity was not checked, and a fresh discharge, almost in their faces, which caused them enormous loss, was unable to repulse them.

Ere long, assailants and assailed were contending hand to hand. It was a fearful combat, in which men only loosed their hold to die, and in which the conquered, frequently dragging down the conqueror in his fall, strangled him in a last convulsion. For nearly half an hour it was impossible to judge how matters went; the shots and the blows of axes and sabres followed each other with marvellous rapidity.

At length the Indians fell back: the wall had not been scaled. But the truce was not long; the Indians returned to the charge, and the struggle recommenced with new obstinacy. This time, in spite of the prodigies of valour, the smugglers, surrounded by the mass of enemies who attacked them on all sides simultaneously, were compelled to fall back on the house, defending every inch of ground; their resistance could not last much longer.

At this moment shouts were heard in the rear of the Indians, and Wilhelm rushed upon them like a hurricane at the head of his band. The redskins, surprised at this unexpected attack, fell back in disorder, and dispersed over the country. Leon, taking advantage of the opportunity, dashed forward at the head of twenty men to support his ambuscading party and complete the defeat of his enemies. The pursuit did not last long, however, and the smugglers returned to the hacienda, for the Indians had vanished like shadows.

Two hours passed without any incident. Leon gave orders to repair the damage done by the enemy, and then went to the young ladies, in order to learn how they had endured this fearful assault. On entering the room, he stumbled over the body of an Indian. The captain recoiled; a cold perspiration bathed his face; a convulsive tremor seized upon him, and he was on the point of losing his senses. A terrible thought crossed his mind; he feared he should see the young ladies killed. Looking sharply about the room, he saw them crouching in a corner, and a cry of delight burst from him.

"Oh!" he exclaimed, "what has happened here?"

Maria, without answering, took the torch, which was burning in a ring against the wall, and illumined the Indian's countenance.

"Tcharanguii!" he exclaimed.

"Yes," she said, "and it was this that killed him." She displayed with savage energy the pistol that she held in her hand.

"Oh!" said Leon, falling on his knees, "Heaven be thanked!"

"Captain, captain!" Wilhelm shouted, as he rushed into the room, "here are the Indians!"

Leon hurried out. The fight had recommenced between his men and the Indians. Day was beginning to break, and discovered an entire army of Indians forming a circle round the hacienda.

"Comrades!" Leon said, in a thundering voice, addressing the smugglers, "we cannot hope to conquer, but we must die like brave men."

"We will!" they replied, with an accent of sublime resignation.

They were only twenty-nine in all, for sixty had been killed in the first two attacks.

"Do not let us waste our powder," Leon added; "but make sure of our aim."

The horizon was gradually growing clearer, and friend and foe could perfectly distinguish each other. There was something painful in this spectacle of twenty-nine calm and stoical men, who had all made a sacrifice of their life, and were preparing with heroic carelessness to support the onrush of thousands of implacable enemies.

All at once Leon uttered a cry of surprise; he had just recognised the grand chief of the Moluchos, who was advancing at the head of a portion of the army to carry the hacienda by storm.

"Diego!" he shouted.

"Leon!" Tahi-Mari replied.

And then turning to the fighting Indians, he commanded them to stop.

Then, rushing towards the man who had been his friend, he said—

"You here! Why, unhappy man, you must wish for death!"

"Yes," Leon replied.

"Oh! I will save you!"

"Thanks, Diego. But will you also save those who are with me?"

"Those who are with you have killed five hundred of my men during the night. Oh! the incarnate demons! Yes, I ought to have suspected it; you alone were able to withstand an army for a whole night in a dismantled ruin. Save them," he added—"no, it is impossible."

"In that case, good-bye," Leon said, as he prepared to turn away.

"Where are you going, brother?"

"To die with them, since their death is resolved."

"Oh, you will not do that?"

"Why should I not do it? Why have you forgotten, that you were for a long time their leader, but will now sacrifice them to your blind fury?"

"Oh! I cannot let the Soto-Mayor family escape thus!"

"That family left me at the Parumo of San Bautista, after the Indian bullets had killed the general's wife."

"Are you speaking the truth?"

"I have only two ladies with me."

"Wait!" said the chief of the redskins, and returned to his band.

Leon said a few words to Wilhelm, who dashed into the house to inform the young ladies that they were out of danger, but only on condition that they wrapped themselves so carefully in their rebozos that their features could not be recognised.

Leon saw Tahi-Mari talking with great animation for about ten minutes among the Molucho chiefs: at length they separated, and Diego returned to him.

"Brother," he said to him, "you are an adopted son of the Moluchos; you can retire withersoever you please with the men whom you command, without fear of being disquieted."

"Thanks, brother," Leon said; "I recognise you in that."

"Where will you go?" Diego asked again.

"To Valparaíso."

"Good-bye."

"Why good-bye; do you never wish to see me again?"

"How?"

"Listen; in a week I shall be free from any engagement. Where will you give me a meeting?"

"At the Rio Claro," said the Indian chief.

"I will be there."

The two friends parted as in the happy days of their friendship, and then the captain joined his men, while the Indian put himself at the head of his army again.

"To horse!" Leon then said.

The smugglers obeyed; and then forming a close squadron, they left the hacienda at a canter, having the two veiled ladies in their midst. The Indian army made way for them to pass; and the twenty-nine men rode with head erect through the dense ranks of the Moluchos, who watched them pass without evincing the slightest impression. Six days after, Maria and Inez de Soto-Mayor were in safety behind the walls of the convent of the Purísima Concepción.

CHAPTER XXV
THE ARREST

The appearance of Valparaíso had greatly changed. It was no longer the careless, laughing town which we have described, echoing from morning to night with gay love songs, and whirling round with a wild sambacueca. No! its gaiety had faded away to make room for sombre anxieties. Although its sky was still as pure, its sun as hot, and its women as lovely, a veil of sadness had spread over the forehead of the inhabitants, and chilled the smile on every lip. The streets, usually so full of promenaders and so noisy, were gloomy and silent. The shops—nearly all deserted and closed—no longer displayed to purchasers from all countries those thousand charming trifles of which the Creoles are so fond.

Numerous troops of soldiers were encamped in all the squares; strong patrols marched through each district, and the ships anchored in the bay, with nettings triced up and ports opened, were awaiting the moment for action; while at intervals the beating of the drums or the dull ringing of the tocsin, terrified the timid citizens in their houses, where they hid themselves under triple bolts and locks.

What was occurring, however, was sufficient to excuse the terror of the alarmed population. Tahi-Mari, the great Molucho chief, at the head of the twelve allied Araucano nations, after seizing the forts of Araucas and Tulcapel, and massacring their garrisons, had taken Valdivia, which he plundered, and continuing his march with more than two hundred thousand Indians, had subjugated Talcahueno, Concepción, Maule, and Talca. In spite of the desperate efforts and courage of General Don Pedro Sallazar, who at the head of six thousand men had vainly attempted to arrest the invader, the Spanish army, conquered in five successive actions, was dispersed, leaving Tahi-Mari at liberty to march upon Santiago, the capital of Chili.

Only one resource was left Don Pedro Sallazar, that of collecting the relics of his defeated army, and entrenching himself on the banks of the

Massucho, in order to dispute its passage with the Indians, who were preparing to cross the river. This he did with the help; of four thousand men, whom Don Juan brought to him, though not without difficulty.

The President of the Republic had called under arms all the youth of Chili, and in the towns, pueblos, and villages, the citizens had eagerly placed themselves at the disposal of the military authorities, who had armed and sent them off to Valparaíso, which was selected as headquarters, owing to the proximity of that town and Santiago.

On the eighth day after the arrival of General Soto-Mayor's daughters at the convent of the Purísima Concepción, at about midday, three or four thousand men, forming the volunteer contingent, were piously kneeling in the Plaza del Gobernador and attending the divine service, which the Bishop of Valparaíso was celebrating in the cathedral for the success of their arms. In all the towns of the republic, novenas and public prayers had been ordered, to implore heaven to save the country from the immense danger which menaced it.

When mass was ended, the soldiers rose to their feet and closed up in line. Then a brilliant staff, composed of general officers, at the head of whom was the commandant of Valparaíso, came out of the cathedral and stood on the last step of the peristyle. The governor stretched out his arm as a signal that he wished to speak, and the drums beat a prolonged roll. When silence was re-established, he said:—

"Chilians! the hand of God presses heavily upon us: the ferocious Indians have rushed upon our territory like wild beasts; they are firing our towns, and plundering, burning, massacring, and violating on their passage. Soldiers, you are about to fight for your homes; you are the last hope of your country, who is looking at you and counting on your courage; will you deceive its expectations?"

"No!" the volunteers shouted, brandishing their weapons frenziedly. "Lead us against the Indians!"

"Very good," the general continued; "I am happy to see the noble ardour which animates you, and I know that I can trust to your promise. The President of the Republic, in his solicitude for you, has chosen as your commander one of the noblest veterans of our War of Independence, who has claimed the honour of marching at your head—General Don Juan de Soto-Mayor."

"Long live General Soto-Mayor," the soldiers cried. The general, upon this, stationed himself by the side of the governor, and all were silent for the sake of listening to him.

"Soldiers!" he exclaimed, in a fierce voice, and with a glance sparkling with enthusiasm, "I have sworn to the President of the Republic that the enemy should only reach Santiago by passing over our corpses."

"Yes, yes, we will all die. Long live General Soto-Mayor!"

At this moment the doors of the cathedral, which had been shut, were noisily opened; a religious band could be heard; the bells rang out loudly; a cloud of incense obscured the air; and an imposing procession, with the bishop at its head, came out under the portico, and ranged itself there while singing pious hymns. On seeing this, soldiers and generals knelt down.

"Christians!" said the bishop, a venerable, white-haired old man, whom two vicars held under the arms, "go whither duty summons you. Save your country, or die for it. I give you my pastoral blessing."

Then, seizing a magnificent standard, on which sparkled a figure of the Virgin, embroidered in gold, he said—

"Take this consecrated flag. I place it in the hands of your general, and Nuestra Señora de la Merced will give you the victory!"

At these words, pronounced by the worthy bishop, a perfect delirium seized upon his hearers, and they swore with many imprecations and with tears in their eyes to defend the flag which General Soto-Mayor waved over their heads with a martial air, and to conquer or die in following him. The volunteers then marched past the staff and the clergy, and returned to their cantonments at the Almendral.

The general had already taken leave of the governor, as the troops had completely evacuated the square, and was preparing to return to the mansion which he had inhabited since his arrival from Valdivia, when he heard his name pronounced behind him just as he was on the point of mounting his horse. He turned his head quickly, and uttered a cry of joy on recognising Captain Leon Delbès.

"You here!" he said.

"Heaven be praised, I have found you, general!"

"Where are my girls?" the old gentleman asked, anxiously.

"Saved."

The general opened his arms to the young man, who rushed into them.

"Oh, my friend, what do I not owe you! My poor children! for mercy's sake take me at once to them. Where have you left them?"

"At the convent of the Purísima Concepción, general, as I pledged myself to do."

"Thanks! Come then with me; while we are going we will talk together, and you will tell me how I can recompense the eminent service which you have done me."

"General, I beg you do not revert to this subject. When I started to seek the two young ladies who had been torn from you I accomplished a duty, and I cannot and will not accept any reward."

The general looked at Leon, seeking to read his thoughts in his face, but he could not divine anything.

"Ah!" he answered, "we shall see. Caramba! You are a man of heart, but I have a desire to be a man of my word. Let us hasten at once to the convent, for I am longing to embrace my poor girls."

"But, general, my presence may perhaps be inopportune—I am only a stranger, and—"

"Sir! the man who devoted himself to save my children cannot be regarded as a stranger either by them or me."

The captain bowed.

"Let us start," Don Juan continued. "You are on foot, so I will send my horse home."

"Pray do not do so, general, for my horse is waiting a few yards off."

Leon whistled in a peculiar manner, and almost immediately the general saw a horseman, leading another horse by the bridle, turn out of the Calle San Agostino. It was our old acquaintance, Wilhelm.

"Here it is," said Leon.

Wilhelm had come up, and after saluting the general, said to the smuggler, in a low voice:

"Captain, here is a letter which has arrived for you, and which Master Crevel bade me to give you, adding that it was very pressing."

"Very good," said Leon, taking it and putting it in his pocket, without even looking at the handwriting. And he leapt on his horse.

"Follow us," he shouted to Wilhelm.

"All right, captain."

The two gentlemen rode off in the direction of the convent, escorted by Wilhelm, and followed by the general's servant. On the road the general overwhelmed Leon with questions as to the way in which he had contrived to find his daughters; and the captain described his expedition to him. When he came to the rescue which he accomplished by pretending to deliver Inez and Maria from the possession of the fiend, the general could not restrain a burst of laughter.

"On my word, captain, what you did there denotes on your part great boldness and profound skill. I knew that you were a courageous fellow, but I now see that you are a man of genius."

Leon tried to defend himself against such a flattering qualification, but the general insisted, while repeating the expression of his gratitude. In this way they reached the convent gates, and the general and Leon went in. Here again the young man was obliged to repeat to the curious abbess the details of his Odyssey.

The general yielded to all the transports of a real joy, and never tired of lavishing the tenderest caresses on those whom he had thought eternally lost. It was then that the memory of the beloved wife who no longer lived returned to him with all the greater force. Heavy tears poured from his eyes, and were mingled with those of his daughters.

"My children," he said to them, "Heaven has recalled your mother from my side, and your brother, Don Juan, is at this moment exposed to all the horrors of civil war. Hence I should only have you to cherish if my son succumbed beneath the blows of our cruel enemies. Remain here, then, my children, in this holy house, until the re-establishment of peace restores us better days."

"What! are you going away again, father?" Inez asked.

"I must. I have been intrusted with the command of a division, and I owe the little blood left me to the defence of my country."

"Oh, Heaven!" the young ladies exclaimed.

"Reassure yourselves: I hope to see you again soon: the walls of this convent will preserve you from external dangers. I leave you here without anxiety, until I return to be present at your taking the veil, my good Maria, and your marriage with Don Pedro Sallazar, my dear Inez."

The young ladies made no reply, but simultaneously glanced at the smuggler, whose face was extremely pale.

"It is to you that I confide them, my sister," the general continued, addressing the abbess. "Watch carefully over them, and whatever may happen, only act on my orders, or those of my son, if I am killed, as regards Maria's taking the veil or Inez's departure, for the war may—produce great changes and unforeseen catastrophes."

"You shall be obeyed, general," the abbess replied.

The general embraced his daughters for the last time, and prepared to depart; but at the moment of separating from their father they appeared visibly affected. Maria looked at Leon, striving to read in his face an encouragement to confess to the general the slight inclination she felt for a conventual life. The captain understood the maiden's desire, but his face did not speak, and hence Maria's lips did not move.

On her side Inez appeared to have formed some violent resolution, for with purpled cheeks she addressed the general, while repressing the beating of her heart.

"Father," she said to him, with an effort, "before you leave us, I wish to say a few words to you without witnesses."

The tone in which these words were uttered produced a certain impression on the general.

"What have you to tell me, my child?"

"You shall know directly, father."

"Allow me to withdraw, general," said Leon; "besides," he added, "I have some business to settle, and—"

"Señor, Inez has secrets to reveal to me," the old gentleman said, with a smile. "I will let you go; but only on condition that you come and see me tonight before I set out for Santiago."

"I shall not fail, general."

"Good-bye then, for the present, captain."

Leon bowed, and after exchanging a few compliments with the persons present, left the room. The abbess also retired, though somewhat reluctantly, followed by Maria, and the general found himself alone with Inez. Let us leave him and his daughter together for a moment, and accompany Leon, who found Wilhelm waiting at the gate.

"What is the matter with you?" he asked him, as he mounted his horse; "you have a very singular look today."

"Well," the German replied, "it is because I see some fellows I do not like prowling about here."

"What do you mean?"

"Nothing, except that we had better be on our guard."

"Nonsense, you are mad!"

"We shall see."

"In the meanwhile, let us make haste, for Diego is waiting for us at the Rio Claro, and time is slipping away."

The two smugglers rode off in the direction of the spot fixed by Diego for the meeting he had given the captain. Leon was thinking of the scene which he had just witnessed at the convent, and was asking himself what Inez could have to say to her father. Wilhelm was looking around him suspiciously. They rode on thus for about ten minutes, when just as they were turning the corner of the great Almendral street and preparing to leave Valparaíso, a dozen alguaciles barred their passage.

"In the name of the law I arrest you, Señor Delbès!" one of them said, addressing Leon.

"I beg your pardon," the smuggler said, laying his hands on his pistols, and raising his head.

Wilhelm followed his example.

"Shall we drop them?" he asked, eagerly, in a whisper.

"We two could certainly kill eight!" Leon replied; "but I fancy that would do us no good, as we are beset."

In fact, the first two men were joined by other ten, and a large band of serenos speedily surrounded them.

"Surrender!" said the man who had before spoken.

"I must do so," Leon replied; "but tell me why you arrest me?" Then he bent down to Wilhelm and whispered—"You know where we were going; proceed there alone, and tell Diego what has happened to me."

"All right; trust to me."

"Gentlemen," Leon continued, "I have asked you for what motive you arrest me; will you be good enough to tell me?"

"We do not know," the head of the serenos answered. "I have orders to make certain of your body and the rest does not concern me. For the third time, are you willing to follow us peaceably?"

Leon reflected for a few seconds, and answered in the affirmative.

"In that case, uncock your pistols."

He raised his arms and discharged his pistols in the air.

"Why, what are you about?" the sereno exclaimed; "you will give an alarm!"

"You told me to uncock my pistols, and I did more, I unloaded them. What more would you have?"

"Enough argument; march!" said the man.

"March!" the captain repeated.

And surrounded by a strong squad of police, Leon was carried off to the governor's house. This arrest, and the two shots heard in this part of the town, had brought to the spot a large number of curious persons. Wilhelm mingled among them, and joined the mob that was awaiting the prisoner coming out.

Ten minutes passed, and at the expiration of that time Leon reappeared, escorted by twenty serenos, who led him to the Calabozo, situated on the Almendral, at no great distance from the Convent of the Purísima Concepción, where he was safely placed under lock and key. Wilhelm understood that he would have no hope of seeing his captain again by waiting longer.

"Good!" he said to himself, "I know where to find him now: let us make haste to go and warn Diego or Tahi-Mari, for I really do not know what to think of our friend and foe, the captain's lieutenant."

Whereupon the worthy German buried his wide spurs in his horse's flanks, which started at a gallop in the direction of the Rio Claro.

"No matter; all this does not appear to me clear," the smuggler muttered. "Well, we shall see."

Night was beginning to fall. As he left the town, the angelus was ringing in all the churches, and the tattoo sounding in all the streets of Valparaíso.

CHAPTER XXVI
THE SCALP

It was about ten o'clock at night. It was cold and foggy; the wind whistled violently, and heavy black clouds coming from the south dropped heavy rain upon the ground. Between Valparaíso and Rio Claro —that is to say, in the gorge which had many times served as a refuge for the smugglers, and which our readers are already acquainted with—Tahi-Mari indolently lying at the foot of a tree, was rolling a papelito in his fingers, while lending an attentive ear to the slightest sounds which the gust conveyed to him and at times darting glances around him which seemed trying to pierce the obscurity.

"Ten o'clock already," he said, "and Leon not yet arrived: what can detain him? It is not possible that he can have forgotten the hour of our meeting. I will wait longer," he added, as he drew his mechero from his pocket and lit his cigarette, "for Leon must come back to me—he must absolutely."

Suddenly a sound so light that only an Indian's ear could seize it, crossed the space.

"What is that?" Diego asked himself.

He rose cautiously, and after concealing his horse in a dense thicket, hid himself behind the trunk of an enormous tree close by. The sound gradually drew nearer, and it was soon easy to recognise the gallop of a horse at full speed. A few minutes later a rider turned into the clearing; but he had not gone a few yards when his horse stumbled against a stone, tottered, and in spite of the efforts of the man on its back, slipped with all four feet, and fell.

"Der Teufel! Carajo! Sacrebleu!" Wilhelm shouted, as he fell, borrowing from all the languages he spoke the expressions best adapted to render the lively annoyance which he felt at the accident which had happened to him.

But the German was a good horseman, and the fall of the horse did not at all take him unawares. He freed his feet from the stirrups and found himself on his legs. Still, on looking around him, he noticed that the clearing which was deserted on his arrival, had become peopled, as if by enchantment, by some fifty Indians, who seemed to have sprung out of the ground.

"The deuce!" thought Wilhelm; "I fancy there will be a row, and I am afraid that I shall come off second best."

At this moment a shrill whistle was heard, and the Indians disappeared so rapidly that the German rubbed his eyes to see whether he was awake.

"Hilloh!" he asked himself, "is this an apparition, and are they demons or men?"

Then, seeing that he was really alone, he busied himself with raising his horse.

"There," he continued, when the animal was on its legs again, "I will wait till Señor Diego arrives. Plague take the spot; it does not appear to me so sure as formerly, and our ex-lieutenant might have chosen another."

"Here I am, Wilhelm!" Diego said, suddenly, as he stood before the smuggler.

"Well, I am not sorry for it, lieutenant," the German answered, phlegmatically.

"What do you want here?" the other asked him, sharply.

"I have come because the captain ordered me to do so, that is all."

"Why did Leon send you in his place? I was expecting him here."

"Ah, that is another matter, and you must not be angry with him."

"But," Diego continued, biting his moustache savagely, "what does he expect me to do with you?"

"Hang it all—whatever you like."

"But where is he?"

"He is arrested."

"How!—arrested?"

"Yes; and it was before being imprisoned in the Calabozo, that he ordered me to go in all haste and warn you."

"Arrested!" the half-breed said, stamping his foot; "that scoundrel of a Crevel has betrayed me, and shall pay dearly for it."

"Crevel, do you say, lieutenant? Well, it is possible; and yet I do not think so."

"I am sure of it."

"Why so?"

"I sent him a letter which he was to deliver to Leon, and in which I warned the latter of the danger that menaced him."

"A letter, you say; and when did you send it?"

"This morning early."

"Ah!" said Wilhelm, "I have it."

And he told Diego how—as Leon had gone out when the letter arrived at Crevel's—the latter asked him to deliver it to the captain, and that when he received it, he put it in his pocket without reading, absorbed as he was in his conversation with General Soto-Mayor.

"What! is the general at Valparaíso?" Diego asked, interrupting the smuggler.

"Yes, lieutenant; but he will not be so for long."

"Why not?"

"Because the governor had just given him command of the new body of volunteers, who are going to reinforce the Chilian army at Santiago."

"That is well."

Tahi-Mari whistled in a peculiar way, and an Indian appeared. The chief of the Molucho army said a few words to him in a low voice. The Indian bowed as a sign of obedience, and, gliding through the herbage, disappeared. Wilhelm looked on at the scene, whistling to give himself a careless air. When the Indian had gone, Tahi-Mari turned to him, and laid his hand on his shoulder.

"Wilhelm," he said to him, "you love your captain, do you not, my lad?"

While uttering these words his searching glance was plunged into the smuggler's eyes, as if questioning his thoughts.

"I love the captain? Der Teufel! do you doubt it, lieutenant?"

"No! that will do; you are an honest fellow."

"All right."

"But listen to me. Will you save him?"

"Certainly. What am I to do for that?"

"I will tell you. Where is Leon's band?"

"At Valparaíso."

"How many men does it consist of at this moment?"

"Forty."

"Would they all die for their captain?"

"I should think so."

"In that case, you will assemble them tomorrow at Crevel's."

"At what hour?"

"Eleven o'clock at night."

"Settled."

"Pay attention that Crevel does not open the door to any persons who do not rap thrice, and say Diego and Leon."

"I will open it myself."

"That will be better still."

"After that, what are we to do?"

"Nothing; the rest is my business: remember my instructions, and be off."

"Enough, lieutenant."

Wilhelm remounted his horse and set out on his return. At about a league from Valparaíso he met the column of volunteers marching to Santiago, and gaily advancing while singing patriotic airs. Wilhelm who was not at all desirous of being arrested as a suspicious person for travelling at this hour of the night, drew up by the wayside, and allowed the men to defile past him. When the last had disappeared in the distance, the German returned to the high road, and half an hour later re-entered Valparaíso, puzzling over the remarks of Tahi-Mari, whose plans he could not divine.

In the meanwhile, the volunteers continued to advance, filling the air with their martial strains. They formed a body of about four thousand men; but of this number only one-half were armed with muskets—the rest had pikes, lances, or forks; but their enthusiasm—powerfully inflamed by the copious libations of aguardiente which the inhabitants of Valparaíso had furnished to them—knew no limits, and made them discount beforehand a victory which they regarded as certain.

These soldiers of the moment had been selected from the lowest classes of society, and retained a turbulence and want of discipline which nothing could conquer. The citizens of Valparaíso, who feared them almost as much as if they had been Indians, were delighted at their departure, for, during their short stay in the town, they had, so to speak, organized plunder, and made robbery their vocation.

General Soto-Mayor did not at all deceive himself as to the qualities of the men whom he commanded, and perceived at the first glance that it would be impossible to obtain from them the obedience which he had a right to demand. In spite of the repeated orders which he gave them at starting to observe, the greatest silence on the march, through fear of being surprised by the Indians, he found himself constrained to let them act as they pleased, and he resolved to let the army bivouac on the road, while he proceeded to his country house, whence he could dispatch a courier to Santiago, requesting officers to be sent him who could aid him in restoring some degree of order among the men he commanded. It was evident that such a disorderly and noisy march exposed them to be murdered to a man in the first ambuscade which the Araucanos prepared for him.

It was about one in the morning when the volunteers arrived at the general's country house. It was plunged in profound obscurity; all the shutters were closed, and the watch dogs barked mournfully in the deserted courtyards. After ordering a halt for some hours the general proceeded towards his residence. At the sound of the bell a heavy footfall was heard inside, and a grumbling voice asked who was knocking at such an hour, and what he wanted.

When the general had made himself known, the gate turned heavily on its hinges, and Señor Soto-Mayor entered, not without a painful contraction of the heart, the house which recalled to him such affecting recollections. Alas! long past were the happy days which he had spent in this charming retreat, surrounded by all those to whom he was attached, and resting from the fatigues of a gloriously occupied life.

The old gentleman's first care was to send off the courier, and then, after taking out of the manservant's hand the candle which he held, he entered the apartments. This splendid residence, which he had left so brilliant and so animated, was now solitary and deserted. The rooms he passed through, on whose floor his foot echoed dully, were cold; the atmosphere which he breathed was impregnated with a close and unhealthy odour, which testified the little care the guardians of the house had displayed in removing it; on all sides were abandonment and sadness.

At times the general's eyes fell upon an object which had belonged to his wife, and then they filled with tears, while a deep sigh issued from his oppressed chest. At length, after visiting in turn all the apartments in the house with that painful pleasure which persons feel in evoking a past which cannot return, the general opened the door of the room which had served as his bedroom. He could not restrain a start of terror. A man, seated in an easy chair, with his arms folded on his chest, seemed to be awaiting somebody.

It was Diego.

"Come in, my dear general," he said, as he rose and bowed courteously.

"Señor!" said the general.

"Yes; I understand. It astonishes you to see me here: but what would you have? Circumstances allowed me no choice; and I am sure that you will pardon me this slight infraction of etiquette."

The general was dumb with surprise at the sight of such audacity. Still, when the first flush of indignation had passed, feeling curious to know the object of the person who behaved to him so strangely, he restrained his anger and awaited the result of this singular interview.

"Sit down, general, pray," Diego continued, keeping up his tone of assurance.

"I thank, you, sir, for your politeness in doing the honours of my house; but before aught else, I should wish to know the reason which has procured me this visit."

"I beg your pardon, general," the other replied, with a slight tremor in his voice; "but perhaps you do not recognize me, and so I will—"

"It is unnecessary, sir. I remember you perfectly well; you are a smuggler, called Diego the Vaquero, who abandoned us after engaging to escort us, as did Captain Leon Delbès, in whose service I believe you were."

"That is perfectly correct, general; still the name of Diego is not the only one which I have the right to bear."

"That concerns me but slightly."

"Perhaps not."

"Explain yourself."

"If the Spaniards call me Diego, the Indians call me Tahi-Mari."

This name produced the same effect on the general as an electric shock.

"Tahi-Mari!" he exclaimed. "You!"

"Myself!"

A flash of hatred animated the eyes of the two men, who seemed measuring each other like two tigers brought face to face. After a moment's silence, the general continued:

"Can you be ignorant that I have round the house in which we now are four thousand men ready to hurry up at my first summons?"

"No, general; but you do not seem to know that I, too, have in this house two hundred Indians, who are watching each of your movements, and who would rush on you at the slightest signal I gave."

The general's lips blanched.

"Ah! I understand," he said. "You have come to assassinate me after killing my wife, for now I no longer doubt but that it was you who had us surprised in such a cowardly fashion in the Parumo of San Juan Bautista."

"You are mistaken, general: it was not I who made you a widower; and it was in order that none of my men should tear from me the prey I covet, that I have come myself to fetch it."

"But what impels you to be so furious against those of my race, so that the name of Tahi-Mari may be equivalent to that of the murderer of the Soto-Mayors."

"Because the Soto-Mayors are all cowards and infamous."

"Villain!"

"Yes, infamous! and it is because I have sworn to exterminate the last of the accursed family that I have come to take your life!"

"Assassin!"

"Nonsense; a Tahi-Mari fights, but he does so honourably—face to face. Here are two swords," Diego continued, pointing to the weapons lying on a cheffonier, "choose the one you please; or if you like, you have your sabre, and here is mine. On guard! and may heaven protect the last of the Tahi-Maris, while destroying the last of the Soto-Mayors!"

"I have a son who will avenge me," the general exclaimed.

"Perhaps not, Señor Don Juan, for you know not whether he is dead or alive."

"My son!—oh!"

And the general, overpowered by a feverish excitement, furiously drew the pistol which he had in his belt and discharged it point-blank at Diego. But the latter was following his movements, and at the moment when the general's hand was lowered at him, he cut through his wrist with a sabre-stroke. The general uttered a cry of pain, and the bullet broke a mirror.

"Oh, oh!" Diego exclaimed, "ever treacherous; but we are too old enemies not to know each other, and hence I was on my guard, general."

The old man, without replying, drew another pistol with his left hand and fired. But the badly aimed shot only grazed slightly the Indian's chest;

and the bullet, after making a scratch along one of his ribs, entered the panel of a door. Diego bounded like a lion on the old man, who had fallen to the ground, and whose blood was streaming from the frightful wound he had on his arm. Then he seized his long white hair, pulled up his head violently, and compelled him to look him in the face.

"At last, Soto-Mayor, you are conquered!" he shouted.

The old man collected the little strength left him in a supreme effort; his eyes sparkled with fury, his countenance was contracted with disgust, and he spat in his enemy's face. At this supreme insult Diego uttered a frightful howl, and then drew his knife with a demoniacal grin.

In the meanwhile the sound of the pistol shots had spread an alarm among the volunteers, and a party of them rushed tumultuously into the house. When the soldiers entered the general's bedroom, after breaking in the door, they found the window open and the old man stretched out on the floor, bathed in blood. In addition to the horrible mutilation of his arm, he had a hideous wound on his head, from which the blood streamed down his face. Diego had scalped the unfortunate Don Juan de Soto-Mayor.

A cry of horror burst from every mouth, and they hastily gave the wounded man all the care which his wretched condition required.

CHAPTER XXVII
THE CAPTURE OF THE CONVENT

Since the invasion of the Araucanos, Crevel's hostelry had lost much of its old splendour. No longer was heard the clink of glasses or the smashing of window panes which the noisy customers broke while discussing their affairs. The bottles remained methodically arranged on the shelves that lined the shop, and the time when Crevel earned a few piastres a month, merely by counting as new the cracked ones which his customers threw at his head in the guise of a peroration, had passed away. The most utter vacuum had taken the place of the overflow.

At the most, not more than one or two passers-by came in during the course of the day to drink a glass of pisco, which they paid for, and went off again directly in spite of all the efforts and cajolery of the banian, who tried to keep them in order to talk of public affairs and cheer his solitude.

On the day after Leon Delbès' arrest, however, the house offered, at about ten in the evening, a lively appearance, which formed a strange contrast with the calmness and tranquillity which the state of war had imposed on it. The shop was literally encumbered with customers, who smoked without saying a word.

The silence was so religiously observed by them that it was easy to distinguish the sound of the rain falling outside, and the hoofs of the police horses which echoed dully on the pebbles or in the muddy pools which covered the soil.

At nightfall the worthy landlord, who had not seen his threshold crossed since the morning by a single customer, was preparing to shut up, with sundry execrations, when an individual suddenly entered, then three, then four, then ten—in a word, so large a number that he found it impossible to count them. All were wrapped in large cloaks, and had their broad-brimmed hats pulled down over their eyes so as to render their features unrecognisable.

Crevel, agreeably surprised, prepared to serve his guests, with the assistance of his lads; but though the proverb says that it is impossible to have too much of a good thing, the extraordinary number of persons who seemed to have given each other the meeting at his house assumed such proportions, that our landlord eventually became alarmed, as he did not know where to house the newcomers. The crowd, after invading the ground floor room, had, like a constantly-rising tide overflowed into the adjoining one, and then ascended the stairs and taken possession of the upper floors.

When ten o'clock struck, forty customers peopled the posada, and, as we said, not a single syllable was exchanged between them. Crevel comprehended that something extraordinary was taking place in his house; and he sought for means to get rid of these silent guests by affecting preparations for closing his inn, but no one appeared to catch his meaning. At this moment a sereno offered him the pretext which he was awaiting by shouting outside—

"Ave Maria purísima las diez han dado y llueve." The stereotyped phrase of the night watchman, though accompanied by modulations which would make a cat cry, produced no impression on the company. Hence Crevel resolved to speak.

"Gentlemen," he said aloud, as he stood in the middle of the room with his hands on his hips, "it is ten o'clock, you hear, and I must absolutely close my establishment."

"Drink here!" the customers replied, in chorus—accompanying the sentence by dealing vigorous blows on the table with their pewter measures.

Crevel started back.

"Really, gentlemen," he tried to continue, "I would observe to you that—"

"Drink here!" the topers observed, in a voice of thunder.

"Ah! that is the game, is it?" the exasperated landlord cried, who felt all his courage return with his passion. "Well, we will see whether I am master of my own house."

He rushed towards the door, but had not taken a step in the street, when a newcomer seized him by the arm and unceremoniously thrust him back into the room, saying, with a mocking air—

"What imprudence, Master Crevel, to go out bareheaded in such weather! You will catch an awful cold."

Then, while the banian, confused and terrified by this rude shock, was trying to restore a little order in his ideas, his addresser, behaving just as if he were at home, and assisted by two customers, to whom he gave a signal, fastened the window shutters, bolted and locked the door as well as Crevel's lads could have done it.

"Now let us talk," said the newcomer, as he turned to the stupefied landlord. "Do you not recognise me?" he added, as he doffed his hat.

"Monsieur Wilhelm!" Crevel exclaimed.

"Silence!" the other remarked.

And he led the master of the posada into a retired corner of the room.

"Have you any strange lodgers here?" he asked him, in a low voice.

"No! if you know this legion of big demons who have collected in my house during the last hour—"

"Well! I am not alluding to them. I ask you whether you have any strangers lodging here. As for these gentlemen, you must know them as well as I do."

"From the cellar to the garret there is not a soul beside these gentlemen; but as I have not yet been able to see so much as the end of their noses, it was impossible for me to recognise them."

"These are all men belonging to the captain's band, you humbug!"

"Nonsense! In that case, why do they hide their faces?"

"Probably, Master Crevel, because they do not wish them to be seen; and now send your lads to bed, being careful to lock them carefully into their attic, and after that we will see."

"Then, something is going to be done?"

"When you are told you will know. In the meanwhile, execute my orders."

"All right! all right!"

And Crevel, without any further urging, went off to carry out the order he had received, with the promptitude of a man who knows how to obey when he hopes to makes a profit by his obedience. When he had left the room, Wilhelm turned to his comrades, who, during the conversation, had remained motionless and apparently indifferent to what was going on.

"Up, gentlemen!" he said to them.

They all rose.

"Call down your companions from upstairs," Wilhelm said again.

One of the men went upstairs, and two minutes after the whole of the smugglers were collected round the German.

"Are you all here?" he asked.

"Yes," they replied.

"Armed?"

"Yes."

"You know that we have assembled to deliver the captain?"

"Yes; we are ready."

At this moment three knocks were heard on the outside shutter.

"Wait," said Wilhelm. "Silence!"

He walked to the door.

"What do you want?" he said.

"Diego and Leon," a voice replied.

"Very good."

The door was opened, and Tahi-Mari entered.

"Diego!" the smugglers exclaimed, joyfully.

"Myself, lads," the half-breed answered, as he cordially pressed the hands offered him. "I have come to help you to deliver Leon."

"Bravo! long live Diego!"

"Silence, my friends! we must be prudent if we wish to succeed, for we have two expeditions to attempt: hence we must arrange our plans carefully in order to make no mistake. The first is against the Convent of the Purísima Concepción."

The smugglers made a face.

"The second," Diego continued, without appearing to notice the effect which the word convent had produced on the smugglers, "is against the Calabozo, where the captain is locked up."

"Good!" the smugglers said; "we are listening." He then explained to them all the details of his plan, and when everything was settled, they prepared to set out.

"Hilloh, though," Diego suddenly exclaimed, "what has become of Crevel?"

"He has gone to lock up his lads," Wilhelm replied.

"A good precaution; but he is a long time over it."

"Here he is," a smuggler remarked.

"Señor Don Diego!" Crevel said with amazement, on perceiving the ex-lieutenant of the band.

"Good evening, Crevel. I am delighted to find you in such good health."

"Thanks, caballero, but you are too obliging."

"Come, make haste, take off your apron, put on your cloak, and come with us."

"I?" the landlord said, with a start of terror.

"Yes, you."

"But how can I be of any service to you?"

"I will tell you. Captain Leon informed me that you stood well with the sisters of the Convent of the Purísima Concepción."

"Oh, oh! up to a certain point," Crevel answered.

"No false modesty. I know you possess the power to have the gates opened whenever you think proper, and hence I invite you to accompany us for that purpose."

"Oh, Lord! what can you be thinking of?" the startled banian remarked.

"No remarks; make haste, or by Nuestra Señora de la buena Esperanza, I will set fire to your hovel."

A heavy groan escaped from Crevel's breast as he prepared to obey. It was striking half-past ten by the cathedral dock. A second later the Voice of the sereno croaked close to the posada.

"Ave Maria Purísima, las diez y media han dado y señora," he cried.

"It seems that it has left off raining?" said Wilhelm. "All the better."

"Come, make haste," said Diego, with a sign to the German.

"I understand, lieutenant."

Wilhelm crept out of the posada, whose door was only on the jar. A moment later, a fall, a stifled groan, and a whistle were heard.

"Let us be off," Diego went on, pointing to the door, through which Crevel passed meekly. All the smugglers glided out of the inn, and walked a few yards behind each other, careful to remain in the shadow, and preserving the deepest silence. A few minutes after, they came up to Wilhelm, who was bearing on his shoulders a bundle, whose shape it was at the first glance impossible to recognise.

"Here is the sereno," he said; "what shall I do with him?"

And the German pointed to the bundle on his shoulders, which was nothing else, in fact, but the hapless watchman.

"Take him with us," Diego answered. "A passer-by might liberate him, and that would be enough to raise an alarm."

"Very good," said Wilhelm, and he followed the party.

The smuggler had simply waited for the sereno at the corner of a house, and when he saw him at a convenient distance, lassoed, gagged, and bound him, and threw him across his wide shoulders, no more or less than if he had been a bale of goods.

The band proceeded toward the Almendral. All the serenos they met underwent the same fate as the first; like him, they were prevented from stirring or shouting, and taken on a smuggler's back. Thanks to this clever manoeuvre, they reached the walls of the convent without obstacle. Eight serenos had been captured during the walk, and when they reached their destination Diego ordered his men to lay them at the foot of the wall which surrounded the convent. Then he turned to Crevel and said—

"Now, compadre, we have reached our destination; we are in front of the convent; and it is your business to get us inside."

"But, in Heaven's name, how do you expect me to do that? You do not reflect that I have no means to—"

"Listen," Diego said, imperiously. "You understand that I have no leisure to discuss the point with you. You will either introduce us into the convent—in which case this purse, containing two hundred and fifty gold onzas, is yours—or you refuse, and then," he added, as he coldly drew a pistol from his pocket, "I blow out your brains with this."

A cold perspiration broke out on Crevel's forehead, who knew Diego too well to insult him by doubting his intentions.

"Well?" the other asked, as he cocked the pistol. "Do not play with that thing, lieutenant; I will try my best."

"To give you a better chance of success, here is the purse," the half-breed said, throwing it to him.

Crevel seized it with a start of delight which it would be impossible to describe; then he walked toward the convent gate, while racking his brains as to how he should contrive to earn the money and run the least possible risk. A luminous thought crossed his brain, and it was with a smile on his lips that he raised the hammer to knock. All at once the half-breed stopped his arm.

"What is it?" Crevel asked.

"It has struck eleven long since; everybody is asleep in the convent, and so it would perhaps be better to try some other method."

"You are mistaken," the banian replied; "the portress is awake."

"Are you sure of that?"

"Hang it all!" the other replied, who had his plan, and was afraid that he must restore the money if Diego drew back from his resolution; "the convent of the Concepción is open day and night to people who come in search of medicines; so leave me alone."

"In that case, go on," said the leader of the party as he let go his arm.

Crevel did not allow the permission to be repeated, and, through fear of a fresh objection, hastened to let the knocker fall, which echoed noisily on the copper boss. Diego and his men were standing in the shadow of the wall. A moment after, the trapdoor was pulled back, and the wrinkled face of the sister porter appeared in the opening.

"Who are you, my brother?" she asked, in a sleepy voice; "and why have you knocked at our gate at such an hour?"

"Ave Maria Purísima!" Crevel said, in his most sanctified voice.

"Sin pecado concebida. Brother, are you ill?"

"I am a poor sinner whom you know, sister, and my soul is plunged in affliction."

"Who may you be, brother? I fancy I recognize your voice, but the night is so dark that I cannot see your face."

"And I sincerely hope that you will not see it," Crevel mentally remarked; and added aloud—"Oh, sister, you know me perfectly well. I am Signor Dominique, the Italian, and keep a locanda on the Port."

"Oh yes, I remember you now, brother."

"I fancy she is nibbling," Crevel muttered.

"What do you want, brother? hasten to inform me, in our Saviour's name; for the air is very cold, and I must continue my orisons."

"My wife and two children are ill, sister, and the reverend pater guardian of the Carmelites recommended me to come and ask you for three bottles of your miraculous water."

"Good gracious!" the old woman exclaimed, her eyes sparkling with delight; "three bottles!"

"Yes, sister; and I will ask your permission to rest myself a moment, for I am so fatigued that I can scarce stand."

"Poor man!" the sister porter said, pityingly.

"Oh! it would really be an act of charity, sister."

"Señor Dominique, pray be good enough to look about and see that there is no one in the street, for we are living in such bad times that it is impossible to take sufficient precautions."

"There is nobody, sister," the banian answered, as he made his comrades a signal to hold themselves in readiness.

"In that case, I will open."

"Heaven will reward you for it, sister."

The creaking of a key in a lock could be heard, and the door opened.

"Come in quickly, brother," the nun said.

But Crevel had prudently withdrawn, and made way for Diego. The latter seized the portress by the throat, and pressing her neck in both his hands like a vice, whispered in her ear—

"One word, wretch, and I kill you!"

Horror-struck by this sudden attack, the old woman fell back unconscious.

"Deuce take the old devil!" Diego said, angrily; "who can guide us now?"

He tried to recall the sister to her senses, but seeing that it was impossible to do so, he made a sign to his men, who had rushed into the convent after him, to gag her and bind her securely. Then, after leaving two smugglers as sentries at the gate, he took the bunch of keys with which the portress was entrusted, and prepared to enter the building occupied by the nuns.

It was no easy task to discover in this immense Thebaïs the cell occupied by Doña Maria—for our readers will have understood that the object of the expedition attempted by Diego, was to carry off that young lady. It remains for us now to explain what the half-breed intended to do with her, and by what reasons he had been urged to commit such a deed.

We must say in the first place, that Diego had the most lively desire to attach to his cause, Leon, whom he knew to be a man of bravery and energy, and was urged to do so not only because he intended to give him a command in the Araucano army, but also because he had no sooner parted with Leon after the altercation which they had while escorting the family of General Soto-Mayor, than he regretted the rupture, now sought every means in his power to effect a reconciliation with Leon, the only person in the world he loved.

The first thing he did for this object was to grant Leon what the latter had demanded so pressingly, the liberation of Don Juan, the old general's son. He knew that he must not dream of thwarting his friend's love for Maria, and awaited the end of this love in order to act, thinking that the captain, at the moment when he saw himself on the point of being separated from her whom he loved, would not recoil from the idea of carrying her off. When he afterwards came across him in the half-burned hacienda, and delivered him from the false position in which he was placed, Diego did not at all suspect that one of the females with him was no other than Maria; and great was his surprise when the result of his enquiries told him that Leon had himself conducted the young lady back to the Convent of the Purísima Concepción.

Certain that Delbès had only acted thus in obedience to the chivalrous promptings of his heart, and not wishing him to be the dupe of the honourable feelings which had dictated his conduct by losing Maria for ever, the half-breed resolved to restore her to him in spite of himself by simply carrying her off; and he calculated that the rumours and scandal produced by such an event, would prevent the Soto-Mayor family from offering any opposition to the marriage. We see that although this reasoning was brutal, it was to a certain extent logical.

Now, in order to carry off Maria, she must be found, and it was this that embarrassed Diego and his men, once that they had entered the convent by stratagem. At the moment, however, when they were beginning to lose all hope, an incident produced by their inopportune presence came to their assistance. The smugglers had spread through the courtyards and cloisters, careless of the consequences which their invasion might produce, and with shouts and oaths seemed desirous of searching the convent from cellar to garret.

The nuns, habituated to silence and calmness, were soon aroused to this disturbance, and believing that the fiend was the author of it, they hurriedly leaped from their beds, and, scarce clothed, ran to seek shelter in the cell of the abbess, while uttering heart-rending cries of terror. The latter lady, sharing the error of her sisters, had hurriedly dressed herself, and assembling her flock around her, advanced resolutely toward the spot whence the noise proceeded, holding in the one hand a holy water brush, and in the other her pastoral staff, with the intention of exorcising the demon. Suddenly she perceived the smugglers, but ere she could utter a cry Diego rushed toward her.

"Silence!" he said; "we do not intend you any harm; leave us alone."

Dumb with terror at the sight of so many armed men, the women stood as if petrified. All at once, Diego noticed a novice who was clinging convulsively to her companions.

"That is the girl!" he said to his men; "it is she whom I want!"

And joining actions to words, he seized Maria, while the other smugglers kept back the abbess and the other sisters, who were more dead than alive. Two men gagged the young lady, and prepared to carry her off.

"Let us begone!" said Diego.

"Villain!" the abbess at length exclaimed, thinking of the terrible account which she would have to render to General Soto-Mayor, "if you have the slightest fear of heaven, restore me that young lady!"

"Silence!" Diego replied.

And pointing a cocked pistol at the abbess, he forced her to be a spectatress of what was going on. At this moment, another young lady, with agitated features and garments in disorder, rushed toward the half-breed, and, clinging to him, shrieked despairingly —

"My sister! — give me back my sister!"

Diego turned, his eyes sparkled, and his face assumed an expression of hatred which made the nuns turn pale.

"Oh, oh!" he said, with a ferocious joy; "Inez here?"

"Yes, I am Inez de Soto-Mayor, and this is my sister; for mercy's sake, restore her to me."

"Your sister? Yes, I will restore her to you, but not yet;" and seizing the poor girl in his powerful arms, he raised her in his arms, and threw her over his shoulder.

"Now, let us be off, my men," he shouted to the smugglers, who stood round him gloomy and silent, as if ashamed of their cowardly conduct. Ten minutes later, no one remained in the convent but its peaceable inmates. Once outside, Diego ordered Wilhelm and Crevel to carry Maria to the posada kept by the latter, with instructions to deposit her in the green room. Then wrapping Inez in a poncho, he entrusted her to two other smugglers, whom he led into a little lane, where a man on horseback was waiting. This done, he rejoined his band, who advanced prudently towards the Calabozo, keeping in the shadow of the walls, and redoubling their precautions.

This time they would not have to deal with harmless women, but with soldiers. And let us say it in praise of the men whom Diego commanded, they were desirous of fighting with enemies capable of defending themselves, in order to expiate the disgraceful part which they had played in the affair of the convent.

A sentry was walking up and down in front of the prison, and a cavalry picket was stationed a short distance off. The smugglers had dispersed, and anxiously waited till Diego should form a decision. The latter was cursing the presence of the cavalry, and knew not what he had best do. All at once the prison gate opened: two torches gleamed in the obscurity, and Diego saw the Governor of Valparaíso come out, and, at his side, Captain Leon Delbès, with whom he was conversing.

The half-breed made a sign to his men to conceal themselves in the doorways, and walked alone toward the two gentlemen, while feigning the movements of a belated passer-by. The torch bearers had re-entered the prison, and the governor was mounting his horse, and taking leave of Leon.

"I thank you, general," the latter said, "for the eagerness you have displayed in setting me at liberty."

"On learning your arrest, captain, General Soto-Mayor hurried to tell me that he would be answerable for you, and to beg me to release you from prison, which I should have done sooner had I not been compelled to be absent from Valparaíso the whole day, for an affair of the highest importance."

"Pray believe, general, in my deep gratitude."

"Do not forget, if any misadventure were again to happen to you, to apply to me, and I will hasten to come to your aid."

Leon bowed his thanks for the last time, and the two gentlemen parted. The general, followed by his escort, returned to the palace, and Leon walked toward the Calle San Agostino. He had not gone twenty yards when he came face to face with Diego, who had turned back to meet him.

"Good evening, Leon," he said to him.

"Diego! you here! what do you want here, imprudent man?"

"I came to save you, but I see that you do not require my assistance, and I congratulate you on it."

"Thanks, brother!" Leon answered, with emotion. "As you see, I am free."

"In that case, I have only to withdraw with the men who joined me for this enterprise."

The smugglers had left their lurking places, and thronged round their captain.

"Thanks, my friends, thanks for what you intended to do. I shall not forget it."

"Now," Diego continued, "I have nothing more to do here, and so I am off. Good-bye, Leon; you will soon hear from me."

"What! are you going?"

"To join my friends. And you?"

"I intend to remain at Valparaíso."

"Good! I need not repeat that, whenever you like to join us, you have only to come."

"Thanks, brother! I have not forgotten it."

"Once again, good-bye."

"Let me at least accompany you."

"No; do you go to Crevel's, for your presence may be necessary there."

"What do you mean by that?"

"You will soon learn."

And, without further explanation, Diego proceeded to the spot where the smugglers who guarded Inez were waiting for him. The man on horseback dismounted. Diego took his place, and, throwing Inez across the saddle, he dashed off at full speed along the Santiago road, shouting—

"Each his share! I have mine!"

The two smugglers rejoined their comrades, and then the band divided in two parts: one moiety returned to Dominique, the Italian's, where they were lodged, while careful to hide from their landlord the compromising part which Crevel had thought proper to make him play in the drama at the convent. The other smugglers scattered about the obscure hostelries of which there were such a large number on the Almendral.

CHAPTER XXVIII
AN INDIAN VENGEANCE

It was a frightful thing to see Diego's headlong gallop along the road from Valparaíso to Santiago. In the shadows of the night, the shapeless group of the horse, and the two human beings it bore, made the sparks fly out of the pebbles on the road. The animal's powerful hoofs bounded along, pounding everything that they settled on, while its outstretched head cleft the air. Its ears were erect, and from its open nostrils issued jets of steam which traced long white tracks in the darkness.

The horse dashed along, uttering snorts of pain, and biting between its clenched teeth the bit which was covered with foam, while blood and perspiration poured from its flanks, which were torn by the spurs of its impatient rider. And the greater its speed grew, the more Diego tortured it, and tried to make it go faster. The trees, the houses, and rocks disappeared with an extraordinary rapidity on either side of the road.

Inez, half dead at the moment when the half-breed dragged her from the convent, felt herself recalled to life by the movement which the horse imparted to her body. Her long hair trailed in the dust, and her eyes, raised to heaven, were bathed in tears of despair, grief, and powerlessness. At the risk of dashing out her brains against the stones, she made extraordinary efforts to escape from her ravisher's arms.

But the latter, fixing on her a glance whose expression revealed ferocious joy and lubricity, did not appear to notice the horror which he caused the maiden; or rather, he appeared to derive from it a source of indescribable pleasure. His contracted lips remained dumb, and only at intervals allowed a shrill whistle to pass, destined to redouble the ardour of his steed, which, exasperated by the pressure of its rider, hardly touched the ground, as it were, and devoured the space like the fantastic courser in the German ballad.

"Stay, child," Diego said, suddenly, as he raised Inez on his horse's neck, and compelled her to look at a country house which they were passing; "here is your father's house, the haughty General Soto-Mayor, call him to your assistance."

And a savage grin succeeded these words.

"Father!" the maiden cried, whom he had freed from her gag—"father!—father!"

This cry died away in hollow echoes, and the house disappeared again in the dizziness of this mad ride and the horse still galloped on. Suddenly Inez, collecting all her strength, leaped forward with such vivacity that her feet were already touching the ground, but Diego was on his guard, and ere she had regained her balance, he stooped down without checking his horse, and seizing the maiden by her long hair, he raised her, and placed her again before him. A sob burst from Inez' chest, and she fainted.

"Oh! you will not escape me," the half-breed shouted; "I have you, and no one in the world will be able to tear you from my hands!"

In the meanwhile, day had succeeded darkness; the sun rose in all its splendour, and myriads of birds saluted the return of the light by their joyous carols. Nature was awakening gaily, and the sky of a transparent azure, promised one of those lovely days which the blessed climate of South America has alone the privilege of offering.

A fertile and deliciously diversified landscape stretched out on either side of the road, and became blended with the horizon. The maiden's lifeless body hung on either side of the horse, following all the joltings which it imparted; with her head thrown back, and covered with a livid pallor, eyes closed, lips blanched and parted, teeth clenched, neck bare, and bosom heaving, she palpitated under the large hand of the Vaquero, which pressed heavily upon her.

At length they reached a devastated hacienda, in which a hundred Indians, painted for war, were encamped. Tahi-Mari gave a signal, and a horse was brought him. It was high time, for the one which had borne him from Valparaíso hardly halted ere it fell, pouring from mouth, nostrils, and ears a flood of black thick blood. Diego got into the saddle again, caught up the maiden in his arms, and prepared to continue his journey.

The Indians, who doubtless only awaited the coming of their chief, imitated his example, after throwing a few flaming logs upon the roof of the hacienda, in order to leave a trace of their passage. Ere long the whole band, at the head of which Diego placed himself, dashed forward, surrounded by the cloud of dust which they raised.

After a few hours' ride, whose rapidity surpasses all description, the Indians saw the lofty steeples of the capital of Chili standing out on the horizon, beneath a cloud of smoke and fog which hung over the city. The Araucanos turned slightly to the left, galloping through the fields, and trampling down the rich crops that covered them. In about half an hour they reached the first Indian sentries, and they soon found themselves within the camp of the twelve Molucho tribes.

Let us examine for a moment the state in which the war was. As we have already said, after several sanguinary combats, the Chilians, suddenly attacked by the Araucanos, who had invaded their territories on all sides at once, to the number of 200,000, had been, in spite of prodigies of valour, completely defeated and compelled to retreat.

The Moluchos had surprised their enemies without giving them time to assemble. The population of Chili was only composed, at that time, of two million and a half, scattered over a territory of vast extent, nearly as large as Germany. The towns are very remote from each other, and the means of transport are almost unknown. We can therefore understand the difficult position in which the besieged found themselves.

The Chilian army, which should be composed of 10,000 men, never consists of more than 7,000, scattered through distant garrisons; and for that very reason it is very difficult to assemble it under pressing circumstances. The soldiers, usually recruited by force, are, as a rule, thorough scamps, whom peaceful people fear as much as the Indians, for they know that when they pass into a province they plunder, burn, and violate absolutely as if they were in a conquered country. Hence the government only quarters a very small number in the great centres of population, removes them as far as possible, and subdivides them so as to be able to keep them under more easily, and never allows a whole regiment to remain in the same province at once.

What became of this organization when the Araucanos declared war? The Chilian government, attacked simultaneously on all sides, was unable, in spite of all its efforts, to collect a force sufficiently imposing to boldly face the Indians and drive them back. Hence, the only chance was to check their advance by harassing them and having outpost fights, by means of which it was hoped that they might be discouraged, and induced to return to their forest fastnesses.

These tactics were certainly good, and had often been employed successfully. This time again they would have, in all probability, succeeded, through the military science and discipline of the Spaniards, if they had not had to contend against this countless mass of Indians, and above all, if the latter had not been commanded by Tahi-Mari. The Molucho chief had not indulged in idle boasting when he told the Ulmens of the twelve nations that he was acquainted with all the resources of the Spaniards, and was certain of conquering them.

In fact, after dashing on Valdivia like a starving tiger on the prey it covets, his road as far as Santiago had been one triumphant progress, in which he overthrew, destroyed, and plundered everything, and left behind him a long sanguinary track, marked at intervals by numerous horribly mutilated Spanish corpses. Advancing with a sword in one hand and a torch in the other, this modern Attila wished to reconquer the Chilian territory by wading up to his knees in Spanish blood.

Nothing was sacred to him, neither age nor sex; old people, women and children, were pitilessly tortured. The twenty years which he had spent in traversing the various countries of America had proved of service to him, by familiarizing him with strategic ideas and the mode of employing military forces, through watching the manoeuvres and exercises of the Spanish armies, whose entire strength consisted in skilful tactics. Tahi-Mari's first care, therefore, was to employ the ideas which he had acquired in introducing a species of discipline in the ranks of the Moluchos.

The Chilians no longer understood the method of fighting the Indians. They no longer had the skirmishes to which they were accustomed, but real battles, fought according to all the rules of warfare, whose observance on the part of Araucanos beyond measure surprised them.

In this way victors and vanquished had arrived beneath the walls of Santiago. The Indians, after pushing on a reconnoisance even in the suburbs of the city, had boldly halted a short distance from its gates, and were bravely preparing for a storm. A frightful terror had seized on the inhabitants of Santiago. The richer emigrated in crowds, while the rest prepared, like the troops, to offer a vigorous resistance.

The President of the Republic had smiled disdainfully, when he saw from the ramparts the enemy getting ready for a serious attack; but when he had distinguished the perfect concord with which this multitude acted—with what skill the posts were established—taking advantage of the slightest accident of ground, and only operating with the most consummate prudence; selecting with discernment the weakest spots of the fortress, and holding the river Mapucho above and below the city, so as to let no succour or provisions reach it—his forehead became wrinkled with anxiety, and a deadly fear seized upon him; for he understood that his enemies were guided by an experienced chief, whose military genius would easily overcome the obstacles opposed to him, if time were granted him to take his measures and establish himself securely in the position which he occupied.

It was then that the President of the Republic, no longer doubting the imminence of the danger which the country was incurring, made an energetic appeal to the patriotism of the Chilians; an appeal to which they responded enthusiastically by hurrying up from all sides to range themselves under his banner. But time was needed for this succour to arrive, and to come the enormous distances that separated it from the capital. In order to gain this time, the president feigned a desire to treat with the Indians, and pave the way for negotiations.

The redskins had established their camp in the smoking ruins of the charming country houses which surrounded the city, and whose magnificent gardens, now, alas! devastated, seemed to make Santiago stand out from a basket of flowers. Nothing could be conceived so filthy, repulsive, and frightful as the appearance of this camp, forming a girdle round the city. It was hopeless to look for parallels or covered ways; not even a sentry could be seen watching over the common safety.

The camp was open on both sides, and at first sight it might have been supposed deserted, had not the dense smoke rising from the wigwams, made of branches and erected without any apparent order, proved that it was inhabited. A gloomy silence prevailed day and night in this strange camp, and no human being was visible there.

The Chilians, though thoroughly acquainted with the crafty character of their enemies, had allowed themselves to be trapped by this semblance of neglect and carelessness. Two days after the Moluchos sat down before the city, a strong Chilian patrol, consisting of two hundred resolute men, left the city about midnight; and, deadening the sound of their footsteps as far as possible, advanced into the very centre of the camp without being disquieted. Everybody seemed asleep, and no sentinel had given the alarm. The leader of the expedition, satisfied with the result which he fancied he had obtained, was preparing to return to Santiago to report the result of his reconnoisance to the besieged, when, on turning back, he found every line of retreat interrupted, and a countless swarm of Indians surrounding him.

The officer who had fallen into the trap did the only thing that was left him: he fell bravely at the head of the men whom he commanded. On the next morning, at sunrise, two hundred heads, scalped and horribly disfigured, were thrown by the Moluchos over the walls of Santiago. The Chilian Spaniards took the hint, and did not repeat the experiment.

When Tahi-Mari entered the camp with his band, the Indians flocked up tumultuously, and received him with loud yells of delight. He made them a sign of thanks, and without checking his pace, went toward his lodge, in the doorway of which Shounon-Kouiretzi, crouching on his heels, was gravely smoking. On seeing the commander he said—

"Tahi-Mari is a great chief; is he contented with his journey?"

"Yes," Diego replied, laconically. "My brother will watch at my door, and allow no one to enter."

"My brother can trust to me; no one shall enter." And the Indian began smoking again, impassively. Diego went in, carrying Inez, wrapped up in a poncho. After removing her bonds, he laid her on some sheepskins, thrown in a corner of the hut, which served him as a bed. Then he fetched a calabash of water and dashed the contents in her face, but Inez still remained motionless.

On seeing this, Diego bent down and devoted to her the greatest attention, in order to recall her to her senses; anxiously consulting her pulse, raising her in his arms, tapping her hands, and employing, in a word, all the means usual for restoring a fainting person. For a long time his efforts were sterile, and life seemed to have abandoned the poor girl for ever.

"Can she be dead?" Diego muttered.

And he began attending to her again. At length a sigh burst from Inez's bosom, she languishingly opened her eyes and uttered a few broken words in a faint voice. All at once she rose.

"Where am I?" she screamed.

Diego, without answering, fell back into a dark corner of the lodge, and fixed a serpent glance upon her.

"Where am I?" she repeated. "Maria! sister! how I am suffering! Oh, Heaven!"

Her memory gradually returned, and everything flooded back to her mind. Then a shudder of terror agitated all her limbs, her haggard eyes wandered around, and she perceived Diego.

"Oh, that man!" she said, as she hid her face in her hands. "I am lost! Great God, I am lost!"

Diego issued from his corner, and with his eyes fixed on her, slowly advanced toward her. Fascinated by the half-breed's sparkling glance, she fell back step by step, with her arms stretched out, and displaying signs of the most violent terror.

"Leave me, leave me!" she murmured. She thus reached the walls of the hut, clung to the intertwined branches, and stood motionless, while still looking at her persecutor, who walked toward her with an ironical smile.

"Leave me!" she repeated, unable to offer Diego any other resistance but her tears and her despair. But he was not the man to be affected.

"Leave you!" he answered; "do you fancy that I brought you all this distance to restore you innocent and pure to those who are dear to you? Undeceive yourself; henceforth you belong to me, and you will not leave this spot till you have nothing left to refuse me."

"Oh, mother, mother!"

"Your mother is dead, and no one can come to your assistance—do you hear; no one?"

"In that case, kill me," Inez cried, as she threw herself at the half-breed's feet.

"No! it is your honour, not your life, that I must have."

"But what have I done to you? Great Heaven, I am only a poor girl, and you cannot be so cruel to me without a motive."

"No, you have done nothing to me, and I feel for you neither hatred nor love; but you are the daughter of General Soto-Mayor. Your family dishonoured mine, and you will be dishonoured to expiate the crimes of your relatives."

"Oh, that is frightful; you will not act thus, because you know very well that I am innocent."

"Your ancestor dishonoured the wife of my grandfather, and she has still to be avenged."

"Mercy, mercy!"

"No! eye for eye, and tooth for tooth!—for you the shame, for me the vengeance!"

"In your mother's name, pity!"

"My mother!"

This word produced such an impression on the half-breed that he bounded with rage, and his face assumed a fresh expression of rage and fury.

"Ah, you speak to me of my mother! Mad girl! you do not know, then, that she found herself one day in the path of a Soto-Mayor, and that he brutally and cowardly plunged her into ignominy in order to satisfy a moment of brutal desire?"

"Oh, Heavens!" Inez sobbed.

"You do not know that while the poor woman was grovelling in despair at his feet, and imploring him, in the name of her God, to spare her, the villain laughed and caught her in his arms. Do you now understand why I forbid you invoking my mother's name?"

"Oh, I am lost!" Inez said, broken-hearted. "For the man who avenges himself on the child of his enemy has no heart."

"Yes, you are lost! But if you fancy that my revenge, in seizing you, has spared your father, you are mistaken, for he died by my hand."

"Woe! woe!" the girl shrieked, mad with grief.

"Yes, crushed by my blows, as I will crush all those of your race! No, you will not escape me! It is now your turn to cry and groan—your turn to implore in vain."

And, with the howl of a wild beast, the Indian, whose eyes were bloodshot, and his mouth foaming, rushed frenziedly at Inez and hurled her back on the sheepskins. Then ensued a horrible and nameless struggle, in which the groans of the victim were mingled with the wild panting of the savage. Inez resisted with the violence of despair, but soon, crushed by the half-breed's grasp, she lay helpless, left to the mercy of the man who had sworn her dishonour.

"Brother," said Long-Scalp, appearing in the doorway, "two Spanish chiefs, followed by several lanceros have come to offer propositions of peace to the toqui of the twelve nations."

"Who are the chiefs?" Diego asked.

"General Don Pedro and Colonel Don Juan de Soto-Mayor," the Indian replied.

A smile of triumph played round the half-breed's lips.

"Let them come! let them come!" he said.

"Does my brother, Tahi-Mari, consent to receive them?"

"Yes," Diego continued, assuming his Indian stoicism. "My brother will assemble the great chiefs around the council-fire, and I will come thither."

Shounon-Kouiretzi bowed and retired.

"The betrothed and the brother. They have arrived too late," Diego said, so soon as he was alone.

And he left the hut, in order to preside at the council. Inez was motionless on the couch of Tahi-Mari, the great chief of the Araucanos.

CHAPTER XXIX
THE GREEN ROOM

After wrapping himself carefully in his cloak, Leon pensively went along the streets leading to Crevel's inn. Diego's last words incessantly reverted to his mind, and he asked himself why the Indian had recommended him so eagerly to proceed to the posada. Another peculiarity, also, kept his mind on the rack; he had seen Diego take from the hands of the people waiting for him a large parcel which had all the appearance of a human body. He had also fancied that he heard a dull and plaintive groan from this bundle. "What could it be?" Leon asked himself in vain.

At length he reached the Calle San Agostino. The door of Crevel's inn was ajar, and a bright light illumined the interior. Leon went in. Crevel, seated at his bar, was talking in a low voice with Wilhelm, who, with his arms leaning on the chimney, was probably telling him some improper anecdotes, for the two men were laughing most heartily. The unforeseen arrival of the captain alone arrested the flow of their hilarity, and they exchanged a meaning glance which did not escape Leon.

"Still up!" the latter said.

"We were waiting for you, captain," Crevel answered.

"Thanks; but I would advise you to extinguish your lights, for people might be surprised at seeing them so late."

"That is quite true," said the landlord.

"Give me the key of the green room," Leon continued. "I need rest, and I will throw myself on the bed for an hour."

Crevel and Wilhelm looked at each other again, and winked in a most peculiar way.

"Did you hear me?" Leon resumed.

"Oh, perfectly, captain," the landlord replied. "You can go up, the key is in the door."

"Very good; in that case give me a light."

"You do not require it, for there is one in the room."

"Ah! now I see that you really did expect me."

"Eh, eh, I am not the only one."

"What do you mean?"

"I? Nothing, captain. Go up and you will see."

"See what?"

"I beg your pardon, captain, I forgot that it did not concern me, and that—"

"Come, Master Crevel, will you have finished soon or not? Of whom and of what are you speaking? Make haste and explain yourself."

"Why of the little Señorita up there—by the gods!"

"A woman in my room! Tell me, Wilhelm, do you know what Crevel is talking about?"

"Well, captain, you must know that—well—since—"

"Ah! I really believe that it would have been wiser to go upstairs and look for myself, you scoundrels."

And he prepared to ascend the stairs.

"Ah!" he said turning round and addressing Wilhelm; "do not stir from here without my orders, my boy, for I may want you."

"That is sufficient, captain."

Leon went out of the room, and, as he did so, heard the landlord, who was fastening his door, say to the German—

"The captain is a lucky fellow."

"That comes of being good-looking, Señor Crevel," the other replied.

More and more puzzled, the captain continued to ascend, and soon stood before the door of the green room. Crevel had told the truth, the key was in it, and a light could be seen gleaming through the cracks. The greatest silence, however, prevailed inside. After a moment's hesitation, the young man turned the key and entered, but at the first step he took he stopped and uttered a cry of surprise.

A young lady, seated in a chair, and dressed in the white garb of the novices of the Purísima Concepción, was sobbing and hiding her face in her hands. At the captain's cry, the girl started and quickly raised her head—it was Maria de Soto-Mayor.

Leon dared not believe his eyes. Maria in the green room! How did she happen to be here in the middle of the night? What could have happened? By what concourse of extraordinary events could she expect his coming? Wild with delight at this sudden apparition, the captain fell on his knees, murmuring—

"Oh, niña! bless you for being here."

And he tried to seize her hand and press it to his burning lips. Maria leaped out of the chair in which she was seated, and flashed at him a glance of supreme disdain.

"Whence, sir," she said, "do you derive the audacity to present yourself thus to me?"

"Señorita!" Leon said, surprised and discountenanced by Maria's hurried movement.

"Leave the room, sir," she continued, "and spare me at least the shame of listening to your remarks."

"Good Heaven!" Leon exclaimed, who began to suspect some infamous machination; "what have I done that you should treat me in this way?"

"You ask me what you have done? in truth, I do not know whether I am dreaming? would you learn it from me, then, and pretend not to know?"

"Oh, Maria! I am ignorant of the meaning of this: but on my mother's soul, I swear that a thought of insulting you never crossed my mind."

"In that case, sir, how do you explain your unworthy conduct?"

"I do not know to what you are alluding."

"Your presence here, sir, is a sufficient proof that you expected to find me here, even if you thought proper to deny your share in the abominable scandal which you have caused. Ah, Leon! could I suppose that you would offer me this outrage by publicly dishonouring me?"

"Oh!" Leon exclaimed, "there is some infernal mystery in all this. Maria, once again I swear to you that your every word is an enigma, and I ask you how it comes that I find you in this inn room when I believed you at the Convent of the Conception?"

Maria felt her convictions shaken by the accent of truth with which these words were imprinted: still, being unable to believe in the smuggler's innocence—so long as it seemed to her impossible that any other than he should have dreamed of tearing her from the convent—she resumed, though in certainly a milder tone—

"Listen, Leon. Up to this day I believed you a man full of honour and loyalty. Now the action which you have committed is infamous; but tell me that it was suggested to you by some wicked creatures. Tell me that you have obeyed an evil inspiration, and though I could not forgive you, for you have ruined me, I would try to forget and pray Heaven to efface your image from my heart. For mercy's sake let us leave this den as quickly as possible, and do not prolong a captivity which covers me with infamy."

"Do you want to drive me mad? Good Heaven! what can have happened during the hour since I left prison?"

"Prison!"

"Yes, señorita, the day before yesterday, after the visit which I paid you in the general's company, I was arrested and taken to the Calabozo, whence I was released scarce an hour ago."

"Can that be true?"

"Yes, on my honour."

"But, in that case, on whose authority did the man act who entered the convent at the head of his bandits and carried me off by main force?"

"Oh, Heavens!" said Leon, "that man! Oh, I understand it all now. Tell me, Maria, did you recognise his features?"

"Stay—yes, yes, it was certainly he."

"Who?"

"Your friend, who accompanied us on the journey to Valdivia."

"Diego!" Leon exclaimed.

"Yes, Diego."

"Oh, woe upon him, then!"

And seizing the bell rope he rang violently. In about a quarter of an hour, Crevel thrust a startled face through the half-open door.

"Do you want anything, captain?"

"Yes; send up Wilhelm at once."

The banian disappeared. Leon, suffering from a furious agitation, walked up and down the room displaying all the signs of a passion on the point of exploding. His face was pale; his muscles were contracted, and his eyes flashed fire. Wilhelm came in. At the sight of him Maria gave a start of terror, but Leon reassured her.

"Fear nothing, señorita; you are under my protection."

The German understood that he had committed some folly.

"Wilhelm," Leon said to him, fixing on him a scrutinizing glance, "listen carefully to what I am going to say to you, and answer me."

"Very good, captain."

"Where did you go the day before yesterday, after my arrest?"

"To Rio Claro, to find the lieutenant."

"What did he say to you?"

"He told me that he wished to deliver you, and gave me the meeting for last night at ten o'clock."

"He came here? What next?"

"Next, captain," the German said, twisting his hat between his fingers. "Well, it was—"

"Speak the truth; I insist on it."

"Well, the whole band was assembled."

"And what did you do?"

"Lieutenant Diego told us that you loved a novice in the convent of the Purísima Concepción, that he had sworn to make her yours, and we must carry her off."

"And then?"

"Then he led us thither, and by his orders we carried off the señora and brought her here to Crevel's, while Diego went off with another girl."

"Another, do you say?"

"Oh, Heaven!" Maria exclaimed.

"But who was it? Will you answer?" Leon commanded him, with a rough shake.

"On my word, captain, it was Doña Inez, the sister of Doña Maria."

"Malediction!" Leon said, furiously.

"Oh, my sister!—my poor sister!"

"The infamous fellow!" the young man continued; "what frightful treachery! Henceforth all ties are broken between us. This, then, was the vengeance he coveted!"

Then, addressing the German, who was looking at him anxiously, he said—

"Wilhelm, there is not a moment to lose; assemble our men, and let them all be here within an hour."

"All right, captain."

And the German dashed down the stairs at a tremendous pace. Leon then turned to Maria, who was sobbing.

"Courage, Señora. I cannot take you back to the convent, where you would no longer be in safety; but will you join your father at Santiago?"

"Do not abandon me, Leon, I implore you," she answered. "You alone can protect me. Oh, my poor sister!"

"If I cannot save her, I will avenge her in an exemplary manner."

The maiden no longer heard him. Absorbed in her grief, she dreamed of the fatality which had weighed on her ever since the day when her eyes first met Leon, and derived from them the love which was destined to change the calm life which she led at the convent into such terrible trials. Still, on seeing near her Leon—whose eagerness in lavishing attentions on her was incessant—she gave him a look of ineffable sweetness, while asking his forgiveness for having suspected him of complicity in the outrage of which she had been the victim.

"Maria," Leon said in reply, as he covered her hand with kisses, "do you not know that I would joyfully sacrifice my life at a sign from you?"

"Forgive me, Leon, for I should die if your love ceased to be as noble and pure as your heart."

"My love, Maria, is submissive to your wishes; it is the most fervent worship—the purifying flame."

"Leon, my sister is perhaps at this time abandoned defencelessly to the insults of her cowardly ravisher."

"Let me first restore you to your father, and then I will do all in my power to save your sister."

"What do I not owe you for so much devotion?"

"Have you not told me that you loved me?"

"Yes, Leon, I love you, and am proud of it."

"Oh, thanks!—thanks, Maria! God will bless our love, and I soon hope to tell your father of it. May he but approve of it."

"Does he not owe to you the life of his children? Oh, when I tell him how I love you, and how generous your conduct has been, be assured that he, too, will love you."

While the two young people were indulging in dreams of happiness and the future, Wilhelm was executing the captain's orders, and Crevel's posada was again filled by the members of the band. An hour had not elapsed when he came to tell Leon that everything was ready for departure.

"In that case," Leon said to him, "all you have to do is to select the best horse you can find in the landlord's corral, and get it ready for señorita Maria."

"All right, captain," Wilhelm answered, who knew no phrase better fitted to display his obedience than the one which he habitually used.

"All along the road to Santiago you and Joaquin will keep constantly by her side, and watch her carefully so that no accident may happen to her. Do you understand?"

"Yes, captain."

"In that case make haste, and here is something to hasten your movements," Leon continued, taking from his pocket some onzas and handing them to the German.

"Thanks, captain. You can come down with the niña whenever you like, for we shall be ready in a moment."

Very shortly after, in truth, Wilhelm was standing before the inn door, holding two horses—one for Leon, the other for Maria. When left alone with the latter, the captain took from under his cloak a large black manta, which he threw over the young lady's shoulders, and pulled the hood over her face.

"Now," he said to her, "let us go."

"I follow you," Maria answered.

Leaning on the young man's arm, she cautiously descended the stairs, and found herself in the midst of the smugglers who had invaded the convent. But, knowing that she was in perfect safety by Leon's side, she manifested neither surprise nor fear. Assisted by him, she mounted her horse, seized the reins, and placed herself resolutely in the first rank between Wilhelm and Joaquin.

The captain, after giving a final glance at his band, to assure himself that everything was in order, leapt upon the back of his mustang, and gave the order to start. The smugglers then proceeded at a sharp trot across the Almendral in order to reach the Santiago road.

CHAPTER XXX
THE CONFESSION

General Soto-Mayor had been hurriedly raised by the volunteers, whom the report of the two pistol shots had attracted to his room, a surgeon attached to the reinforcing column was summoned, and hastened to dress the old gentleman's frightful wounds. The terrible pain which the scalping caused him, and the immense quantity of blood he had lost, had plunged him into a profound fainting fit, from which it seemed impossible for him to recover. Upwards of three hours passed before he gave any signs of life. At length a faint sigh issued from his oppressed chest: he made a slight movement, his eyes opened slightly, and he muttered in a low and broken voice—

"Something to drink."

A servant brought him a bowl filled with a potion prepared by the doctor.

"Oh!" he said, a moment after, "my head is burning; what frightful pain!"

The surgeon begged him to be silent, administered a second potion, and a few minutes after the patient's eyes closed. He had fallen asleep.

"That is what I wanted," the surgeon said, as he felt his pulse and looked at him attentively.

"Well, doctor," an officer asked, "what do you think of the general's state?"

"I cannot say anything about it yet, gentlemen," he answered, addressing the persons who surrounded the old gentleman's bed; "his wounds are very serious, and yet I do not believe them mortal. We have numerous examples of scalped persons who have been perfectly cured. Hence it is not the wound on the head that alarms me the most, although it is the most painful. Tomorrow, as soon as I have removed the bandages, I shall be able to tell you what we have to fear or hope. Now, be kind enough to withdraw;

thanks to the potion, the general is enjoying a calm sleep, but the slightest noise might disturb him. I will instal myself at his bedside, and not stir till he is either dead or saved."

Upon this the doctor dismissed all the persons who filled the room, drew an armchair up to the bed, sat down in it in the most comfortable posture, took a book from his pocket, and prepared to spend the night as well as he could in reading. The peons accompanying the general, on seeing their master in so pitiable a state, unloaded the baggage and carried it into the casa. Then each resumed possession of his lodging, while congratulating himself in his heart at being no longer compelled to expose himself to the dangers of war.

After the misfortune which occurred to the general, the officer who took the command of the volunteers in his place sent out heavy patrols in all directions in pursuit of the Indians; but their search had no result, and they returned one after the other without discovering the slightest sign which could put them on the track of the assassins. They were, therefore, obliged to give up for the present all thoughts of taking vengeance for the odious attack which had been committed on the person of General Soto-Mayor.

Still this affair exerted a salutary influence over the mind of the volunteers. At the sight of so terrible a fact as the one which had just occurred, they understood how necessary prudence was when engaged with enemies so invisible and formidable as the Indians. They, therefore, began subjecting themselves to the claims of discipline. In consequence, they ceased their cries and songs, and fulfilled their military duties much more seriously than they had hitherto done.

The rest of the night passed away calmly and peaceably, and with the exception of two or three false alarms which the sentries in their inexperience gave, nothing happened to disturb the tranquillity of the volunteers encamped under the walls of the Casa de Campos. At sunrise, when the country illumined by the hot beams had lost the sinister and gloomy aspect which darkness imparted to it, the Chilians, who, without confessing it, had been in a state of real terror, gradually regained courage and recommenced their gasconade, though it was moderated by the recollections of the night.

At about eight in the morning the general woke up, and though he was very low and his weakness was extreme, the long sleep which he had enjoyed seemed to have greatly relieved his sufferings. The doctor, after carefully counting his pulse, began removing the bandages which he had placed. The appearance of the wounds was excellent; the flesh offered no extraordinary signs of inflammation—in a word, the patient was going on as well as could be expected. The wounds were washed, fresh bandages put on, and another potion made the general fall back almost immediately into the lethargic sleep from which he had roused himself.

When midday came, the suppurating fever set in with great intensity. The old man uttered inarticulate cries, made fearful efforts to leap out of bed, and talked with extraordinary vivacity, making unconnected remarks, whose meaning it was impossible to understand. The names of Diego, of Tahi-Mari, and of the different members of his family incessantly returned. The general was evidently suffering from some horrible delirium aroused by the terrible scene of which he had been the victim on the previous evening. Four powerful men were scarce sufficient to keep him down in his bed.

From three to four o'clock in the afternoon an improvement took place; the fever relaxed, the sick man's eyes lost that frightful stare and expression of wildness which terrified his attendants. He recognised his domestics, the doctor waiting on him, and even the officers who surrounded him. Everything led to the hope that the general would be saved; such at least was the opinion of the surgeon, who expressed it loudly.

At about six o'clock, the officers whom the general had dispatched to Santiago, returned to the country house, bearing the instructions of the President of the Republic. The officer who commanded the expedition in the general's place, opened and read them. They were formal.

The president gave orders to General Soto-Mayor to proceed by forced marches on the capital, which was in the greatest peril: he added that he could send him no officers, in spite of his urgent request, and concluded by requesting the general to read the despatch to the soldiers, in order to make them understand how much he reckoned on their patriotism in answering the appeal of the menaced country.

The officer intrusted with the interim command obeyed the orders which he received. He assembled the troops, read to them in a loud voice the contents of the despatch, and made them a short speech, in which, while exalting the powerful help which they might afford to the inhabitants of Santiago, he asked whether he could really reckon on them. A universal and enthusiastic outburst was the response to the general's speech, and immediate preparations were made for the departure.

The commandant—who did not wish to abandon General Soto-Mayor defencelessly in his house, which was open to all comers, and might at any moment be invaded by the Indians—chose from among his volunteers fifty men, to whom he entrusted the defence of the casa, after exhorting them to behave properly, and placing them under the command of an alférez. Then, this duty fulfilled, he took leave of the surgeon, after recommending him to neglect nothing in restoring the general's health, and took the road to Santiago at the head of his volunteers.

The night passed without any incidents worthy of record. The men left in charge of the house had closed the gates and had entrenched themselves in the interior. Toward morning they heard the sound of a horse galloping at full speed. They had scarce time to notice the rider, who departed rapidly, after halting for an instant before the house. Some inarticulate sounds reached the ears of the sentries, but before the latter could think of challenging, horse and rider were a long distance off. It was Diego returning to Santiago with his victim.

The general's state was satisfactory; the fever had considerably decreased, the wounds continued to offer the most favourable aspect, and with the exception of the atrocious sufferings he felt in his head, the old gentleman had regained a little calmness. Suddenly a loud sound of horses was heard on the road, and a servant hastened into the sick man's chamber, announcing that Captain Leon Delbès had just arrived, and had important news to communicate to the general. The surgeon tried to oppose the interview which Leon requested, alleging that his patient needed absolute repose; but, on the repeated entreaties of the latter, he was obliged to consent, though resolved to put a stop to it whenever he thought it advisable.

The captain, as we know, had left Valparaíso in the company of Maria, with the intention of proceeding under the escort of his band to Santiago, where he expected to find the general. But, while passing in front of the country house, he was astonished at seeing; the gates open, and a picket of lanceros in the courtyard. Not knowing to what to attribute the warlike appearance which this peaceful mansion had assumed, he halted his band and went up to the gate for the purpose of enquiring. The old manservant, who had been left as guardian, and had admitted his master two days previously, was at this very moment occupied in front of the house, and Leon questioned him.

The worthy man then told him in the fullest details the assassination attempted on the person of his master, and the hopeless efforts which had been made to discover the perpetrators. On listening to the narrative, the captain trembled and guessed at once that Diego must have passed that way. In truth he was the only man he knew capable of committing a similar crime and surrounding it with such mystery. Moreover, the project of vengeance which Diego nourished against the Soto-Mayor family, sufficiently indicated him to Leon for the latter to entertain no doubt as to his guilt.

Locking up in his bosom the feeling of horror which the half-breed's deed inspired him with, the captain returned to Maria to announce to her that her father, rather seriously wounded, was at the moment at the Casa de Campos, and hence it was unnecessary to go farther, and if she saw no inconvenience, he would at once place her in his hands. The young lady who, in following Leon, had no other object but to join her father and place herself under his protection, begged to be at once led to him. But, on Leon remarking that her unexpected presence might be fatal to the general, by causing him too lively an emotion, she consented that Leon should warn him first.

The captain led his band into the courtyard, and then sent a footman to the old gentleman to request an interview. When he entered the general's bedroom, and found him lying on a bed of pain, with his head wrapped up and his face more livid than that of a dying man, he felt affected by the deepest compassion. It was in fact a melancholy sight to see this old man, who had but a few days previously been so strong and robust, now broken by suffering and lying there horribly mutilated.

"Señor Don Juan, it is I, Leon Delbès," he said, addressing the wounded man.

The general offered him his left hand, and a smile played round his bloodless lips.

"Have you any new misfortune to announce to me, captain?" the old man said, in an almost unintelligible voice. "Speak—speak."

Leon started at the sound of this faint voice, and held his tongue, not daring to tell an unhappy man who was on the brink of the grave of the new misfortune which had fallen on him without his knowledge. The general noticed the young man's agitation, and felt that he had guessed aright.

"It concerns my daughters, does it not?"

"Yes, general," Leon replied, hanging his head sadly.

"Are they dead?" the old man asked, with a tremor in his voice.

The surgeon read in his face the nature of the feelings he was undergoing, and seemed to fear the captain's answer, but the latter hastened to speak.

"No, general, they are alive, and one of them accompanies me."

"But the other?"

"Is no longer in Valparaíso."

"What has happened, then, at the Convent of the Conception?—speak."

"It has been attacked, general."

"I understand," the old man said, "one of my daughters has fallen again into the hands of the Indians—the name of her who is left me?"

"Doña Maria, general!"

"And it is again you who restore her to me, my friend. Thank you, and Heaven grant that I may soon be able to reward you in the way you deserve."

Leon gave a gesture of refusal.

"Oh! I know how a noble heart like yours should be rewarded."

Leon bowed and made no answer.

"But, for mercy's sake, tell me what you know with reference to Inez, and do not be afraid of grieving me, for I am resigned to undergo all the misfortunes which God may send me as an expiation for my sins."

The young man then told him of the rape of Maria's sister, while carefully holding his tongue as to the circumstances under which he had recovered the other young lady. Then he told him of his intention of going to Santiago to find Diego, in whose power Inez was. On hearing that it was Tahi-Mari, who had robbed him of his child, the general, in spite of his courage, felt tears of grief bedew his eyes.

"O God!" he exclaimed, "punish me if I have offended you, and I will bow my head beneath the punishment but will you allow this man, this villain, to heap up crime upon crime, to strip me of what I hold the dearest?"

There was a moment's silence, which the old gentleman was the first to interrupt.

"My friend," he said to Leon, "you told me that Maria had been saved by you, and yet I do not see her."

"She awaits your permission to present herself to you, general."

"Let her come—let her come!"

A peon was ordered to go and fetch Maria, who was kneeling in her mother's room, and soon after, the maiden was standing before her father; but on seeing the condition in which the murderer had left him, she could only sob. The old man made a sign that he wished to embrace her.

"My daughter," he said, after pressing his lips on the novice's virgin forehead, "since the walls of a convent have not protected you from the fury of my enemies, and I know not whether I shall ever see my other children again, you will henceforth remain with me, if," he added, "Heaven grant me the strength to live."

"Oh, thanks, father—thanks! for the convent is death, and I wish to live to love and cherish you."

"What do you say?"

"Forgive me, father, but I suffered so deeply at being separated from those whom I love."

"This is strange! and yet your sister Inez asked three days ago to speak to me in private, and asked my permission to take the veil in the Convent of the Conception, as she was determined not to marry Don Sallazar, who loves her. I believed that it was you, child, who had persuaded her to this."

"Oh, no!" Maria murmured.

The doctor, who had hitherto contented himself with displaying the dissatisfaction which he felt on seeing the general fatigue himself with talking, thought it prudent not to allow the interview to go on, and made an observation to that effect.

"Thanks, doctor," said the general, "for the interest you take in my cure."

"General," said Leon, "the doctor is right; my presence is no longer necessary here. I will hasten to Santiago, and ere long I hope you shall hear from me. Señora Doña Maria does not require my services further, and so I will retire."

"Oh, father!" Maria could not refrain from saying, "if you only knew how brave and generous he is!"

The general made no reply, and seemed to be reflecting.

"Doctor," he said, suddenly addressing the surgeon, "you must arrange some plan for transporting me to Santiago."

"What are you thinking of, general?" the other exclaimed, falling back a couple of steps, so great was his surprise; "it is impossible."

"And yet it must be," the old man remarked calmly. "If my son is still alive, he is at Santiago with General Don Sallazar; I wish to see them."

"What?" said Leon.

"Once again, it is impossible," remarked the doctor, who was grieved to see the obstinacy with which his patient supported his resolve.

"You, Captain Leon," Don Juan continued, "will go on ahead, since you still offer me your assistance, which has been so precious to me; we shall meet at my cousin's, Senator Don Henriquez de Castago."

"But, general?"

"But, doctor, you will do whatever you like; have a litter made, or invent any mode of transport that you please, for I intend to go to Santiago with my daughter Maria, even if I die on arriving."

"At least, wait a week."

"It is your opinion that I cannot be removed today?"

"Most certainly."

"Well, I will wait till the day after tomorrow; between this and then prepare all that you want, and do not trouble yourself about the rest. If an accident happens to me, the blame will rest on myself alone."

"General!"

"I have spoken, and I warn you that, if you do not consent, I shall blow out my brains, or rather tear off my bandages, and die here."

And the old gentleman prepared to suit the action to the word.

"Stay!" exclaimed the surgeon, who found himself compelled to yield, "I will act in accordance with your wishes."

"Very good," the general replied; "and now I will try to take some rest, for my strength is exhausted, I feel."

Leon prepared to bid farewell to the general, and leave the country house.

"Good-bye, my friend," the patient murmured; "in two days we shall meet again, or, if not, it is to you—you alone—I confine the care of guarding Maria. Go, and may Heaven aid you to find Inez."

Leon bent his knee before the old man.

"Sir," he said to him, with profound emotion, "my life and heart belong to you; take one and break the other if you like, for I can no longer conceal from you the secret that devours me—I love your daughter, Doña Maria."

"Father, father!" Maria also exclaimed, as she fell on her knees by the side of the general's bed; "forgive me, for I love him in return."

As his sole answer, Don Juan de Soto-Mayor held out his hand to the young people, who covered it with kisses and burning tears. A glance of ineffable happiness was exchanged between the smuggler and the novice.

"Now I am strong," Leon exclaimed, as he rose. "You shall be avenged, Don Juan."

And he rushed out of the house. In a second, all his men were ready to start.

"Companions!" he shouted, as he leaped on the back of his mustang, "to Santiago at full gallop!"

A whirlwind of dust rose, enveloping men and horses, who disappeared on the horizon. Two days later, a young lady on horseback was riding by the side of a litter carried by two mules, in which lay an old man, and a military surgeon and fifty lanceros escorted them. They were Maria de Soto-Mayor, the general her father, and the doctor, who were proceeding to Santiago.

CHAPTER XXXI
THE CAMP OF THE MOLUCHOS

When Tahi-Mari reached the council lodge, the great Molucho chiefs were already assembled. A compact crowd of Indian warriors silently surrounded the approaches of the lodge, and pressed forward to hear the resolutions which were going to be formed by the Ulmens.

On perceiving the formidable toqui of the Moluchos, the warriors respectfully fell back to let him pass, and Tahi-Mari entered the hut. His face was haughty and frowning, and everything about him indicated pride and resolution. He sat down on the trunk of a tree reserved for him, and which enabled him to survey the assembly. After looking round him for a moment, he began to speak—

"For what purpose have my brothers, the Ulmens of the twelve nations, assembled?" he asked.

"The pale-faces," Huachacuyac replied, "have sent two great chiefs to discuss peace with us."

"The Spaniards," Tahi-Mari continued, "have two tongues and two faces. My brothers must be on their guard, for they wish to deceive them by false promises, while they are preparing the means to destroy them."

"Matai," said the Ulmens, "our brother is learned: he is a great warrior; he will judge."

"What is the opinion of my brothers? We cannot refuse to receive the messengers of peace," Huachacuyac remarked.

"My brothers speak wisely: let the Spanish chiefs be brought in, and we will hear them."

A movement took place among the Indians; Shounon-Kouiretzi went in for a moment, and returned almost immediately, conducting General Don Pedro Sallazar and Colonel Don Juan de Soto-Mayor. They were unarmed, but their bold bearing and haughty brow showed that they did not experience the slightest fear at finding themselves at the mercy of their barbarous enemies.

A dozen lanceros, unarmed like them, halted at the lodge-door. Shounon-Kouiretzi motioned the two officers to sit down on trunks of trees not so high as the one employed by the chief, then after lighting a calumet, he handed it to Tahi-Mari, who smoked it for an instant and restored it to him. The latter then presented it to Don Pedro Sallazar, who passed it to Don Juan. The calumet soon went the round of the assembly and returned to Tahi-Mari, who finished it. After this the toqui threw the ashes towards the strangers, saying, in a loud voice—

"These chiefs and the soldiers who accompany them are the guests of the Ulmens of the twelve Molucho nations: the warriors will respect them till sunset."

This ceremony performed, there was a profound silence.

"What do the Spanish warriors desire?" Tahi-Mari at length said; "the white chiefs can speak, for the ears of my brothers the Ulmens are open."

Don Pedro Sallazar rose and said in Indian, a language which he spoke with considerable facility—

"Grand Ulmens of the twelve nations, you, oh formidable toqui, and all you red warriors who are listening to me, your great white father sends me to you; his heart bleeds at seeing the numberless misfortunes which war has caused; his ears are filled with the complaints of mothers reduced to despair and of children who are weeping for their fathers killed in action. The country is devastated, the towns are only piles of ashes, and the rivers and streams whose waters were so limpid are now corrupted and fetid with the number of corpses they bear along. His mind being saddened by these terrible calamities, and wishing at length to restore tranquillity and abundance to this unhappy land, your great white father asks of you through my voice that the axe should be buried between us, peace be re-established among us, and the redskins and palefaces henceforth form one united nation. Let my red brothers reflect: I have spoken."

Don Pedro Sallazar sat down again, and Tahi-Mari immediately replied—

"The Ulmens of the twelve great nations have never desired war; they have avoided it as long as they could, and now endure it. It is not the Molucho nation that dug up the hatchet. It is now three hundred years since the Spaniards landed in our country. Our tribes had no liberty upon the seashore, but the palefaces pursued them as if they had been like wild beasts, and compelled them to take refuge in the deserts of the Andes. Why, after tearing from the poor Indians the fertile and sunlit lands which they possessed, are they now trying to rob them of the uncultivated plains and reduce them to slavery? Why do they wish to destroy their religion, and their laws, and drive them into the eternal snows? Are not the Indians and Spaniards sons of the same Father? Do not the priests of the palefaces themselves say so? Let my brother the Spanish chief answer."

"Yes," said Don Pedro, rising, "the great chief of the Moluchos is right; but why renew old quarrels and revive ancient animosities? Is not the country vast enough to support us all? Why should we not live in peace together, each following our laws and professing our religion? We are ready to grant our Indian brothers all they ask that is just and equitable. I have come here to listen to the propositions of the Ulmens, and the great Spanish chief will ratify them if they are reasonable."

"It is too late," Tahi-Mari replied, rising in his turn; "the Moluchos are resolved to regain their liberty, which was unjustly torn from them; they are tired of living like wretched vagabonds on the snow-covered mountains; now that they have descended into the plains warmed by the sunshine they do not wish to leave them."

"The Ulmens will reflect," Don Pedro resumed. "They must not let themselves be led astray by a slight success; the Spaniards are powerful, and victory has ever been on their side up to this day."

"And then, too," said Don Juan, rising in his turn, "what do you hope to obtain? Do you fancy yourselves sufficiently strong, even if you succeed in capturing Santiago, to contend against the immense forces which will come to crush you from the other side of the Great Salt Lake? No; the war you are waging is a senseless war, without any possible object or result. Commenced under the persuasion of an ambitious chief, who employs you to carry out schemes of which you are ignorant, you are only instruments in his hands. Believe my words and those of General Sallazar; accept the frank and loyal peace which we propose to you. This man, whom you have appointed your toqui, is abusing you and deceiving you, and driving you towards an abyss into which you will fall if you do not listen to the voice of reason, which addresses you through our lips."

A lengthened tumult and menacing effervescence followed these remarks of the young man. The chiefs anxiously questioned each other in a low voice. Don Juan's bold language had produced a certain impression on them, and some of them recognised its correctness. Tahi-Mari alone remained impassive; not a muscle of his face had moved, and the trace of any emotion might be sought in vain upon his countenance. When the effect produced by Don Juan's speech was slightly calmed, he rose, and giving his foe an ironical glance, he said —

"The young Spanish chief has spoken well, and if he does not count many years he has a great deal of wisdom. Peace is good when loyally offered."

"And we do offer it loyally," Don Juan remarked eagerly.

"Ah! my brother must pardon me," Tahi-Mari said, with a sarcastic smile.

"That demon is meditating some roguery," Don Pedro said, in a low voice, to his companion; "we must be on our guard."

"My brothers the Ulmens," Diego continued, "have heard the words pronounced by the two Spanish chiefs, and if they were really the expression of their thoughts I would join my voice to theirs in urging you to accept the peace they offer; but unfortunately here is a proof of the bad faith which regulates their conduct."

Tahi-Mari drew from under his poncho a paper, which he slowly unfolded, while a quiver of curiosity ran along the ranks of the Indians, and the two Spanish officers exchanged glances in which anxiety was visible.

"This despatch, my brothers, was found this very day upon a Spanish soldier, who was the bearer of it. My brothers, the Ulmens, will listen to me as I read it; and then see the amount of confidence which they ought to place in the sincerity of our enemies."

"We are listening;" the Ulmens said.

"This is it," Diego remarked, and read:

"'My dear General,—The Indians are pressing us closely, and have placed us in a most precarious position; still I hope to gain a few days by making them proposals of peace, which will have no result, as you can easily imagine; but will give the reinforcements you announce to me time to come up. Do not delay, for I am anxious to deal a decisive blow, and drive the rebels for ever from these parts.'"

"This letter, signed by the President of the Republic, is addressed to the general commanding the province of Coquimbo. My brother can consult: I have spoken," and Tahi-Mari resumed his seat.

A movement of fury seized the Ulmens, who rushed on the Spanish officers with the intention of tearing them to pieces.

"Back, all of you," Tahi-Mari shouted in a thundering voice, "these men are inviolable!"

The Indian stopped as if by enchantment.

"The word of an Ulmen is sacred," the half-breed continued. "Let these chiefs return to the lodges of their white brothers; my brothers will show these perfidious Spaniards that the great chiefs of the twelve Molucho nations are as merciful as they are powerful."

Don Pedro and Don Juan, after escaping the peril that menaced them, prepared to depart.

"A moment," said Tahi-Mari; "you will not leave the camp alone; follow me."

And leaving the council lodge, he pointed towards his wigwam, in front of the two officers and their escort of lanceros, who had awaited them at the door.

On reaching the door of his abode, Diego went in, but came out again almost immediately, holding by the hand a veiled female.

"There," he said, addressing Don Juan, "take away this girl, who wearies me, and whose verses no longer possess any charms for me; perhaps she will succeed in pleasing some of the soldiers, for she is Spanish."

Then with a rapid movement he tore off the veil that concealed the prisoner's features, and pushed her towards the officers.

"Inez!" the latter exclaimed, in horror.

It was indeed Inez; though not to be recognized by others but them, as her face had assumed so strange an expression, and her eyes were wandering. She turned her head in all directions, looking stupidly around her, and then suddenly folding her arms on her chest, she sang with an accent of ineffable sadness the following lines from an old dance song:—

"From the corner,
From the corner of the Carmen
To the rock,
To the golden rock,
I have seen a,
I have seen a girl descend,
Singing,
Singing the Sambacueca."

"Oh!" Don Juan murmured in despair; "great Heaven, she is mad."

"And I have not even a sword," Don Pedro exclaimed, wringing his hands furiously.

"Ah, Don Juan de Soto-Mayor, you did not expect I fancy, to find your sister in Tahi-Mari's lodge? Take her back, while awaiting the end of my vengeance; for, as I told you, I do not wish to have anything more to do with her; and you, Señor Don Pedro, are you not her assumed husband?"

"Wretch! why did I not listen to the feeling of aversion, with which you inspired me, when I saw you at the house of General Soto-Mayor? I ought to have killed you before you made me fall into the trap which you and your gang laid for us in offering to escort us."

"Coward!" Don Juan said in his turn, his eyes full of tears; "kill the brother after dishonouring the sister, for I hate you and defy you."

And, raising his hand, he sprang forward to strike Diego on the face; but the latter at once guessing the young man's intention, seized his arm and held him as in a vice.

"I need but to give a signal, and your head and that of your companion roll at your feet; but I will not give it."

And with a sudden push he threw Don Juan far from him.

"Begone," he said coldly, "for no one will touch your person, which is sacred to all in this camp, our two families no longer reckon insults and wrongs, Don Juan, and this one will be requited with the rest."

During this time poor Inez, apparently not noticing what was going on, was crouching in a corner, and with her head in her hands and her long hair covering her face, was humming in a low voice a hymn to the Virgin. Without making any reply to Diego the young men walked up to Inez and made her rise. She offered no resistance, but continued to sing—

> "'The birds in the sky,
> The fishes of the sea,
> The wild beasts of the forests,
> Celebrate her glory.'"

"What is the matter, Señor Caballero?" she suddenly asked, as she broke off her chant and looked at her brother, "you appear sad. Would you like me to sing you a pretty sequidilla?"

> "'Señorita, señorita,
> Raise your little foot.'"

"Oh," said Don Juan, "what madness! Inez, my sister, recognise me. I am Juanito, your brother, whom you love so dearly."

A flash of intelligence passed into the maiden's eyes, and a smile played round her lips.

"Juanito!" she said. "Yes, yes," she exclaimed clapping her hands, "listen—"

> "'Juanito is a brave,
> A brave whom I love,
> A handsome fellow dressed,
> All in cloth—"

A hoarse burst of laughter interrupted the song.

"Why try to arouse her memory?" Tahi-Mari said, with a shrug of the shoulders.

"Oh!" Don Juan exclaimed, turning to him, "all your blood will not suffice to avenge us."

"As you please, caballero: but in the meanwhile be off, or I cannot answer for your safety."

"Not yet," said a thundering voice, which vibrated through the air.

A great disturbance broke out in camp, and a man covered with perspiration and dust proceeded towards Tahi-Mari's hut. It was Captain Leon Delbès, on seeing whom Diego turned pale, but remained motionless. Leon advanced toward him thrusting aside every obstacle that barred his progress.

"What have you done with General Soto-Mayor's daughter?" he asked, fixing his eyes on the half-breed's.

The smuggler's entrance had been so unexpected, his action so extraordinarily rash, that all the Indians who witnessed the scene stood as if petrified with admiration and amazement. On hearing Leon's question Diego looked down, but made no reply.

"What have you done with her, I ask you?" the captain repeated with a passionate stamp of his foot.

At this moment the young lady, to whom nobody paid attention, leant on his shoulder, and with a charming smile began singing again in a sweet and melancholy voice—

> "Seated at the corner of a street,
> They tell me that my chuca sells,
> They tell me that she sells flowers."

"Oh!" Leon exclaimed, "I understand it all now. Unhappy child! unhappy father!"

And quick as thought, he drew a pistol from his girdle, and placed the muzzle against the half-breed's chest. The latter, calm and haughty, raised his eyes and looked at Leon, without making the slightest motion to escape death. The young man trembled, and let his weapon sink again.

"And yet I cannot kill him!" he said, the first feeling of surprise over. The Indians rushed furiously on him to make him pay dearly for this insensate attempt.

"Stay," Diego said, "this man is an adopted son of the Moluchos, and I forbid you touching him."

The Indians fell back.

"Is this the way in which you avenge yourself?" Leon exclaimed. "What! instead of attacking your enemy face to face, you cowardly carry off a child to make her your victim! Oh! I curse the day when my hand clasped yours for the first time: I believed you to be a man of heart, and you are a ferocious brute. I no longer hate you, I despise you."

"Leon, your heart is no longer your own; it belongs to a Spanish girl, and a cloud covers your mind; one day you will render me justice."

"Never!" Leon replied, "never! I curse you, and I swear by the ashes of my mother, that if you let me leave this place, my vengeance shall pursue you; you will ever find me on your road ready to fight you and overthrow your plans."

"Your will be done, brother: my hand will never be laid upon you to ask an account of your outrages. But woe to the Spaniards who have broken our friendship!"

"Speak no more of friendship, since you have crushed my life and destroyed my happiness for ever."

"Are you saying the truth?" Diego asked, feeling doubt glide into his mind.

But already the captain, followed by Don Pedro, Don Juan, and Inez was crossing the camp, through a triple row of Molucho warriors, who watched without daring to attack them, though their desire so to do was great. They soon reached the spot where their horses were waiting, and half an hour later were all four at the house of Senator Don Henriquez de Castago. While all proper care was being given to the unhappy Inez, Leon Delbès told the two officers—in what state he had left General Soto-Mayor, and of; his speedy arrival at Santiago accompanied by Maria. When he had finished this painful narrative, Don Pedro and Don Juan, struck by the same misfortunes, displayed toward Leon the most lively feelings of esteem and friendship, while complimenting him on the attachment which he had not ceased to display toward the Soto-Mayor family.

"Sir," Don Pedro said to him, "if during the course of our unhappy journey to Valdivia, I for a moment misunderstood your noble qualities, forgive me, for today I declare to you it is a friend who sincerely offers you his hand."

Leon pressed the general's hand warmly.

"Don Juan and I are going to inform the senate of the result of our mission; you remain in this house till the general arrives."

The smuggler bowed, and the three men separated, respectively enlightened as to the feelings of esteem which they professed for each other.

CHAPTER XXXII
THE SACK OF SANTIAGO

Leon's first care on reaching Santiago had been to inquire after the residence of Don Henriquez de Castago, and to inform him of the visit which General Soto-Mayor intended to pay him. At the same time he told him of the purpose of his own journey. Don Henriquez eagerly placed his house at the smuggler's disposal, and told him of the perilous mission which was being attempted at that very moment by General Don Pedro, and his cousin, Colonel Don Juan, in going to the toqui of the Araucanos to make him proposals of peace. It was then that Leon, after quartering his men, set out in all haste for the camp, in order to obtain news of Inez, and at the same time help the two officers if they were in danger. We know what occurred in consequence of this exploit.

Two days after these events, General Don Juan de Soto-Mayor and his daughter Maria arrived at the capital of Chili. Thanks to the numerous precautions which the surgeon had taken, the old gentleman had suffered but little through the journey, and the state of his health was more satisfactory than might have been supposed. So soon as he reached the house of senator Don Castago, he was put to bed, and Leon took upon himself to inform him of the release of Inez, the outrages of which the poor girl had been the victim, and the madness which had resulted from them. The general begged her to be brought to him, and when she was in his presence he embraced her, and covered her with tears.

Inez could not at all understand her father's grief, whom she did not at all recognise; but struck by the old man's suffering appearance, she at once installed herself by his bedside, and would not quit it again. Her madness was gentle and melancholy; she spent long hours without breathing a syllable, or sang to strange tunes snatches of songs which she had formerly known.

On her side, Maria, attentive and devoted even to self-denial, lavished on Don Juan the most affectionate care, and the old man discovered at each moment in his daughter the germs of the noblest qualities of the heart. Leon's name was never pronounced by the general without arousing in her thoughts of joy and happiness; but, understanding what kindness and gentleness her father had displayed in not spurning the smuggler's love for her, she silently awaited the moment when she would be able to yield entirely to the happiness of belonging to the man whom her heart had selected.

The general, as we may suppose, had been beyond all expression surprised on hearing the community of feeling between the captain and Maria; but penetrated with gratitude for the eminent services which the young man had rendered him, he heartily desired that an opportunity might offer itself to fill up the distance that separated Leon's rank from his. But it was no easy matter.

In the meanwhile, the position of the Chilians shut up in Santiago was beginning to grow serious. The Indian lines were being gradually drawn closer round the town, intercepting the communications with the exterior, and preventing news from being received. The provisions would soon run short; want was already being felt in the poorer districts, and wretched people, with worn and haggard faces, might be seen wandering about the streets and loudly demanding bread.

General Sallazar had succeeded, it is true, in crossing the Masincho after a glorious battle with the Indians, and entered Santiago; but it was far more difficult to drive away the besiegers who surrounded the city. Situated in the heart of the Chilian republic, the capital is at a great distance from the frontier; and as it had no reason to apprehend foreign attacks, owing to the impassable deserts that separate the states, it had not been fortified.

Attempts had been made hastily to throw up a few breastworks, but workmen were wanting. Discouragement seized on the population, and the inhabitants, terrified at the sight of the Indians, filled the churches with their lamentations, and offered up vows and novenas, instead of combating their enemies energetically, and dying courageously in defence of their homes.

Eight days passed thus, and during this period Leon distinguished himself greatly by making daring sorties at the head of his men, in which he captured herds of cattle or flocks of sheep, which revictualled the town and restored a little courage to the population. One evening, after carefully visiting all the posts with Don Juan, General Sallazar, Leon was preparing to take a few hours of indispensable rest after a fatiguing day, when suddenly the bells of all the churches began pealing, shrieks were heard, and soldiers galloped through the town, shouting, "To arms! to arms!"

The Indians were beginning the assault by attacking the town on all sides simultaneously. The danger was imminent, and there was no time for hesitation. The salvation of the whole population was at stake. The three gentlemen shook hands silently, and rushed in different directions.

The night was dark and rainy; the west wind howled furiously in the hills near the town, and from time to time a dazzling flash rent the horizon, and preluded the rolling of the thunder which was blended with the sharp sinister crash of the musketry fire. The drums beat, and bugles brayed; the churches were crowded with women and children, who, piously kneeling on the slabs, prayed God, the Virgin, and the saints to come to their assistance.

The tumult was frightful. The cries of the wounded, the hurrahs of the combatants, and above all, the war yells of the Indians, who bounded like panthers upon the last defenders of the town. All this formed a din rendered more horrible still by the sight of the fire which was beginning to tinge the sky with a red and ill-omened glare.

Tahi-Mari, naked to the waist, his hair in disorder, and his features contrasted by the thirst for carnage and destruction, held an axe in one hand and a torch in the other. He was seen rushing at the head of a band of veteran redskins into the thickest of the Spanish battalions, cleaving a bloody track for himself—felling and pitilessly massacring all those who dared to oppose his fury. Santiago was one immense crater—the fire embraced the whole city; its devouring flames had dissipated the darkness, and spread around a light which allowed the dark outlines of the combatants to be seen as they struggled with the sublime energy of despair.

A countless swarm of Indians had invaded the town, and fighting was going on on all sides. The Spaniards disputed the ground inch by inch, and the streets, the squares, and the houses were the scene of a horrible massacre. Tahi-Mari, ever in the first rank of the Indians, excited his soldiers by his shouts and example. All was lost, and the Chilian capital had at length fallen into the power of the Araucanos. The burning buildings fell in with a crash, burying beneath their ruins assailants and assailed. The churches were given up to pillage, while the women and girls, torn half naked from their houses or from the foot of the altar, endured the last violence which their cruel victors inflicted upon them.

All hope of flight or rescue seemed annihilated; the redskins, drunk with carnage and spirits, rushed furiously upon the relics of the despairing population. It was at this moment that the President of the Republic, followed by a few devoted soldiers, formed a hollow square on the Plaza de la Merced, in the centre of which he placed all the aged persons, women, and children, who had escaped the fury of the Indians.

Suddenly loud shouts were heard, and three heavy bodies of men, commanded by Don Juan, General Pedro Sallazar, and Leon Delbès, debouched from three different streets. In the centre of the one commanded by Leon, was old Don Juan carried on a litter, with Maria and Inez by her side. Leon placed the persons whom he had saved in the centre of the square formed by the President, and called on Don Juan and Don Pedro's detachments.

"Now," he cried to the President of the Republic, "fall back, while we support you."

"Do so," he answered.

And the square fell back with all those whom it contained. "Forward!" Leon shouted, "kill! kill!"

And the three bands, facing the startled Indians, threw themselves upon them and commenced a frightful butchery. The square De la Merced was literally encumbered with combatants. The Moluchos, incessantly pushed forward by their comrades, who arrived to their help, fell impassively beneath the lances and sabres of the Spaniards, who protected the flight of the President as he retired and took in his charge all those persons incapable of bearing, arms. The fugitives soon reached the city gates.

The contest had lasted more than an hour. A countless number of corpses covered the ground and formed a rampart for the Spaniards, who redoubled their energy. At this moment Tahi-Mari appeared in the square. At a glance he judged the position, and rushed upon the Spaniards. The shock was terrible. Don Pedro and Don Juan recognised their common enemy, and cutting their way through the dead and wounded, both attacked him at once.

"Ah!" Diego shouted, "we meet at last, then."

"Yes," Don Pedro retorted, as he aimed a sabre cut at him, "and for the last time, I hope."

"You have told the truth," said Diego, as he parried with the handle of his axe the blow aimed at him; "die, then!"

And he cleft his head open. The unfortunate Don Pedro stretched out his arms, rolled his eyes wildly, and fell from his horse, murmuring the name of Inez. The Spaniards uttered a cry of grief, to which the Indians responded by a shout of triumph.

"It is now our turn," Tahi-Mari exclaimed, as he dashed towards Don Juan.

"Yes," the young man replied, "our long standing quarrel will be at length decided."

The two enemies rushed upon each other with clenched lips and bloodshot eyes, fighting furiously, caring little about dying, provided that one killed the other. But at each instant a crowd of Indians or Spaniards, drawn by the moving incidents of the fight, came between them and separated them. When this happened they made extraordinary efforts to come together again, overthrowing the obstacles that were in their way, and constantly seeking each other, only one thought occupied them—that of satiating their vengeance; every other consideration was effaced from their minds, and forgetting the sacred interests which they had to defend, they only thought of their personal hatred. Ere long those who separated them fell back, and they found themselves once more face to face.

"Defend yourself, Tahi-Mari," Don Juan shouted, as he dashed at the Indian chief.

"Here I am," the latter shouted, "and you are about to die."

Suddenly leaping from his horse, he cut the sinews of the colonel's horse with a blow of his axe. But Don Juan probably expected this attack, for when his horse fell uttering a long snort of pain, he was standing with his feet freed from the stirrups. Then began, between these two men, a combat impossible to describe, in which rage and fury took the place of skill. Tahi-Mari wielded his terrible axe with unparalleled dexterity; Don Juan had his sabre welded to his wrist, and followed the slightest movements of the other.

Each observed the other, and calculated the value of his blows. Eye on eye, chest against chest, panting, with foreheads streaming with perspiration, and their features violently contracted by hatred, they watched for the decisive moment. Don Juan was bleeding from two deep wounds; he felt his strength becoming exhausted, and felt as if he could no longer hold his sword. Tahi-Mari had also received several wounds, not dangerous, it is true, but which were, for all that, visible on his face and movements.

All at once, the half-breed, profiting by the fact that his enemy, who had constantly been on guard, left himself uncovered, aimed a blow at him with his axe. Don Juan raised his sword, but only parried imperfectly, and the axe was buried deeply in his shoulder. Collecting all his strength, he had to keep his feet; but tottering involuntarily, he fell to the ground, heaving a deep sigh. Diego burst into a yell of triumph, and rushed upon the young man.

"At last," he said.

At the same moment he received a violent blow, and he fell back blaspheming. He rose with lightning speed, and saw Leon Delbès before him, who had rolled him in the dust by dashing his horse's chest at him.

"Oh!" the Indian exclaimed, as he let his axe fall, "always he between this family and me!"

"Yes, I! Tahi-Mari—I, whom you must kill before you can reach your enemies—I, who have sworn to tear your victims from you: attack me. What are you waiting for?"

A combat seemed to be going on in Diego's mind, and then he remarked, as if speaking to himself:—

"No, no; not he, not he! the only man who ever loved me on this earth. Now, for the other," he added, as he looked furiously around him, "he can never have enough of Spanish blood."

And slipping on one side, he rushed back into the thick of the fight.

"What!" cried Wilhelm, who had just stationed himself by Leon's side, "will you let that hyena escape, captain?"

"Yes!" Leon answered, as he shook his head sadly, "my hands shall not be dyed with that man's blood; his life is sacred to me."

"That is possible," the German grunted, "but it is not so to me! And then, again, the opportunity is too fine, and it is doing a service to humanity."

And before Leon could prevent his design, he raised his rifle to his shoulder, and fired. Diego made an enormous leap, turned half round, stretched out his arms, and fell with his face on the ground. The captain rushed towards him and had to raise him; the Indian looked at him for a moment, his eyes were fixed on his with an expression of ineffable tenderness, and pressing his hand forcibly, he said in a low voice—

"Thanks, thanks, brother, but it is useless; I feel that I am going to die."

Suddenly, by a supreme effort of will, and aided by the smuggler, he succeeded in gaining his feet again. Then, his black eyes flashed with pride and triumph.

"Look!" he exclaimed, "they are flying, those cowardly Spaniards are flying! I die; but I am the victor, and almost avenged."

And he found sufficient strength within him to utter his terrible war cry. Suddenly, a jet of black blood rose to his lips; his body stiffened with a horrible convulsion, and he fell dead. Still, his eyes were open, and his lips, curled by a smile of bitter irony, seemed to defy his conquered foes, even after he had drawn his last breath.

"Back, der Teufel! back, or we are lost!" Wilhelm exclaimed, as he seized the bridle of Leon's horse and pulled it back.

"Oh!" the smuggler said, as he wiped away a tear, "that man was made of iron."

"Stuff, why pity him?" Wilhelm said, carelessly; "he died like a soldier."

The fall of Tahi-Mari, which was not known to the Indians for some minutes, did not at once check the order of the battle. Leon's band, which had advanced too far, had extraordinary difficulties in effecting a retreat, and joining the debris of the army marching on Valparaíso.

The Moluchos, deprived of the man of genius, who had conceived the plan of this daring campaign, and who was alone capable of bringing it to a satisfactory conclusion, henceforth were a body without a soul. Dissensions broke out among them, each chief claiming to succeed the great Tahi-Mari, and they could not come to any understanding. The league of the twelve nations was; broken; the Ulmens no longer acted harmoniously, and soon undertook isolated expeditions, which had disastrous results.

The Indians were for nine days masters of Santiago; at the end of that time, the Spaniards, who had vigorously assumed the offensive, expelled them from the capital, and pursued them even beyond their frontier line. Of the 200,000 men who had invaded the Chilian territory, 40,000 at the most succeeded in regaining the inaccessible llanos which serve as their retreat. The others found death in the land which they had for a moment hoped to conquer. Such was, through the imbecility of the chiefs, the result of this enterprise, which, if better conducted, might have changed the fate of South America.

Six months after these events Leon Delbès was married at the church of La Merced to Doña Maria de Soto-Mayor. The old general and his son,

Don Juan, who had both recovered from their wounds, were present at the ceremony, offering up vows for the happiness of the young couple. Inez lived for a year without regaining her reason, but her madness had become a sort of gloomy and taciturn melancholy, which nothing in the world could remove. She expired one day without pain, for her death-agony was a pallid smile, in the midst of which her soul fled away.

As for the secondary characters of the story, we will mention their fate in a few words. The band of smugglers was broken so soon as Leon left to go and live with the general. Wilhelm, for his splendid conduct on the night of the capture of Santiago, was given a commission as lieutenant in the Chilian army. The worthy abbess of the Convent of the Purísima Concepción continued to sell her aqua milagrosa at the fairest price. And one fine day, Master Crevel, tired of the annoyance the police inflicted on him, placed the ocean between them and him by returning to France.